THE HOLLOW FORTRESS

THE HOLLOW FORTRESS

PART I OF

THE BARRETT O'BYRNE TRILOGY

B. L. VAN VORS

ALDER HOUSE PRESS

❖ ❖ ❖

TAOS NEW MEXICO

15 14 13 12 11   1 2 3 4 5

ISBN 978-0-615-36950-1

Designed and typeset by Mina Yamashita
Composed in Minion Pro,
an Adobe Original typeface designed by Robert Slimbach
Display composed in Charlemagne

THIS BOOK IS DEDICATED IN GRATITUDE TO:

L. Frank Baum, Robert A. Heinlein, Louis L'Amour,

C.S. Lewis, Doris Lessing, John D. MacDonald,

A. Merritt, J.K. Rowling, Mark Twain, J.R.R. Tolkien,

and Roger Zelazny

PROLOGUE

Afghanistan
The Hindu Kush,
Sunday, May 3rd

"BEAUTIFUL COUNTRY," Jolly remarked.

Army Special Forces Lieutenant Barrett O'Byrne grunted agreement. It was beautiful country, high in the Hindu Kush and largely untouched by the carnage that had ravaged the rest of Afghanistan.

Both men were lying prone on a granite outcrop above Bashar Hasem Pass, scanning the valley below through 100x Nikons. The SAT link had squirreled an hour before and they were forced to rely on direct visual contact with their quarry.

"Maybe they'll surrender peacefully," Barrett said.

Jolliteau gave him a wry glance.

Barrett chuckled. He'd only been with the team three weeks. He knew in Jolliteau's mind he was still on probation.

The big sergeant suddenly tensed, the binoculars tight to his eyes. "There! They're in the open—that cliff wall—seven, eight clicks."

Their target was a small group of Taliban suspected of a recent raid on the police station at Dar As al Maari—at least they were thought to be Taliban. They'd gotten good descriptions from the villagers, nine young men, short beards, dirty robes, AK-47s, and black headgear. Taliban. Yet they were headed north into the Pamirs. Taliban usually retreated to the southwest, to their hidden redoubts in the tribal country along the border.

So, why north? North was high country, home of the mysterious Nuristanis, a people whose allegiance to Islam was questionable even by liberal standards.

And other behavior didn't add up. The usual Taliban M.O. was to kill or mutilate their victims, at least hold them hostage. After taking the station, instead of killing the cops, this band had just tied them up and left them alive. They took food, a little cash, and the station's two U.S. donated HumVees. Witnesses could recall none of the jihadist rhetoric associated with the Taliban. The vehicles had been found at the eastern base of the pass, abandoned where they ran out of gas.

It was telling. But what it told was anybody's guess.

Bashar Hasem Pass was low for the region, no more than five thousand meters, but their helicopter had developed mechanical difficulties early on. The team pushed ahead on foot, without rest for most of the day. *Diwangi*, mountain sickness, was not to be taken lightly. A dull throb at his temples alerted Barrett to early symptoms. He broke open a cellophane pack of diomox pills, washing them down with a gulp of canteen water, noticing Jolliteau's eyes on him as he did so.

Odd, he thought, first the chopper, now the Sat link. Even their GPS units were acting up. *Almost as if—.*

He stopped. Technology was technology, prone to failure at any time, more so in these ancient mountains. No reason to make it more than it was.

It was late spring and the valley below was in full bloom. It was warm for the altitude, close to eighty-five degrees. Barrett loosened the checkered scarf around his neck, taking advantage of a cool breeze blowing up from the valley. He caught the unmistakable scent of citrus and jasmine blossoms. A thousand feet below the Abar River tumbled from high clefts into ice blue pools as it wound its energetic way toward the plains of Bamiyan.

Out of the shadows of the cliff the men they followed were easy to spot, nine of them, moving up the narrow trail that led to the mountain village of Bet Al Nuri.

Not good, Barrett thought. No one wanted a firefight in a friendly village—especially not with evening coming on.

A narrow and deceptively fragile looking rope bridge spanned the gorge and the river below. Paulus and Conagher, the team's two scouts, had already crossed.

"Finally some luck," said Jolly. "Looks like they've stopped."

Through the binoculars Barrett could see the men had halted in a small clearing just off the trail. From their animated gestures it appeared they were arguing.

"Time to move, Lieutenant."

Barrett nodded and Jolliteau raised his hand in the 'Go' sign. Immediately the other members of the team scrambled to their feet and began working their way down the steep moraine, taking cover among boulders and fallen slabs of granite.

Barrett holstered his binoculars and stood, swaying slightly as he did so. It was then that he heard the music, faint at first, then more definite, carried by the same soft breeze that had earlier perfumed the mountain air.

The music was foreign, unfamiliar, yet something about it compelled his attention. A reed flute. Drums. A man's voice, resonant and filled with longing, as though the singer called upon God Himself to deliver him of some great sorrow. His voice ran counterpoint to the flute's piercing demi-quaver and the rhythm of the drums. As if in answer came a chorus of women's voices, clear and melodious. The music enfolded him. Barrett found himself holding back tears.

The late afternoon sun reflected gold off the snow capped peak of Tirich Mir, at seven thousand meters the highest mountain visible from their position. Suddenly and without warning the peak flashed a brilliant green, lighting up the sky.

For Barrett the effect was extraordinary. At that moment something opened in him, or opened to him. A memory, as faint and haunting as the music, agonizingly intimate.

If only—if only—.

If only what? The thought escaped him.

"The light?" he blurted out. "Did you see that light? It was—."

Jolliteau was staring at him, concern showing on his dark features. Concern, or something else?

The music had stopped. Barrett looked back at the mountain. Once again the peak was gold, now darkening into a tarnished bronze. A sudden, agonizing sense of loss overcame him, followed by foreboding, like a dark cloud over the sun.

"You O.K., Lieutenant?"

Barrett steadied himself against a large rock. *Shake it off. Breathe.*

The thin mountain air found his lungs, but he couldn't shake the feeling that a door had opened to something higher, something vital, and that he had missed it, and by missing it his life was about to take a very dark and dangerous turn.

CHAPTER 1

Oxfordshire, England
October 27

WILLIAM HAMILTON WINFORD, III, Billy to his friends, Lord Winford to his neighbors, was busy coding in new instructions for King Leonidus when the doorbell rang. It was a real bell, pre-WW-1 vintage, made of resonant bronze that had to be manually struck. It had been made for another age when servants had been expected to answer its call.

Billy ignored it. All his rooms were let and his lodgers had their own keys. He was engrossed in his programming.

'Let's see, now. What would motivate Leonidus? Virtue? Duty? Glory?' How do I program that?

The bell ringer was insistent. 'Go away,' Billy mumbled, half to himself.

The ringing continued. A door inside the manor slammed. "I'll get it, you lazy sod! Play with your silly toys. Let an old woman do your work!"

Billy sighed. Meg, his oldest and most irascible lodger and the only one with a room on the first floor, shuffled to the door. He would hear about this later.

He turned back to the monitor. The battling figures froze on the screen. *Motivation? Let's see—is there such a thing as selfless glory?"*

The computers were the few artifacts in the house not from an earlier era. Eight quad-processing Mac G6s daisy chained on a customized RAID circuit, were connected to the internet by a super broadband Lambda Rail tributary, the same line used by nearby Oxford University. It was a perk for which he had spent a great deal of money.

On tables scattered around what was once the old manor's drawing room, were a half dozen 42-inch monitors. On five of the screens Greek and Persian soldiers were doing their best to kill one another. The sixth displayed the shifting numbers and icons of his code. On a wall, mounted between portraits of long dead relatives, a giant Sony 103-inch OLED waited to display newly rendered sequences. A worn leather sofa and several equally abused chairs faced the screen. But for now, the screen was dark.

'Lets see—how do I write an algorithm for virtue? What is the impulse behind virtue? Not talked about much these days. The Mahabharata went on about it, Plato, and Timeaus? No, that was more arcane—other worlds and all. The Greek word for virtue was 'arete', wasn't it? 'Valor in war'.'

A sound brought him out of his thoughts—a man's voice.

He tapped the keys, studied the results and frowned. This was going to take time.

Footsteps approached. *Meg had actually let the fellow in.*

He lifted himself out of his chair, favoring his bad leg. Before he'd moved four steps the door swung open.

The room was dim to better view the monitors. His first impression of the visitor was that of a street person, unkempt dark hair, week's growth of beard, worn military fatigues. He carried a single, water-stained duffle bag. A rectangle of light from the hallway window had fallen on the duffle and Billy's eyes fixed on it—tan canvas, a faded area where the nametag had been removed.

Meg was hovering behind the man like an excited crow. "Don't just stand there like a piked fish," she cackled happily. "Don't you recognize your best mate?"

My best—? Billy blinked and stared.

"Barrett? Barrett! My God! Is that really you?"

Barrett O'Byrne managed a peculiar smile, thin and weary.

"Hello, Billy. A little the worse for wear, but it's me, alright."

"You're supposed to be in Afghanistan! Why didn't you call?"

Billy wanted to rush forward and embrace his friend, but something stopped him—wariness—a reserve uncharacteristic of the Barrett he knew. "What happened to you, man? You look like you fell off a fishing trawler."

"Close enough."

Barrett glanced around the room, his blue-green eyes expressionless. The monitors were all new, big flat screens, not the bulky old CRTs Billy had replaced. He noted the images frozen on the screens, the red battle cloaks, armor and short-bladed swords.

"Greeks and Persians. Thermopylae?"

Honoring the change of subject, Billy pressed a key that started the battle going again.

"Precisely. I've been programming different takes. If the Greeks hadn't kept retreating behind fixed fortifications after every battle, I'm certain they could have won."

Barrett gave a tired laugh and shook his head. "Leonidus had 300 men, Billy. The Persians had over a million—maybe two million."

"Actually the Greeks started with 6,000 men," Billy said, warming to the subject. He could almost forget that more than two years had passed since he and Barrett last sat down in this very room, replaying and dissecting old battles—nearly two months since Barrett had sent a postcard from Kabul, a picture of a small, mud-walled Mosque, with an Apricot tree in front. It hadn't been real news—only that he was enjoying the billet, felt he was doing some good—typically, Barrett—bright and optimistic.

"Leonidus sent the others back, all but his 300 Spartans. What most historians overlooked, what I think Leonidus overlooked, was right up to the end the Spartans had dominated every battle. At one point they actually came within a few hundred meters of Xerxes himself."

"Great God! You haven't seen each other in years, and all you can talk about is some musty old battle! Can't you see your friend is hungry?"

Billy looked up, realizing Meg was still standing in the hall, just beyond the doorway.

"Thanks, Meg. We're fine."

He stepped past Barrett and closed the door. They could hear the old woman sputtering as she shuffled off back to her room.

"Not much has changed, I see," said Barrett, a glimmer of humor breaking through.

"Dried up old cow. I should have booted her out years ago. I've lost more than one lodger because of her. You're the only one she ever liked, you know. Always wondered how you managed."

Billy paused, apologetic as the truth of what Meg had said sunk in. "Sorry. You do look a bit peaked. What time is it?" He looked at his watch, a 27-jewel admiral's chronometer, its case carved from a single block of rose gold by Baume and Mercier in 1936. It had been his grandfather's.

"Almost six. I had no idea it was so late. We can talk over supper."

Barrett nodded. His eyes watched the nearest monitor where soldiers engaged in endless battle.

"Nice animation. Langton's work? Artificial life? The players are making decisions without your input?"

"Good on you. Langton's math, with a few derivations."

"Why do you think 300 men, or even six thousand, could defeat thousand-to-one odds?"

There was an edge to the question that told Billy it was more than just polite curiosity. He wondered at that. "Simple, really. The Greeks were winning. The Persians couldn't bring their numbers to bear. Take Hannibal when he defeated the Romans at Cannae, worse odds, granted, but basically the same situation. If Leonidus had just kept on, the Greeks could have reached Xerxes and cut off the head of the snake. The Persian Empire was top heavy. Besides, weren't you the one who always argued that odds don't mean that much?"

A bleak sort of emptiness seemed to settle on Barrett. "Did I? Must've been drinking. Besides, you wouldn't want to upstage the Oracle of Delphi, would you—Greece saved by its wooden walls and all?"

Barrett felt immediate regret. He knew how cynical he sounded—blaming it on lack of sleep and hunger, really. It had been days since he'd eaten a decent meal.

"You mentioned food?"

"Of course. You're staying, aren't you? Your old room?"

"Billy—I uh—I'm kind of broke right now."

"Don't be absurd. Come along. Your old room it is—but first, food. Let's see what's in the larder."

CHAPTER 2

EXCEPT FOR THE COMPUTERS, little had changed in the old house, that Barrett could see. The kitchen with its art deco appliances and large stone hearth was exactly as he remembered. Most of the meals were eaten at the large oak table. The formal dining room was rarely used. Lodgers, currently five, Billy told him, came and went at all hours.

Barrett's recent past was a nightmare, his future uncertain. But this moment almost brought meaning back to his life.

He'd finished off his second bottle of beer and was chewing the last shred of meat from a cold leg of mutton when Billy finally got around to asking. "So, are you going to tell me about it?"

Barrett put down the bone and wiped his hands on his napkin.

"I left the army."

Billy nodded, noting the places on Barrett's khaki shirt where his name and rank used to be.

"It wasn't a court martial, if that's what you're thinking. Mind if I get another beer?"

"Help yourself. And bring that wine over here, if you would."

Barrett grabbed the last beer from the refrigerator and an open bottle of wine from a nearby counter—Chateau Margaux, 1992. Billy had always enjoyed good wines. Now that his financial house was in order, he apparently could afford them.

Barrett poured a glass and handed it to Billy.

"Old times."

"Old times."

They toasted. Barrett remembered happier days. His year at Oxford, sponsored by the army, had been one of the few truly enjoyable years of his life.

"You were telling me why you left the army," reminded Billy.

Barrett shrugged. Then, after a pause. "We aren't the good guys anymore."

"We? You mean America? Western capitalists? The Corporatocracy? I thought we beat that beast to death."

Billy smiled, but his eyes showed concern. *Well, maybe he had reason.*

"But we didn't kill the beast, not really—policies, politics—maybe. But we— I at least—never really questioned the whole set up, the institutions, the system, the rhetoric that holds it all together."

Billy nodded. "An existential crisis, is it? Rather a profound one, I gather. I doubt it came about by reading Marx, or Ayub Qutub. You were never one for ideology. What was the tipping point?"

Barrett took a swallow of beer, studied the beads of condensation on the glass, surprised to find it already half empty.

"We were trailing some Taliban. At least we thought they were Taliban. They'd raided a police station, stolen some food, couple of HumVees. Didn't hurt anybody. That was odd in itself, knowing how brutal they can be. We caught up to them the next day, a valley up in the Pamirs. Beautiful country. High mountains, like you see in dreams."

He stopped as a memory surfaced, the moment atop Bashar Hasem Pass when he'd heard that strangely affecting music, seen the flash of green light, felt the wholeness it had brought, and the feeling of loss and foreboding that had followed. *Why was he remembering it now? Must be the beer.*

"Were they?" Billy asked. "Taliban, I mean?"

"Huh? Oh, no. Not actually. Just a bunch of idealistic Muslim kids from Kashmir. They'd come to Afghanistan to fight the Infidels, deserted after a couple of months when they decided the Taliban were ignorant thugs, reading things into the Qur'an that weren't there, twisting it to their own purposes. The whole experience turned them off. Just kids, you know. The oldest couldn't have been over eighteen."

"And—what happened?"

"We got an order to hold them. A chopper was on its way—a little unusual. Flying a helo in those mountains is difficult at the best of times, more so at night. But we figured no big deal. Some spook or other would show up, find out what we already knew, tell us to confiscate their weapons and let them go, which is what we would have done anyway. There was an ongoing amnesty. The prisons were overcrowded."

Barrett sighed. Months had passed and it still hurt. It would probably always hurt. He took another swallow of beer.

"There was a village. Few clicks up the valley, friendlies by all account, but you can never really tell. We put out pickets and set up a cold camp and waited for the chopper. Shouldn't have bothered with the cold camp. After all, it was their valley. They knew we were there."

"Who? The villagers?"

"Nuristanis, local militia—big burly guys in Karakul coats carrying Kalashnikovs—eight, or nine, maybe more. They left some guys in the rocks."

Barrett hesitated, remembering the men who'd shown up out of the twilight gloom that terrible night. "Courteous fellows. Proud, manly, but not macho like the Taliban. None of that silly schoolboy bravado."

Billy took a sip of wine, set the glass down. "This doesn't end well, does it?"

Barrett seemed not to hear. He was back in the mountains. "The Nuristanis didn't have any love for the Taliban, either. Bandar, their chief, invited us to their village. Muslim kids as well. Jolly, my Sergeant, had been a linebacker at Auburn. This fellow hovered over him, must have stood six foot five. Spoke English and said he'd been to Eton."

Billy asked, "You told them the helicopter was coming?"

"Sure. Didn't want it to be a surprise. Bandar said they'd decided to wait until it arrived. I figured they were curious. So I called it in, told command we had company. Friendlies. 'Just wait for the chopper', they told me. We built a fire, brewed some tea, passed around MREs, and sat around talking—my guys, the Nuristanis and the Muslim kids. I figured it was a good thing—hearts and minds, and all."

A log fell in the hearth, sending embers across the well-worn tile of the floor. "You've heard of the 'The Salvador Solution'?"

Billy nodded. "The helicopter—?"

"Helicopters—plural, two of them, unmarked. CSARs, those new combat rescue choppers landed with an entire interrogation team, complete with little black bags and a platoon of contractor protection. They wanted the Kashmiri boys, all of them, field operation."

Barrett's face had darkened, shadowed with pain and rage. "I'd always wondered how the Nazis were able to find so many sociopaths to do their dirty work. Didn't have to look far, apparently. Makes you wonder about the human race."

"Try the wine," said Billy. "It's quite good, really." He pushed the bottle toward Barrett.

"Are you trying to get me drunk?"

"Absolutely. I suspect it will mitigate the self pity."

"Damn it, Billy."

He caught himself. Billy was watching him with an amused smile.

"There's a glass behind you."

Barrett poured the wine. "Long way from the village reds we used to drink. You've moved up in the world."

"It came at a price. I was forced to sell a good part of the estate to sort things out. They're building a new mall, hideous thing. As a child I used to play in the woods there. There was a stream, and a cave in the hillside."

Billy held up his own glass while Barrett poured. He turned the glass in his hands, watching the hearth light reflecting off the wine.

"It must have been difficult," said Billy, speaking softly—almost as if he was speaking to himself, "turning those boys over to be tortured."

"Enhanced interrogation, please," Barrett interjected.

Billy looked up, "I've heard Afghans, Nuristanis in particular, do not offer their hospitality lightly."

Barrett nodded. "They shared tea with us, a meal, trusted us. It was a matter of honor."

CHAPTER 3

BARRETT WOKE WITH a throbbing headache and a sour taste in his mouth. He'd been dreaming of a green field bordered by a vast and forbidding forest. Animals lurked in its shadows and an alien sun shone overhead. Something about it was familiar, beautiful and familiar, and he hadn't wanted to let it go.

He glanced at his watch, an Army issued Rolex Submariner, the one thing of value he'd managed to hold on to during the long journey from Kabul.

8:45. He'd slept nine hours, his first decent night's sleep in weeks.

He dragged himself out of bed and threw open the window curtain. Across the gables he could see the morning's distant traffic stalled on the new Oxfordshire Expressway. There had been a time, not long ago, when the view from that window had been a forest, streams, and countryside. He wondered if his dream had been nothing more than a memory of that bucolic past?

When was progress actually progress, and when was it something else? Billy's careful leasing out of the estate's land to developers, painful as it must have been, had allowed him to keep his beloved manor. It had even made him a wealthy man, though you couldn't tell by the way he lived. Little had changed in that regard, save, perhaps, the quality of his wine and the capacity of his computers. He certainly no longer needed to rent out rooms. Barrett suspected he still took in boarders because he liked having people in the house, even old Meg, though he would never admit it.

His own room was warm enough, but he still found himself shivering, imagining damp mist seeping through the windowpanes into his bones. Winter was approaching. The days grew shorter. He had a disturbing sense of the world closing around him.

The thought was interrupted by a knock at the door. He opened it to find Billy, a large cardboard box in hand. "Good, you're up. Found these in the attic. Thought you might find them useful."

He pushed into the room, setting the box on the unmade bed. He took a small, rose-colored glass bottle from a shirt pocket. "Try one of these."

Barrett examined the bottle. It contained a number of very large pills. There was no label. He looked up, questioning.

"Nothing extreme," soothed Billy. "Roots, herbs and flower tops, I imagine. Elyse made them up. Good for headaches, jet lag and hangovers."

"Two out of three. How'd you guess?"

Barrett popped a pill, swallowing without water. "What's in the box and who's Elyse?"

"One of my lodgers. Open it."

Barrett removed the lid. There were clothes inside. It took him a moment to recognize the civilian clothes he'd left behind after he'd completed his Master's studies; shirts, pants, even underwear. "You kept these?"

"Forgot all about them 'till this morning."

Barrett glanced down at his stained boxer shorts. When was the last time they'd been washed? A week ago?

"I—I don't know what to say."

A woman, a girl really, passing by in the hall stopped and peered in. Tall, nubile, milky-smooth skin, disheveled auburn hair. She was dressed for a night out—heels, waist length faux fur coat and an expensive-looking silk shift, so short and clinging it was clear there was nothing underneath.

"Letting out the room, are you, Billy?"

The question was accusatory and Billy ignored it. "Just getting in, Alice?"

The girl shrugged. "Twit left me at Kensington. Paid for the cabbie at least."

Pert nose, full lips—even beneath the streaked makeup Barrett could see she was exceptionally pretty, possibly even beautiful. Her brown eyes were full of mischievous humor.

"You going to introduce us?" she asked, pretending to notice Barrett for the first time.

Her accent wavered between upper crust and Liverpool. Late teens or early twenties, he guessed.

Billy stepped between them. "Barrett O'Byrne, meet Alice Smith. Alice, meet Barrett. Barrett's a friend, and I'm not letting the room out. He's a guest. And you look like you could use some sleep, so on your way."

The girl studied Barrett with a frankness that made him acutely aware of his dress—or lack of it.

"Barrett, is it?" Her voice dropped into an imitation Bacall, husky and theatrically seductive. "Well, Barrett, I'm just down the hall. And call me Ally," she added with a sudden bright smile. "Alice is so very beige, don't you think?"

"You know the rules, Alice. No business here."

"Meanie."

The girl stuck her tongue out, gave a toss of her hair, smiled again at Barrett and turned to leave. "Besides," she said, glancing back over her shoulder. "Who said it had to be business?"

Billy closed the door. "Student," he said, as if in apology. "French Literature. Likes this room, says it has more light than hers. Pays her way by—well, you can guess. Her home life wasn't particularly stable—father abuse and all that. Bright girl, though."

He gave an exaggerated sniff of the air. "You could use a bath, you know. There's a razor in with those clothes. No shaving cream. Maeve might have some. She won't mind."

"Maeve?" said Barrett, thinking still of Alice.

"Shared bath, remember. Maeve lets the room next door—lead singer in an all-girl Irish band—'Celtic Maids.' They're on tour in Wales for a month. Pubs and clubs, mostly."

"Maeve, Elyse, Alice, Meg? Billy, are all your lodgers women?"

"Only if you call Meg a woman. Frankly I rather like to think of her as a bat, or maybe a crow of some sort. And, no pop psychiatry, please. Wounded birds make me feel more manly. The truth is women tend to be gentler on the old place. You do remember Nelson?"

Barrett grimaced. He remembered Nelson all right, an odious giant who'd sat number five on the Oxford rowing team a while back. Barrett had the misfortune of sharing the bathroom with the man—drains clogged with coarse black hair, crap in the toilet, sweat-drenched workout clothes tossed about at random, drunken late night rants and a continuing stream of loud and unattractive women. Billy finally evicted him, an act that had taken more than a little courage. Nelson was a bully, known for his temper. Barrett had stood ready to help if things turned ugly, but Billy had stood his ground, bad leg and all.

They'd celebrated when Nelson moved out. "Remember that oath we took? What did we call ourselves?"

Billy drew back his shoulders. "Knights of the Blasted Heath, we are. Never lie. Stand up to bullies in all their forms. Be loyal to friends. Do the right thing even if it means death or dismemberment."

"And of course, always behave honorably toward women," said Barrett, smirking.

"Always. Though I take it by your tone you no longer agree with those sentiments?"

Barrett felt a sudden irrational anger. *'What do you know about it?'* he wanted to shout. *'Holed up in this bloody mansion, playing fantasy games where everything is black and white. The real world isn't like that!'*

But the anger subsided quickly, leaving him feeling ashamed. He knew how deeply Billy felt about that stuff; honor, service, nobility.

"The difference between a truly noble person and a commoner isn't birth," Billy had once said. "The common instinct is to drag everyone down to his level. A noble person, on the other hand, recognizes real worth and quality, and does his best to raise themselves up to those standards. 'I can be as good as any man,' rather than, 'no man is better than me.'"

A rationale of the gilded class, Barrett thought. Still, there had been a time, not long before, when he'd believed much the same himself.

"Breakfast will be ready in the kitchen when you're ready."

Billy left, closing the door behind him. Barrett reminded himself why he'd come back to England. He'd spent all but his last few dollars bribing a mate on that Spanish freighter—and now he needed money. Billy had done enough, just letting him stay here. Fellow Knight of the Blasted Heath or not, he could not ask him for more.

During his time at Oxford, Barrett had put in a few months as a junior officer on a DOD procurement team, their job, to acquire human assets for work in Iraq. Their contact had been a man in London, and he had an appointment with him tomorrow afternoon. He hadn't seen the fellow in two years, but they'd always gotten along well enough. Hopefully, there would be work.

He sorted through the box of clothes, picked out jeans, a tan safari shirt, and a blue Cardigan. There was also a pair of expensive Bernini loafers he'd forgotten he owned. The clothes had a faint but cloying smell of mothballs, Billy's doing, as if he knew Barrett would need them someday.

The bathroom had changed dramatically since the days he'd shared it with Nelson. Spotlessly clean, embroidered linens, jars of bath salts, scented candles everywhere, an entire shelf of delicately packaged cosmetics. Barrett felt awkward and out of place, as though he'd stumbled into a lady's boudoir.

He shaved using a razor and lathered bar soap while waiting for the tub to fill, cutting himself only once. There was a jar of shaving cream on the vanity but he didn't feel right using it, an expensive boutique brand that must have cost the girl a day's pay. He cleaned the vanity with a wash cloth, turned off the tub faucet and eased into the water. Whether due to Billy's herbal pills or the first hot bath he'd had in weeks, he couldn't say, but his headache was gone.

His thoughts drifted to the girl, Alice, Ally. Young, pretty, sexy, if a little slutty.

He laughed at that. A little slutty? She'd been about as subtle as a dock whore. 'Hey, sailor! Looking for a good time?' Unfortunately, at the moment, he couldn't afford the price of a kiss from a Barcelona streetwalker.

Probably best. His limited experience with commercial sex had always left him feeling diminished somehow, less than the man he hoped himself to be.

What was missing? The challenge? The mystery? Love? Had he ever been in love? An adolescent crush or two, attractions based more on physical attraction than anything higher. What was love anyway but a clever marketing strategy, invented to sell lipstick, deodorants and thong underwear.

How long had it been? The German sisters in Athens, the Indian 'bibi' in Peshawar. He'd had one date with that U.N. worker in Kabul, but she'd been recalled two days later after a bombing had destroyed her clinic. As for the Afghans, forget it. Even to show interest in an Afghan woman was to risk a blood feud.

Four nights—four out of a thousand and one. He'd have done better in a monastery. Best not to think about it, though he supposed this current musing on carnality was healthier than dwelling on the past.

He felt sick. Images smashed through his defenses, *Jolly, running, his head exploding, screams, the clatter of automatic weapons, a Kashmiri boy in a futile attempt to shield his younger brother, Paulus falling, then Cisco, fire and cordite smoke, Bandar, there at the end.*

You had your orders! There was nothing you could do! Nothing you could have done! A lie! He could have done something. He should have done something. Done what was right!

Even if it means death or dismemberment.

The attack passed more quickly this time. Still it left him sweating and drained.

He took in a deep breath. The trembling eased. He was alive. He was thankful for that. It meant there was still time.

Time? Time for—what?

He looked around, found himself lying in the familiar tub with the big lion's feet, surrounded by that absurdly feminine bathroom. The bath water had grown tepid and in his mouth he could taste the sweet copper taste of blood. He'd bitten his tongue again.

He found Billy in the kitchen, frying up a pan of scrambled eggs. "Exactly on time," Billy announced, studying the eggs judiciously before shoveling them onto plates, one of which he handed to Barrett. "A little scrub and some fresh clothes and you look both like the old Barrett and a new man entirely, if that's possible. Sit. Sit."

A platter of fried ham was already on the table along with a pitcher of fresh orange juice, biscuits, butter and what looked liked a jar of homemade Apricot jam. A wisp of steam rose from the teapot. "Pill help?" Billy asked, joining him at the table.

"Headache's gone. Thanks."

"Thank Elyse when you meet her. Her concoctions usually do the trick. Tea?"

Barrett nodded. Billy poured two cups, adding a teaspoon of sugar to each. "Still insist on going to London today? You're sure this fellow can help?"

"He was straight enough back then. It depends on what's available.

Pay's up."

"Bugger the train, then. Take Isabel. She hasn't been out for a while, could use a good spin."

"Isabel?" Barrett was startled. "You'd let me take Isabel?"

"I worry about her sitting too long. Oil gets mucky, tires get flat on the bottom, seals dry up. I'd drive you myself, but this Leonidus thing has me snaveled."

Isabel was one of Billy's prides, a 1958 Jaguar Custom Phaeton inherited along with the title and estate from his late father, who had inherited the estate from his father. Billy's parents had both been physicians, unstintingly (Billy would say insufferably) zealous in their work for the World Health Organization, and who cared little for either the manor, or the car. Billy had spent his childhood being dragged like baggage from one festering hole of humanity to another, Gamboa, Ratanagua, Utter Gamesh, Katai, Pomadoji, places most had never heard of and, if they had, would more than likely avoid.

It was at Pomadoji where he'd had contracted a rare form of *scolio femoritis,* the disease that had left him with his bad right leg and an intense dislike for foreign travel. He'd once said it was only luck he hadn't contracted Ebola or been killed by mercenaries, which had been his parents fate.

"Don't worry about petrol," said Billy. "Her tanks are full and insurance is paid. You'll be doing me a favor. After all, what are friends for?

Chapter 4

"Sorry you came all this way for nothing, Lieutenant. If I'd known how to reach you, I'd have told you not to bother."

Piers Pontson, owner and sole agent for World Wide Manpower, Ltd., folded his arms across his chest and leaned back in his chair—not exactly hostile, but definitely not inviting. When Barrett had called to arrange the meeting three days earlier, Pontson had been both friendly and encouraging. "Young officer with your training and background? We'll find something to suit."

Unlike large contracting companies like Blackwater and Severus with their thousands of employees and armies of lawyers and lobbyists, Pontson worked alone, representing individuals—ex-intelligence agents, and military specialists—who were unable or unwilling to make their connections through regular channels.

Stocky and blunt-spoken, Pontson appeared to be doing well despite the economy, or perhaps because of it. His new office was on the nineteenth floor of the Branson Building. Expensive tribal rugs lay over thick Berber carpeting. The bookcase lining one wall held magazines, journals, and books on military history. A workstation with an array of sophisticated computer hardware took up a quarter of the room. The window behind Pontson's desk displayed a panoramic view of the Thames River. Three of London's bridges were visible in the distance.

"You're saying there are no jobs?" asked Barrett, somehow knowing the answer, but wanting to know the reason for the change in the man's attitude.

"Not for you. Considering your situation I'd be a bloody fool to take you on. Frankly I'm surprised you didn't bother to mention it."

"Mention what? What are you talking about?"

"The little detail about your desertion."

"Desertion?"

Pontson noted Barrett's stunned expression with a frown. "Don't tell me you didn't know? After your call I did some checking. You've been listed."

"That's impossible! I'm on terminal leave. Here!" Barrett fished two slim sheets of paper from his wallet and shoved them across the desk. "My orders."

Pontson made no effort to look at them. "My information says you faced a court martial for refusal to obey an order during an engagement in which a number of your men lost their lives."

Barrett fought down a sick feeling. "That's not how it was."

"But the event happened?"

"It happened. But I never refused an order. I was the only legitimate officer there. The others were contractors—an interrogation team. As for being court martialed, that's a joke. An open hearing is the last thing they'd want."

"You're saying it's a setup?" Pontson appeared to relax. "That would explain some things."

"Explain what? Who said I'm wanted for desertion?"

"Certain sources—nothing I can corroborate yet. It did smell a bit, if you know what I mean. Unfortunately, guilty or not, you put a burr up someone's arse—someone with clout."

Pontson picked up the orders, giving them a quick glance before handing them back to Barrett. "Easy enough to forge, of course. Proves nothing. I thought you said you were in Spec Ops. Those were issued by an intel outfit."

Barrett started to reply, then realized he'd never really looked at the orders, accepting them on faith.

Pontson was right about the issuing authority, 24th Army Intelligence. The authorizing signature was gibberish, the name printed beneath it, a man he'd never heard of, Colonel A. Bestair.

"I didn't know what command I was in. We were transferred out of Spec Ops two days after we got back to Kabul. My team—what was left of it—was broken up, assigned to units outside the country. I was the last to go. A Major, Harriman or something, brought my orders to me at the BOQ."

Barrett stopped, grimacing at his own naiveté. He should have been more wary, but accepting the leave had seemed the easiest way out of an untenable situation.

On some instinctual level he must have known it wouldn't be that simple.

Why else did he refuse the MAC flight to Salonika and hop that civilian convoy out of Kabul? He hadn't been thinking straight, not since that night.

But why charge him with desertion? The last thing they would want was a court martial, with its public forum and rules of evidence.

Another darker thought entered his mind. Why that flight? MAC flights left Bagram for the West every day. What had been waiting for him in Salonika?

"All sorts come to me these days," Pontson said. "Economy being what it is. Ex-cops, bully boys, soldiers and intel types, even the occasional 'Beau Geste,' wanting to join the Foreign Legion. If they're healthy and have some training, I can usually find them work. Unfortunately most of my business these days involves Americans."

He paused. "You do understand what I'm saying?"

Barrett had difficulty speaking, his emotions careened between despair and growing rage.

A deserter! How dare they!

Pontson stood and held out his hand. "Check the want ads, Lieutenant. There's work there, for someone willing. And remember, you're not alone."

He emphasized this last by tightening his grip as Barrett took his hand, as if the words were somehow meaningful.

Odd.

Barrett left. Outside the office the secretary barely acknowledged him as he passed toward the elevator. A man and a woman, both carrying briefcases, called out to him to hold the door. He ignored them. The door closed with a pneumatic hiss and he was alone.

He felt trapped, as if forces unseen were already closing in. Pontson seemed straight enough, but Barrett suspected he would be on the phone to— to whom? Someone who accused him of being a deserter?

And why the advice about the want ads? He couldn't use his passport, not now. He was in the country illegally. He had no visa, no work permit. There must be an underground labor market, but he was doubtful it would be advertised.

CHAPTER 5

BARRETT LEFT THE BUILDING and drove aimlessly, collecting his thoughts. He saw a small park and stopped. Leaving Isabel at the curb, he navigated his way through the nannies, prams and joggers toward an unoccupied bench.

Heavy dark clouds were building in the east. A storm, announced earlier by the BBC, was expected later that evening.

A sharp jolt broke him from his thoughts. "Hey! Watch it!"

A figure, average height, wearing a grey woolen greatcoat and a floppy grey hat, disappeared into the crowd. A newspaper, apparently dropped during the collision, lay on the sidewalk. Barrett reached down to pick it up.

The London Times showing today's date was folded in thirds, as though ready for a newsboy to deliver. He started to throw it in a nearby trash receptacle when something caught his eye. The employment section was folded to reveal an ad circled in red ink:

TRAVEL AND ADVENTURE
WANTED: Man in his twenties to early thirties. Must be brave, honorable, in good health and fit, skilled in the martial arts, particularly swordsmanship. Time of service undetermined. Excellent pay and benefits. Contact S., Langton Manor, Langton Vale, no later than 12:00 midnight, October 28th.

Barrett looked around, half expecting to find someone watching him. But no one in the sea of humanity flowing through the park appeared to be the least interested in either him or the newspaper in his hand.

He read the ad again, then a third time.

A prank. Has to be—.

Irritated at himself for half believing, he again started to throw the paper away. Then, almost as an afterthought, he stuffed it into his coat pocket.

CHAPTER 6

THE SUN HAD ALREADY SET by the time Barrett arrived back at Winford Manor. He left Isabel in the carriage house and entered through the servant's entrance. He ran into Meg below the stairs. "There you are, Lieutenant. Been wondering when you'd get back. Billy said to tell you he's out. Went off with Elyse. They should be back soon. He's a bit worried about you, you know."

"I know. I've got it sorted out, though."

Barrett had a strange fondness for the old termagant, which surprised everyone, especially Billy. She spoke her mind right enough but beneath it all she had a warm heart. The truth was, he found himself often appreciating her sensibilities, however harshly expressed.

"I've a pot o' tea on."

Meg's room was really a suite, with an attached bathroom, small kitchen, and adjacent parlor. During his year at Oxford he'd often taken tea with the old woman. She'd told him stories of living in London with 'The Major', her husband, who'd lost an arm in the Falklands. Barrett had listened more than he'd talked, which was one reason he was the one living person Meg had never spoken a bad word to or about. That, and the fact that he reminded her of her husband, she said, gone these many years.

Clearly she hoped to talk, while Barrett wanted nothing more than to lay back in a warm bath and put all thoughts from his mind. "I had some fish and chips from Andy's on the way back. Maybe later."

"I'll keep the kettle warm. You've that look The Major used to get when he was troubled. Sometimes it does good to talk things out. We close ourselves in—can't see the forest for the trees."

Had Billy broken his promise and told her something? Not likely. More probably it was just him, ex-army Lieutenant Barrett O'Byrne, wearing his problems on his sleeve. He would have to watch that. No good involving others.

Safe in his own room he shed his shoes and did a series of martial art forms while waiting for the tub to fill. He'd spent a summer in China after graduation from the Point, studying Yin style Pa Qua from Grand Master He Xiang Bao. The workout had become habit, almost an addiction, but the past weeks he'd been neglecting it. By the time he'd finished he was damp with perspiration.

Fifteen minutes and sweating—he couldn't allow himself to go that slack again. He turned off the bath water and did another half hour of Phoenix form, concentrating on the movement, stilling his thoughts as the form required.

He was interrupted by a knock. "Barrett?"

"Come on in, Billy."

Billy entered, accompanied by a girl. At first glance she didn't look over twenty. Petite, not over five two, with fine features and flaxen curls. Her blue eyes were made larger by thick, horn rimmed glasses. She wore a long flowing print dress and sandals. Barrett could easily imagine her with a garland of daisies in her hair.

Elyse, he decided, the maker of the remarkable headache pills.

Billy introduced them. He was smitten, Barrett saw. Well, good for him—about time.

"Had a pint and some chips at the Flying Dutchman," Billy said. "Walked the entire way." There was a note of pride in his voice.

"Walked? That's two miles, at least! "

"Closer to three, actually. Elyse has been working on my leg. Getting around much better these days."

"Most of the problem wasn't the disease," Elyse broke in with appealing earnestness. "He was compensating. We've been releasing the contractions, strengthening the muscles. He's doing quite well."

She put her hand on Billy's arm. The movement was both prideful and affectionate, so subtly endearing that Barrett felt a sudden rush of envy.

"I was about to take a bath."

"Oh, don't mind me. I grew up with five brothers. I'm off anyway. Women's group tonight—I've got to manage. Pleased to meet you, Lieutenant O'Byrne. Billy speaks very highly of you."

Her English was upper class with just the feathery hint of a dialect. Barrett, who was good with languages, tried to place it—not Irish, northern Scotland, perhaps. Good education, older than she first appeared. Twenty-three or -four.

"Just Barrett, please."

"Barrett, then. Good evening, Barrett."

She turned back to Billy, standing on her toes so she could kiss him on the cheek. "Take a hot bath tonight with your salts. You did well today."

After she left Billy closed the door. "She asked to meet you," he said somewhat sheepishly. "She approved, though for the life of me I can't understand why."

"You could tell?"

"She's very open with her feelings. She'd let me know if you weren't right. She's very intuitive."

"She's also very pretty."

Billy grinned. "You think so?"

"Very. In a fey, hippy, creature of the forest kind of way."

Billy laughed. "Certainly different than the society types my neighbors keep trying to set me up with. He glanced at the closed door. "I'm quite fond of her, you know."

Coming from Billy the statement was a declaration of undying love. "How long have you known her?"

Billy pulled out a chair and sat down, stretching out his bad leg. "She answered my posting about six months ago. First time we met she took one look at my leg and said, 'I can help that.' I took her for one of those New Age Twinkie people. Made me a bit angry, actually. I'd had my fill of therapies, you know. Lots of promises, but nothing helped, really. But she worked on it, certain movements, a massage sort of thing she does. Gave me herbs, some exercises, makes sure I walk on it—weight into the hips."

Billy lifted the leg and dropped it again. "Bit played out now, I'm afraid. How was London?"

"Interesting."

"Interesting interesting? Or interesting like the Chinese curse?"

"More like the Chinese curse." Barrett slumped back on the bed. "Billy,

I'm uh—I'm in some trouble."

"No work?"

"Not really." He hesitated, wondering how much he should say. "I'm leaving in the morning."

Billy had been kneading his leg. He looked up in dismay. "Morning? I'd rather hoped you'd be around a bit longer. I could use help with this Leonidus thing. Not quite sure how to go about it. If it's money—?"

"No. It's not money—not just money. I learned something in London. It's best you not know. It could spill over."

Billy nodded as though not surprised. "I didn't mention it last night. You needed to talk. But I did feel you were being a bit simple about the whole thing. They wouldn't let you just go like that, resign your commission and walk off, unattended as it were."

Once again Barrett was caught off guard by his friend's perceptiveness. "The leave was phony, a set up. I've been declared AWOL, deserter—but not publicly—at least, not yet"

"Of course. They would need to discredit you first. You will let me help? Fellow Knight of the Blasted Heath and all. I'm not exactly without resources."

Something in the way Billy said that last, the confidence, the absolute certainty, made Barrett pause. Billy had changed since they'd last been together, and it wasn't just the improvement in his walking. He'd been so absorbed by his own problems he hadn't taken time to appreciate it.

The publication of Billy's book the past year, 'Asymmetrical Warfare in the 21st Century,' had earned him a certain reputation, along with several large consulting contracts. Billy had never actually named his clients. Still, how many people in the world were there interested enough in Billy's particular area of expertise to pay him good money for advice? Terrorist groups, predatory corporations, and most current governments excluded, of course. He knew Billy too well to believe his friend had slipped over to the dark side.

Billy was his friend. If nothing else he deserved to know the score. "When I leave I want you to promise me you'll forget I was ever here."

"Pish. I won't do any such thing."

"Billy, these people—."

"Sorry. One for all and so forth. No use arguing."

Barrett gave up. "All right. You asked for it. I'm relieved of all responsibility." But even as he said the words he knew it was a lie. He'd put his friend at risk the moment he'd showed up at Winford Manor.

He left Billy sitting thoughtfully on the bed. The bath water wasn't yet cold, but close enough. He was toweling off when Billy entered, the newspaper he'd picked up in London in his hand.

"What's this about? I found it on the floor."

"What? That paper?"

"The ad you circled. TRAVEL AND ADVENTURE?"

"I didn't circle it. I found it like that on the sidewalk."

"Found it? And it was already circled? Strange, don't you think? You called, of course."

"It's a joke—has to be. Beside, look at it—no phone number. And the date? That's tonight. I don't even known where Langton Vale is."

"It's a two hour drive—some sort of ancient battlefield thereabouts— rather a mystery, I gather, hard to date. Wouldn't mind visiting the place myself." Billy looked at his watch. "It's not yet seven. Plenty of time."

"Are you nuts? Now? Besides, there's a storm coming."

"Worth a try."

"Billy, I don't think—"

"Don't think then. Get dressed. Afterall, what do you have to lose?"

CHAPTER 7

BARRETT UNDERSTOOD BILLY'S AFFECTION FOR ISABEL. The ancient Jaguar was as much a work of art as it was a machine. Her leather upholstery and burled walnut trim had been rubbed and polished so many times during her half century of life, they seemed to exude a warm glow. She cruised along at a stately sixty miles an hour, the sound of her 175 horsepower, and straight six aluminum engine little more than a soothing whisper.

With the traffic and some wrong turns, the drive took them two hours longer than Billy had predicted. It was closing on eleven when they saw the sign pointing to the village. Even in the glare of Isabel's headlamps its faded letters were barely legible—*Langton Vale, 3 miles.* The hands on Isabel's analog clock read 10:47.

"We'll make it," Billy murmured cheerfully. "We still have more than an hour."

Barrett slumped back in his seat. He'd tried to catch some sleep during the long drive but a growing and unaccountable apprehension had kept him awake. The closer they came to Langton Vale, the more apprehensive he became. He tried to dismiss it as concern about the future.

"The coincidence intrigues me," said Billy. "Finding that newspaper exactly when you did, right in front of you, particularly after that fellow mentioned looking in the want ads." He slapped Barrett on the leg. "Come on. Wake up. Full alert now."

Barrett scowled. "I should never have let you talk me into this."

The night seemed to agree with his darkening mood. A full moon rose over the trees, its pale light in stark contrast to the black clouds of the approaching storm. Clusters of houses began to appear, many with the plaster and beam construction of an England two hundred years gone. Sporadic lightning flashes added to the sense of the unreal. A ground mist was forming in the woods, flowing into the hedges and fields bordering the road.

A two pump Enco station on the edge of the village proper still had its lights on and Billy turned in. They hadn't seen another car since leaving the main highway.

Odd to find a station open so late at night with hardly any traffic. Still it was a stroke of luck. They needed directions and Isabel was down to a quarter of a tank. Grand old dame she was, but her twelve miles to the gallon was not going to cure global warming.

The night was surprisingly warm, almost humid. An attendant emerged from the station. The man fit the quaint character of the village itself, dressed in knickers and shapeless wool.

"I'll do that," he muttered gruffly. "How much ye be needing?"

Billy stood by the car, stretching his leg. "Whatever she'll take."

"A she, is it?" The attendant eyed Isabel appreciatively as he primed the pump.

"Surprised to find you open this late," said Barrett.

"Always open Samain night, leastways 'til the women finish their doings at sunrise."

"Samain? Barrett had heard the term but knew little of what it meant, a Celtic holy day of some sort.

"Halloween," supplied Billy. "Leastways, its precursor. Full moon tonight, some unusual astrological alignments this year. Elyse is into it. She's got the others, Meg and Maeve, Alice even, involved in some ritual thing back at the house."

Barrett stared in disbelief. "Are you serious? It's Halloween night and you didn't tell me? Is that what this is about? A ruse to get me out of the house so your daffy boarders can chant at the moon?"

Another thought occurred to him. "The ad! It's a Halloween prank!"

"Nonsense," said Billy, unperturbed. "I didn't plant that ad. The fact it's Samain night should be irrelevant."

"Irrelevant?" Barrett was at a loss. It was the girl. Billy had always been so logical, so sensible. Any other time he might have said the change was for the better.

"Is there a Langton Manor around here?" he asked, turning to the attendant, half hoping the answer would be no and that would end it.

Instead the man nodded. "Aye, two miles up the road. Can't miss it. Lies atop Battle Hill, it does. Gate to the property's locked when no one's about."

"No one's there?"

"Gerlach, the caretaker, disappeared July last. Some say with the family silver. Others not so sure—me wife, for one. She's other ideas I won't repeat."

Barrett felt an unaccountable sense of relief. He shot Billy a look.

"Someone's there now, though," the man went on, seemingly contradicting himself. "Lights and such. Been seen walking odd hours about the downs. Wife says the Squire's back."

Barrett stood, trying to balance his emotions, a strange mix of anxiety and exhilaration. The man put the nozzle back on the pump. "Hundred and eight quid, even."

Grumbling, Billy payed cash. "Price of petrol keeps going up we'll all be walking. You're wife's in a coven?"

"Aye. She's Mistress. We've a cottage adjunct Notting Wood. Druid stone's there they use—and the wood's themselves, of course. Good night to ye." The man touched a finger to his hat and disappeared back in the station.

Barrett turned to Billy. "Coven?"

"Old Religion's common enough in these country villages." Billy climbed back into the Jaguar. "We'd better be on. Midnight's not far off."

The macadam road changed to cobbles as they entered the village proper. The shops were quaint and well kept. Neatly painted signs announced 'The Green Man Boutique,' 'Wild Hunt Antiques,' and 'Battle Hill Crystals and Potions'. In daylight Barrett imagined it would be charming and picturesque, a place for a weekend escape from frenetic city life. At night, this night at least, it seemed oppressive and medieval, with only an occasional street lamp lighting the way. Mist drifted in from the forest and hung low to the road, curling up stairways and lampposts. Shadows prowled in the narrow alleyways.

They slowed as they passed the only building in town that was brightly lit. A wooden sign over the door bore a lion and unicorn, rampant. "Local pub," said Billy, stating the obvious.

The Lion and Unicorn.

Barrett found the name unsettling, though he was uncertain why. Through the pub's paned windows, patrons could be seen crowded against the bar, pints in hand. No women, he thought darkly. Probably out in the forest, throwing runes and dancing naked.

The road reverted to a pale macadam as they left. A round hill loomed to their left, separated from the road by a wide meadow and encircled by a high stone wall. Atop the hill, silhouetted against the rising moon, was a large and forbidding edifice.

They drove another mile before arriving at the entrance. An iron gate stood open, the driveway beyond was lined on both sides with great shaggy oaks. Wind, ominous and smelling of fall harvest, filled his nostrils as Barrett lowered his window for a better view.

"Gate's open," said Billy, again stating the obvious. For the first time that night he sounded uncertain.

Barrett glanced at his watch. The luminous hands read eleven minutes past eleven. The clock on Isabel's dash read exactly the same. 11:11. The second hand seemed to slow as it made its way around the dial.

The drive was narrow, built for an earlier time. Weeds, a foot high in places, clogged the cracks between the bricks.

"No one's been up this in months," said Barrett.

"Maybe there's another road," said Billy.

Lightning flashed again, followed seconds later by the rumble of thunder. After the eerie silence Barrett found the sound oddly comforting.

The driveway wound about for another quarter of a mile before they came abruptly to a circular courtyard. The three-storied house loomed over them, it's gables and stone walls covered with dead and dying ivy and the patina of centuries.

Billy left the motor running and Isabel's headlamps on as they got out. A gust of wind whispered through the trees and rattled the gutters.

"Spooky old place," said Billy.

Barrett thought he saw movement in an upstairs window, a curtain blowing in a draft. The light from Isabel's headlamps spilled sideways across a large knocker in the shape of a lion's head.

Billy hesitated as he lifted the knocker. "Wouldn't want to wake anybody,"

"As Elyse says, 'Nothing ventured, nothing gained.'" Billy let the knocker drop. A dull boom sounded inside as it landed on the striker plate.

Seconds passed.

Smirking, Barrett was about to speak when—.

"Good evening. May I help you?" said a voice.

"Holy Mother—!" Startled, Billy did a half turn, almost colliding with Barrett.

Someone was standing in the gloom near a high hedge. It was difficult to make out features; medium height, dark greatcoat, a floppy hat of equally indeterminate color.

"I didn't mean to startle you," said the apparition. "I was out walking and saw the lights of your car. You're here about the notice, I presume?"

The figure moved closer, still hidden in shadow.

"Yes, the notice," said Billy, recovering quickly. "It's legit, then?"

"Quite legit, I assure you. I'm around the side, cook's apartment. Follow me, please. Quickly, now. We haven't much time."

Without looking back to see if they were following, the figure vanished down a path.

"Extraordinary," said Billy. "What do you make of that?"

Barrett didn't answer. The enigmatic dread that had been growing in him since nearing the village had returned with a vengeance. The feeling was so strong it took an effort of will not to grab Billy by the arm and bolt to the car.

Vexed with himself, he took a deep breath and shrugged. "Nothing ventured, nothing gained. Right!"

"Good," said Billy. "My thought exactly. Hold a minute, would you."

Billy limped to the car where he switched off the engine and headlamps and pocketed the key. He returned brandishing a small flashlight taken from the glove box. "Ready."

A large drop of rain splattered the cobblestones. Then more. The long expected storm poured down in earnest.

CHAPTER 8

THE SITUATION WAS SO FOREIGN to Barrett's experience, he had no framework for comparison. The creepy atmosphere was enough to give goose bumps to a gravedigger.

A jagged fork of lightning lit up the sky, followed by crackling thunder. Rain clattered against the gutters and streamed over the cobblestones. They followed the path past stilled fountains, gardens gone to seed, and mulberry trees that hadn't been pruned in decades. By the time they'd rounded the corner of the house the rain had drenched them to the skin. Their host waved to them from a doorway. "Inside—put your coats by the fire."

They were ushered into the warmth of a comfortable drawing room. A sofa and two overstuffed chairs circled a small stone fireplace. Three oil lamps lit the room. A grandfather clock in the corner chimed the half hour: 11:30.

As their host removed the soggy hat, a shock of grey hair fell to her shoulders.

"I say," said Billy. "You're a woman!"

"I'm Sianiave Langton. Current Squire of Langton Manor. Squiress, if you prefer. I placed the notice."

"Why?"

"There's a tea pot on the stove in the kitchen. Who is the applicant?"

"Applicant?"

"For the post! I believe the notice indicated one man. Singular. Which of you is it?"

Billy dropped the flashlight in a pocket of his coat and hung it on the rack by the fire. "Uh, it's Barrett, my friend here."

"Good enough. Kitchen's through that door. Be a good fellow and brew up some tea while we talk. China Keemun is all I have, I'm afraid." As she spoke the woman began hustling Billy toward the nearest of two doors that led from the room.

"Wait a minute!"

Without thinking, Barrett had grabbed the woman's arm, finding it to be as well muscled as that of a young athlete. She looked at his hand, not quite in annoyance, more as though amazed he'd had the temerity to touch her at all.

Apologetic, he released his grip. "Sorry. But before anyone goes anywhere I'd like to know what this is about."

"Impossible. There are aspects to the work that can't be discussed with anyone but the applicant."

"It's all right," said Billy quickly. He regarded the woman for a moment, then nodded. "You won't find better than him, you know."

She smiled. It was a kindly smile, with no hint of irony. "I know."

Then, as though having said too much, she swept an oil lamp off a side table and shoved it into Billy's hands. "Take this. Electricity has been off for a bit. There's food in the icebox, cheese and viands. Help yourself. I know I'm being short, but there really isn't much time.

"One caution," she added. "Stay in the kitchen. Do not, under any circumstance, enter the main house. It's not—," she hesitated, searching for a word. "safe."

"Okay. Kitchen only."

Billy left, the door closing behind him. Barrett faced the woman. "Alright, you've got my attention."

"First sit down. I have some questions for you."

There was something in her tone, not demanding exactly, or rude, more the voice of someone confident in her abilities and used to being in charge.

He tried to place her and came up blank. Her grey hair, full and straight, was modestly groomed. She wore little if any makeup. A gold earring with a single blue stone hung from her right ear, and there were three large rings on her fingers, one on her left hand and two on her right, each set with a stone, of yellow, red and green. She wore elegant leather boots, a simple white cotton blouse, and khaki slacks that could have come from any high-end shop in the world. Her English was so free of accent it was almost an accent in itself. Judging by the fine wrinkles around her eyes he guessed she was in her sixties or seventies, though in the right light she might pass for younger, perhaps much younger, judging by the easy way she moved and the surprising strength he'd felt in her arm. Her nose was slightly crooked, as if broken and never set right, and there was a small scar on the left of her chin. Her eyes were a startling shade of emerald green. Other than the glint of sharp intelligence, they gave little away. One thing was clear. Here was a woman to be reckoned with.

He sat on the nearest sofa. The woman took a seat in a chair across from the fire, facing him.

She took a long stemmed clay pipe from a wooden box on the coffee table and began packing it with tobacco, though of a type he'd never seen before—grey shreds, like desert sage.

"Your name?" she asked.

He opened his mouth, then hesitated. He'd been about to give his name as Michael Coerte, the name on his phony passport. Billy had already given away his real name, he remembered.

"Barrett," he said, feeling a curious sense of relief at not having to lie. "Barrett O'Byrne. And you are really are a Langton. Si-an-a—?" He stumbled over the name.

"Sianiave. And yes. I am a Langton, the last Langton. As for the work, it's exactly what the notice indicated. Since you've taken the trouble to answer it I presume you feel you meet the requirements?"

"They seemed fairly straightforward."

"Your skill with a sword?"

"I was captain of both the fencing and archery teams at West Point, and I've studied kendo, not that—.

"West Point? An officer? May I ask what rank?"

She had an irritating way of asking questions, abrupt almost to the point of rudeness.

"Lieutenant, recently resigned."

"Your age?"

"Twenty six, more or less. Look—"

"More or less?"

"I was raised by foster parents. No one knew my biological parents, or the exact date of my birth."

"An orphan. How intriguing. Well, Lieutenant O'Byrne, or would you prefer I call you Mr. O'Byrne?"

"Barrett's fine."

"Barrett, then. Isn't twenty-six a bit old to still be a lieutenant? One would assume that a West Point man with any capacity at all would have risen to the rank of captain by now. Did you enter university late?"

"I was in Special Ops. Rank doesn't come easy."

"Of course."

The look of amusement on the woman's face indicated she understood exactly, or didn't believe a word of it.

A small flame seemed to sprout from a finger as she lit the pipe. Barrett couldn't see a lighter. A match, probably, hidden in her hand. Neat trick, that. She took a puff, and let it out. The smoke was grey but definitely not tobacco— not sage or marijuana either. It had a pleasing, meadowy scent, though nothing he recognized.

"One more question," she said. "Then it's your turn."

He braced for the question he knew must be coming, unsure as to how to answer. He couldn't tell her the truth, that he was a wanted man, wanted as a deserter with possible terrorist connections. Yet for some reason the thought of lying, of lying to her, was unthinkable.

The Squiress of Langton took another puff on the pipe and leaned back in her chair. As she exhaled, the smoke formed into shifting strands that curled toward the ceiling. Her fathomless green eyes caught and held his. The connection was intimate, almost physical.

"Have you, Lieutenant O'Byrne, ever asked yourself what compelled you to engage in martial pursuits such as archery and fencing?"

The question was so oddly phrased, so different from what he'd expected, for a moment Barrett sat speechless.

Billy stood, mesmerized, both by the enormity of the kitchen and what it contained. Despite the light from his lamp, much of the room was lost in shadow.

It was as if he'd entered a museum exhibit, or wandered onto the set of a period piece. The appliances were even older, much older actually, than the ones at Winford Manor. The refrigerator truly was an ice box—the kind they had at the turn of the last century where a block of ice was slammed into a compartment—not just a figure of the old woman's speech. The gas range was a twelve burner dinosaur, it's center griddle massive. Two large ovens, each sufficient in itself to provide for a small bakery, sat on either side. Utensils and copper pots hung from overhead racks. There were four large porcelain sinks and a huge woodblock table. An entire wall consisted of nothing but cabinets of chinaware, enough to serve hundreds.

The Squires of Langton had done some entertaining in their day, he thought.

He tried to place the current owner, if indeed she was the owner, in this context. If truly a Langton, she was the keeper of a great family history, and secrets, surely many secrets. His own family, the Winfords, had once been well-regarded members of the British aristocracy. He prided himself on his knowledge of British history, particularly its military history, which among the English was inseparable from the whole. But about the Langtons he knew nothing. Who were they? How had they come by their fortune? How had they come to build their manor on Battle Hill, and why did it appear as though the place hadn't been inhabited for a hundred years?

An ancient battle had taken place in the region, possibly on this very hill. The particulars were vague—4th or 5th century, Rome in decline, the period when the first tales of King Arthur had begun to surface. King Arthur also was known as Artos the Bear, who in all probability had been a local patrician or tribal chieftain of some sort. Yet there was no mention of Arthur in any tales associated with this particular battle, nor of Romans for that matter. Artifacts uncovered at the site were thought by most scholars to be of Celtic origin, though unique in design and workmanship.

In the 1920s an amateur archaeologist, a German named Piter Dietrich, claimed to have found a sword while digging in the area. What was remarkable was that the sword was wrought of finely folded steel and was still in relatively decent condition. As steel of any quality was rare among the Celts, the archaeological community immediately determined it to be of a later period, possibly even a forgery. Suspicion fell on Dietrich, whose amateur career then came to an abrupt and humiliating end. Those same authorities dismissed the site as having no great significance. Perhaps a Norse incursion—though in those days Viking raiders tended to stay nearer the coast.

A battle of more import than the academics realized had taken place here. Billy was convinced of it. The battle's origin and outcome might remain a mystery, but its lasting effects were clearly alive in the local populace. Over the years, dozens more artifacts had been discovered, from brass spear tips to tarnished axe heads—these usually found by local farmers tilling their land, or children playing in the fields—yet not one skeletal remain had been uncovered. Perhaps they'd been burned, or taken to another location for burial.

The Battle of Langton Vale was one of those queer historic anomalies reputable archaeologists avoided, much like Grail research or tales of Atlantis. 'Career enders' they were called. Sir Harold Bingham had mounted a serious excavation of the battlefield in 1939. That ended with the outbreak of World War II and the archaeologist's unexplained death less than three weeks after work on the site had begun.

❖ ❖ ❖

"Intriguing," murmured Billy. "Very intriguing."

He set his lamp on the prep table. A copper tea pot, half filled with water, was on the stove where Sianiave had said it would be. Judging by its condition it was one of the few pieces in the kitchen that had been recently used. A tin of China Keemun tea was on the counter next to the stove, along with teaspoons, a bowl of sugar, slices of lemon, a box of matches, and three porcelain tea cups.

Three? Almost as if she'd been expecting them?

He glanced at his watch: 11:44. Sixteen minutes to midnight. She seemed to be in a hurry. Why? The possibility others might arrive in answer to the notice was of small concern. Barrett would be the best man. But best for what, exactly?

Squiress Langton was a presence, that was certain. Once she introduced herself, Billy had no doubt about her authenticity. He was relieved more than he cared to admit. It had troubled him deeply to see his friend in distress.

Unlikely as it first appeared, the notice in the newspaper had given him an excuse to get Barrett alone for a few hours and examine possible courses of action—a loan, perhaps. Barrett would refuse an outright gift. The ad had seemed a flight of fancy, though Elyse had pounced on it immediately.

The thought of Elyse comforted him. Her openness to the unexpected, her faith in the extraordinary. She wouldn't question any of this—not at all. She had remarkable intuition about people. He wondered what she'd make of Sianiave Langton.

Si-an-a-vee. Celtic sounding, *a bit exotic, but still in fine shape*, he thought. Billy immediately trusted her, though he didn't know why.

He lit the burner on the stove. A new, five-gallon tank of natural gas stood on the floor near the stove, a line jerry rigged to the stove's backside. There was no electricity, just gas brought in bottles. According to the man at the petrol station, the caretaker had vanished some time ago under suspicious circumstances. It seemed Ms. Langton had not been long in residence.

While he waited for the water to boil, Billy wandered about the kitchen opening drawers, peering into cabinets. There was little enough in the 'ice box'—a slab of ice, a block of cheddar cheese, a loaf of bread, milk, and a few other odds and ends that included a half eaten roasted chicken in a plastic take-out tray.

Was it something to do with the house? Was she claiming the estate from dysfunctional relatives, tracking down the caretaker who'd purloined the family silver? Judging by the stash of silverware in the drawers, they hadn't pilfered much. The house was just the sort of place thieves and vandals would target.

Billy put a single tea bag in each cup along with slices of lemon. The water was taking its time to boil.

Two large swinging doors on the far side of the room appeared to move, as though touched by a draft. The doors led to the main part of house?

Can't hurt to look. You don't have to enter, just a peek.

Billy pushed open one of the doors just far enough to see into the space beyond. It was as dark as a cave, and at first he had no desire to enter. But then a flash of lightning lit up a vision, and Billy was transfixed.

"My lord!"

The lightning had shown a great hall with a high ceiling and many door-ways leading to who knew where. The walls were richly paneled in dark wood, the floor set in a pattern of black and white marble. But it was neither the floor nor the walls that drew his attention. Wondrous things, swords, shields, battle axes, spears and pikes, weapons of a kind and design he'd never imagined filled the gallery. Surely they weren't local.

Forgetting both the water boiling on the stove and his promise not to leave the kitchen, Billy almost stumbled in his hurry to get the lamp.

CHAPTER 9

'WHAT COMPELLED YOU TO ENGAGE IN MARTIAL PURSUITS such as archery and fencing?'

Barrett stared at the woman, struggling to hide his emotions. Why he reacted so strongly to this question, he had no idea, only that the moment she asked it, his heart constricted into a cold ball, and a strange, almost painful throbbing gripped his head.

The previous questions had been tailored to lead him along a certain line of thought, a technique that might have come straight from the pages of a military interrogation manual. Tease the subject with obvious questions, then, when they least expect it, hit them with a kicker. Knock them off balance. Let them think you know far more than you really do—that you already know the answers.

What answers? *What could she know? What was there to know?*

Barrett took a breath. The buzzing subsided. Without waiting for an answer the woman took a puff on her pipe, her green eyes cool and appraising. "Your turn," she said.

Outside the storm had increased in fury, the lightning and thunder incessant. Buffeted by the wind the rain sounded like a drum rattle against the window. Outside there was a loud crack as a falling branch struck the side of the house. Sianiave's eyes went to the clock. 11: 49. Eleven minutes to midnight.

Barrett cleared his throat. "This job—?

"Bodyguard of a sort. I've always admired a man who can use a sword well. It shows a certain strength of character."

"Is it you?"

"Excuse me?"

"Are you the principal? The body I'll guard?"

"Heavens no." She laughed, as though the thought was absurd. "I'm just an agent. It's a woman, though, a girl, really."

"Is she coming here? You've been watching the clock."

"No. She's not in England. And I am concerned about the time, very concerned. We must be on our way shortly or we'll miss the rendezvous. And since we don't have much time, and since you appear to have the necessary qualifications, you have the job. You begin immediately."

"Hold it. I haven't said I'll take the job. About the fee?"

"Fee?" Now she was amused. "Of course, five hundred a month, with a contract of six months. If the job ends sooner, you will be paid for the full six months. In the unlikely event it takes longer all parties will be free to re-negotiate."

"Five hundred—what? Dollars? Pounds? Euros? That's not enough to— ."

From somewhere she materialized a coin, flipping it to him, "Of these, coins of the realm. I'm unsure of the current exchange rate, but whatever it is, I trust it will be sufficient."

Barrett caught the coin in the air, surprised by its weight. It was crudely minted, but he had little doubt it was gold, very fine gold. It reminded him of a Spanish piece of eight, struck from a single gold bar, the figures imprinted with a hammer and die.

Energy costs, immigration, global warming, wars, the growing public uncertainty about the world economy, all had combined to drive the price of gold well north of a thousand dollars an ounce.

"That's crazy," he murmured, calculating the value of five hundred such coins. He turned it in his fingers. Heads showed the bust of a woman. The coin was worn, making it difficult to discern details, but the effigy had a look both of compassion and wisdom, much like the Chinese deity Kwuan Yin or the Hindu Green Tara. Tails featured a lion and unicorn rampant, the same images as the pub sign in the village. As with the sign, he felt the same sense of familiarity.

Coin of The Realm? Which realm?

"Where did you get it? And why the largesse?"

"You'll earn it. I assure you. As to where I got it, you'll find out soon enough."

She opened a drawer on the sofa's end table taking out a small leather pouch which she tossed on the table in front of him. "There are ten more in that purse. Call it an advance. Now, please. We must be going. Say good bye to your— ."

A scream from deep within the house cut her off. Barrett jumped from his seat. "What the hell!"

Sianiave was also on her feet. "Your friend! I told him not to go in there!"

Barrett, already halfway to the kitchen door, hardly heard. Sianiave hesitated only a moment, then grabbed up her walking staff and followed.

Outside, the storm was growing ever more violent, the lightning and thunder so frequent now, it was as if the house itself lay at the center of a pitched battle. Barrett ran through the kitchen. The scream had come from beyond. He slammed through the double doors just as Billy came stumbling toward him.

"Jeezes, Billy! What's wrong!?"

"Barrett! We have to get out of here! Something's in there—a bloody nightmare!"

Billy kept looking over his shoulder as if expecting whatever it was he thought he saw might appear at any moment. Shadow shapes, caste by a shifting orange light danced across the walls. There was an acrid odor of smoke. It took Barrett a moment to realize what he was seeing. "Fire!"

Billy paled even further. "Bloody hell! The lamp! Wait, don't go in there! Barrett!"

"The whole house could go up!"

Billy stood immobile as Barrett ran into the hall, torn between terror and guilt at his cowardice. Guilt won over. He pulled a sword loose from a wall and started to follow when Sianiave stopped him. "What did you see in there?"

Billy's mind was already at work, rationalizing the irrational, blocking out the unthinkable. "I don't know. Something—something fearsome—."

He weighed the weapon in his hand, suddenly unsure. "A shadow—I don't know. I thought—." He caught himself, realizing she appeared neither surprised, nor angry, just grimly purposeful. "It was real? You're saying it's real?"

The look on her face gave him the answer. "My God—Barrett!"

Barrett was in the dining hall, struggling to pull a burning tapestry from the wall. The shattered oil lamp lay nearby, its flames spreading with improbable speed.

The room itself was huge, the ceiling easily thirty feet high. Tarnished suits of armor stood guard at the doors. The great table at its center was encircled by chairs for a multitude. Tapestries, battle flags and ancient implements of war decorated the walls. The doors of a hallway opened to the far side, disappearing into darkness.

Barrett gave up trying to save the tapestry. The oak panels behind it were already ablaze, the flames leaping from panel to panel as if alive. for the first time he noticed the sword in Billy's hand. "What are you doing with that thing? We have to call the Fire Department."

"There's no phone service here," said Sianiave, who had entered behind Billy. Her attention was focused more on the darkness in the opposite hallway than on the burning wall.

"Do you have a cell phone?" Barrett had left his new one back in his room. Billy had never owned one, considering them a modern horror.

"Cell phone?"

"A cell phone, we need to call—." He stopped. It wasn't shock. She really had no idea what he was talking about.

She turned away. "It's not important. We're late already."

"You could lose the house!"

Her lack of concern was both frustrating and unnerving. Did she want the place to burn? They might hold Billy responsible. "We'll drive to the village!"

He took off running as Billy struggled to keep up. "Barrett, I saw something in there—honestly!"

Barrett didn't answer. He was beginning to suspect Billy might be right. It was clear the woman was hiding something. She was behind them now, walking slowly, looking over her shoulder, watchful and alert. He didn't think it was because of the fire.

They ran through the kitchen, grabbing their coats in the drawing room. Outside the storm was in full fury, the lightning flashes coming so close together it may as well have been daylight. Barrett had to shout to be heard above the thunder and driving rain. "I'll drive! Where are the keys!"

Billy handed them to him without objection. Barrett threw himself into the driver's seat, inserted the ignition key and pressed the starter button. There was no response, not a sound from the engine. "Damnit! It's dead! You must have left the lights on!"

"No. You saw me. I turned everything off."

"Where's the hood latch?"

"Hood? The bonnet! There. Down to your left."

Barrett pulled the latch and jumped out of the car. Billy joined him, shining his flashlight into the engine compartment as Barrett lifted the hood.

"My God! What—?"

The question trailed off into impossibilities. What had once been Isabel's beautiful, polished aluminum engine now looked like nothing so much as a lumpen blob of grey wax melted over the steel undercarriage.

Barrett glanced at his watch. Five minutes to midnight. Someone was having them on. But who, and why? And what could do that to the engine? Lightning? Must be, though some half-remembered lesson from Physics 101 told him it was impossible.

He fingered the coin in his pocket, shoved there when he heard Billy's scream. The pouch containing ten more coins was still lying on the table—an advance, she said. Maybe the offer was still open.

Flames were visible through the lower windows now, flickering against the glass. At this rate the entire mansion would be gone in a flash. Billy put a hand on Isabel's fender. "Sorry, old girl."

The rain seemed to be easing. In the direction of the village not a light was visible.

"Where's Miss Langton?" Barrett asked.

CHAPTER 10

SIANIAVE APPEARED SUDDENLY from around a corner of the house. The lightning and thunder continued unabated, but the wind had ceased and with it the rain. Instead of the greatcoat, Sianiave wore a long wool cape, its hood thrown back exposing her flowing grey hair. "Well, Lieutenant, time is short. Do you accept the commission?"

Barrett's thoughts felt suddenly and unaccountably leaden, disoriented, as though in an opium dream. "The fire—?"

"Forget the fire! Do you accept the commission!?"

He shook his head, trying to clear it. Billy elbowed him. "Say yes."

"But—."

"Of course he does!"

Barrett nodded feebly.

"Good enough." Sianiave shoved the bag of coins into Barrett's hand. She had grabbed them from the table. "The contract is agreed upon and witnessed. Now follow me. Your lives depend on it!"

The arbor led to a rusted iron gate, hidden in the ivy. A stone path lay beyond, winding down through thickets of overgrown roses. At one time the roses had bordered the path. Now gone wild, they covered much of the hillside. Mist was rising like steam from the dense foliage.

"Our car? The engine—?

Sianiave struggled with the rusted latch. "Dammit it, man! Gather your wits! The creature your friend saw in there is real! It's working on your mind!"

The words meant little to Barrett, but Billy swayed as though he'd been punched in the stomach. "Real? Good Lord."

"What you saw was only a thought form, otherwise you'd be dead. It's been trying to break through since last evening. The Binding on the house is old, weakening. The fire will end it—there!"

The latch came free. With the metallic grating of hinges long unused, the gate opened. At the same moment a horrifying shriek came from inside the house, slicing through the night like the cry of a banshee. The sound was so savage and dissonant, so full of insane hatred, Barrett had to fight back nausea.

"It's through! Run!" With that Sianive flew through the gate and down the path.

Barrett gazed at the burning mansion as though entranced. His thoughts were sluggish. Nothing seemed quite real. He regarded the bag of coins in his hand, its meaning momentarily lost.

Billy grabbed his arm. "Barrett! Run!"

Billy's touch broke the spell. Abruptly, as if jarred awake, Barrett came to himself. "I'm with you!" He shoved the bag of coins under his belt and started after Sianiave, Billy close behind.

The path led downward, its stones covered in dessicated rose petals slick with rain. Billy followed in a stumbling half-gait, slipping more than once on the wet grass, the thicket's sharp thorns tore at his clothes and skin. At first Barrett easily outpaced him, slowing often to allow Billy to catch up. But the further he ran, the more difficult movement became, every step more and more of an effort, as if the dullness that had been attacking his mind had decided to focus instead on his body.

"Barrett! Wait!" Billy was breathing heavily, obviously in pain. "Give me a moment. It's this downhill thing."

"We have to keep going. We're almost down."

Despite his words, Barrett was glad for the respite.

Above them angry red flames had burst through the lower windows of the house, shattering the glass, torching the trees and hedges and engulfing the west side of the mansion. There was something both frightening and compelling about the sight. "It's my fault," Billy groaned. "Such treasures there. Artifacts, weapons, all lost—."

"The fire spread too fast. Look at the flames. The color is too red—not normal. Besides, the woman doesn't seem upset about it."

Billy pondered that, then shook his head. "Whatever she's afraid of, it's real," he said. Then, thoughtful, "You know, without Elyse I never would have made it this far."

"Keep that thought. Marry her when you get back."

"She's certainly like no one—." Billy froze. "Look!" He pointed back up the hill.

"I see it! Get down!"

A figure had appeared on the hill, silhouetted against the flames. It was manlike in form, yet of greater size than any man could be. A splitting pain clawed at Barrett's head. His stomach turned over in a queasy, sickly, gurgle. Never had he felt such revulsion. "What the hell is that?"

Billy was silent.

As they were, hidden by the thicket and the gathering mist, it should have been impossible for anyone standing above to see them. But the creature slowly turned its head, as if somehow sensing their presence. With another unearthly scream it pushed through the gate and moved swiftly down the path after them.

Barrett helped Billy to his feet. "Time to go. Can you make it?"

"I'd bloody well better."

The path ended in a meadow at the bottom of the hill, a large standing stone dominated its center. Overhead, the storm clouds were parting, and the moon became fully visible. Its light reflected off the dull surface of the stone, luminous. Sianiave stood beside the stone, bathed in moonlight. "Here!" she cried. "It's almost on you!"

Within that circle of light was safety, Barrett knew, though why he was certain of this he had no idea. Close behind them, too close, he could hear the heavy footfalls of whatever it was that pursued them.

"Run! Run!" cried Sianiave.

Barrett was within a few yards of the circle when Billy cried out again and fell. He looked back to see Billy on the ground, clutching his bad leg and writhing in pain.

"Leave him!" cried Sianaive. "It's you the thing wants!"

Near as it was, Barrett still couldn't bring his pursuer into clear focus. Just feet away, it remained wraithlike, as dark and insubstantial as a shadow, yet as real and inexorable as death. Its breathing was labored, its rank breath stank of effluvium and decay. Its features were a vague and malevolent distortion of the human—tiny pointed ears, the stub of a nose, a lipless gash for a mouth. It was hairless, its small reptilian eyes as pitiless as death itself. A spiked mace swung from its right hand, back and forth like a pendulum, teasing.

Barrett moved to his right, hoping to draw the thing away from Billy, but it was wasted effort. The creature ignored the feint, stepping past Billy as if he didn't exist. Its attention was on Barrett alone.

"Such a weak little monkey." Its voice was a rasping whisper.

The thing was evil, Barrett knew. He'd never thought in such terms before but it was the only word that fit. Arrogance, cruelty, perverse lusts and a venomous hatred of all things human—the creature reeked of it.

He stood, indecisive. Time seemed to slow. How do you defend yourself against a monster wielding a mace? His revulsion had become stomach wrenching. He tried to back away, but it was like moving in thick honey. He could hear the creature's voice in his head, sly and seductive—'weak—so weak—effort is pointless—no hope—weak—.

The mace snaked out. From somewhere Barrett found the strength to duck and the ball missed his head by less than an inch. Instinctively he dropped into Crane Fights Snake, kicking out with his left foot at the creature's knee. But his effort was slow and powerless.

The creature laughed and swung the mace. Spikes tore furrows of cloth and skin from Barrett's shoulder. The ball continued, arcing around with impossible speed. This time it struck his shoulder square, crushing bone and tendon and knocking him backward on the wet grass.

Just before he lost consciousness Barrett heard Sianiave calling out. The language was strange, though the words seemed familiar, part of the same distant and ephemeral memory as the images of lions and unicorns—and a woman's face on a gold coin.

Crazy. Everything was crazy. Just a dream, a dream only. Billy really ought to marry Elyse. He's a good man. True to a fault. He deserves happiness. Someone deserves happiness.

If only—if only—.

A blinding light.

Then darkness.

CHAPTER 11

BARRETT OPENED HIS EYES.

As a foster child, he once spent eighteen dreary months with a family of devout Christians, Dominionists who believed Armageddon would soon cleanse the United States of nonbelievers and Christ would reign supreme for a thousand years. The creature that had attacked him fit well with their beliefs—one of Satan's minions if not the Evil One himself. But neither the feather bed on which Barrett lay, nor the rock-walled room, matched their idea of hell—nor heaven, for that matter.

Purgatory?

He was breathing. He could feel his heart beating strong and steady. His vision was unimpaired. If anything, it seemed sharper than usual.

In all probability he was still alive, though it was possible he was dreaming. Still, the bed and bedding felt real, solid. The room looked real enough. If he was dreaming it was the most vivid dream he'd ever had.

The room was unusual, definitely not a hospital room, at least none he was familiar with. It looked more like a granite cave whose walls had been dressed by stonemasons—high ceiling, corners rounded and uneven.

He was lying on his back in a large, four-poster bed, its canopy tied in swales to the posts. He was swathed in hand-stitched sheets of white linen, fresh pillows and duvet of thick goose down, judging by a feather poking from the duvet.

Two doors led from the room, arched, fashioned from heavy wood planks, banded in hammered iron. The door to his right was larger and more substantial, with a dead bolt the other lacked. He guessed that door led outside.

Outside? Where?

A heavy wood table, several chairs, and a large dresser comprised the rest of the furnishings. Torch brackets bolted to the walls were unlit.

Where was the light coming from?

He raised his head. High above, a window had been cut through the stone, multipaned, of an uneven oblong shape. Sunlight streamed through.

Altitude. High altitude. He was in the mountains.

There had been rumors of a monastery high in the Pamirs, a cave system inhabited for millennia by monks reputed to have magical powers, a name—Abshar. This had been in the very region where he and his team had encountered the Kashmiri boys.

Was he was back in Afghanistan? Had everything that happened since that night been nothing but a dream? It made a certain sense, but the details didn't add up. Every instinct told him that wherever this was, it was not Afghanistan.

He sat up, his body obeying without argument. There was no stiffness, only a slight tenderness in his shoulder. He was dressed in an unbleached linen shift not unlike a hospital gown but of finer cloth and rougher cut. He winced, remembering the pain of the creature's mace smashing into him. He pulled open the shift and found only yellow bruises where the spikes had torn into his flesh.

If it was fantasy, where had he gotten the bruises? But if his memory was true, and a monster had slammed twenty pounds of spiked mace into his shoulder, why was there so little damage? Hard experience taught him something about the human body and the effects upon it of violent trauma. The shoulder was an especially delicate and complex mechanism. That blow should have done serious damage. It *had* done serious damage. Of that he was certain—damage needing surgery, followed by months of therapy.

He rubbed his chin—four, maybe five days beard growth. Where was he? Who had brought him here? Was he crazy? Drugged? He considered the possibilities, rejecting them all. His mind felt clear. Exceptionally so, in fact.

René Descartes; I think, therefore I'm—what?

An image came to him. 521. Descartes, a foot soldier outside the gates of Prague the day the city fell. One of Barrett's professors had used that moment as a metaphor for the ascendancy of human reason. Until that fateful day Prague had been a center for such villified practices as alchemy, mysticism, and magic. Descartes, of course, had gone on to become one of reason's greatest champions.

There was a logical explanation for everything.

The sound of the latch lifting on the smaller of the two doors brought Barrett to alert. The door cracked open and a face peered in, red-bearded and friendly.

"Good. You're awake."

The man pushed open the door with his foot and entered. He was carrying a large tray. "Viands and drink, if you're up to it."

Seen fully, the fellow was one of the most extraordinary-looking individuals Barrett had ever encountered. He stood, Barrett guessed, a good five inches less than his own six two. But whatever he lacked in height he more than made up in breadth. His chest was broad as a door, his limbs in proportion to his mass. He was dressed in garb that looked for all the world like a Viking yeoman's, complete with sandals and fur leggings.

"Who are you?" asked Barrett.

The man placed the tray of food on the table. "Aye. You've got questions. Understandable. Not many survive a morghul's blow, not to mention being yanked here without proper preparation as you were. You have a great many, no doubt. Questions, I mean. I'll answer what I can of them. But you'll be wanting a bite to eat first."

Barrett swung out of bed, surprised at how easily his body moved. He felt twenty-two again, his age during the summer he returned from training in China and in the best shape of his life.

He stretched and yawned, languorously, like a bear waking from winter hibernation. He looked down at the food the man was setting on the table: a loaf of bread, four large red apples, and several thick cuts of some red meat. There were also two huge tankards containing some brownish liquid—cider, beer, or cold tea—what it was, he couldn't tell.

The fellow was right. He was hungry, ravenously so. "What time is it?" he asked.

"Late afternoon. Sianiave told me to pass on her regrets she was unable to be here when you woke."

Startled, Barrett looked up. "Sianiave!? She's real!? She's here!?"

"Real enough, but not here. Left this morning. Back in a few days, she said. I'm not one she confides things to." He held out his hand. "I be Osmodon of Linsraden, Sianiave's liege man."

Barrett took the offered hand, his own almost lost in the massive paw. Given his size, the man's grip was surprisingly gentle. Barrett had little doubt, had he so wished, the fellow could have crushed his hand as easily as if it were an egg.

"Barrett O'Byrne."

"Aye. Barrett of Amra. She told me your name. I've been watching over you for two days now, after Sianiave did the healing. If I'm to be your weapons instructor, I need to scree your mettle."

Amra? Scree? Healing? Morghul? Liege man? Weapons instructor? Question after question, all hinting at a mystery Barrett's reason told him could not be. For the moment he put them aside—thirst and hunger before his need for immediate answers. "Pleased to meet you, and thanks for the food. You'll join me?"

"Aye. Glad you asked."

Osmodon picked up a tankard and settled into a chair. "First rule of the traveler—never pass up a meal or the chance to drink good ale. One thing I've learned about the Lady Sianiave, she stocks the best." He raised the tankard. "*Y'ol bol'sun!*"

Surprisingly, Barrett knew the toast. He'd first heard it from a Kirghiz rug dealer in Kabul. "*May there always be a road.*"

He raised his own tankard, though unlike Osmodon who wielded his with one hand as easily as if it were a pint glass, Barrett was forced to use two. He drank, hesitatingly at first, not sure what to expect, then with dawning pleasure. It was ale, rich and heavy, better tasting than any he could recall.

"You're a traveler?" he asked, wiping his mouth with his sleeve.

Osmodon picked up a slab of mutton. "Aren't we all travelers on a journey into the unknown? But aye, Linsraden is many leagues off and I've been gone now these forty-four years, a pilgrim teaching arms and fighting to the worthy and the willing—and some not so willing, I admit—and perhaps not so worthy."

"Linsraden? Is that in the north countries? Sweden?"

"I've never heard of this Swe'den. Linsraden is Linsraden, loveliest holding in all the world—Asgar's temple on the cliff above, white houses below, white sailed ships in the harbor and the blue sea beyond. Leastways that's how it's still pictured in my mind. It's gone now, of course, burnt by the Black Fleet, our people scattered, killed, or taken south as slaves and sacrifices."

Whatever Barrett thought about the man, there was no denying the sadness that had fallen on him. "I took it on as a fault of mine," Osmodon went on. "But I couldn't foreswear my father. There'd been word of the Fleet, but not believing they'd come that far north he refused my advice and instead led us inland to Danemar—a goose chase, as it turned out."

The big man shrugged, biting into the mutton, nearly devouring it in a gulp. "I've come to terms. My father is long dead, as are the others who rode with us that day. The women stay most in my mind—warm, lovely things—as feminine as field flowers, but savage fighters when they'd a mind. They left their mark."

Barrett tried to place the accent, a slight brogue, neither Irish nor Scottish. It reminded him of Billy's friend, Elyse.

Billy! How could he have forgotten? "Billy! That thing—!"

"I was not present, of course," Osmodon said, unperturbed. He wiped mutton grease from his beard with the back of his hand and tore off a piece of bread. "Regretful, but I hear you gave an account of yourself. Few can stand against a morghul without knowing the shields. Its foul thoughts cloud your wits and suck your will. Believe me, I know. Yet not only did you stand, Sianiave said you even managed a blow. As for your friend, once you were through, my guess is the beast simply left him and departed."

"Your guess? Billy wasn't five feet away!"

"Morghul's are vicious and evil, yes. But never think them stupid. It was you he was after. Sianiave, at least, was not concerned."

Barrett felt lost. This was impossible, the very conversation, mad. His eyes rested on the larger of the two doors, looking for an escape to some place of sanity. "What's outside?"

"Why, the outside, of course. It isn't locked. Sianiave has no need of locks. Not here."

It had been said as an invitation and Barrett took it as such. He walked over to the door. Osmodon eyed him like a concerned father watching over a child. After a moment's trepidation, Barrett threw back the bolt and pulled up on the heavy latch. The door swung open to a draught of frigid air.

Outside was a small veranda, little more than a ledge. A low wall, no higher than a man's knee, was the only thing that stood between the ledge and what must have been a two-thousand-foot drop. A river moved below, a silvery ribbon winding through an impossibly steep canyon.

He fought a rush of vertigo. But it was not, at first sight, so great a shock as might have been. He'd suspected they were in the mountains—but which mountains? The peaks looked higher, sharper angled, far more dramatic than either the Rockies or the Alps. It could have been Alaska, though more likely the Andes or Himalayas.

How had they gotten him here?

Raptors circled in the distance, condors, hawks—eagles? With a slight tilt of its wings, one broke loose from the flock as if curious about this new thing that had appeared in its world. It soared toward where Barrett stood on the ledge.

As the full dimensions of the bird became clear, Barrett gasped in disbelief. "Holy—."

It was an eagle! But there was no eagle in the world, no bird in the world, so impossibly large. The thing was as big as a small plane.

Reason no longer held. He fell back against the wall. His breath caught in his throat as he stared up at the impossible.

He felt a warning hand on his shoulder. "Best come back inside, lad," said Osmodon, not unkindly. "The eagles here aren't generally known to carry off grown men, but one can never be certain."

CHAPTER 12

Barad'An, Anor
April 21

PRINCESS GWYNDOLYN—Ren to her family and friends—pulled back on the bowstring, stilled her thoughts as she'd been taught, and released the arrow. It sped to the straw target, hitting the bull's-eye with a gratifying thunk.

"By the gods!" cried Fletcher, as he and Ren both hurried closer to assess the target. "Ren, I believe you've done it!"

Ren had known the arrow would find its mark as soon as she'd let it go. It had struck the very center of the circle, nudging against Fletcher's own arrow, a feather's width further out.

She lowered her bow, struggling with an undefined emotion. Fletcher was captain-major of the wall guard and the greatest archer in Anor. He had been her instructor for ten of her seventeen years. Now, for the first time, she had bested him. She should be elated. Why did she feel only emptiness, sadness?

This was a passing, she suddenly realized—one for which she had not prepared. She'd come to the wall to keep her old friend company, for she knew how tired he got, standing the long vigils. The contest had been an afterthought, a way to break the tedium.

Mabry Fletcher was no longer a young man. In less trying times he would have retired years ago to his farm in Osting Garth. But his wife and sons were dead, his farm burned along with the other outlying estates. When Artos left, taking the cream of the young knights with him, the incessant battles bleeding away the rest, he'd had little recourse but to continue in his post. She could never have defeated him in his prime.

The old man grabbed her up in his burly arms, his weathered face beaming with pride. "A great day! Truly a great day!"

"What?" she mocked, a lop-sided grin hiding her true feelings. "—that you were beaten by a girl half your size and a seventh your age?"

"Absolutely, child. Every teacher dreams of such a day, the day he knows the teaching is done, his skill and knowledge passed on." He set her down again and bowed. "I only wish I had prepared a trophy. This moment should be remembered."

Ren struggled to find a suitable reply, something that would lift the sudden weight that had settled on her. But no words would come. She barely managed to hold back tears.

He pulled the winning arrow from the target. "I'll have it mounted."

"Now you're teasing me. Really, it was just luck—and only fifty paces."

"Six out of ten is hardly luck. As for distance, your strength will develop. I, for one—." He was interrupted by a cry from the nearest watchtower.

"RIDERS APPROACHING!"

They ran to the parapet, the contest forgotten. Below and in the distance a group of mounted men had emerged from the forest, riding at full stride for the city gate.

"It's the king!" shouted Fletcher even as the tower watchmen took up the call. It was impossible to mistake Nightmare, the king's great black stallion. At least three dozen horsemen, Uruks by their look, were in close pursuit.

Fletcher shouted orders. "Open the gate! Call out a sortie! It's King Cuchulain and he's hard put!"

Battle trumpets sounded as the orders were passed down the wall. Slowly, with the twanging of ropes drawn taut and the grinding of wooden gears, the great gate began to rise. Ren watched the scene below unfold with mounting despair.

So few—.

Her grandfather had ridden out that morning with nine knights and five squires. She counted only seven returning. She spoke their names out loud as she recognized their colors and horses—her grandfather Cuchulain in the lead, Aerindir and Abdelar, Bors, Prince Corwin, Squire Caswell. Was that Old Knockpine?

Where were the others? She feared the worse. With less than fifty experienced knights and fewer trained squires left in the city, every loss was felt, every death an irreparable blow.

"Archers prepare! Pikemen to the gate!"

Ren was old enough to remember a time when the land between Barad'An's wall and Arden Forest had been a bustling city in its own right, with a shifting population nearly as large as that within the city. There were makeshift shops, market stalls, tented pavilions, smithies, corrals, and forage barns to service the once vital caravan trade.

All gone now, burned by raiders or cleared for defense. Now there was just two miles of scarred grassland, only ancient grey oaks that stood like sentinels to mark the Great North Road. They had been planted the same year as the laying of the city's cornerstone, and no one had the heart to cut them down.

The king was less than half a mile from safety. Astonishingly, their pursuers didn't stop as they neared the wall. Eastern Uruks (by their dress) gave chase, mounted on wiry little steppe ponies. Did they actually think to attack the wall itself? Seven times in its long history, the wall had withstood armies.

With the sight common to her lineage, a sight some muttered bordered on the unnatural, Ren suddenly understood. They weren't after ransom. They meant to kill her grandfather!

Why? Uruks were tribal nomads from the Blasted Lands, little more than bandits. What would the death of Cuchulain gain them, save more enmity?

A horse stumbled with an arrow through its shank, spilling its rider. "No! Get up! Get up!" Ren found herself crying out loud, her hands clenched so tightly her knuckles were white.

"Belarane, Old Knockpine! Get up!"

She knew Belarane well. He had bounced her on his knee, though he was an aged man even then. He always smelled of cinnamon.

As if hearing her words, Belarane rose up, sword drawn. Aerindir and Abdelar broke from the king, horses rearing as they turned back to help. Belarane waved them on. "Stay with the king!"

The enemy was upon him. Ren watched as he fell, cut to pieces under rearing hoofs and flashing scimitars.

"The sortie!" cried Fletcher. "Where's that damned sortie!"

Trumpets sounded as knight after knight galloped out through the gate, many not even in battle dress. The Uruk charge wavered, then broke, flailing their curved swords and shouting curses as they retreated back to the forest.

All but one. Riding at full gallop, a large Uruk, a captain by his size and bronze ornaments, slid his bow from his shoulder, nocked an arrow, rose in his saddle, and let fly, all in one seemingly effortless motion. Ren watched in horror as the arrow arched toward Cuchulain with inhuman accuracy, striking through the king's right shoulder even as he reached the safety of the wall.

"Grandfather!"

Throwing down her bow she ran for the nearest ramp, pushing through soldiers coming up from the courtyard below.

In the plaza, pages were saddling nervous horses for knights hurrying to the field. Dogs barked, pigs, goats, and geese ran amok while citizens stood rooted, staring in fear as their bloodied king passed through the gate, a black feathered shaft piercing his right shoulder.

Ren pushed her way into the throng. "Let me through! Let me through!"

Cuchulain dismounted, staggering as he did so, doing his best to hide his pain. "Grandfather!" cried Ren, but he turned away when she moved to help. "Keep back, child!"

She started to object, but the words caught in her throat when she saw him sign to her silently.

Our lives are in danger.

Ren stood, shocked. Never before had she seen anyone use that sign, not since, as a child, the High Priestess Saolin had taught her the hand language.

Something was terribly wrong and it wasn't just the fallen knights or the arrow in her grandfather's shoulder. All of her senses snapped to alert. She looked at the nearest faces, searching for anything amiss.

"Bors!" cried the king, motioning to the big knight by his side. "Help me with this bloody dart!"

"Sire, we should get you to the healers —"

"Later," barked Cuchulain. Then softly, "There's no time." In hand code he signaled *poison.*

It took all of Bors' long years of training to keep the emotion from his face. He glanced up at the other knights mounted nearby, still waiting for the king's orders. Had they also seen the sign? He couldn't tell, for like himself, their faces gave nothing away.

Ren certainly had seen it, her eyes widening in alarm.

With only a grimace that showed his pain, and careful not to touch the arrow's metal tip, Cuchulain broke off the offending point, then dropped to one knee. Using both hands, Bors took hold of the shaft and pulled it free.

"There's bleeding, sire. It should be bandaged."

"Let it bleed," grunted Cuchulain. He wrapped the arrowhead in a scarf, placing it in his saddlebag. He turned to Ren. "Find Saolin. Bring her to my chambers."

Another hand sign, visible only to her and Sir Bors—*trust no one.*

Cuchulain grabbed his stallion's reins and mounted. "Carswell!" he cried to his squire. "Bring the priest—half an hour—no sooner and no later, by force if necessary! Corwin, Aerindir, Abdelar! Attend me!"

With that, the king, surrounded by Corwin and two of his remaining knights, angrily spurred the big stallion and sped through the hastily parting crowd.

Concern for her grandfather was uppermost in Ren's mind, but she also tried to make sense of his actions. The signal he'd given her was to be used only in the most dire of emergencies. *Immediate danger*?

But from whom? And why Saolin? Her grandfather hadn't spoken ten words to the priestess in years. And what did that lying blatherer of a priest know of anything?

"Bors? What happened out there?"

The knight was close to exhaustion himself, his green and black battle dress stained head to foot with blood. "Best you obey the king. I fear you'll have answers soon enough."

He spoke softly, so only she could hear. He took up the reins to his own horse and swung back into the saddle. "Don't tarry, though. The dice are rolling."

With that he turned his mount and rode out through the gate to join the hunt for the Uruks.

Ren studied the crowd, like herself, fearful and uncertain.

CHAPTER 13

SQUIRE CARSWELL HAD HIS ORDERS, and by his reckoning it was about time. "You two! Geoff, Pentwyn! Come with me!"

A hard man of no particular brilliance but deeply loyal, Carswell had been the king's squire for forty years, sacrificing land and a title to serve his king. During the Rift he had allied himself with Artos. But when Cuchulain had banished Artos from the kingdom, Carswell had stayed back and remained steadfast. He had never questioned that decision, though in hindsight, it was clear Artos had been in the right. The squire's morality was simple: Remain true, even if it meant death—even the death of a kingdom.

Carswell's two men-at-arms had been standing nearby. He didn't really expect trouble. Despite the priest's pretentious title and claims to holiness, Glays was, in Carswell's mind, little more than a peddler selling charms and fairy tales to a vulnerable citizenry. Glays would never confront a tested warrior, certainly not the king's own squire. Carswell was of the Old Faith, sore put when Cuchulain had given Glays the Old Right Temple, reestablishing it as a church dedicated to his strange religion and vengeful god.

When Carswell and the two men-at-arms approached the church, he saw twelve of Glays' white-robed ruffians waiting expectantly near the tower steps. The cleanliness of their dress was in sharp contrast to his own blood-soaked garments, so stained it was difficult to make out his colors of brown and yellow.

A sallow man with the two gold stripes of a captain smirked as he moved to block the way. "Apologies, sirrah. The church is closed today."

"Stand aside! I'm here by the king's order!"

"Squire Carswell. Of course. I hardly recognized you under all that filth. Did you fall off your horse?"

Carswell knew the man slightly and had no use for him—one of the itinerant mercenaries Glays had hired to populate his so-called temple guard. Insolent fellow. Any other time he would have called him out for such rudeness, but he was on the king's business.

"Now you know me! Stand aside!"

The man was defiant. "I'm afraid not, good squire," he murmured, his feigned courtesy belied by an irritating sneer. "Church grounds are sacrosanct. Weapons are not allowed. You can leave your sword and dagger here with me. I'll take good care of them—and your men, too, of course."

"My men?"

"Certainly. The bishop will see only you. Your men must wait here."

"He expects me?"

"Of course." The man tapped his forehead meaningfully. "Divine sight, you know."

It was clear the fellow didn't believe his own words, though several of the younger men in his troop raised their eyes heavenward.

Carswell stood for a moment, carefully turning over his options. He had little doubt the three of them could handle this pack. The king's orders had been explicit. "Use force if necessary."

His hand moved to the hilt of his sword. For a brief moment the smirk left the popinjay's face, and he took a step back.

Carswell hesitated. More than a small number of citizens stood with the priest's men. Cuchulain had not said why he wanted Glays brought to him, though he could guess.

"You've nothing to fear," said the man, again with mocking courtesy. "The bishop is alone, sirrah."

Carswell unbuckled his belt, handing sword and dagger to Pentwyn. A smaller dagger remained hidden in his boot. "Wait here. I won't be long."

He shoved past the captain and climbed the remaining steps to the church entrance, though he still did not think of it as a church. It had been built in the Old Days, on a hill within the city, taller than the royal palace. It was almost an exact replica of the Old Left Tower—Yu'an Tara's Temple—visible on a twin hill on the eastern side of the city. It had been built first and was the structure which gave the city its name—Barad'An—The Tower of 'An.

The priest's offices were to the right of the great columns and up another flight of stairs. Like most of the knights who had remained with Cuchulain after the Rift, Carswell was no longer a young man. He hadn't slept well the previous night. Now, after the battle and subsequent flight, he was near exhaustion. By the time he reached the door to the inner sanctum he was breathing heavily. He rested for a moment. Then, irritated at his own fatigue, he pushed through the unlocked door.

The room was large and round, with a high, vaulted ceiling. Save for a few poorly rendered portraits of pasty looking men with yellow rings above their heads, the walls were bare.

Carswell had been in that room before, when it had functioned as a temple to the Old Faith, and before the priest had arrived. Shelves had lined the walls then, filled with manuscripts and books bound in leather. Now, Glays stood alone, peering through a narrow window with a spyglass. From the window you could see the city below and the forest and hills in the distance. Divine sight, indeed. This was how the priest had known of his coming.

"Ah, Carswell," said Glays. "Good of you to come. The sortie knights are returning without much success, it would appear." He lowered the spyglass, turning to face the squire. "You were with the king. What brings you here?"

"You are to come with me. The king's orders."

Glays nodded agreeably. "Of course. I saw the arrow strike him. A nasty wound, I fear. I will bring my surgeon."

"I'd sooner put the the king in the hands of the Uruk who shot him than that rat-faced magician. You'll come alone, priest—and now. The king awaits."

Glays wore a voluminous white robe woven of silk and hemmed in gold. A gold cross hung from his neck on a gold chain and jeweled rings decorated his fingers. His dress had become more elaborate with each passing year, Carswell thought dryly.

"Come, my good squire," Glays murmured. "You of all people wouldn't deprive our king the best medical help simply because of personal dislike. Gothmog is really quite clever with wounds, you know."

Carswell was tired, and he was losing his patience. "Saolin will serve. Come."

"As you wish. But would you look at this first? I'd like your comments." Glays held out the spyglass.

Again Carswell hesitated. It seemed a reasonable request, at least reasonable in tone. Only twice before had he looked through a spyglass. Such artifacts were exceedingly rare and worth their weight in gold—the art of their making lost a thousand years before. What harm could it do?

Cautiously he took the glass and put it to his eye. Beyond the wall he could see the knights returning, as Glays had said. The glass brought him so close he could almost read the furrowed lines on Bors' face.

Glays moved closer. "And below, good squire? Below on the stairs? Tell me what you see."

"The stairs—?"

Carswell lowered the glass. He didn't need its amplifying powers to see that something was terribly wrong. Two of the white robed guardsmen were down, their blood staining the marble steps. Pentwyn and Geoff were standing back to back, pikes lowered, bleeding from a dozen wounds as the remaining guardsmen circled in. A spear caught Pentwyn in the chest and he went down.

"What have you done!"

A long-bladed dagger appeared in the priest's hand. Carswell turned, but it was too late, and he cried out more in surprise than pain as the blade found its mark in his side. He grabbed the priest's hand to no effect. Glays was strong—stronger than he'd ever suspected. The spyglass dropped to the floor, shattering.

Face twisted in rage, Glays used both hands and the full weight of his body as he drove the dagger in, its sharp blade cutting through liver and bone, into the squire's rib cage. "You half-wit! Do you or your idiot king think to command me, God's true Messenger?"

Carswell struggled, but he knew he was lost. His grip was weakening. There was blackness at the edge of his vision. He cursed his stupidity. Who could have suspected the priest to have such strength. He had failed in his duty—failed his king. That knowledge troubled him more than the certainty of his own death.

Then, as sometimes happens in that single moment before a man's life is snuffed out, Squire Carswell had a vision—the priest kneeling on a marble floor of intricate design—a knight standing over him, his sword raised. The knight was unfamiliar to Carswell. He was covered head to foot in blood, but the angles of his face showed strength and resolve—a good man.

The sword swept down.

Carswell looked into the priest's maddened eyes. "You'll die beneath the sword before spring is done," he said.

A moment later the squire's hand slipped from the knife. A groan escaped his lips as the priest's weapon found his heart.

Glays held on to the hilt until he was sure Carswell was dead. The man's last words had unnerved him. Not the words so much as the tone in which he spoke them—neither frightened nor angry—simply stating a fact already known.

He gave an involuntary shudder. He'd have Gothmog perform a cleansing later. For the moment there was much to do. He looked down at the shattered spyglass. Shame, that.

He pulled the dagger from the squire's body and turned back to the window. Men were dragging off the bodies of the dead pikemen, others washing the blood from the steps. Absently, he wondered how many of his own men had perished in the fight. No mind. Martyrs to the Faith.

"Gothmog!"

A sallow faced little man in a black tunic appeared from behind a curtain, a slender dagger in his right hand. "It went well, m'lord?"

"Well enough."

Glays studied the body on the floor. "Pity poor Squire Carswell, a brave and faithful man. Unfortunately he seems to have succumbed to wounds suffered earlier in battle."

Gothmog licked his thin lips. "I can use the heart, if it's not too damaged."

"Take the body away. Have someone clean up this mess."

Glays wiped the blade of the dagger on his robe, then tossed it on a nearby table. "I'll need fresh robes. Meet me in my chamber, and bring your bag. The king awaits."

CHAPTER 14

SAOLIN HECATE, HIGH PRIESTESS of the Yu'an Tara Temple, was already on her way to the king's bedchamber when Ren found her. A statuesque woman with flowing white hair, she was a severe beauty who had refused to succumb to age or weakness. Two Sisters attended her. Each wore the blue robes of their order and carried the small, brass bound chests that contained the tools and potions of their trade.

"Saolin! Wait!"

"Gwyndolyn! Good. You can help. I was told Cuchulain already removed the arrow."

Saolin was perhaps the only person, man or woman, who still called Ren by her birth name, Gwyndolyn.

Ren was short of breath. Arriving at the temple, Saolin had already gone on her way to treat the king. "He believed it to be poisoned."

Saolin frowned. "Since when do Uruks use poison?"

They rounded a corner, nearly colliding with Aerindir and Abdelar as the two brothers exited the king's bedchamber. Abdelar's usual good nature was dampened, his face set. "Ren, we were sent to find you. I fear your grandfather is failing."

Ren's heart fell. It was what she had feared.

Aerindir's jaw was clenched. His visage, hawklike and intimidating at the best of times, was a portrait of controlled rage. "It was no common Uruk's arrow. He grows weaker by the minute. Unless you have something more in those boxes than datura and devilsbane, priestess, the king will pass within the hour."

"We shall see," said Saolin, moving past Aerindir. "Come, Sisters."

The pikemen guarding Cuchulain's chamber stepped aside as the Sisters approached. Abdelar caught Ren's arm before she could follow, motioning her to a nearby alcove. Aerindir stood nearby, as if on guard.

Abdelar spoke urgently. "Ren, there's little time. Listen carefully. Your grandfather must speak with you. But you must quit his chamber immediately afterward. Do not stay, much as you might wish. We must leave the city."

"Leave the city?"

"Your grandfather will explain. Aerindir and I will be waiting at the stables. Go directly there. Do not return to your chambers. Bring nothing and tell no one. Your life and more depend on it."

"Abdel, what's happening?"

"Please—." Abdelar stopped, grabbing her hands almost painfully in his. The intensity was so unlike him. "*Winter has come.*"

Ren's darkest fears were suddenly realized. The words were one half of a code phrase drummed into her from childhood, more urgent than the king's hand sign. She had never heard them spoken in earnest, not even during the Rift, when her uncle Artos had rebelled with his knights and the priests of the Right Temple.

Almost as though someone else was speaking through her, she replied, "*The fire must be tended.*"

Abdelar relaxed his grip. "We'll be waiting." Motioning to Aerindir, the two knights hurried off, neither looking back.

Ren's mind was a swirl of conflicting thoughts. Of all the knights in Barad'An she was closest to Abdelar and Aerindir. They had always treated her as their sister, protective, loyal and wise. She could never doubt them.

Winter has come.

Mortal danger threatened. What had happened out there in the forest? Flee the city, the people she loved? Flee from what, and to where?

She caught herself, remembering her teachings, the stilling of the mind, *come to what is, come to the present. Put real effort to real effect.*

Cuchulain!

Two pikemen guarding the door stood to attention as she approached— good men, though like so many left in Barad'An, in their evening years.

Saolin and the two acolytes were already at work stripping away Cuchulain's blood-soaked shirt. They wore thin lambskin gloves, for protection. Prince Corwin, the only other person in the room, stood nearby watching them work with quiet concern.

Her grandfather's face was ashen and soaked in sweat. With a nudge, Saolin turned him on his side, to better reveal his wounds. Blood, now turned to a black ichor, oozed from both the front and back of his shoulder. There was a foul smell of bile. Horrified, Ren imagined she could see tiny, wormlike shapes moving in the ichor.

"Carlyn, hand me the dragonsroot salve. Katrin, some water, and two of those poppy balls. Be careful! Don't let that foulness touch your skin."

Saolin barked this last as Sister Katrin lifted up the shreds of the king's ruined shirt, carefully dropping them into a bedpan.

"Ren!" rasped Cuchulain when he saw his granddaughter. His voice was frail—dry as dust. "Thank the Fates. Come!" He struggled to sit up, his body trembling in pain and fever.

Saolin steadied him. "Do not move, old man."

Sister Carlyn was from Eldemere. Ren had known her years before as a playmate. She barely acknowledged Ren now as she handed Saolin a jar of a greenish salve which the priestess rubbed carefully on the king's wounds. The ichor bubbled, then settled. The sickening movement in it, for the moment, stilled. The two acolytes began a low chant, tracing healing symbols in the air with their fingers.

Cuchulain's eyes were steady with purpose. "Abdelar has spoken with you?"

Ren nodded, hardly trusting herself to speak.

"You understand?"

"Save your strength, grandfather. Please."

"There's little left to save. I'm for it. All Saolin can do is stave the pain."

"Don't say that," Ren protested. "You're still strong!"

Saolin shook her head. "This was no common poison, child. Dark work, woven by a master. Your grandfather is right. The best I can do is ease the pain."

Cuchulain sighed, "Not a small gift, old woman. There are things I still must do."

"Swallow these." Saolin handed Cuchulain two green balls the size of olives. Ren held back tears as her grandfather choked them down.

"Can't Sianiave help?"

"Perhaps, if she were here, but she's not." There was a hint of bitterness in Saolin's reply. She'd never gotten along with the sorceress, Ren recalled.

The poppy balls were taking effect. The tremor in Cuchulain's hand lessened. For a brief moment color returned to his features and his voice steadied. "Saolin, you must leave, go into the forest. Take the Sisters. Glays hates women, the Sisters most of all."

"Glays?" Saolin stood back indignantly. "Leave? Because of that—that swine?"

"He will be steward and regent when I pass, or have you forgotten?"

"How could I forget. You agreed to it against my advice."

"I had little choice. Tradition demands that a man—."

"Tradition be damned! Your stubborn adherence to tradition caused Artos to leave."

Cuchulain sighed. There was deep regret in that sigh. "This I admit. Which is why I must send Ren away, now."

"NO!" cried Ren.

Cuchulain ignored the outburst. "I can still command my granddaughter, but of you, Saolin, I can only entreat." He stifled a cough as he reached out for Saolin's hand. "Take the Sisters and go to Marduk. You'll be safe there, at least for a time."

"I won't abandon the temple, certainly not to that loathsome creature. Wouldn't he love that—Barad'An all to himself and his despicable god."

"It is not just his god who helps him in this."

"Not his—then—?" Saolin's face blanched in sudden realization. "How do you know this? How could I not know this!?"

"Glays has been patient, and they've planned carefully. You are not at fault. Until this morning, even I was uncertain. It was Corwin who brought word. We can only hope the priest is not yet aware we know. For myself, there is nothing. I beg you. Leave the city!"

A violent tremor shook Cuchulain. He fell back against the pillows. The blood welling up from his wounds had turned dark again. Saolin's face softened. With a touch that was surprisingly gentle, she reached down and stroked his cheek. "Save a seat beside you in Velkela, my king. I feel I won't be far behind."

Ren had known Saolin her entire life. There was a veil, something between them that precluded intimacy. Still, she respected the woman, for her strength and wisdom, and her dedication.

Were those tears in the old woman's eyes? Clearly there was more between Saolin and her grandfather than Ren had imagined.

"Come, Sisters," said Saolin. "We must gather our things."

She turned to Ren, "Farewell, child. You were always a good student. I'm sorry we couldn't have been closer."

The two acolytes took up their chests and followed Saolin from the room. Prince Corwin, who had been watching, and whose face gave away nothing of his own thoughts, approached the bed and, bowing low to Cuchulain, said. "I will also take my leave, sire."

Corwin had been a mystery to Ren. Dark-haired, of indeterminate age, he had a strength that belied his slender good looks. Of all the knights, save perhaps Abdelar and Aerindir, he was the best at arms. He had inhabited their lives for as long as she could remember, most often at times of crisis. No one knew or said from whence he came. Sianiave, who knew him as well as anyone, never discussed his origins. Ren may as well have asked about the wind.

"Even you cannot stop this storm, my friend," rasped the king, his voice weakening even as he spoke. "And you have your own work to do."

Corwin's smile was grim. "This is my work, sire. But in this matter I will follow your wishes, for I see no other course." He removed a dagger from his boot, lethal and businesslike in its lack of adornment, and laid it on the bed.

Cuchulain moved the knife under a sheet, away from sight but near his right hand. With a nod to Ren, and a look she did not understand, Corwin turned and left the room. Alone now with her grandfather, the dying man reached out to her.

"Grandfather—."

"Hush. There is little time. You must go to Ellohir, in Gallian."

"No. I won't leave you. I won't leave the city."

Cuchulain stopped. In the long hall outside they could hear the sound of marching feet.

"Please, Grandfather."

"Hear me out! If I had lived, I may have been able to hold the city. It is not yet in your power. Glays will control Barad'An. You alone stand in his way, and Ellohir can protect you. You must stay there until the time comes for you to return."

Ren could hear the guards arguing outside, barring the way to intruders. Her grandfather's voice was barely a whisper. "Go. Aerindir and Abdelar are waiting."

The door opened and Ben Shafter, the senior of the two guards, peered in. "It's the bishop, sire. He demands to see you."

"Is Carswell with him?"

"No, sire. The bishop is accompanied by twelve of his temple guard, for your protection, he says." The old pikeman cleared his throat, uneasy. "He's brought his surgeon."

"Gothmog! That weasel! Grandfather, you musn't." Ren was desperate.

"Ben, escort my granddaughter. You are relieved of duty. Go home to your wife."

"Sire?"

"Now, Ben. Send Jorald home as well."

Ren felt the very walls closing in on her. Why was he releasing his guards? Where were his knights? He seemed to be giving up without a fight.

Or was he? Glays was not alone, he'd said. Clearly Saolin had understood something Ren had not. Who or what could cause that obdurate old woman to flee?

Winter has come.

And then that elusive sense of knowing, the intuition that was both the bane and blessing of her lineage, engulfed her. Not the who or the how, but the why. Cuchulain, knowing his fate, was protecting his people, those he most loved and trusted, by sending them to safety.

Her grandfather was an obstinate man, not fond of taking council, at times as unyielding as a stone. In his recalcitrance he had driven her uncle from the city, but it was this same stubbornness that for more than sixty years had allowed him to hold the city together against an ever-encroaching dark-ness. For all his faults, she loved him dearly.

He nodded as understanding passed between them. Not trusting herself to say good-bye, Ren bowed and backed away. Ben Shafter escorted her from the room.

CHAPTER 15

GLAYS PACED RESTLESSLY in front of the door that led into the king's private chambers. He had waited ten years for this day, but now his patience was wearing thin.

An aged pikeman had stopped him. Twelve of his best guardsmen stood poised and ready behind him. He didn't count Gothmog, a weapon best used in the dark. The little magician stood there now, in shadows, black bag clutched tightly against his chest.

The priest's eyes fell on his captain, Borson Brand, young, predatory, ready to kill at a word. He'd acquitted himself well on the steps. They'd lost only three men while subduing Carswell's escort—not a mean feat.

He could end this charade now, kill them all—that miserable shell of a king and all his pagan lackeys—except the girl, of course. He wanted her alive. Killing Saolin before he took charge of the city might provoke dissent. Too many of Barad'An's citizens still believed her puerile superstitions. He would hang her and the other witches from the great oaks in front of the city. That would cure them of their blasphemies.

Why wait? Do it now. Brand was watching him expectantly, waiting for the order, lean and anxious, like a hungry wolf.

One factor alone made the priest hesitate, the same uncertainty that had kept him waiting in the hall like a supplicant. Aerindir, Abdelar, Bors, the other knights, they could be dealt with. Saolin, the Sisters, he dismissed as irrelevant. But Prince Corwin—.

Corwin was inexplicable, therefore dangerous. He once ordered Gothmog to conduct a ritual scree of the man, an attempt to learn what he could of this adversary. Gothmog selected a young girl as a proxy for the ritual, hanging her on hooks in his dungeon. But the attempt had failed disastrously. He'd encountered a shield so powerful it had blasted him from his circle. The brazier had begun a jerking dance, spreading hot coals across the floor. The girl had begun screaming madness about goblin worlds and machines that spit death—this, moments before her heart burst from her wasted body.

According to Gothmog, one wall, made of stone and four feet thick, had melted into a churning maelstrom, a malevolent labyrinth of a thing. He'd been so unnerved by the experience he'd lain useless in his bed for three days. For his part Corwin seemed not only to have survived the sorcerer's assault unscathed, but showed no sign he'd even been aware of it.

Glays stopped in mid-pace, remembering the look on the magician's face, a look of absolute horror. What had he seen to disturb him so?

When Cuchulain had arrived through the gate with the arrow in his shoulder, Glays had been so confident his time was at hand he hadn't bothered to consult his spies. It occurred to him he wasn't really sure who was attending the king—the witch priestess, of course, and her acolytes, Princess Gwyndolyn, Bors?

He, himself, had seen Aerindir and Abdelar leave, crossing the playing field and heading—where? Why would they leave the king's side now? And why were there so few guards nearby?

Something was amiss. Ten years—he'd been waiting for this day ten years. *Caution, caution.*

The heavy chamber door swung open abruptly. Ren emerged, eyes straight ahead, followed by the grizzled pikeman who'd challenged him at the door. Why was she leaving? Was Cuchulain already dead?

"Princess Gwyndolyn? You're leaving now, with the king so ill? I understand the arrow was lethal, poisoned." He placed a hand on her shoulder as though in condolence.

Ren looked at his hand as though it were some unsavory thing and struggled not to show her disgust. The nails of the priest's hand were long and carefully manicured, with rings on every finger. One held a large ruby in a gold setting. The hand smelled of lavender.

She forced herself to meet his eyes. "Actually grandfather is recovering well," she lied, forcing a calm she didn't feel. Lies did not come easily to her. Anger, quickly hidden, showed in the tightening of the man's mouth.

Glays managed a nod. "Good news indeed, if such is the case. Our Lord is mighty. Blessed be our Lord. But there is a matter of some importance I would discuss with you. If the king is mending, as you say, I would have you wait."

Ren smiled, as though amused. "Wait? For you? When there are so many more important matters to attend to?"

Wench!

His fingers dug painfully into her shoulder. Ren suppressed a grimace. The pressure eased almost immediately, yet his reaction gave him away. He was not master of himself. His emotions, his vanity, held sway.

More disturbing was the aggression he'd displayed. She was uncomfortably aware of her own vulnerability. Glays was easily a foot taller and a hundred pounds heavier than herself, and now she was aware of his strength. His small, slate-colored eyes were windows on the arrogance, the ambition, and the cruelty that drove him.

She sensed something else, a thing both leering and possessive. She remembered the words of Meg, her handmaiden since birth. It had been the night of her first moon. "You are a woman now, and exceedingly beautiful. There'll be men who will want you for that beauty. They won't use just flowery words or trinkets to win you. They'll try to take you. You must pluck the weeds before they take root."

"I can take care of myself, Meg," Ren had argued. At that age her visions of men took the shape of tall, handsome warriors, like Abdelar or Corwin, certainly not loathsome pigs like Glays.

Meg's wisdom was earthy, but more often than not Ren had found it far more practical than the obscure utterances of the Sisters.

Pluck the weed—.

"Remove your hand," she said, using the voice of command taught to her by Sianiave—voice without fear or doubt.

The priest blinked, staring at the diminutive figure before him as though he couldn't believe what he'd heard. For a moment he appeared confused, but his anger quickly returned. His jaw clenched tightly. Ren was sure he was going to strike her.

An amused chuckle from across the hall broke the tension. Glays looked up, his eyes narrowing. Prince Corwin leaned against a pillar, his right hand fingering the pommel of his sword. "Problems, bishop?"

Behind Glays Gothmog slunk further back into shadow.

"Certainly not." Glays turned back to Ren. "We'll speak later, m'lady."

He turned away, as though dismissing her from his thoughts. "Captain Brand, wait here with your men. Come, Gothmog!"

Gothmog spat on the floor and followed the priest into the bedchamber.

CHAPTER 16

"WE'D BEST BE GOING," urged the old pikeman. For a brief moment he wasn't sure the priest's soldiers would let them pass. He motioned to the other guard. "Jory, you're relieved. Go home. These fellows will look after the king now."

Jorald grunted in surprise. "You sure, Ben?"

"Go home. King's orders. I'll escort the princess to her quarters."

Jorald hesitated, uncertain. The street trash the priest had gathered about him couldn't protect their hats in a low wind, but Ben Shafter was as good a man as there was in the king's service, and with the princess herself standing there the order had to be obeyed.

He shrugged, lowering his pike. "If you say so, but I'm not liking it."

Corwin followed behind as Shafter and Ren moved off. Once out of sight of the guardsmen, he stopped. "Ren, there isn't much time. Your grandfather will stall as long as he's able."

"The dagger—"

"He's very weak. I doubt his chance for success. I must leave you here." He put a hand on Shafter's shoulder. "Keep an eye out, Ben."

"M'lord, why don't we just do him ourselves. Like Jory said, that rabble couldn't—?"

"I wish it were that simple, but this goes deeper than Glays. Until it's sorted out we'll follow the king's wishes. Take Ren to the stables. Aerindir and Abdelar are waiting."

"The stables —?" Sergeant Shafter frowned as he realized the plan. The stables could only mean one thing. Ren was fleeing Barad'An. The thought troubled him deeply, but he saw the sense of it.

Benjamin Shafter of the royal house guard was old by any man's standards, both in years and experience. He'd served Cuchulain for over sixty years, and King Cynbromir before him. He'd survived many a battle, but none with so dark an outlook as this. The world had changed this past hour. That was the truth of it.

The king had given him his leave. He could retire with honor, spend his remaining days tending his garden with the missus, watch the grandchildren grow up—but in a world ruled by Glays?

He straightened. Whatever the future, he had one last task to complete before his oath was fulfilled.

Corwin took Ren's hands, leaning forward to kiss her cheek. "It's up to you now."

With those portentous words, he saluted Shafter and left.

Ren stood silent. Despite her beauty, her rank, the facade of strength, she was little more than a child—a child left to deal with matters beyond her experience. The weight of a kingdom would soon be on her shoulders.

"Come on, Ben," she said. "We're on our own."

Ren set the pace. Shafter settled into the loping rhythm of the battle run he learned as young foot soldier. He took consolation in the fact that he'd brought his short pike to work that day instead of the heavier *cavalieret*, his Horse Killer.

He followed Ren across the Gathering Courtyard, skirting obsolete gardens, and down a broad stair overrun with hollyhock, then across a weed-choked gaming field where Ren paused for a moment, seeming to study the ivy-covered wall beyond.

"M'lady?"

Ben caught his breath, but one thing he knew, this was not the way to the stables. Then, with a sudden movement, Ren pulled aside a section of ivy to reveal the opening of a narrow, arched tunnel. For all his years of service in the palace he had never known of its existence.

"It will save us half a mile," said Ren. Sweeping aside cobwebs and spiders, she disappeared into the darkness. Head bowed to avoid the low ceiling, and against his better judgment, the old pikeman followed.

The tunnel sloped downward, growing ever darker. "Stairs here," whispered Ren. "Watch yourself."

Shafter nearly tripped as his foot touched the first stair. Ren, surefooted as a cat, had already vanished. Thankfully, after twenty or so harrowing steps, there was light ahead. The stairs led to one of the many aqueducts that once irrigated the city. Now, it was dry and lichen covered, lit by shafts of sunlight filtering through overhead ducts.

They ran down the aqueduct for several hundred yards before coming to another flight of stairs which ended at a landing and a low oak door. Ren pulled open the door and they emerged into a grove of plum trees just to the west of the Moon Gate, the smallest and least used of the five gates that led into the palace complex. The gate was open, and Shafter saw no guards about. In fact they'd seen no one since leaving the King's Quarters.

The market square lay on the other side of the gate. Unlike the palace, its streets were filled with people, shopkeepers and émigrés, soldiers, bully boys, prostitutes, housewives, beggars and artisans, all appeared to be staring up at the palace as though awaiting a sign. A woman and a young girl with worried faces stood aside as they passed.

Ren avoided the throng by cutting down the narrow alleyway that separated the page quarters from the palace wall. From there, it was only a few hundred yards to the east entrance of the stables.

Aerindir and Abdelar led three saddled horses from the staging paddock when they arrived. The two knights had changed from their bloodstained garb into tough leather traveling clothes. Both were heavily armed, swords and daggers at their sides, full quivers across their shoulders, longbows in hand. The saddle bags were bulging, and there were bedrolls.

The horses shifted, anxious in anticipation. Ren recognized them as three of the fleetest and sturdiest mounts in the city.

"Ren!" cried Abdelar. "Thank the stars!"

Shafter leaned over a hitching post, struggling to catch his breath and doing his best not to dishonor himself by throwing up. "Sorry, M'lady. I haven't had a run like that since the Battle of Neddley Vale, long twenty years hence."

"You did well, Ben," said Ren gently. "Your oath is fulfilled. Go home to your wife."

He rubbed the back of his hand across his mouth and straightened. "I'll wait to see you off, if you please."

Abdelar tossed Ren the reins to Light, a speckled buckskin gelding and a horse she'd ridden many times. She was pleased to find they'd brought her tournament bow, a beautiful, deadly thing, fashioned of layered oak and ironwood, and strung with catgut. She'd left it in her apartments. Now it was attached to her saddle horn along with a full quiver. Her sword *Asin* was there as well, along with a dagger and sword belt, which she quickly buckled around her waist.

"A troop of the priest's guard are headed this way," said Abdelar, mounting his own horse, a big roan named Glaerindor.

Aerindir steadied Stormcloud, named for the dark grey of his coat. He lifted himself easily into the saddle just as the great horn of Barad'An sounded. The horn was set in an iron collar atop the Palace Tower, blown only on two occasions—to announce the city under attack, or the passing of a king. Its mournful resonance echoed from the stones of the city. Ren knew it was the sign for which the people had been waiting.

"He's gone," whispered Abdelar, as if not quite believing it.

"Mourn later," growled Aerindir. "Now the priest rules in Barad'An!"

Ren had been well schooled, both in the martial arts of the knights and the subtle arts of the Sisters. Even so, a wave of grief threatened to undo her. Grief not just for her beloved grandfather, but for a king, and the city and people he'd ruled for over half a century. Her city and the people she loved with all her heart.

A city and a people she was about to abandon.

Light reared, almost pulling the reins from her hand. At the far end of the stables a double column of white robed Guardsmen approached.

"Ren!" cried Abdelar. "Now!"

She needed no urging. Light steadied as she leapt into the saddle. Without another word she spurred the gelding forward, out the paddock gate, and down the cobbled road that exited the city, Aerindir and Abdelar close behind.

Ben Shafter watched until they were gone from sight. *Those three are for it,* he thought to himself, half wishing he was young enough to join them.

By the time the three riders had reached the plaza the great gate was already grinding down. A platoon of guardsmen blocked the way. Ren didn't rein in until they were almost on top of them.

"Out of the way, you louts! I'm Princess Gwyndolyn of Anor."

"I know who you are!"

A bullnecked man stepped forward, a commander, by his gold piping. This surprised Ren, for she'd never seen him before. How many others had Glays secreted into his private army, unbeknownst?

"Aerindir and Abdelar, you are under arrest as traitors! Throw down your arms. Princess, you're to come with me!"

Adbelar laughed. "Treason is it?"

The two knights had slung their bows across their backs and drawn their swords, positioning their anxious mounts on either side of Ren. The priest's man stood unblinking—sure of himself. "No need for you to die here. Surrender now and you'll be given a fair trial."

"Fair trial, my buttocks."

Sunlight gleamed off Abdelar's sword as it arched through the air. The man's head landed on the cobbles where it rolled for several feet before stopping at a guardsman's boot. The headless body collapsed backwards. A shower of blood sprayed those standing in its wake.

For a brief moment the only sound that could be heard was the retching of a young recruit who'd been drenched in the ghastly shower. His face was mottled purple in outrage; he raised his pike and charged. "Murderers! You'll die for this!"

"Not today," said Aerindir calmly. He gave a slight twitch to Stormcloud's reins. The stallion reared, its forehooves taking the man in the chest, crushing his ribs.

The other guardsmen moved in. "Kill the pagans! God is great! For God and fellowship!"

Ren shoved a dirk through a man's eye as he tried to drag her from her horse. She broke another's thumb with a quick movement, then sent him sprawling to the cobbles with a kick to his face. "The gate!" she cried, urging Light forward as she drew *Asin*, but too many blocked the way.

Battle horns sounded behind them. Ren parried a pike thrust, shoving Asin's point into her attacker's unprotected throat. Glancing backward she saw riders approaching, twenty at least. Her hope vanished when she saw the riders were all wearing the white cloaks of the templars.

Too many.

The gate was almost down. Aerindir and Abdelar had taken out half of the original company of guardsmen, but those who remained had pulled back, taking up a position directly in front of the gate. There was no way to get through those pikes. Not without risking the horses.

Suddenly the downward descent of the great gate stopped. Wooden gears shifted, slack ropes tightened. Slowly the great gate began to rise.

"What?" cried a guardsman. "Lower it! Lower the gate!"

The words changed to an incoherent gurgle as a white-feathered arrow struck his eye. Another man died with an arrow through his heart. Another, then another went down.

"Fletcher!" cried Ren. There, above on the rampart, stood her mentor, bow in hand.

Preoccupied as she was, she still marveled at his accuracy. Every arrow found its mark.

"Ride!" yelled Fletcher. "Ride!"

Ren and her protectors spurred their mounts through the gate and out to the open field.

From his perch on the wall, Captain Fletcher watched until they crossed the field and vanished into the dark line of Arden Forest. A dozen or so riders, those who'd managed to escape his arrows, were at least a quarter of a mile behind.

A dozen only? Aerindir and Abdelar would make stew meat of them, as would Ren, for more than anyone else in the city, he knew what she could do. He would have skewered more of the bastards but he'd run out of arrows—this and the fact that his drawing arm ached as though a hot spike had been driven through it.

He removed a corncob pipe from a pocket under his chest plate, packed it with *suph* and lit it with a flint. Might as well have a smoke before they came for him—ready for the dungeons, unless they butchered him on the spot.

Whichever way it went, it wouldn't be long.

He took a puff of smoke and sat down with his back to the stone parapet. Whatever his fate, he'd lived a good life, and he missed his wife Helga, now long dead. His men would have joined him, but he'd ordered them down. Politics wasn't his forte, and the sounding of the great horn had said it all. The king was dead. Glays would be steward, though it wouldn't be official until the Conclave.

Ren was safe.

All considered, the royal archer of Barad'An was well pleased with himself.

CHAPTER 17

Slopes of the White Mountains
April 22

TRAVELING BY SLED IN THE MOUNTAINS had proved exceedingly dangerous. Barrett was glad to be clear of the ice flows, avalanches, and unexpected crevasses that had slowed their progress. They were making better time now. The snowfield at the skirt of the mountain sloped gently toward a broad expanse of forest. They had almost reached the tree line when, unexpectedly, Osmodon slammed down on the sled's brake.

"Hold up, Bear! Whoa, dogs!"

The big sled ground to a halt. The dogs, eleven of them, barked happily, tongues lolling, and settled into the snow. Bear, the big lead animal, looked back, puzzled by the stop. Barrett wondered himself. The forest was less than three miles off and there were still several hours of daylight remaining.

"Is there a problem?" Sianiave asked.

"An odd sound," said Osmodon, jumping down from the rattan carriage. "Runner's my guess." He peered under the carriage, knocking away ice that had accumulated on the runners. "As I feared, split near through. We'll be running on frame before long. Should've been quicker around that last snag."

Sianiave threw back her fur hood and removed her snow goggles—a piece of whittled wood with thin slits cut for vision. She used a hand to shade her eyes from the glare. "The snow's melting earlier than usual. You couldn't avoid them all."

Barrett welcomed the break. Riding in the sled's carriage was more taxing than it appeared—leg muscles constantly flexing and relaxing to compensate for the motion. They'd been traveling for three days now and his legs were tired and sore.

"Can you fix it?" he asked Osmodon.

"It'll take time."

"We don't have time." Sianiave swung down beside Osmodon. "Can we make it to the forest?"

"With no more snags and luck stays with us."

"Snow will be thinner under the trees. If it can't be fixed, we'll walk. Ardendell isn't more than a league."

Barrett wondered at Sianiave's stamina. He was even more amazed at how much her physical appearance had changed since she'd arrived four days ago. When they'd first met, he'd imagined her to be sixty-five, even seventy years old. She now looked twenty years younger. Even the color of her hair was different, not grey, but silvery blonde. He decided she was the most unusual women he had ever met. Also the most irritating.

The change in her appearance wasn't any more dramatic than the change in himself. Gone was his depression, the angst, the constant inner dialogue of guilt that had been stirring in his head ever since that night in the Pamirs. Physically, he felt stronger.

No, not felt. He was stronger. Ten days of Osmodon's ironhanded training had put him into a shape he hadn't known since that summer in China, studying Pa Qua with Grand Master He Xiang Bao. But that didn't explain half of his new found strength. It was as if gravity itself was less in this world, gravity in all its manifestations, psychological as well as physical.

His hand fell to the sword at his side. The brass and leather scabbard strapped to the outside of his furs felt as comfortable as his combat rigging had felt in Afghanistan. Forty-four inches of razor-sharp steel with quality equal to a five-body *katana*. He could wield it as easily as he had the lightweight sabers and épées of his college days. In tests of strength, he'd occasionally come close to besting Osmodon—surprising them both. On Earth, the Earth he'd known, he could imagine Osmodon competing in strongman competitions—tossing tree trunks, boulders, and blocks of pig iron for sport.

"We'll camp in the trees tonight," said Sianiave decisively. She pointed to the forest below and a dark line of trees in the distance. "There's a river there, the Dunenwine. It flows to a large lake, the Dunenmere. Ardendell lies on its eastern bank."

"How far?"

"A league, possibly more."

Barrett groaned. Ardendell was a way station, a village where Sianiave hoped to leave the sled and purchase horses for the remainder of the journey. The broken runner was a problem. He didn't look forward to hiking thirty miles knee-deep in snow.

"Let's go!" said Sianiave, clambering back into the sled. "We're already days behind."

"The mistress calls," sighed Osmodon, taking one last look at the runner.

Once on board he let out a piercing whistle. The sled took off with a jolt and the barking of dogs. Barrett could now hear the sound that had alerted Osmodon, a thin abrasive hum coming off the right front runner, deepening its dissonance even as they neared the forest.

Barrett had learned a great deal since he'd arrived in this world. Tor Eyrie, the place where he first awoke, was a series of habitable caves high in a colossal mountain range, the White Mountains. It lay just beyond the northern march of a kingdom called Anor. He'd learned this from Osmodon during his recovery.

From his own experience in high mountains he'd guessed Tor Eyrie's altitude to be near seventeen-thousand feet, though the usual perceptions didn't apply here—the size of the eagles, for example. He watched them from the terrace as they soared overhead, graceful, majestic, improbably large and yet, strangely nonthreatening. The sky itself exhibited a similar contradiction, broader, more blue, yet somehow familiar. The thin air shouldn't have sustained him, yet he felt strong, and revitalized.

Some part of him remembered this place—this world—a world where colors were more vivid, darkness darker, light lighter, the mountains higher, the very air more alive. During the day a glorious sun shone down upon them. At night the stars twinkled like lamplights, scattered in constellations that were alien in ways he couldn't describe.

If the sun was king of the day, then the moon was queen of the night, for though she carried the same markings as the earthly moon, here she appeared brighter and a good deal larger.

Since leaving Tor Eyrie, Barrett had witnessed vast blue glaciers, frozen waterfalls a thousand feet high, herds of caribou as large as elk, and elk the size of Percherons—these, and other breeds he'd never before encountered. Once, they had spotted a bearlike creature lumbering across an ice floe. Even at a distance it had appeared big enough to swallow a man whole. He had a nagging sense he should know about these things—had known about them. That taunting familiarity had helped him accept it all.

In the end, it came down to observable facts. He still felt hunger and pain. Who was to say the world he came from wasn't the dream, and this one the reality. This world felt more real. He decided the sensible course was to take it all at face value. Whether he was on another planet, in another dimension, or in another time, hardly mattered.

He was a soldier. He had accepted a job. His clothes, including his coat, were missing, but they had given him new ones. The bag of coins Sianiave had given him were in the pocket of his new fur coat.

She wasn't present when he first awoke. In her absence, she had assigned Osmodon to be his counsel and weapons instructor. With little else to do, he had thrown himself into training with a fury. During their breaks Osmodon had answered what questions he could.

Tor Eyrie was only a small part of a network of connecting caves. Most were sealed, either intentionally or by time and the elements. It was said they'd once housed a great monastery. Water was still drawn through a series of ingeniously engineered ceramic pipes. Hot water came from a mineral spring deep in the mountain, supplying the kitchen and baths.

Merchants brought supplies to the Tor from Ashar'Apu, a village in the river valley below. The villagers clearly held Sianiave in high regard, a regard they extended to her guests. They believed her to be descended from the ancient sorcerers who had once occupied the monastery.

"Do you think it's true?" Barrett had asked Osmodon. "That she's descended from a race of sorcerers?"

"Can't say," he replied. "Some matters she doesn't talk about."

"How long have you known her?"

That question brought a rueful chuckle. "Met her at a tavern in Barad'An, if you believe it. She caught the eye of every man in the place when she walked in, but she sat at my table. Came directly to it, as though it were me she sought. I was a bit full of myself in those days. My only thought was to bed her.

"Bought her a drink," Osmodon continued. "Tried to soften her up, truth be told. Four flagons later I was dead drunk, and she was still sober as a Sister. That's when she offered me a job. I was low on funds, not thinking too clearly. And she brought out this bag of empresses."

"Empresses? Coins?"

"Aye, fifty of 'em. She wanted me to escort her to Minador, a city to the west of Barad'An, ten leagues, maybe. Got in a skirmish or two, nothing difficult. Can't say the same for the next one, though."

"Next one? What? Another job?"

"Aye. That one nearly cost my life."

Osmodon had seemed unwilling to say more, and Barrett didn't press the subject. "You say you've been with her ten years."

"Ten, did I say? Seems more like a century. I may have mentioned, there's things she doesn't talk about, and much is beyond my ken. But she pays well, and keeps me busy."

Barrett had formed a picture of Osmodon and the woman who had hired them both. Osmodon was a good man. Sianiave had not only captured his loyalty, she provided him with a noble purpose. Exactly what purpose, he couldn't or wouldn't say, but clearly he believed it to be worthy.

Despite her sometimes thorny disposition, Osmodon had come to trust Sianiave, and offered his fealty. "She's earned it," he said, half jokingly. "Frankly I was surprised when she accepted, but knowing her as I do now, I suspect she planned it all along."

Osmodon claimed to know little about why Sianiave had brought Barrett to Tor Eyrie. He never asked Barrett where he came from, or why, and Barrett found it easier to keep mum on the subject. In the end Barrett simply said that Sianiave had hired him to protect someone, a girl, he thought. Why she chose him, he had no idea. He was just an ordinary soldier from another country.

When Osmodon heard this, he let out a bellowing laugh. "Sianiave don't waste time with anyone. She has her reasons."

He'd paused, sitting back to study Barrett thoughtfully. "Aye, soldier you may be. But ordinary? I think not. Your skill with a sword is too great."

Barrett took a moment's pride in the compliment, as Osmodon was, himself, a formidable swordsman.

The big man was also an enthralling storyteller. One evening, after a brutal day of training, they'd tapped a keg of Sianiave's ale. Osmodon had filled the evening with tales of fighting, womanizing, and sorcery.

Barad'An was a city in the south, he'd explained, once the capital of a great empire, now fallen into hardship. Cuchulain, its king, was a fool, a brave fool, but a fool nonetheless, reliving past glories while his kingdom fell into decay.

Artos, Cuchulain's nephew, was by all accounts strong and true, with keen intelligence and almost preternatural instincts that once had been the hallmark of his line. Osmodon had first traveled to Barad'An to offer his fealty to Artos, but he had arrived a fortnight too late. Artos was gone, banished by his uncle. Jealousy, some said, or a disagreement over some matter, or by guile, or sorcery. Ten years passed and there had been no word of him.

Barrett found Osmodon's tales fascinating, but assumed them to be little more than fairy stories.

He related more easily to the villagers who lived below Tor Eyrie, at least those hardy few who traveled twice weekly up the narrow pass to bring supplies and food. Both in manner and dress they reminded him of the Afghans he met in the Pamirs. Even their language seemed oddly similar, though when Sianiave had appeared a week later, she had quickly dissuaded him from such ideas.

"What language are we speaking?" she had asked when he'd brought up the subject.

"Speaking? Now? English, of course."

She'd looked amused. "English? Really?"

"Of course it's English!"

"Try saying a word describing something from your world. Something you don't see here."

Tor Eyrie was lit with candles, torches, and oil lamps. The image of a light-bulb sprang to his mind, but when he tried to name it, no word would come, at least none that made any sense. He tried speaking of computers, cell phones, airplanes, automobiles, all with the same result. The more he struggled, the more the words—even images—escaped him. After several minutes of intense effort his head began to ache.

Sianiave was sympathetic. "Don't fight it. Such things don't exist in this world. They can't exist in this world. You might be able to draw a picture, use written symbols, but I would advise against it. Words, images, thoughts, they send out—resonances. The effects, if not properly guided or applied, can be calamitous."

"We're speaking English now!"

"No. You hear it as English, because that is what you know. But English doesn't exist in this world. No more than those other things you could imagine but were unable to name."

She stopped and grew serious. "There are correspondences between the worlds, of course—otherwise you wouldn't be here. We couldn't be here. But they aren't the ones you imagine. That's why the appearance of the morghul in your world is so troubling. It knew the dangers, yet still it crossed the boundary. It risked more than you can imagine, just to get at you."

"Me?" Barrett had winced at the memory, the revulsion he'd felt, the pain of the creature's mace slamming into his shoulder. "Why me?"

What was so special about him that some monster from another world would apparently take great risks to seek him out?

CHAPTER 18

THE RUNNER GAVE OUT five minutes into the forest, nearly toppling the sled. "That's it," said Osmodon eyeing the damage. "It would take half a day's work to whittle a new one."

Sianiave tossed a leather satchel on the ground. "Don't bother. This forest is too thick for the sled in any event. We'll make better time walking."

She looked up through a break in the canopy where the half moon rose against a deepening orange sky. "It will be night soon," she added, frowning.

Barrett sensed caution in her words. The first night out from Tor Eyrie they slept in a cave high in the mountains. The second night they stayed in the ruins of a temple so old, even Sianiave couldn't recall the god for which it had been built. This forest felt different, less protected. Barrett remembered the eagles, and the bear-like creature he'd seen lumbering across the ice floe.

They made camp next to the damaged sled. Barrett collected firewood while Osmodon fed the dogs, tossing them the cakes of dried meat that had been their fare since leaving Ashar'Apu. Growling and barking, the dogs fought over the meal, but in the end all were satisfied.

Sianiave sorted through the supplies, deciding what to take and what to abandon. By her reckoning Ardendell was still two day's march south, but it could be more. She put necessary items in a pile—bows, arrows, swords and daggers, oil and sharpening stones, flint, cooking utensils, and rope. They would keep their coats but could do without the other furs, though they were pleasant to sleep on. They'd keep the food, of course, even if game was plentiful.

The coins she carried were heavy, but that couldn't be helped. They needed horses and tack. This far north, neither would come cheap. Further south there would be other expenses. They had other means of acquiring what they needed, of course, but sorcery would draw sorcery to it, like light draws darkness.

The air beneath the trees was still and heavy. Drifts of snow settled in the hollows and against the tree trunks. In some patches spring grass already peeked through the damp forest loam.

Twilight settled and the forest grew deathly quiet, as if the trees themselves were holding their breath. Even the dogs, chewing on the last of their meal, perked up their ears as if they sensed something lurking in the darkness.

Barrett dropped an armful of broken branches on the snow. "That should do it."

Sianiave barely glanced up from her work. "We need more for a watch fire, enough to burn through the night. This is an old forest. It has little fondness for humans."

"That bear we saw? Might it come for the food?"

"The dogs can deal with bears."

That gave Barrett pause.

"Is there something you're not telling me?"

"Just keep your sword at the ready."

"Something's off," said Osmodon, returning from feeding the dogs. "Dogs sense it. Forest's too quiet." He was carrying an armful of harnesses, which he tossed into a pile by the sled. "They won't be needing these. It's a long way back to Ashar'Apu."

"You're sending them back?" Barrett had grown fond of the dogs, especially Bear, the big lead animal. It seemed friendlier with them around, not to mention safer. At night they cuddled like puppies, keeping one another warm.

"They'll be of little use to us from here on. No, it's best we loose them. Come morning I'll give them a good feed. Their home's in the mountains and Bear knows the way. They'll be safer than us, I ken."

Osmodon set about building the fire while Barrett went to gather more wood. His search took him further and further from the campsite as dry wood became increasingly harder to find.

A sound, a soft 'hu', startled him. He looked up to see two large yellow eyes peering down from an overhanging branch. He dropped the wood and drew his sword. Another 'hu', low and inquisitive, was followed by the flutter of wings as an owl left its high perch and soared into the night.

Feeling foolish, Barrett sheathed his sword and began reclaiming his wood. Off to his left, a flickering light had become visible through the trees. The light cast black shadows that seemed to move from tree to tree as if alive. Firelight—Barrett realized with unexpected relief. Osmodon had started the fire.

He hefted the wood in his arms. It was enough, he decided. If Sianiave wanted more, she could get it herself.

When he arrived back at the campsite, the meal was ready—black tea, dried fruit, dried meat, and biscuits. They ate in silence. The forest had a way of dampening conversation. Even Osmodon, normally so loquacious, spoke little.

Barrett arranged his sleeping furs against the trunk of an oak. He lay back, facing the fire, watching the embers as they rose like fireflies into the night. The pungent odor of burning wood and the crackle of the fire were comforting. The air was so still, the smoke rose straight upward. The dogs had settled down.

Sianiave tamped leaves into the bowl of her pipe, lighting it in the same manner as she had that first night at the mansion. Barrett noticed that neither she nor Osmodon faced the fire. Instead they sat obliquely, their eyes continually returning to the darkness between the trees, their weapons within arms reach.

Barrett shifted his position. Staring directly at a fire obscured vision. He should have known better, but the comfort of the furs, the quiet pleasure of the fire, the mysterious nature of the forest itself—all had an intoxicating effect. It made him forget the dangers that might lurk beyond the campfire.

He moved his eyes back and forth as he waited for them to adjust. He noticed Sianiave watching him. The firelight reflected off her green eyes and golden hair.

Golden?

He stared in fascination. Her hair, more silvery than blonde that very day, now appeared full and golden. Her face looked younger now, no older than thirty-five. The uncomfortable thought came to him that Sianiave was not only an extraordinary woman, but an extraordinarily beautiful woman. Even the crooked nose and the scar on her chin enhanced her beauty.

Had the appearance of age been an act, a disguise? If so, she was a master illusionist. Was she now her true self, or was this the illusion? If Osmodon was to be believed, she was a sorceress. How many fairy stories had he read as a child, warning of the sinister shape-shifting abilities of witches?

"You still believe this to be a dream?" Sianiave asked, smiling, as though aware of his thoughts.

"I'm no longer sure what to believe."

Smiling, She took a deep puff on her pipe, letting it out in a series of smoke rings.

"Don't tease the lad," growled Osmodon. "His answer was as sensible as any I've heard. Who can know the truth of such matters? Not even you, I suspect, with all your witch knowledge. The desert people have a saying, 'Life is a caravan of dreams. Dogs bark, and the caravan moves on,' whatever our thoughts or beliefs about it."

Sianiave sent another smoke ring skyward. "The desert people are wise."

Barrett had the uncomfortable feeling he was missing something, something of vital importance, but any thought he had on the matter was cut off by a cry from deep in the forest. It lingered, then trailed off.

"What in hell was that!?"

"Quiet!" hissed Sianiave. Both she and Osmodon sat motionless, listening.

A second howl, this one closer. Sianiave jumped to her feet. Osmodon grabbed both his sword and battle axe. "Keep your back to the fire, lad! They fear fire!"

Barrett stumbled as he buckled on his sword. "They? What's out there?"

"Wolves!" said Sianiave, sticking her sword point first into the snow for easy reach as she took up a bow.

"You're worried about wolves and not bears?"

"Arden wolves, lad," said Osmodon. He was peering into the forest as though intent alone could pierce the darkness. The dogs were whimpering, all except Bear who had gotten to his feet, facing the direction of the howls as if to protect the others.

Seconds passed. Something moved, or were shadows playing tricks? Barrett blinked and rubbed his eyes. Was he imagining them? Red lights appeared in a line in the forest, like malevolent fireflies.

Eyes, he realized with a shock. There were shapes behind them, wolf-like, yet unlike any wolves he'd ever seen—huge and lean, with matted hair. Their heads, fanged and snouted, were disproportionately large, even for such massive bodies. He counted at least a dozen of the beasts.

"They're hungry," said Sianiave, nocking an arrow. "They're working up their courage. That big one, by the oak there? He'll come first. I have one shot, then it's blades."

"Their heads," said Osmodon. "Take off their heads."

There was a glint in the big man's eyes and a fierce grin on his face. Sianiave drew her bow. "Beware an old man in a cloak."

"What?"

Barrett hadn't finished his question when Sianiave released her arrow. It struck the big wolf in the eye just as it charged. The beast fell to the snow, snarling in agony, but not yet dead.

The wolves attacked. Osmodon decapitated one with a stroke of his axe. Sianiave dropped her bow, taking up her sword in time to slice the top off a wolf's head. Turning quickly, she disemboweled another. Any other time Barrett might have enjoyed sitting back to admire her skill, for she moved with lethal grace. But the battle was on him. In the bloody minutes that followed, he lost all sense of time.

He aimed for their heads, but often had to settle for quick thrusts and slashes at lesser targets. From nowhere, a beast leapt, grabbing his sword arm in its jaws, its weight throwing him back-first into the flames. With his left hand he drew his dagger and gutted the animal, rolling away just in time to avoid catching fire.

Then, as quickly as it had begun, the battle was over. The few wolves that were left backed slowly away, then turned and vanished into the forest.

Barrett stood, breathing heavily. Carcasses, limbs and heads of dead and dying wolves lay about. Osmodon was covered head to foot in blood and entrails.

"Well, that was a bit of fun."

"Fun?" muttered Sianiave caustically. "Do you realize the danger if even one of us had fallen?"

Her eyes rested on the big wolf she'd first shot, still alive, the arrow still embedded in its right eye. The wolf snapped viciously as she approached. "I'm rather fond of wolves in general, but these things aren't really wolves, any more than trolls are human." With one swift stroke of her sword she took off the beast's head. "Bloody evil creatures."

She wiped her blade on the creature's fur. "How are the dogs?"

"The dogs?" Osmodon looked as though he'd been slapped. "The dogs!"

He ran to the tree where the dogs had been resting. Of the seven near the tree, not one remained alive, torn apart by the wolves. Seven of eleven, Barrett thought. The other four had either run off or been dragged away.

Osmodon was trembling, whether in rage or grief, Barrett couldn't tell. Spotting the body of a dead wolf, Osmodon kicked at it. "Bloody damned beasts! The dogs got one, at least. Good and faithful creatures they were. I should have looked after them better."

"It's not your fault," said Sianiave. "Dogs are no match for Arden wolves. We were lucky to survive ourselves. Maybe some escaped. I don't see Bear."

Osmodon turned away as though he hadn't heard. With slumped shoulders he walked slowly back toward the fire. Never had Barrett seen a man look so forlorn.

"He has a soft heart," said Sianiave, sighing. "But we've other worries now. We must move the camp. Wolves aren't the only predators in this forest. The smell of blood will bring more evil enemies—wyverns, trolls, beings you don't want to think about."

"Wyverns? Trolls? I hope you're joking."

She flicked a piece of gore off her coat. "Do I look like I'm joking?"

It took them only minutes to pack. Osmodon helped, but said little.

Barrett had put one last pot in his backpack and was tying the laces when a sound caught his attention, a moan or whimper. It was low, barely audible, and came from the forest. "Do you hear that? It sounds like a wounded animal?"

Sianiave closed her eyes, then nodded. "That's no wolf. It's one of the dogs."

"You can see about it," said Osmodon dully. "I don't have the heart."

"Of course," Barrett said, and then went toward the forest.

The fire still burned strongly, but beyond its light the forest was black as ink. On the far side of a large willow, between darkness and dancing shadows, Barrett found Bear, his head resting mournfully on the flanks of another dog.

"Bear! It's Bear!"

Bear, thankfully, wasn't hurt. The other dog, a young female, had been eviscerated, half her stomach torn out. She lay on her side, barely breathing, every now and then a soft whimper escaped. She barely reacted when Barrett stroked her head. Bear glanced up, an unspoken plea in his eyes.

"I'm sorry. There's nothing I can do."

Bear settled his head back against the female, forlorn. Barrett knew he should kill her, end her pain. Thankfully the decision was taken from him. She lifted her head one last time, nuzzled Bear's nose with her own as if to say good-bye, then was gone.

"I'm sorry, boy."

For a moment Bear lay unmoving. Then his head picked up, suddenly alert. He gave a low, guttural growl and leapt to his feet.

Something was there, in the darkness between the trees. More shadow than substance, its appearance was so out of context that Barrett immediately assumed it to be either Osmodon or Sianiave.

"Ozzy?"

Not Osmodon, nor Sianiave. This figure wore a cloak, its face hidden beneath the cowl. Besides, if it had been either one of them, Bear wouldn't have reacted as he did.

The figure stood silent, ominous. Barrett suddenly remembered Sianiave's warning—*Beware of an old man in a cloak.*

He glanced back at the camp. Sianiave and Osmodon were walking toward him, oblivious of the figure in the woods.

"Who are you? What do you want?" Barrett questioned.

He heard the hiss of a dry chuckle. The specter was less than ten feet away. How had it come so close?

He drew his sword. "Stay where you are!"

Another hiss. The cloak seemed to shimmer, then dissolve, like black ink on black water. Barrett found himself staring at the yellowed fangs and vulpine eyes of the largest wolf he'd ever seen.

He barely had time to raise his arm before the creature leapt, its weight driving him against a tree and knocking the sword from his hand. His forearm, protected by the thick fur coat, was the only thing that stood between his neck and the beast's slavering jaws. He fumbled desperately for his dagger.

There was a sudden jolt, and the weight fell away. Possessed by rage, Bear had charged into the beast headlong, tearing at its flank, tooth and claw. Barrett grabbed his sword just as the wolf regained its footing. The sharp blade cut deep into the creature's neck. Another swing and the head rolled free.

Barrett fell back against the tree, shaken, while Bear continued to vent its fury on the headless torso. Sianiave and Osmodon arrived, blades in hand. Bear made one last attack at the bloodied torso, then fell back, panting.

"Big bloody thing," said Osmodon, lifting a hind leg. "Two hundred pounds or more, even without the head."

Sianiave reached out a hand to Barrett's face. Her touch was gentle as she studied the cuts. "You were lucky. Little more than scrapes."

"You knew—." Barrett could barely get the words out. "The old man—?"

"A characteristic of Arden wolves is that the dominant male is always a shape-shifter. I thought the big male I killed was the alpha, but evidently, I was mistaken."

"Shape-shifter? You mean a *werewolf*?" Barrett was stunned.

"No. Those are rare indeed and don't travel in packs. Shape-shifters use a mind trick, an illusion. How's your hand?"

Barrett flexed his fingers. "Looks worse than it is."

"Good. We don't have the time to spend on another healing. We'll clean those cuts. The gods know what filth that thing carried."

Bear trotted up to Barrett and dropped the wolf's gruesome head at his feet.

Osmodon laughed. "A gift for you."

CHAPTER 19

THEY SHOULDERED THEIR PACKS and started off, trudging deeper into the forest. Osmodon carried a small oil lamp and led the way. For Barrett, the lamp's elfin light called up a dim, almost forgotten memory. He was lying in a crib, a woman looking down at him. She had long, dark hair and her lips were bright red. In his infant's mind she appeared exceedingly beautiful. She stroked his forehead, whispering the words *"Always remember, child. The darker the night, the brighter shines the candle."*

His real mother? Barrett didn't know.

Though Osmodon's lamp was barely the size of a pint glass, the dark forest magnified its light. He wondered if it might not attract the very beasts they hoped to avoid. Bear, trotting protectively alongside, seemed to share his concern, tracking back and forth, attentive to every sound and shadow.

"You've a bond now, lad," said Osmodon, commenting on the dog's vigilance. "Bear's taken you as family."

"How do you figure?"

"That female you found him with was Nettle, his eldest pup. Must have broke his heart, not being able to protect her and the others."

"Sounds like someone else I know," Barrett said, grinning.

"Aye, mayhap. It's our job, you see—taking care of others. That's why he gave you the thing's head—his way of saying, 'See, I did my job.'"

Barrett spent most of his childhood shunted from one loveless foster home to another. The longest he'd stayed with a family was a year and a half with the Dobson's, a juiceless couple whose sole purpose was to make life miserable for anyone who didn't agree with their tortured vision of religion. Yet there had always been a stray or a neighbor's dog around to give him comfort.

Leaving the dogs had always been more difficult than leaving the families.

The O'Byrne's were the exception. He took their name as his own, though he had known them for less than a year. But those few short months almost made up for the previous seventeen years of beatings and empty promises.

His sophomore year at West Point, the O'Byrnes had left for Cabo San Lucas in "Jung's Dream," their fifty-two-foot motor sailer. They never arrived. The Coast Guard suspected drug pirates, for the weather had been mild and both Bob and Nancy were experienced sailors. Neither they nor "Jung's Dream" had ever been seen again. It was as though they'd vanished from the face of the earth.

"The dog's full name is Beonard," said Osmodon, breaking Barrett from his thoughts. "'Strength of the Bear.' Barrett means 'Heart of the Bear.' Heart and strength—you two are a match."

"I thought there was no corollary here with—." Barrett stopped, unable to find a word for "English" that made any sense.

Sianiave, following behind Osmodon, glanced back over her shoulder. "I never said there weren't corollaries, only that they aren't the ones you imagine."

The answer was typical of her. "How can you know what I imagine?"

"Experience has to come first."

Just answer the damn question, he wanted to shout, but his irritation was short-lived. He remembered trying to tell Osmodon what it was like in his own world. As much as it hurt his ego to admit it, he was the child here, though the longer he remained, the more familiar the place became—even this gloomy forest. It was the memory of his own world that was fading.

Osmodon had stopped. He studied the line of a depression that led into the darkness. "What do you make of this? A path, I ken, but no tracks I can make out."

Sianiave moved closer. It was impossible to see beyond the range of the lantern light. The darkness was near total. "It's going in the right direction. You've a concern?"

"Animals usually take the easiest route. Yet I see no tracks."

The path was cluttered with fallen trees and tangled undergrowth. To Barrett, it looked inviting—its lack of animal tracks more plus than minus.

"Let the dog decide," suggested Sianiave.

"Good enough. Bear! Come here, boy."

The dog trotted up to Osmodon, tail wagging. Osmodon stoked his ears, then pointed. "This way, yes or no?"

With a bark Bear leapt over a fallen tree and disappeared down the path. Several minutes later he reappeared, barked twice, then ran down the path again for ten feet before he stopped, looking back at them.

"Satisfied?" said Sianiave. Her smile said she'd known all along what the answer would be.

Barrett, for one, was glad to be walking on easier ground. They'd been on the march for well over an hour, stumbling over roots and branches and struggling through snowdrifts. The fight had taken more out of him than he cared to admit. He was exhausted. His legs ached and his pack chaffed his shoulders. Even Osmodon looked done in. Only Sianiave seemed untouched by the hardship, appearing stronger the further they traveled.

They crossed over a small stream. A paving stone was visible under the flowing water, then more stones further up the bank. They were following what appeared to be an ancient road.

When Barrett pointed it out, Osmodon showed little interest. "Aye. Reckon so, straight as it is. Question is, where does it lead?"

He turned back to Sianiave. "M'lady, shouldn't we be looking for a place to camp? It's been a long night, and I for one —." He stopped abruptly, raising his lantern. "Hello. What have we here?"

A large cottage stood in front of them, two storied, stoutly built of logs, slate, and stone. Stone stairs led up to a wide porch and the windows were shuttered. Above it all towered a massive stone chimney.

As they drew nearer, Barrett saw that skilled labor had gone into its construction. The stones had been carefully laid. The wood was grey with age but solid looking and finely joined. Geometrical figures had been carved into the shutters; five- and six-pointed stars, triangles, and spiral labyrinths. An octagon decorated the front door.

Sianiave gave a satisfied nod. "Good. We'll have a roof over our heads."

Barrett's right hand moved unconsciously to the pommel of his sword.

Sianiave had no such reservations. She was halfway up the stone steps. "Come along. It's safe."

"She's probably right," said Osmodon, obviously sharing Barrett's concern as he studied the building. "She usually is. Doesn't look like anybody's lived in it for years."

Dried vines covered one side of the house and weeds were pushing through cracks in the foundation. Branches from nearby trees had worked their way under the eaves, pressing against the stone walls. A well in front had collapsed in on itself, and the porch was covered in a thick mat of dead leaves and snowdrift.

Bear bounded up the steps after Sianiave. "Good enough," muttered Osmodon, his eye on the dog. "But I'm still keeping my sword handy."

Either the cottage door had been left unlocked, or among her other skills Sianiave was a master locksmith, for she had it open by the time the two men reached the top of the steps. The door was made of heavy timbers, banded with iron. The latch and lock had been artfully forged.

Inside was a great room. A stone hearth dominated the far wall. There were several pieces of rough-hewn furniture, shelves, a table and chairs, but little else. Wooden stairs led to the upper floor. Firewood was stacked neatly in a corner. Sianiave dropped her pack and started tossing logs into the hearth.

The logs were so dry they didn't need kindling. Sianiave lit them in the same way she lit her pipe, a trick Barrett had yet to fathom.

"This was the ferryman's cottage," she said.

"Ferryman? We're near Ostengarth! We've reached the river, then."

"You'll hear it in your dreams tonight. There are bedrooms upstairs but I think it best we sleep by the fire. There is a bath in back."

"I take it the ferryman doesn't live here anymore," said Barrett, eyeing the empty room.

Sianiave explained, "Ostengarth was once the main crossing for the Great North Road. There was a garrison of border rangers nearby, a sturdy lot. We'll see their tower in the morning, though it's surely in ruins now. It was already that way the last time—." She suddenly stopped.

"When was that, m'lady?"

"It's been a while." she said softly.

Osmodon set his axe and sword near the door, arranging what bedding he had in a corner near the fire. "So the ferry's no more. How do we cross?"

"There's no need to cross." Sianiave found her pipe in a pocket of her coat and sat back in a chair in front of the fire. "We'll see the road in the morning. It parallels the river for a ways, or used to. Cynbromir, Cuchulain's father, recalled the garrison eighty years ago. Weeks later, forest bandits burned Ostengarth to the ground. This house we're in was the only building left standing, and the ferryman the only person who escaped."

"How'd he survive?" asked Osmodon. "This place is no fortress."

"No. But then that ferryman was not an Ostengarther, or a ferryman for that matter. He was trained in Megida by the Brotherhood."

Osmodon looked up in surprise. "A wizard?"

"Aye. The year that Kosha Khan sacked Megida, he took refuge here and cast a binding."

"A binding. That explains it. Must have bled out onto the path. Animals sense such things." Osmodon gave Sianiave an accusing look. "You knew all along."

"What's a binding?" asked Barrett. He set his pack down opposite Osmodon. The things Sianiave and Osmodon spoke about casually meant little to him. Despite recent experience he still had trouble believing in wizards, or magic. He had seen things that mystified him, but understood none of it.

"A binding is a spell," Sianiave said, "cast to protect a thing or place from, shall we say, disruptive forces."

"The manor house, when we met. You said the fire had weakened the binding."

"That was not a natural fire, as you might have guessed. And that house was older than it looked, far older—and one must consider the strength of the original spell. The summoning of a binding is not a spell for a novice. The ferryman was an adept. No one knows how old he was when he arrived here, but he tended the Ostengarth ferry for many years. He was a kindly fellow, but with little heart for his true calling.

"A friend and I were once guests in this very house," she added. "The year the garrison was disbanded."

Sianiave had spoken offhandedly, but Barrett sensed something else—sadness, perhaps. And then he realized what she had said.

"The year the garrison was—but that was eighty years ago!"

Sianiave looked at him, amused. "Let's just say I wasn't young, even then."

"That's impossible! That would make you—."

Osmodon sighed sympathetically. "Don't fret on it, lad. Imagine how I felt, realizing the girl I was trying to bed was old enough to be my grandmother."

"Enough," said Sianiave.

"Or great, great, great, great—."

"I said that's enough!"

With a look of amusement, Osmodon rolled onto his side. "Don't wake me early. I haven't felt so done-in in years." With that he fell instantly asleep.

Sianiave tamped a mix into her pipe. Barrett watched her, incredulous. Maybe time was different here. Maybe centuries didn't mean centuries. Maybe she and Osmodon were playing with him.

"Get some sleep," she said.

The fire eased the chill in the room. Bear curled up in front of the hearth. With his coat for a blanket and his pack for a pillow, Barrett lay back. The last thing he saw before falling asleep was Sianiave seated in the chair by the fire, quietly smoking her pipe, lost in thought.

That night he dreamed, not of wolves and sorcerers, but of harsh lights and unfamiliar faces hidden behind green masks. He couldn't understand them, but their eyes showed concern, and there was a troubling urgency in their movement. In horror, he realized they didn't see him! How could they help if they didn't see him?

He cried out in terror—*They don't see! They don't see!*—repeating it over and over. *They don't see!*

A hand stroked his head, soft and comforting. A woman's gentle voice, *"Some see, child. Some see. You aren't alone. Trust me. All will be well again."*

The images of lights and masks shimmered, changed, became sunlight reflecting off of an emerald-green pool. The music of a stringed instrument, a mandolin or lyre, played nearby. The smell of pine needles and spring flowers, a beautiful girl swam naked in the pool, bathing under a waterfall, green eyes and golden hair.

Tears welled in his eyes.

CHAPTER 20

MORNING LIGHT FOUND A CRACK in the shutters and fell across Barrett's eyes. Osmodon, already up, was crouched by the fire baking biscuits and heating a pot of snow for tea and porridge. Sianiave was nowhere to be seen.

"Sleep well, did you, lad?"

Images of harsh lights and green masks, the feeling of abject terror, were now fading. What stayed with him was the image of the girl in the pool. "Very well," he said, and meant it.

He stood and stretched. His body was nowhere near as stiff as it might have been. Despite the growing rankness of his clothes and a foul taste in his mouth he found he was in surprisingly good spirits.

Osmodon seemed to share his mood. "Right place, this cabin, spells or no. Sianiave's out collecting firewood," he added, flipping over a biscuit. "Said we should replace what we use. Took the dog with her."

"She's collecting wood and you're cooking? Interesting."

"She wanted to be by herself, I reckon. This place has some meaning for her, though I've no idea why. Ten years working for the woman and she's more of a mystery to me than when we met."

There were a dozen questions Barrett wanted to ask, about Sianiave's age, the change in her appearance. What was the "great purpose" she pursued that Osmodon followed without question?

"No running water," grunted Osmodon. "Better outside anyway. No telling how many years a man wastes, pissing indoors."

Barrett dug out the utensil Osmodon called a "bum brush," along with the furred stick that served as a tooth brush and the powder that passed for toothpaste. Outside the morning was surprisingly warm, the sun now rising above the trees in the east. Bluebirds, jays, and robins were busy, and the air smelled of honey and pine smoke. New grass was sprouting up between patches of melting snow. All about the cabin leaves were turning green. It was an altogether different place from the witch's cottage he imagined the night before.

He breathed in a deep lung full of the crisp air and headed for the nearest tree.

Sianiave returned some minutes later with an armful of wood and Bear at her heels. With a satisfied grunt she dropped the wood by the hearth.

Barrett and Osmodon, half through their breakfast, looked up in surprise. She had doffed her heavy furs, wearing instead tight buckskin pants and a brightly woven vest over a cotton shirt. She sported calf-high leather walking boots. Her golden hair, no longer hidden under a fur cap, was tied into a single braid that hung halfway down her back.

She is beautiful, Barrett thought. More than beautiful, radiant. But it wasn't just her hair or her change of clothes that caught him off guard. Nor were they the reason Osmodon, who'd seen her earlier that morning, was also staring open mouthed.

Sianiave was smiling. Not the amused half smile they were used to, or the sad smile of vanished memories, but a smile that glowed from the inside, bringing sparkle to her features. For the first time since Barrett had known her, she actually appeared to be happy.

"I found a boat," she announced, ignoring their stares as she grabbed a biscuit.

"A boat?" Osmodon asked, dumbly.

"A boat. Grounded on a sandbar by the old quay. I fear its owner met a bad end. There are bloodstains on the tiller and gunnel. Lucky for us, though."

Osmodon gave Barrett a questioning glance. Both knew that it would take more than finding an old boat to put her in such a mood—perhaps it was the energy of the place, or the early coming of spring.

Osmodon asked, "And it's finding this boat that's brought such pleasure to m'lady?"

Sianiave looked up from her meal as if startled. "It's a fine morning, and that boat will save us two days, at the least."

"We've been traveling at a good pace. Is it Gwyndolyn that concerns you?"

Gwyndolyn. A not unpleasant shiver ran up Barrett's spine to the base of his neck. It was the first time he could recall having heard the name, yet it struck a chord—reminded him of forest pools, music, and green light.

"Of course I'm concerned about her!" said Sianiave sharply. "Something's wrong. Events are in motion. We leave as soon as we finish eating." The smile had vanished.

"Is Gwyndolyn the girl we're going to meet?" asked Barrett. "Is she a relative?" He was fishing. Neither Sianiave nor Osmodon had been especially forthcoming about his job, though for different reasons. Osmodon seemed to know little more than himself.

"Relative?" Osmodon's eyes crinkled in humor. "Now there's something I hadn't considered. Is she, m'lady—a relative, I mean?"

Sianiave set down her plate. "Osmodon, you've said enough!"

"My apology." Osmodon looked only a little sheepish.

It was early spring in this world, Barrett knew. Early April, Osmodon had told him, though he hadn't guessed the exact day.

It had been fall in that other world, October 28th. Billy had called it Samain, the time of witches, the time when the border between the worlds was at its weakest! That bit of folklore certainly took on new meaning.

Soon after they left the cottage. Sianiave led them down a gently sloping path that took them through the center of what had once been a sizeable village. Here and there a broken wall or foundation peered out from the underbrush. A tall brick chimney was kept from toppling by the elms grown up around it. The stone arch of a doorway stood alone in a meadow shading a jackrabbit as it nibbled on a cabbage plant. Birds and butterflies were everywhere. A fox watched curiously from its perch atop a fallen log as they passed. During eighty years, the forest had reclaimed its own.

The river itself was bordered by a thick copse of alders, the path ending at the crumbling remains of a large stone quay.

"The ferry quay," Sianiave told them. "This is the widest part of the Dunenwine. The waters are slow and deep here. Crossing is almost impossible above, and not much easier below, at least until you come to Ardendell and the Dunenmere."

She pointed to a line of weed-covered paving stones. "The Great North

Road, or what remains of it. It follows the river south a while before turning again into the forest."

On the far side of the river, rising out of the trees, was a stone tower. Its parapet was blackened and fallen into ruin, giving it the appearance of a half-burnt candle. Sianiave regarded it for a long moment, then turned away without speaking.

The boat was lodged on a spit of sand built up on the high side of the quay. It measured six meters long, stoutly built, with a sharp keel and three plank seats. Its green and white paint was cracked and faded. A rust-colored substance stained its tiller and stern gunnels.

"Blood, right enough," judged Osmodon. "Lots of it. Whatever occurred, it was more than likely deadly."

The boat's oarlocks were in working order, but the oars were missing. Piles of flotsam, logs, leaves, and dead branches had built up on the spit alongside the boat. Osmodon used his axe to fashion two logs into functional, if clumsy, paddles.

They stowed their packs in the center of the boat. Sianiave climbed into the stern, near the tiller. Osmodon had to coax Bear onboard. The dog deemed the water more dangerous than wolves. Barrett and Osmodon shoved the little craft into the eddy, then both jumped in. Once in the river stream, Sianiave took over at the helm.

The journey down the river was largely uneventful, though at a point where the river narrowed, Bear leapt up barking, sensing something in a nearby tangle of trees. Osmodon had to pull him back to avoid overturning the boat.

By late afternoon the forest began to thin, the snow, save in the deepest shadows, was almost gone. Meadows appeared, rolling hills with wildflowers and new spring grass. Occasionally they would catch sight of the road, or a standing stone marking its course. Bear ate his meal cake for lunch. Barrett, Sianiave, and Osmodon made do with their staple of dried meat and fruit.

River water quenched their thirst. Barrett found it pure and delicious.

"It comes from mountain glaciers," Sianiave said. "There's little farming now. None in the north, and sheep and cattle are in short supply, too many predators. I would guess there are fewer than two-thousand inhabitants left in all of Anor, where once there were ten times that number. A family with three children is considered large. Most parents are grateful to have one."

"Plague?" Barrett asked.

"Of a sort—and constant war, " Sianiave replied.

Osmodon nodded. "The Uruks see nothing but empty land now, ripe for the taking. They've been bolder with every passing year."

Barrett looked quizzical. "Uruks?"

"You've not heard of Uruks?" Osmodon went on.

"Perhaps by another name," said Barrett. "Describe them."

"Aye," said Osmodon. "A tribal people—fierce, they are. As for the rest, depends who you ask—drug takers, cannibals, worshippers of evil gods who decorate their tents with the heads of slaughtered children. They are ferocious in battle, merciless in victory, murdering the men and raping the women. Those who survive are sold as slaves, or put to work in the brothels of Nibur. Leastwise, so 'tis said."

Osmodon grunted. "No doubt much is true, though I can vouchsafe the fact Uruks are no more cannibals than you or I. Their ways are strange, harsh by our reckoning. I've fought them enough, and respect them, though I'd never admit to it, not with the way things are these days."

"The Uruks aren't the problem, only a symptom," said Sianiave, steering them past a large rock.

"Symptom? Of what?"

Sianiave ignored the question. Barrett had to content himself with listening to Osmodon's tales of his travels among the desert nomads. The stories sounded exotic and somewhat far-fetched, complete with dragons, djinn, and evil princes. But he was no longer the skeptic he had been. He was learning that, in this world at least, more often than not, fantasy was reality.

CHAPTER 21

NIGHT HAD FALLEN when they finally reached Ardendell. The air had grown heavy, and a thin mist was rising off of the water. They had entered into a wide lake, the Dunenmere—its shores invisible in the darkness. Osmodon had been sitting in the bow of the boat, lantern in hand, warning of rocks and snags that appeared all too suddenly out of the mist.

They were debating whether to continue on in the darkness or find shore and make camp, when suddenly the lights of a village appeared to their left. As they drew closer the shapes of gabled roofs and a high wall appeared. A chill settled on them. The chorus of cicadas and bullfrogs that had been with them since sunset, had gone silent.

"So few," Sianiave murmured.

"M'lady?"

"Ardendell is a well populated village, or was. How many lights do you count? Fifteen? Twenty? There should be a hundred. And that wall wasn't there on my last visit."

A few strokes of the makeshift paddles sent the boat gliding into a long, narrow wharf. Bear leapt ashore. Osmodon set his lamp on a piling, tying the boat to a mooring post while Barrett and Sianiave unloaded the packs.

Even in the dim lamplight it was apparent the wharf was in disrepair. The few boats moored nearby were equally neglected. The air smelled of rotting fish.

The wall was built of logs—a stockade. A door leading from the wharf was closed, barred from within. A crudely lettered sign read: "NO ENTRY AFTER DARK."

"Not very hospitable," commented Osmodon.

Sianiave was thoughtful. "They feel the need to protect the town from the waterside."

The water was black and still, reflecting the light from Osmodon's lantern.

The mist had grown thicker, drifting off the lake and rising through the cracks in the wharf.

"Makes my skin crawl," Osmodon muttered, staring at the inky water. "In Linsraden 'twas said grendels prefer such nights."

"Things are worse than I thought if grendels have come this far from the ocean," said Sianiave, shouldering her pack. "But you're right. If we have to sleep outside, it should be away from the lake. The road passes on the far side of the village. There'll be another gate."

"What's a grendel?" asked Barrett uneasily, staring out at the mist-shrouded lake.

Sianiave was already moving off and didn't answer.

"I take it they don't have them where you're from," said Osmodon. "For which you should be thankful. They come out of the water at night while folks are asleep. What they do to their victims is not a conversation I would have on a night such as this."

Hefting his pack and grabbing his lamp, Osmodon started off after Sianiave. Barrett took one last look at the lake and quickly joined the others.

They left the wharf, following the wall around to the far side of the village. There, as Sianiave had guessed, was another gate, this one large enough to drive two wagons through abreast, though it was also closed. A small, unmarked door was built into the gate, a bell rope at its center. A peal sounded when Osmodon gave it a pull.

A small port in the door popped open. A pair of eyes peered out. "Who goes there!"

"Three travelers and their dog," growled Osmodon impatiently. "We've come a long ways and have need of lodging."

"Come back in the morning." The port slammed shut.

"We'll pay," said Sianiave quickly. "With gold."

A moment's silence, then the port cracked opened again. "Gold, you say?"

Sianiave held up a coin. The metal glittered in the lantern light. The eyes widened. "Bless me! Is that an empress?"

"Yours, if you let us through."

"How do I know you're not bandits—or worse?"

"Do I look like a bandit?"

"Fair to say you don't, m'lady. But those with you, bruisers they are, and well armed."

"Of course they're armed. Who travels these days unarmed? Come now. An empress, all your own. More than you make in a year, I wager—just for a kindness."

A moment's hesitation, then, "Pass it through."

Sianiave held the coin up to the port where it was snatched by skinny, arthritic fingers. Another moment—then they heard bolts being thrown, and the door opened.

The watchman was a ferret of a man. He glanced nervously about as he waved them inside. "Hurry. I could lose my job. Work's hard to come by these days."

They passed into a small watch station. There were two chairs and a table, a partially eaten loaf of bread on the table, and a jug of strong smelling ale. A lantern hung from a bracket and a fire burned in a clay stove. A second door lay opposite the one through which they'd entered.

Once the front door was bolted again the gatekeeper relaxed, suspicion replaced with the semblance of a smile. "You'll be staying at the Lion?"

Sianiave studied the man. "Have we a choice?"

"Lion's the only inn still open. Holbert does right well, even with travelers so few these days. Head of the council, he is." There was accusation in his tone, and some bitterness. "What's your business? Perchance, I can be of help?"

"Our business is none of yours," grunted Osmodon, disliking the man.

"Of course, of course. Only it's my job to ask such questions, you see. Names, business, destination, and the like? Council rules, you know."

"This is the way?" asked Sianiave, indicating the opposite door.

"Yes. But your names?"

Barrett found himself staring at the man in utter fascination. It was if he knew everything there was to know about the fellow, his lack of character, his greed, fear, cunning, the absence of anything substantial in his makeup, all was as clear as if he could read the man's mind. Accepting a bribe was common practice for him, and the gold coin had been far too much to pay. Barrett also knew that once they entered the village, he would run and tell someone in order to curry favor.

Feeling Barrett's eyes on him, the man stepped backward as though physically threatened. "I've done nothing! Stay away from me!"

"Barrett!" snapped Sianiave. She shook her head as though in warning, then turned back to the gatekeeper. "We mean you no harm. We're here only for a meal and a night's lodging."

The man's shoulders slumped and he shook his head as though waking from a trance. "Of course, m'lady. The Lion it is. Tell Holbert Old Bob sent you. Old Bob, it is."

Outside, Sianiave took Barrett's arm. "I should have warned you. Try not to stare directly at people when the sight comes to you like that."

"The sight—?"

"We'll speak about it later."

Barrett turned to Osmodon for help, but the big man simply shrugged.

At first glance, Ardendell resembled another village Barrett remembered, though he had trouble recalling a name. Wattle and daub construction, narrow cobbled streets, thatch and slate roofs—there were hitching posts in front of some of the larger establishments, and an occasional covered well. A tallow candle burned in a nearby streetlamp. Others were dark.

It was a town clearly in decline—fallen chimneys, boarded up doors and windows. Few houses looked lived in, though here and there a ray of light from a candle or lamp escaped from under a door or through a shuttered window. Over it all hung the stench of decay.

Barrett couldn't read Sianiave's thoughts, but he sensed both sadness and anger. "This way," she said. "The Lion isn't far."

A rat as large as a cat slipped under a door, disappearing inside. A faded sign over the door read,

COLM & SONS, TINKERS

WEAPONS SHARPENED

HARNESSES, WAGONS, AND KETTLES REPAIRED

Somewhere in the distance a dog barked. Bear turned his head, then ignored the sound. "Fallen a bit has it, m'lady?" Osmodon commented. "I mean since your last visit."

"Yes," she said shortly.

She was sure of her way now, turning down a wide alley. The inn was at the far end, a large three-storied building with a gabled roof. Wrought-iron carriage lamps bracketed the front door. Smoke drifted up through brick chimneys, carrying the smell of fresh-baked bread and roasting mutton. Raucous laughter could be heard inside. Lights shone from the windows on the first floor, but the windows on the upper floors were dark.

The inn was L-shaped, with a wing to their left. To the right, forming a courtyard, were the stables. Barrett had a moment's pause as he stared up at a sign hanging over the front door, a lion and unicorn, rampant.

"Don't read too much into the sign," Sianiave cautioned. "The inn here and the tavern back there have little else in common."

"It's an ancient seal," Osmodon said, giving Barrett an odd look. "Marks the House of Ambergin. Must be known even where you come from."

Barrett kept silent.

At Tor Eyrie it had been Osmodon's job to train Barrett, and he soon discovered that the lad's martial skills surpassed even his own, something he hadn't expected. He himself had studied and taught the warrior arts for more years than he cared to remember. While sparring with swords and in hand-to-hand combat, he'd found his charge using forms he'd never encountered, amazingly deft. What's more, the lad's strength was astonishing for his size, and nearly equal to his own, though he hated to admit it. He sensed nobility in the fellow's character, and respected him for it.

"No farmer's horse, this," said Sianiave. A horse in one of the stalls had caught her eye, a big grey, with intelligent brown eyes and a white blaze on its forehead. She moved closer for a look.

"No, ma'am," came a voice from behind them. "Greywind's a knight's horse."

A boy appeared. He had blonde hair and his feet were bare. He carried a feed bucket. Barrett guessed him to be about fifteen.

"You startled us," said Sianiave, though she didn't look startled. Barrett suspected she'd known he was there. "A knight's horse, you say?"

"Aye, though Master Holbert has rights now. Are you looking to buy a horse?"

"Three horses, actually. I gather you're the stable boy. Have you any suggestions?"

"Master Holbert will sell those two there. He took 'em in payment." The boy pointed toward an adjoining stall where two sturdy ponies were kept.

"Bill and Tarabald—they're farm animals, but good for a day's work, and faithful too. They keep Greywind company," he added, moving to the grey's stall and pouring oats into the feed bin.

"Greywind, you call him? How did an innkeeper come to own a knight's horse?"

The boy stroked the grey's head affectionately. "I found him wandering loose in the forest. Master Holbert took him in, hoping his rider might show up. But it's been over three months now. By law the horse now belongs to Master Holbert, but he has no use for an animal trained for war, and feed costs are dear. He'll sell him right enough."

The boy regarded Barrett. "Sir? Are you a knight?"

Barrett turned. "Who? Me? A knight?"

"Greywind should go to a knight, and you have the look about you."

"He will not be used for farming," said Sianiave, stroking the grey's neck. "That I can promise."

The horse snorted and stamped, but continued to chew on his oats.

"Saddle and trappings?" asked Sianiave.

"Farm rigging for Bill and Tarabald, and battle gear for Greywind. It's how I knew he belonged to a knight."

"What's your name?"

"Will, ma'am. Some call me Wispy Will. I tend to daydream a bit, I guess."

Sianiave reached into a pocket, coming up with three coins, which she gave to the boy. "Take these, Will. I'll trust you to have the horses saddled, fed, watered, and ready to go early, for we'll leave soon after dawn."

The boy stared at the coins in disbelief. They shone brightly, even in the shadowed courtyard.

"Hide them," she said, cupping the boy's fingers around the coins. "Tell no one, not even those whom you trust. Pay off your indenture. Promise."

"M'lady!"

"Your indenture—promise."

"By my heart, I promise, but—"

"You're doing us a service. Have the horses ready to travel in the morning."

The boy stared at the coins in wonder. As they moved toward the inn he ran after them. "The dog! Master Holbert doesn't allow animals in the inn. You can leave him with me. I'll see he's looked after."

"What do you think, Bear?" said Osmodon, scratching Bear's head. "Trust this boy?"

Bear barked once in reply and sidled up to the boy.

"He's in your keeping, lad," said Osmodon. "His name is Bear, and he likes meat, and lots of it. We'll square it with your master."

CHAPTER 22

THE INN'S COMMON ROOM was crowded and homey, a welcome change from the cold night air and the forsaken village. Tavern maids in bright blouses hurried about carrying trays of food and tankards of ale, brushing off groping hands and rude jests with the skill of long experience. An aged minstrel in ragged green clothes and dusty boots strolled between the tables, strumming a six-stringed lyre. The words to his songs were all but lost in the din. Sawdust covered the plank floor and candles and hanging oil lamps lit the tables. A large stone hearth warmed the room. Every now and then a small boy would appear with a log and add it to the fire.

"Leastwise we know where the townsfolk are," commented Osmodon. "I was beginning to think the place bereft of people."

Barrett studied the crowd. The 'sight' he had experienced with the gate-keeper hadn't entirely subsided. Despite the outward show of revelry, there was tension in the room. He noticed more than one man drop a nervous hand to his weapon, as if for assurance of its presence.

It wasn't a celebration that brought them here, Barrett thought. These people were afraid. He saw it in their faces and their overly loud laughter.

As their presence was noticed, the laughter faltered. Even the minstrel stopped his strumming, turning to regard the new arrivals with curiosity. A rotund, balding man in a stained leather apron approached them, his brown eyes sharp and measuring.

There was a flicker of recognition as his eyes fell on Sianiave.

"Welcome to the Lion and Unicorn, m'lady. I am Holbert Holbertson, keeper of this inn. I take by your baggage you're here for rooms?"

He spoke loudly, wanting others to hear, to get the matter of these travelers settled so the room could return to normal.

Sianiave favored him with a dazzling smile. "Thank you, yes—three rooms, and a meal, if you will. We've come a long way and are tired and hungry."

Barrett hid his surprise. Her smile had been enough to quicken the heart of a corpse. Its effect wasn't lost on the innkeeper. "Of course, m'lady. You'll have your pick of rooms. These are mostly local folk, and only five of my rooms are let. For all that, it's better than most nights. Not that I'm complaining, mind you, but we do miss the travel trade."

He stopped, abruptly. "Apologies, m'lady. My troubles aren't yours. Three rooms, you said? There's the King's Suite for yourself, and rooms across the hall for you companions. I'll give you a fair rate for the three."

"That's very kind of you."

The innkeeper's face reddened. "'Tis nothing. For a meal, we offer mutton and cheese. Bread—fresh baked of course. We have flour, though vegetables are hard to come by."

He spotted a booth in the corner where a stout woman was menacing a large, bearded man twice her size. Three younger men also sat at the table.

"You great hairy beast!" scolded the woman. "You're coming now, not tomorrow! Leaving your wife and daughter alone—you should be ashamed! And you three louts—what do you have to say for yourselves?!"

"Big Nelly's wife," Holbert chuckled. "Come to drag him and her boys home."

The woman hauled away the unresisting man. The three younger men, all with the same curly blonde hair and bulk of their father, gathered up their weapons and followed, much to the good-natured jeers of the onlookers.

"Maude! Mary!" Holbert waved over two tavern maids who quickly cleared the table. "Busy tonight, as you can see. You'll have to tend to your own baggage, I'm afraid—leastwise for the time being. I'll send a lad over soon as I'm able."

"We'll manage," said Sianiave, giving him another glowing smile. "And thank you again."

"I'll see to your food myself!" The innkeeper bowed, almost tripping over himself as he scurried off.

"And ale!" bellowed Osmodon after him. "Don't forget the ale!" He slapped Barrett's arm. "You see that, lad? Reminds me of when I first saw her that time in Barad'An. No doubt I acted as much the fool. Did that fellow actually bow?"

Sianiave sniffed. "He was only being courteous."

Osmodon laughed. "Courteous, you say?"

Whatever her motives, Sianiave seemed well pleased with herself. The atmosphere quickly returned to normal. A tavern maid arrived with three large tankards. She returned Osmodon's smile with a blue-eyed wink as she hurried back to the bar.

The ale was thick, dark, and strong. Osmodon finished his in one long draught and called for more. Barrett's head was spinning after half a flagon. Waving off a refill, he looked around the room and his eyes fell on a table near the hearth. A girl sat there alone. So far as he could see, she was the only lone female in the room who was not a tavern maid. Even through the shifting throng and curling smoke he could see she was beautiful, extraordinarily so.

Why was she alone? Was she waiting for someone—her husband, a lover? There was a tankard in front of her, but she didn't appear to be drinking, just lost in thought, not moving.

Her skin was as flawless as alabaster, a mane of black hair fell across her shoulders. Rosebud lips formed an enigmatic smile and a low-cut blouse revealed taut breasts. Barrett guessed she might have been eighteen, though something about her suggested she was older. She looked out of place in the tavern. Despite her beauty there was an unmistakable sense of menace present—of darkness.

The longer Barrett watched her, the more he wanted to stare. Heat seemed to emanate from her, magnetic, as though her body were singing to his—the song settling into his loins. She might be the most desirable woman he had ever seen. Maybe it was the smoke in the room but everything around her began to appear hazy and unfocused.

A prostitute—hardly. Every man in the room would have been at her table begging for favors.

Slowly, as if aware of his attention, she turned her head. He realized he'd be caught staring, but he couldn't take his eyes away.

Their eyes met—hers black and fathomless. She smiled—just a small curl at the edge of her lips—but knowing, full of promise.

"This should keep you for a bit!" The innkeeper, unknowing, broke the enchantment. He balanced a tray on his shoulder and began laying out platters of food—roast lamb, a loaf of bread, and a quarter circle of ripe yellow cheese.

Neither Sianiave nor Osmodon appeared to have noticed either the girl or Barrett's attraction to her, for which he was grateful. The affect she'd had on him wasn't a noble one, though Osmodon would certainly have understood.

When he turned back, she was gone, her table taken by three drunken farmers. The disappointment he felt was almost physical.

Osmodon had hewn a chunk of lamb with his dagger and was tearing into the bread with his hands. Likewise, Sianiave was making do, though with smaller pieces. Hungry as he was, Barrett couldn't take his mind off of the girl. Could he find her again? And if he did, what then?

The innkeeper stood by the table. "M'lady. If I might ask—?"

"Of course," said Sianiave, putting down a slice of cheese and reaching into her pocket. "How much do we owe?"

"Oh, not that—we can settle your account when you leave. No. It's just that you mentioned you've been on the road for a bit. It's been near on a week since we've had any news from the south."

"I'm sorry. But we've come from the north."

"The north—?" He seemed surprised.

"We are traveling south however, and are in need of horses. We've been told you have several you might be willing to sell."

"Why, yes—three, to be exact. But for the life of me, why do you want to travel south at such a time?"

A tavern maid arrived, taking the tray from the innkeeper's hands and pulling on his arm. "Holbert! The tap is broken again. You'd best hurry!"

He shook his head in despair. "Third time this week, and with the coppersmith gone. Please excuse me, but business calls. If you're serious about the horses, we can talk later."

"That was a bit strange," said Sianiave as the innkeeper hurried off again.

"How so?" asked Osmodon, between bites.

"News from Barad'An can't be that hard to come by, even in these times. Yet our host seemed surprised we were even traveling in that direction. Something's not right. I've felt it since we entered."

Barrett wasn't following the conversation. His thoughts again on the black-haired girl. He looked up, realizing Sianiave had asked him a question.

"I'm sorry?"

"Is something wrong?" Sianiave asked. "You seem distracted."

"Fine. Just tired."

"We can all use some sleep. We're in for a long ride tomorrow."

CHAPTER 23

MIDNIGHT APPROACHED, its hour marked by a large water clock atop the hearth. The tavern hall emptied with unseemly speed. The patrons left in groups, three and four at a time as if to give one another courage. Drunken laughter gave way to wariness as they headed into the night, crude weapons in hand.

The girl was nowhere to be seen. Barrett considered the possibility she was but a hallucination, a fantasy conjured up from his own tired and libidinous mind. Or maybe it was the ale.

But no. She was no fantasy, no mirage. Somehow he was certain of that. Her affect on him had been all too real.

The minstrel sat on a chair by the hearth, plucking a quiet lament on his lyre, lost in drink or sad memories, perhaps both. The tavern maids went about carrying off empty plates and flagons, and replacing melted candles. Every now and then, the blue-eyed wench encouraged Osmodon with another mischievous smile.

With a heartfelt sigh Holbert joined them at the table, glad to be off his feet. He brought an ink pot, parchment, and quill pen and proceeded to add up a column of figures—all business now.

"A hundred and seventy-three silver pennies," he announced with a flourish of his quill. "Three horses, their tack, three rooms for a night, this night's meal, heated baths for all, food for your dog, and breakfast for three in the morning—a bargain, I must say. The grey stallion alone is worth that, if I'm any judge—a knight's animal by all accounts, with a fine leather saddle."

Barrett knew little about the value of the local currency, but considering how free Sianiave had been with her gold, the offer seemed a good one. As best he could figure, gold was worth fifty times that of silver, and silver pennies were, from what he could see, rather smaller than the gold "empresses" she'd been handing out. By that account, a hundred and seventy-three silver pennies was less than what she'd given the stable boy.

Sianiave studied the innkeeper's tally. "A knight's horse? We've heard the story, Master Holbert, and while I do not doubt your ownership, what if by happenstance we cross paths with its previous owner? Knights are known to be fond of their horses. As for the other two, they are farm animals, barely larger than ponies, and we have many leagues yet to travel."

"Have no worries there," insisted Holbert. "They are sturdy beasts, good for a hard day's work or a long day's ride. As for the grey, I very much doubt ownership will be contested. There was no livery we could find—no cygnet at all. The beast itself had several wounds, suffered in battle, no doubt. but healed now, of course," he added quickly. "It's probable, with the king's passing, and events in Barad'An as they are —."

"What?!"

The table shook as Osmodon dropped his flagon. "What's that you say!? The king—"

Sianiave looked stunned. "Cuchulain? Dead?"

Holbert reached out a hand as if to comfort her. "My greatest apology, m'lady. I thought everyone knew."

A complex series of emotions crossed Sianiave's features—anger, grief, uncertainty. The death of this king was personal for her, Barrett saw, though he had no idea why. Then, as firmly as if a door had slammed, the practical woman he'd grown used to reasserted herself.

"As I said, Master Holbert, we've been in the north."

"Of course! Flog me if I've upset you. It's a sorry way to learn such troubling news."

"How?" growled Osmodon. "Not old age. That was a hard old man. He had years left in him."

Holbert shook his head sadly. "A morghul's arrow, they say. Tom O'Canter, the minstrel there, first brought tidings. Others have passed through since, but no news of late."

"With Artos gone, and Gwyndolyn not yet of age—." Sianiave had grown thoughtful.

"Aye," said Holbert, nodding. "The priest, Bleys or Glays, whatever his name, didn't wait a day before proclaiming himself steward, and high priest of both Right and Left Towers, if you believe it!"

"Glays?" growled Osmodon. "That puffed up ass? How in the hell did he end up on top?"

"Clever really," mused Sianiave. "By proclaiming himself steward and keeper of both towers, he not only gains control of the city, he becomes archon, and Gwyndolyn's sole guardian. The Sisters would never have agreed."

Holbert nodded. "It's said they had no choice. There's talk the king and the priest signed some charter or other. Few knights were left to argue, and the Sisters are no fighters. And it's come out that the priest has been hiring recruits into his own army for years. Those who oppose him, he hangs or crucifies."

"Crucifies!"

"Nails them to the big oaks as a warning to the opposition. You can smell the stench for miles. I wouldn't have believed it, but we've heard it from more than just Tom."

Sianiave frowned. "How do people here stand?"

The innkeeper glanced over his shoulder, but only the serving maids, the fire boy and the minstrel remained in the room. "A dangerous question, if you ask the wrong folk."

"You've nothing to fear from us."

"You travel south, you say? You could end up facing the question yourselves, not that I would wish such a thing on you—or anyone for that matter."

The innkeeper leaned forward, his voice low. "Fear can work on a man. There was a time when Barad'An was the heart and soul of Anor. The king's men protected the roads and caravans, guarded the borders. In Bran's day it's said a virgin carrying a bag of gold could ride from one end of the kingdom to the other without fear. Well, sore be it, those days are gone, and have been for my lifetime. Barad'An's a hollow fortress now, walled up like an old maid's memories—hanging on to past glories."

"It doesn't trouble you?" asked Sianiave, "the king passing, this priest taking power?"

"Of course it troubles me. It troubles us all. But times change. We've got to mind our own. You've seen the town. Trade's all but disappeared. Travelers grow fewer every year. Even the weather's off, growing warmer it is. A normal year there'd still be snow two feet deep. Bandits and wolves have the forest. People have gone missing—children too. Just last week. Gef, the Woodsman, found a pit surrounded by rune stones filled with bones—human bones, burnt and chewed upon. Uruks, some say, though Uruks rarely venture this far north, and they have naught to do with runes."

"Wildings?" suggested Osmodon.

"Or some other creatures, fairy tales, some say. But the older folk, those that remember, know differently."

"Is this why you built the wall?"

"Aye, though I was against it. It won't hold against an army, or even a determined raiding party, but it makes some feel safer. Few farms left. Or the people packed up and left before they could be burned out. No fishing further than the end of the dock, though on bright days a few of the younger men will take a boat out. Some never return, even then. There's talk something evil makes its home in the lake."

Barrett remembered the dried blood they found on the boat, the black stillness of the lake, and the uneasy feeling of being watched.

"I do well enough," the innkeeper went on. "But it's mostly local folk now. You're the first travelers from the north in more than a fortnight."

Then, as if making a decision, he dropped his voice even lower until almost a whisper. There was anger in it. "You asked how we feel about the priest, m'lady? We follow the Old Way here. For anyone to claim he speaks for the Mother as well as the Father, well, it doesn't sit well with us. Ardendell's a market town, or was. We know when someone's trying to sell us a bill of goods, especially since Princess Gwyndolyn was forced to flee."

"Ren—gone?!"

"Escaped with Abdelar and Aerindir, m'lady. They had to ride over a troop of the priest's guard to do it, leastway as Tom tells it."

Osmodon slapped the table and laughed. "Abdelar and Aerindir are with her! By Asgar, that's some good news, at least!"

Sianiave gave Osmodon a warning look, but the innkeeper didn't appear to notice. He continued, "Left a score of the priest's men lying dead at the gate," he said, grinning. "Tom claims he saw it with his own eyes. He's composing a song about it, sings the finished parts when he's a mind."

"Perhaps he'll sing it for us," suggested Sianiave.

"I'll ask him. It's good, the song I mean, if I do say so. It will travel. Little enough to ask for these days, but you take what you can get."

A shadow seemed to pass over the table as a tavern maid blew out another candle and disappeared into the kitchen. For a time, no one spoke. The minstrel's melancholy strumming had stopped. The fire had burned down to embers, and there was a growing chill in the room.

Barrett shifted in his seat. His sword belt pinched his side and his feet ached. He knew he should be paying more attention to the conversation. Sianiave and Osmodon's reactions told him there was important information. Cuchulain, Aerindir, Glays, Abdelar, Gwyndolyn, names he should know. But the image of the black-haired girl kept intruding into his thoughts.

Where had she gone?

Sianiave slapped four gold coins on the table. "We'll accept your terms, Master Holbert. The overage is for your kindness, and to expedite matters. Have the horses ready at sunrise, with enough bread, cheese, and dried meat to last us for a week. And send the minstrel over. I'd like to hear his story with my own ears."

The innkeeper reached for the coins, then hesitated. "More than fair, m'lady. But surely, after what you've heard, you're not still bent on traveling south? It's said the priest's men are stopping everyone they meet."

"Our travel plans are our own business. You're best not to know them, Master Holbert."

"Of course, m'lady. I'll send Tom over."

Holbert stood to leave, then turned back. "M'lady, it's not my usual policy to speak politics or religion with guests. Certainly not with folk I've just met."

"A wise policy for an innkeeper," Sianiave agreed.

"Indeed. Yet I wouldn't want to leave you with the impression I have a loose tongue."

"You've a reason then, for speaking so candidly?"

Holbert paused, then said, "Years ago, when I was still a boy and my father was keeper here, a knight arrived asking for a meal and a night's lodging. Tall and grim he was, and he carried a long sword. Much like your young friend here. It was summer, and there was a woman with him. Beautiful as the moon she was, even to my young eyes."

Holbert was watching Sianiave's face, as though looking for a reaction. When she didn't respond he went on. "I never knew who the lady was, but she and the man were close, for they took a single room."

"What has this to do with us?"

"M'lady, excuse me for saying this. But when you walked through that door tonight, I was seven years old again. At first I thought it couldn't be, and put the thought aside. But looking at you now, excepting for that scar, you could be that woman."

Sianiave smiled. It was not an unkind smile, but Barrett sensed there was more behind it, some emotion even her stern control couldn't quite hide.

"So you decided to trust us on a childhood memory," she said.

"The lady's face is as clear in my mind now as on the night they arrived."

Osmodon shifted uncomfortably, apparently finding something to interest him in his ale.

"I suppose I should be flattered, Master Holbert. When was this?"

"Eighty years it's been, as I will be eighty and eight this coming June. And you're right. I hardly understand it myself. But there was something else, you see."

"Oh? And what is that?"

"The knight was known to us. He had been a ranger at Ostengarth. His name was Cuchulain, who later became king."

CHAPTER 24

THE MINSTREL'S NAME was Tom O'Canter. His eyes were grey and world-weary, his fine features creased with age. Although his instrument was missing a string, his voice was still deep and pure, and he displayed a youthful exuberance in telling the story of Princess Gwyndolyn's escape.

"The guards had them 'til Captain Fletcher began raining arrows from the wall, and that was a wondrous sight. They rode through the gate, more than a dozen of the guard in chase. That evening only seven of the templars returned, and they weren't happy.

"They told the townfolk that the brothers had kidnapped Gwyndolyn. All knew it was a lie, but templars sprung up everywhere. They threatened anyone who spoke against them. Executions began that very day, right in the street, and on the least pretext. Most people were dumbfounded, not believing such a thing could happen in Barad'An. But I've seen it too often to think Barad'An immune to such evil. I was in Megida when the Kosha Sirdar wiped out the Brothers, and before that in Marduk the day the count lost his mind and opened the gates to the Uruk hoards."

Since he'd joined them at the table Sianiave had been studying the minstrel as if to place him in her memory. The minstrel did his best to ignore the scrutiny, avoiding her eyes when he could. But at his last remark Sianiave nodded as though something had become clear.

Osmodon cocked his head in surprise. "Marduk? That was over a hundred and fifty years ago."

The minstrel gave a rueful smile. "A hundred and fifty-eight, to be precise. I'm a bit older than I look."

Barrett did a double take. *A hundred and fifty-eight?* The man didn't look over seventy. Earlier the innkeeper had claimed to be eighty-seven. Barrett had let it pass. Sianiave could easily pass for thirty now, or younger, and God alone knew how old she was.

How old was Osmodon? Forty, forty-five at most. Maybe Osmodon's insistence on calling him "lad" was more than habit of speech.

"What happened to Captain Fletcher?" asked Sianiave. If she remembered the minstrel from some past encounter, she had decided not to mention it.

"They say he was taken to the dungeons."

"Alive?"

"At the time, though it might have been best were it otherwise. The priest has made his magician dungeon master."

"Gothmog?" snapped Osmodon. "That cockroach should have been daggered years ago."

"You speak as if you know the fellow."

"Only by sight. And that's close enough."

The minstrel grinned. For all his age, Barrett noticed that his teeth were amazingly straight and white. "There was a song in Minador, before the sack of course, about a knight, *'The Last Defender of Linsraden.'*"

Osmodon brightened, "A good song?"

The minstrel replied, "Would you like to hear it? I think I can remember a few lines."

"I think we've heard enough for one night," said Sianiave as the minstrel reached for his lyre. "Master Holbert, if you would show us to our rooms. We've a long way to travel, and must rise early."

"Of course. Your baths should be ready."

Barrett stifled a yawn with his hand. He was tired, the thought of a hot bath now uppermost in his mind.

"I'll be along," said Sianiave. As Barrett and Osmodon followed the innkeeper, she turned to the minstrel, slipping a gold coin into his palm. "For your stories–and your silence."

The minstrel pocketed the coin. "Blessings, m'lady, but you've no worries from me, gold or none. I've little love of Bishop Glays, or his hateful creed. Poets are not welcome in such regimes—neither poets nor artful women."

Sianiave smiled.

"My eyesight isn't so far gone that I'd fail to recognize the Lady Sianiave the moment she entered the room, though it was said you'd left Anor for good.

I also recognized Sir Osmodon, though who your other companion is I've no idea. He has a formidable look about him, but he's in none of the songs I know. He's young yet."

"An itinerant soldier who's offered his help." Sianiave pressed a second coin into his palm. "Thank you, again."

"I owe you thanks, m'lady, for we all have our secrets. I trust you to keep mine." The minstrel stood and bowed. "I wish you well on your journey. I feel a great deal rides on its outcome—for all of us."

"Indeed, it may," said Sianiave softly.

CHAPTER 25

THEIR ROOMS WERE ON THE THIRD FLOOR. Barrett's was small and sparsely furnished, but the bed was passing comfortable, the mattress goose down, the sheets freshly washed and with no sign of vermin.

A window looked out over the slated dormer of the room below, presenting a good view of the shore. The wooden stockade that encircled the village was closer than he would have guessed. In the darkness it appeared as ominous as a prison yard wall. Beyond it lay the mist-shrouded waters of the lake.

Their baths had been drawn, steaming and hot. The boys who fetched the water were seated patiently nearby, copper kettles at their feet. When Osmodon asked if they had other chores to do, being it was late, the oldest boy replied that it was their job to stay, in case more hot water was needed, and to provide fresh towels when the guests had done bathing.

There were questions Barrett wanted to ask Osmodon, but the presence of the boys and the warm comfort of the bath subdued his more complex thoughts. Osmodon was equally disinclined to talk, lying back in the tub and humming a nameless tune.

"She's a comely one, she is," Osmodon said, after a bit.

"Excuse me?"

"The wench who served us. Mary. The blue-eyed lass."

"Oh. That one." For a moment Barrett had imagined Osmodon was talking about the dark-haired girl at the table. "You know her name?"

"Aye. We had a meaningful talk."

As far as Barrett recalled, Osmodon had barely said a word to the girl, much less shared a meaningful talk. But then, his attention had been elsewhere.

"She has a friend," Osmodon said, soaping his armpits with a bar of rough soap. "The slender, flaxen-haired lass behind the bar."

Barrett shrugged. He had paid no attention to the tavern maids. "Morning's, what, five hours off?"

"Aye. But life is short and there's a long road ahead. We can sleep in the saddle."

"What about Sianiave?"

"She'd be the first to recommend it. She knows how anxious a man can get. If there was a fellow around to her taste, she'd be doing the same."

The thought of Sianiave with a man somehow made Barrett uncomfortable. "Thanks anyway. I'm ready for a good night's rest."

"As you wish. But I tell you, you're missing out on one of life's great joys. Who knows when we'll have a chance to lie with a pretty maid again. Do you good. Help the juices flow."

"My juices will keep. See you in the morning."

Barrett stepped out of the tub and a boy handed him a towel. He wrapped it around his waist, gathered up his boots and clothes and returned to his room. He didn't relish the thought of morning when once again he would have to don his filthy clothes.

He tossed the towel on the chair, blew out the room's single candle, and lay face down on the bed, naked. The room was warm enough that a light woolen blanket served. Despite the warm glow of the bath, the late hour, and his complete exhaustion, sleep was slow in coming.

Now, he would have stayed awake for the girl at the table.

He tried to picture her face, but the memory had grown hazy, the image that came to him was constructed of bits and pieces of beautiful women he'd seen. But the carnal ache, the hardening arousal, the certainty of her body calling out to his, these feelings had returned with a vengeance.

A sound outside the door brought him to alert. There was something disquieting about the sound, wet, ichorous, as though someone had dropped a large, sodden sponge on the floor.

Seconds passed and he began to relax, most likely Osmodon, returning from his bath—maybe a last effort to fix him up with the bar maid.

He smiled. Why not? Things had been so dark and strange, why not enjoy himself for a change—just for a night.

He rolled to his side, pretending to sleep, but the expected knock never came. Instead another sound, the quiet metallic click of the latch being tested.

He suddenly remembered he'd forgotten to bolt the door.

He sat up, his hand reaching for his sword. Whoever was on the other side of that door was not Osmodon. Nor would it be Sianiave. The surreptitious nature of the sound was more that of a thief or an assassin.

A bright moon had risen above the mist, casting enough light so that he could make out the latch as it lifted slowly off its catch.

He swung out of bed, the sword raised as he pulled open the door. "All right! Whoever you—."

The challenge caught in his throat. Standing at the threshold was the girl from the common room. No longer in a peasant blouse and skirt, she wore an ankle-length white gown of a fabric so insubstantial it revealed rather than concealed an inhumanly perfect body. A slight breeze from the hallway played with the dress, teasing her black hair. Her lips were red and parted in that same, slight smile.

She stood for a long moment, waiting for him to speak.

"Can I help you?" he stammered, feeling foolish even as he said the words.

"Has it been so long, Eanor?"

Her voice was soft, silken, at once innocent and lewdly intimate. Barrett felt as if he had entered a dream. He was afraid to speak.

"You must invite me in." She said it not as question but a statement, as though reminding him of an obligation.

He hesitated, a strange reluctance come over him.

Again he felt foolish. The question was, why? Why was she there? Who was she? She'd called him a name. Ian—something?

"You have me confused with someone else," he forced the words.

She looked amused. But her eyes darted to the sword in his hand. He sensed her wariness, a brief moment of doubt, even fear. "You have forgotten," she said. "I would not have thought that possible."

Again it was a statement, not a question.

Barrett was in turmoil, the dreamlike immediacy of the moment fighting a heightened sense of unease. Why should he be afraid? It was all too obvious she was unarmed. "I'm sorry," he said. "Please come in."

He backed away, propping the sword against the nightstand. Then, suddenly aware of his nakedness, grabbed up the towel and wrapped it around his waist.

The girl almost seemed to float toward him as she came into the room. He had the disturbing sense her feet weren't touching the floor.

"And if you are not who I know you to be," she murmured, "would it matter so much?"

Barrett's resistance was crumbling. What did it matter? A girl he'd been fantasizing about just moments before, was standing in front of him, obviously willing. Why was he hesitating?

She continued toward him, her eyes locked onto his, swallowing him. He could smell her scent now, musky and exciting. Her skin was flawless, supernally so. Slender fingers reached out, touched his chest and sent an electric charge through his body.

He stood unresisting as she raised her mouth to his ear. "You remember."

Just before their lips touched she pulled away, teasing. Her breath smelled of saltwater and pomegranates. Her eyes pulled him down into deep places under the sea. A pale hand took the towel and coaxed it free.

All innocence was gone now. Her fingers moved to his groin, moved with an unwholesome eagerness. "It's been too long—you've come so far—so hungry."

The warning voice in his head was a scream now, but he was no longer listening. He pulled her to him. Her tongue darted out, meeting his. They fell back on the bed. Her dress seemed to vanish as if woven from moonbeams. She flowed atop him, her mouth and hands growing ever more intimate. Warmth engulfed his groin. He felt a sharp pain as something probed his buttocks, then a pleasure so intense he thought he would explode.

Her fingers, he thought, seemed busy elsewhere. Pain, as her teeth sank into his neck. He was beyond caring. Pleasure and pain had merged into an all-consuming rapture.

The moment of release, so close—.

"RELEASE HIM, YOU ABOMINATION!"

With a hiss of rage the creature that had been feeding on Barrett lifted its head from his neck, turning to see Sianiave standing in the doorway, her right hand holding a sword, in her left, a silver cross.

Barrett opened his eyes to find himself staring into a nightmare—mottled skin like the corpse of an old woman too long underwater, white strands of hair, reptilian eyes, and a split tongue that flicked between needlelike teeth. Worse was the body entwined around his—a translucent sac with long, sucker-covered appendages. Its thin, knotted legs were wrapped around his. The tentacle-like arms clamped over his groin and chest were as strong as iron, seemingly fused into place.

There was no pleasure now, only pain. Barrett writhed in agony, unable to move or even scream. The creature's malevolent eyes flashed angrily between Sianiave and Barrett, unwilling to release its prey.

Sianiave spoke a word and a silvery light flashed out from the cross, lighting up the room. Then she commanded, "BEGONE GRENDEL! BACK TO THE SEA!"

The creature retreated as though struck by a brand. With a cry of frustration it separated itself from Barrett, slid wetly to the floor and dove shrieking through the paned glass to the dormer below.

It flowed off the roof and disappeared over the wall. Moments later there came a splash, as though a large fish had jumped in the lake.

"By Asgar, what the hells was that—?" Osmodon stumbled into the room, sword in hand and wearing only his underwear.

He took it all in at a glance, focusing on Barrett who lay unmoving on the bed. Purple welts were already forming where the creature's suckers and teeth had been at work. Behind Osmodon, blue eyes wide with fright and doing her best to hide her own lack of dress with a sheet, stood Mary, the tavern wench.

"What's all the noise? What's going on here?" Holbert appeared, carrying a metal-capped club. He stared at the shattered window, then at Barrett lying curled up on the bed. "Oh, my," he murmured, blanching.

"Bring water and salt," ordered Sianiave. "Lot's of it! To my room! Quickly, man!"

"Of course. Right away. Right away."

The innkeeper took one last look at the broken window, frowned at the tavern maid as if to say, "We'll talk about this later," and hurried off.

Hugging her sheet tightly about her, the terrified maid gave a cry of despair and fled down the hall.

"Take him to my room," said Sianiave. "That thing might come back. I arrived before it completed its desecration. They don't like to leave victims behind."

Osmodon picked Barrett up as easily as though he were a child and carried him across the hall to Sianiave's room. The room was several times the size of Barrett's, with a larger bed, a table, four chairs, and a couch. There was even a fireplace in which a small fire burned.

"A grendel?" Osmodon asked as he laid Barrett on the bed.

"It must have come up the river from the sea. Our companion has been distracted all night. I was going to check on him when I saw its wet prints in the hall. It probably began its work on him even before we entered the inn."

"Why him, with so many others around?"

"Good question."

"Will he live?" Osmodon asked with great concern.

"We'll see."

For Barrett the horror had momentarily retreated. He felt calm, as though none of this was real, drifting in a fugue state between wakefulness and sleep. His eyes remained open and the pain had diminished. But he was still unable to move.

Sianiave passed the silver cross back and forth over his paralyzed body, singing softly as she did so. Both the words and melody were unfamiliar to him. Nevertheless they had an immediate soothing effect. He felt like a child again, Sianiave singing him to sleep with a lullaby.

Slowly, his physical senses returned, and with them—pain. It grew in intensity until it felt as though his entire body were on fire.

"NOOOO!" The word exploded from him in one great spasm.

Sianiave gave a sigh of relief. "Very good. You're back. You had us worried."

Holbert returned, carrying a bag of salt, a mug, and a large pitcher of water. Sianiave filled the mug with water, stirred in a handful of the salt and pressed it to Barrett's lips.

"Drink it, all of it. They feed on the salt in their victim's bodies. A minute longer and there would have been nothing left of you but a desiccated shell."

With Sianiave's help, Barrett managed to drain the mug. She repeated the dosing. After the third mug, he leaned his head over the side of the bed and vomited. Sianiave made him drink mug after mug until, finally, weak and exhausted, he fell back against the pillows. The fire inside his body had eased, but the wounds where the creature had ravaged him were throbbing painfully.

"What was that—thing?"

"A grendel, lad," said Osmodon cheerfully. "A real live grendel."

"My mind," Barrett rasped, recoiling from the memory. "She—it —."

"Yes," said Sianiave. "It uses crude forms of desire to seduce its victims, attacking where they are weakest. Few ever survive a grendel's assault. Consider yourself fortunate."

Barrett didn't feel fortunate. His throat was raw from salt and vomit, and his entire body ached. But worse than that was the humiliation, the self-disgust at having fallen into the monster's trap.

They attack where you're weakest.

What did that say about him? How could he not have known, not have seen it for what it was?

Holbert was pacing anxiously in the background. "Nothing like this has ever happened here before. The Lion is known throughout Anor to be a safe hostel. If this were to get out—."

"I understand your concern," said Sianiave. "But I suggest you warn the council about what has taken up residence in your lake. Clearly the wall is no barrier. And, without a doubt, it is still hungry."

The innkeeper trembled as the words sank in. "What's to become of us?" he mumbled dully. "What's to become of us?"

CHAPTER 26

Atha'amenth,
Arden Forest
May 23

"SHE'S HOLDING UP WELL," commented Abdelar as he watched Ren at play in the pool below.

Aerindir was seated on a nearby rock, polishing his sword. "She'll do," he said shortly. Abdelar chuckled. Coming from Aerindir that was high praise indeed.

They'd been traveling for fourteen days with little sleep, often eating in the saddle. Gallian and the safety of Ellohir's keep was at least another weary week's travel. In their flight from Barad'An they'd battled the priest's guards, then engaged a band of forest brigands who coveted their horses. Ren had acquitted herself as well as any knight—better then many. Ten of the bandits lay dead, the rest had scattered into the forest. Two, Ren had dispatched herself.

They spent the day camped near the mineral pools of Atha'amenth, a place once known for the blue green of its waterfall and the warmth of its healing springs. It was lost to memory for all but a few. The attending manor house with its many tiled spas had long fallen in ruin, overrun with brambles. But the turquoise waters still infused warmth into the pool in which Ren now swam.

Abdelar watched with pride and some wonder as she ducked under the waterfall, frolicking as though they were on a picnic and not fleeing from mortal danger into a lonely and uncertain future.

Gods, what a woman she was becoming—fit to be queen.

Aerindir hadn't objected to a day of rest. They'd taken precautions, of course, scouting the nearby forest, setting up camp in a copse of alders. There was an animal trail leading out the back—an escape route if one became necessary. Their weapons were always at hand, and while one bathed, two remained on guard.

The brothers had watched over Ren since her birth. They were loyal to her father Prince Ilsidain, son of Ambromir and grandson to Cuchulain. That oath kept them from joining the younger knights who followed Artos into banishment. With Ambromir dead in battle and Ilsidain's suspicious death during a boar hunt shortly thereafter, Cuchulain had become their liege lord. But in truth, it was Ren to whom they gave their hearts, and toward whom they felt most protective. Ren had been twelve at the time of her father's death, the same age as they were when their own father had passed.

Abdelar plucked a string on his lyre and began singing. He had a fine, clear voice and was counted one of the best troubadours in the kingdom. His song told a story of lost love and the betrayal of a sacred city by its mad count. It was a sad and melancholy tune, and the story it told did not end well.

"Can't you sing something merrier?" groused Aerindir.

"I'm composing an ode to Cuchulain. There's a tonal similarity."

"Count Otho was a coward as well as mad. Whatever else you might feel about Cuchulain, he was a good man," Aerindir said.

"Aye. Though headstrong, and far too prideful," Abdelar agreed.

Aerindir sighed, "But a man, nonetheless—and a great warrior."

Abdelar nodded as if Aerindir had made his point. "Hence the tragedy—a man who should never have been king, a great warrior brought down by an Uruk's arrow, and a conniving priest. Not grist for a merry mill."

Without waiting for an answer, Abdelar began:

> *With knights, nobles, and pikemen,*
> *clutched about his bed,*
> *and the Sisters and traitor priest*
> *mumbling sugared phrases*
> *in low and mournful tones,*
> *Cuchulain, in all his glory,*
> *died alone.*

There was a moment of silence. Aerindir grimaced.

"Well? What do you think?"

"In truth? It's dreadful. 'Low and mournful tones'—a cliché. I suppose Corwin is noble enough, but you left out Ren entirely. And anyway, how do you know who was there at the end, or what was said? We were ordered away, if you recall. By Ren's account, Mother Saolin dealt quite tenderly with Cuchulain, surprising as that seems. Further more—."

"Enough!" laughed Abdelar. "I should have known better than to sing a song before it's fully rendered. But you're right. It is dreadful. Something or someone, a woman I'll wager, caused Cuchulain's heart to break early on, and therein lies the key to all his acts, and his failure. Being closed in heart, he was closed to his people, certainly to Artos. The truth of his life escaped him. A tragedy, and not just for a king. At least that's the theme as I see it."

"We all die alone," said Aerindir glumly as he studied the polish on his sword. "And a heart too open is an easy target for a spear."

"My brother, you've managed to summarize an entire philosophy in sixteen words—words I fear that are too well accepted in these dark times."

Aerindir grunted and fell silent. He had learned early on it was unwise to enter into philosophical arguments with Abdelar, who seemed to change sides and positions as easily as a bird hopped branches in a tree.

Perhaps that was his secret. Abdelar had always possessed the uncanny ability to see things as a whole, and to find meaning and hope even in the worst of situations. It was a gift, Aerindir knew, he himself lacked.

Holding a fresh elm leaf above the blade edge, Aerindir let it drop. The leaf touched the blade and fell to the ground, cloven in two. Satisfied, he finishing it off with a dollop of beeswax and burnished it with a chamois.

When this was done he held the sword aloft, the midday sun reflecting off the blade. After forty years he still admired its stark and deadly beauty.

Drakulsyr, Dragonslayer, was its name. Its sister blade, *Daemonsyr*, Demonslayer, lay in its silver-banded sheath at Abdelar's side. Their father had given them these swords on his deathbed. Of all that he could leave them, he told them, these two swords were the most valuable, the secret of their making was lost to the ages. Extraordinarily light, they could cut through oak and iron as easily as other blades clove flesh.

Sheathing Drakulsyr, Aerindir stood to stretch his legs. Ren had come out from under the waterfall and was climbing toward a ledge overhead. How beautiful she was. Long legs, golden skin and golden hair, she stood naked and studied the water below, appearing for all the world like High Queen Gwyneth, or Yu'an Tara herself. She was their hope, he knew. Perhaps their only hope, fragile as it was. Not for the first time he found himself wishing he had his brother's capacity to trust in destiny.

Ren arched into the air in a perfect swan dive, surfacing moments later, laughing as she blew water from her nose. Rather than ease his worry, however, the very gracefulness of Ren's performance reminded Aerindir that she was still little more than a child, and how very vulnerable she was.

Abdelar sang another song, well-known to Aerindir, for it was a song they had chanted as boys for forty nights straight, part of their training as pages. It had been written by the poet Hafist, and later put to song by some long-forgotten minstrel. In his indirect way, Abdelar was reminding him of something.

> *The warrior tames the beasts of his past*
> *So that the night's terrors*
> *can no longer break the jeweled vision in his heart.*
>
> *The brave open every chamber in their past,*
>   *and banish all the mind's ghosts.*
>
> *Only the warrior has the courage to slay past giants,*
>   *and the demons of the future.*
> *The warrior sits in a circle with other warriors,*
>   *gathering the strength to unmask—himself.*

As Abdelar finished his song, a flock of sparrows broke suddenly through the forest canopy and passed over the fall. Abdelar's fingers clamped down on the lyre's neck, stilling it, as the birds circled off toward the west.

He looked at the horses. Moments earlier they'd been chewing placidly on the bunchgrass in a nearby clearing. Now their heads were up, ears flattened in the direction of the trees from which the birds had risen.

Abdelar put down the lyre and stood, buckling on his sword and shouldering his bow and quiver—casually, as though nothing was amiss. Aerindir waved to Ren in a prearranged signal, but Ren was already pulling herself onto the flat rock where she had left her own clothes and weapons.

Had she, too, seen the birds? Aerindir wondered.

He stowed the remaining gear in the bags while Abdelar saddled the horses. Both men moved about their business with a deliberate, deceptively casual efficiency.

Abdelar tied his lyre to his saddle. Ren arrived, her own sword buckled about her waist, her hair a tangled mess. *Enemies?* she asked in hand sign.

Abdelar nodded, his voice low. "We've stayed overlong in any case."

Unwilling to risk the horses on such uneven ground, they left on foot, Abdelar in front, leading them down the narrow trail Aerindir had scouted out the day before. The trail followed the base of the cliff, hidden above and below by boulders, trees, and the cliff itself.

They traveled for perhaps an hour, seeing and hearing little, when, unexpectedly, the trail ended. They paused, confronted by a sea of rolling grassland, dotted here and there by islands of trees and forested hillocks. Far in the distance, half a league off at least, stood a single larger hill. This hill was unforested, with the ruins of an old fort commanding the summit.

"Graylen Tor," said Abdelar. "A garrison once stationed there." This was for Ren's benefit, who had not traveled these lands before.

Aerindir's sharp eyes had been scanning the horizon. "There," he said, pointing.

To their right, still several miles off, was a band of mounted riders, perhaps twenty in all. They appeared to be milling around at the foot of the shallow canyon that led to the waterfall.

"Uruks?" Ren asked.

"My guess, though it's difficult to tell from this distance."

"It's us they're after," said Abdelar.

Aerindir nodded. "Cuchulain suspected the priest had contracted them.

They've sent scouts to the pools, I'd wager, and are awaiting their return. They'll find sign of our camp, and our trail."

Ren had been silent, her eyes closed. "We can't stay here," she said suddenly, as though something had come clear to her.

"The way we took will be difficult for them," said Abdelar, thoughtfully. "They will have to travel single file, and slowly, as did we. Perhaps we should wait here until dark."

Aerindir was looking back up the path from which they came. "They may have split their forces. It's what I would do. Even now some may be coming up behind. I say we go now."

Abdelar regarded their mounts, fighting nervously at their bits. "You're right. We have to trust the horses. We'll make for Graylen Tor. It may still be defensible."

Silently they mounted, the horses calming under their weight. With a nod from Abdelar they started out at a canter, across the open field.

CHAPTER 27

"SPLENDID VIEW," REMARKED OSMODON as he climbed atop the ruined wall to sit beside Sianiave. "But I imagine it was a lonely billet."

Sianiave's attention was focused south, on the horizon. "The road was better traveled in those days," she replied absently.

Her knees were pulled schoolgirl-like into her chest as she puffed on her pipe, her golden hair hidden under a broad-brimmed hat. To Barrett, still struggling to undo the cinch on Greywind's saddle, she looked like nothing so much as a young tomboy.

"You knew this place then?" he asked. He was still unwilling to believe her as old as he imagined, yet no longer able to see her as the grey-haired matron of their first meeting. Her personality had remained unchanged, though he was slowly beginning to appreciate her subtle sense of humor.

"Before my time even, I'm afraid," she answered. "Old Empire. It was a link in a chain of defenses that ran from Monk's Haven on the western coast to Nuribor in the east."

The cinch finally undone, Barrett wrestled the saddle off the horse and set it on a flat stone that once had been part of the keep's long vanished tower.

Sianiave had paid for the horses and certainly had the right to claim the best one as her own. Instead she suggested they draw straws. Barrett had pulled the long straw and the big horse was his. He'd come to the conclusion the game was rigged.

Greywind was a war horse, well trained for that, and unusually intelligent. The horse was also grievously stubborn. Barrett knew little about riding, and nothing about war horses, and this one towered over him at almost nineteen hands. The past few days had been a struggle, as if the horse were master and he the pupil. What's more, Greywind's tack, designed for battle, was far heavier and more complicated than the simple rigging of the two farm animals. Only recently had he learned to dress the horse himself, without having to ask Osmodon for help.

"Different in your land?" Osmodon had observed, watching Barrett in his first clumsy attempt.

"Very," Barrett had replied.

The ancient ruins of Graylen Tor lay about them. Only a small area of the old kitchen still held a roof. There they made camp. The dog lay outside in the lowering sun, chewing on a stick. The horses munched on the clumps of grass that had all but replaced the original stone floor.

It was late afternoon, dark clouds, heavy with rain, moved in from the east. It was because of the approaching weather that Sianiave had decided to make camp at the ruined keep. Two hours of daylight still remained, and the trail up the hill had been difficult. Since learning of the events in Barad'An, she seemed distracted, uncertain whether to continue on to the city as planned, or to set out in another direction. It was Osmodon's conjecture that she was looking for a sign—an omen.

The view from the top was well worth the climb, Barrett thought. The forests of North Arden were behind them now, the surrounding countryside glowed emerald green from spring showers, cut through by seasonal streams. To the west a glimmer of sunlight could be seen reflecting off the Dunenwine as it continued toward the sea. Southward, perhaps a league off, stood a line of low mountains. To the east, barely visible even from atop Graylen Tor, was a ribbon of ochre stained hills.

It had been four days since they departed Ardendell. Barrett's physical wounds had healed, but the disgust he felt for having fallen prey to the creature stayed with him.

They attack you where you're weakest.

He had invited the thing into his room. It drew its power entirely from his own fantasies. It wasn't the first time he had almost been killed by some monstrosity insinuating itself into his thoughts. The morghul, the wolf-thing in the forest, the grendel—all had drawn on his own doubt, fear, and lust.

For Barrett the understanding of his own culpability had come like a physical blow. It wasn't that these demons were stronger than him. Even at his lowest point there had been a voice, some essential part of himself that knew the truth, could see behind the curtain of illusion. And yet the rest of him had refused to listen, lost in the enchantments.

His memories of the world from which he came were increasingly insubstantial, though one memory rose up sharp and clear—the summer he studied martial arts in China. He had lost a sparring match to a fellow student, a boy he should have beaten. His sifu had seen the problem immediately. Though naturally ambidextrous, Barrett had found it easier to think of himself as right-handed.

"Balance is key to everything," his teacher had said. "To defeat an opponent, a clever warrior looks for imbalance, as did that boy to whom you lost."

The rest of that summer his sifu had forced him to train as a left-hander. A month later he fought the boy again, and won.

But that had been physical, and easily correctable. How did one correct an imbalance in one's own mind?

He was loathe to ask either Osmodon or Sianiave for advice. He was a soldier, after all, and a good one. He would work it out on his own.

But as days passed, he realized that it was this very pride and fear of embarrassment that kept him from asking for the help he needed most.

On the evening of their third day out from Ardendell, as they camped near a stand of elms, he cautiously broached the subject with Osmodon.

"Ozzy, you once mentioned something about shields?"

The big man nodded. "Shields against creatures like the grendel, you mean? Aye, but they're not like regular shields, lad. You can't just pick one up in an armorer's shop." He tapped his forehead. "You make them, here."

"How?"

"How do you learn to make anything? Experience, lad—by doing, by surviving, and doing again. Teachers can help, but in the end it's you has to do the doing. In that regard, you've managed rather well, I'd say."

"Of course it must be experience of a certain kind." Sianiave had been eavesdropping. "Experience for experience's sake is at best wasteful, at its worst—useless, even dangerous." She pointed the stem of her pipe at Barrett to make this last point.

Was she accusing him of something—weakness, perhaps? "And how will I recognize the right kind of experience?" he asked.

Sianiave smiled, as if reading his thoughts, then grew serious. "If you truly want to know, remember that you're a stranger here. You can't learn if you're not present, and it's difficult to be present with all those little voices in your head competing for attention."

Her words rang true, but the implication unsettled him and he let the matter drop.

Later that evening Osmodon joined him as he relieved himself against a tree. "She offered you a gift tonight," the big man had said quietly, unbuttoning his breeches and adding his own water to Barrett's. "My advice would be to accept it."

"I've heard it before."

Barrett had spoken irritably. He remembered the mantras and techniques he had studied in China and elsewhere. Even the army had mind control training. *Don't pretend to be a tree! Be that tree! When you aim at a target, be that target!*

"If you had understood what she told you, that grendel couldn't have gotten anywhere near you. Besides," Osmodon added with a good-natured wink, "it's not just the words, lad. It's when you hear them. It's the timing."

Barrett looked up. "Timing?"

But Osmodon merely nodded, buttoned up his breeches and walked off.

CHAPTER 28

"Barrett! Osmodon! Look there! Do you see?"

Sianiave stood on the wall, her attention on something in the distance. Barrett followed her line of sight to a wooded area, perhaps five miles off. At first he saw nothing unusual, treetops, shadows beneath. A light wind blew, heralding the approaching storm. Beside him, Bear lifted his head, his nose searching the wind.

"There!"

And then Barrett saw it, a flash of almost diamond brightness amid the trees, then another.

"Saddle the horses!" cried Sianiave, jumping from the wall and running to grab her saddle. "Quickly! You're about to earn your keep!"

"What is it?" Barrett asked.

Osmodon was already following Sianiave as he threw a saddle on his own mount. "Sunlight off a sword blade—there's a battle our mistress means to join."

"A battle?"

"Weapons only!" cried Sianiave. She slung quiver and bow over a shoulder, and vaulted into the saddle, spurring her pony down the hill without looking back.

Osmodon moved to help Barrett, who was having trouble with Greywind's harness. "You'll soon be better appreciating that long straw you drew," he laughed, buckling a chest strap. "My own pony's a good natured beast, but hardly fit for war."

After the slithery horror of the grendel, Barrett almost welcomed the thought of a physical enemy. Bear barked, as if to hurry him on.

For once Greywind didn't fight his reins. The moment Barrett was in the saddle the horse took off at a gallop, the dog close behind.

"Ho!" cried Osmodon grabbing up his weapons. "Wait for me!"

Barrett soon overtook Sianiave. "Who are we fighting?" he cried as he struggled to hold the big horse in. Greywind was faster than Sianiave's farm pony, and wanted to run.

Sianiave's hat flew off in the wind, her blonde hair flowing wild. Her face, tanned golden from days in the sun, was resolute.

"We'll know when we get there!" she shouted.

Osmodon caught up with them at the wood's edge. The sounds of battle were clear now—curses shouted in a strange tongue, cries of pain, stamping hooves, and metal striking metal. Ahead, in a clearing, two men and a girl were holding off twenty or more attackers, short, bandy-legged men with swarthy skin and kohl-rimmed eyes. Two men stood, their backs against a large oak, protecting the girl between them. Riderless horses milled about. The bodies of three other horses, riddled with arrows, lay nearby.

"Barrett!" cried Sianiave. "Dispatch the archers! We'll handle the riders!"

Barrett saw immediately what she meant. Twelve riders had pulled back, preparing for an assault. Nine had dismounted and stood in a semicircle, bows in hand as they sent volley after volley of black-shafted arrows toward the three defenders by the oak.

With an almost supernatural display of swordsmanship, the two men deflected most of the arrows, but more than one found its mark. Only the girl appeared untouched, as if the men were the archer's only targets. Her own quiver empty, the girl pulled a spent arrow from the tree behind her, nocked and released it. An archer fell, pierced through the neck.

Barrett gritted his teeth. During his college years he had dueled with épées, sabers, and katanas. But never had he fought for his life, and never from atop a horse. Greywind had no such misgivings, sprinting into the line of archers, knocking three sprawling and scattering the rest.

Barrett recalled little of what followed, a violent fog of attacks, screams, and severed limbs. Two of the archers fell under his sword before they could cry out. Another lost an arm as he fumbled for his scimitar. Their crude leather armor offered little protection. One ran, but was brought down by Bear. Another managed to get off a bolt, but to Barrett it appeared to be moving in slow-motion and was easily avoided.

Rearing and snorting, Greywind looked for more enemies, but the archers all lay dead or dying in the grass.

Close by, Sianiave and Osmodon had engaged the main body of attackers. Osmodon's opponents fell before him like wheat under a scythe. With a powerful slash he disemboweled one foe, while with his left hand he pulled another from his saddle to be trampled by the maddened horses. Sianiave was no less lethal, fighting with both dagger and sword.

Led by a large Uruk on a black horse, in a last desperate effort, seven riders broke from the mêlée and charged the defenders at the tree. Despite wounds that would have crippled lesser men, the two men guarding the girl stood their ground. The girl dropped her bow and drew her sword, skewering a man who made the mistake of trying to grab her from his saddle.

Barrett spurred Greywind into the fray. He took off an arm with a swipe of his blade, and knocked another attacker from his horse. The last to fall was the big captain who led the charge. Barrett parried a wild blow, then reversed his grip, driving the point of his sword into the enemy's chest. He pulled the sword free, readying for another thrust, but it wasn't necessary. A shudder passed through the man and he toppled from his horse, dead.

The fight was over.

Barrett took a deep breath and surveyed the carnage. Relief, fatigue, and an almost embarrassing sense of satisfaction swept over him. They had won. He hadn't let anyone down.

The dead, the milling horses—it all seemed so familiar.

Osmodon strode across the field toward him, a cheerful grin on his ruddy face, as though just having finished a pleasant walk in the woods.

"Where's your horse?" was the first thing Barrett thought to say.

"None the worse for wear," laughed Osmodon. "Had to leave him, though. Useless in a fight."

With the blood of half a dozen Uruks still dripping from its blade, Osmodon raised his sword as he saluted the three they had saved. "Aerindir and Abdelar, I presume, and Princess Gwyndolyn, of course. I must say the tales of your beauty and courage have not done you justice."

Gwyndolyn? Princess—?

Barrett saw the girl's face clearly for the first time. Even covered in sweat and blood, her beauty defied description.

Ren regarded them warily. "We are grateful for your help, sirs—but I would ask your names."

Neither she nor the two knights had lowered their weapons.

Osmodon laughed. "Of course. And I don't blame you. I be Osmodon of Linsraden. And this tall fellow with the gaping mouth be Barrett of Amra."

"Sir Osmodon? Sianiave's liege knight?" Ren's eyes widened with relief. "That is she, then? The other warrior?"

Osmodon sheathed his sword and hitched his axe. "Aye, here she comes now."

Sianiave, her pony limping on a wounded leg, was walking across the meadow toward them. "It's been three years," said Ren. "It was said she left Anor for good."

"Well met," said Abdelar.

With that he collapsed to his knees and fell face forward into the blood-soaked grass.

CHAPTER 29

As his horse was swiftest, Barrett took it upon himself to retrieve their packs from the keep. At Sianiave's request Osmodon set about collecting a medicinal plant she called kingsroot, some blooms of which she noticed growing in the meadow. Ren's and Aerindir's mounts had been slain, but the water skins on their saddles were untouched. The clothes in Ren's saddlebags were clean, and these she tore into strips for bandages.

A violent storm swept in just before sunset, but was gone within the hour. The big oak, with its broad canopy of leaves, had served as a shelter for the others, but by the time Barrett returned he was chilled to the bone and thoroughly drenched. Osmodon had built a sizeable fire, but Barrett first tended to Greywind, removing his saddle and giving the stallion a quick rub down with a handful of grass. Then he helped Osmodon drag the bodies of the slain Uruks to the meadow and away from the camp.

The two knights had been stripped of their clothes and lay on blankets near the fire. Sianiave had removed the arrows, thirteen of them, Barrett counted.

The wounds were all in the front, he noted. Neither man had flinched or turned away. Abdelar had gotten the worst of it. His skin was a deathly pale, his breathing shallow. From the look of concern on Sianiave's face Barrett suspected there was little hope. But then he remembered his own shattered shoulder, how quickly it had mended under her care.

He changed into dry clothes and squatted by the fire opposite where Ren and Sianiave ministered to the knights, cleansing their wounds, all the while chanting in an unfamiliar tongue.

The woods were quiet. Osmodon joined Barrett, the dog at his heels.

"Who are they, Ozzy?"

"Who? Aerindir and Abdelar? Every minstrel in the kingdom sings of their deeds. Brothers, they are. Their father was Duke Ranulf of Caerlain, who died from wounds suffered in battle. They were just young lads at the time."

"Brothers?"

"Abdelar's mother was a highborn lady of Caerlain. She died giving birth to Abdelar. Aerindir was born in Nibur to a nomad slave. The red fever took his mother on the journey back to Caerlain. The boys were raised as equals in Ranulf's eyes. It's said he loved them greatly, though never could two men seem so different. In songs they call Abdelar "The Fair," always ready with a song himself, or a bit of philosophy. Aerindir they call "The Dark," he of grim visage and few words—yet never was one more faithful, or more courageous in battle."

"Orphans."

"Aye, like yourself."

Osmodon threw a stick on the fire and sighed. "The world has changed, that's the truth of it. You can't count on the old ways to hold any more. A man has to find his own footing."

A long moment passed.

"Osmodon, why did Sianiave hire me?"

Osmodon chuckled. "I've wondered a bit on that myself. Leastwise until I saw you at work today."

"But what I'm asking is, why me? I saw those two fight, the way they protected the girl, with not a thought to their own safety. With men like those—." Barrett stopped.

"So, you think you're a lesser man? Is that it?"

"Well, no one's writing songs about me."

"Give them time. You're still young."

"Not that young. How old are you?"

Osmodon rubbed his beard. "Me? Let's see. My birthday is coming. May the third, it is. I'll be sixty-seven. Some years to go 'til my dotage."

Sixty-seven! Barrett wasn't sure if he found that encouraging or depressing. "And the girl? Gwyndolyn?"

"Gwyndolyn? Not sure exactly, seventeen or eighteen. Years before her maturity in any event. Which is probably why the priest is so anxious to get his hands on her."

Barrett felt an unaccountable sense of relief. *Seventeen or eighteen.* "She's really a princess?"

"Aye. May be queen some day, if there's anything left to rule after this business with the priest. With Cuchulain dead and Artos gone, she's the end of the bloodline."

"This bloodline? It's important?"

"Sianiave believes so—as does anyone who gives it thought. The family has ruled for two thousand years and done a fair job of it, at least for the first sixteen hundred or so."

"You sound skeptical."

"I do? Well, there's reason. But first let me ask you a question. In your land, what purpose does a king serve?"

"A king?" Barrett started to say, none, that kings in his world served no real purpose. Then, after a pause he replied, "They're heads of state, I suppose."

"Fair enough. And what is the state?"

"The people."

Osmodon slapped his thigh. He had found a subject he obviously enjoyed. "Exactly! The people! And it's a king's job to rule his people, ably and justly. But, we forget this. We think they're above us all. We're made of words, us mortals, and our stories and songs give the words meaning. Some stories say kings are divine, or at least come from the gods. So, we get this doltish notion that people are here to serve the king, when the opposite is true."

"You talk as though you have some experience in the area."

"My father was a baron, not a king. But I've seen how a place can be ruined by one man's poor decisions."

Osmodon frowned, suddenly somber. "Being king has to be the scut work of existence. Few would do it willingly, if they knew the load it carries."

Another long moment passed. The fire burned hot. Seated as he was, Barrett couldn't see the two women, but he could still hear them chanting.

Osmodon shook his head as if waking from a dream. "In ages past it's said that kings were chosen by both towers. They served at the will of the Tower Council for seven years only—the time it took for the disease of separateness to take hold—a sickness that severs the king from the land and his people.

More often than not, the dethroned king was put to death. It was considered an act of mercy, there being no one left who cared if he lived and most wanting him dead."

"This changed?"

"Aye. There was a king, Ambergin, who ruled well and wisely. Ambergin had the sight, but more importantly, he never got the disease. He ruled for 150 years, this with the blessing of both towers. Remarkably, his offspring ruled for centuries more, as kings should, and the land flourished. The kingdom became an empire, by all accounts a fairly decent one. Though I myself am against empires on principle."

"I take it this was some time ago, judging by the ruins we've passed."

"Aye, ages. Over time the blood thinned. But the line of kingship just continued. The people shirked their own responsibility in the matter. The kings began to think the power was owed them. The Tower Council lost the right to decide—squabbled among themselves over trivial matters. There were wars, plagues, fighting among the magisters and priests. Even the weather changed."

"And all this because the kings lost this mystical connection with the people?"

"Not just with the people, with the land itself."

"Where does the girl fit into all of this?"

"Sianiave believes the ability to rule is a learned thing. Both Artos and Gwyndolyn were trained from birth in ways few are privy to. Their blood makes them heirs, but their real birthright is in their training."

"Artos—Gwyndolyn's brother?"

"Her uncle. By all accounts, a doughty warrior—a just and honorable man."

Barrett was thoughtful. He had learned more in the past few minutes than he had in the month he had been in this world. It was clear that Sianiave was working on a large canvas, though he still wondered about his part in it. He had a sudden image of a great machine, an elaborate clock—wheels within wheels, worlds within worlds, spinning and turning. It was a confusing image, and he shook it off.

Across the fire, Ren stretched and rose to her feet.

She was beautiful, Barrett thought, she glowed, though this may have been an illusion of the firelight. After Ardendell he no longer trusted his own feelings. Yet the emotions he felt watching Ren were of a different order entirely—light rather than dark, heart rather than loins.

Had he been hired to protect her? Would he willingly give his life to that end?

She glanced in his direction, but before their eyes met, he looked away.

CHAPTER 30

REN HAD FAITH in Sianiave's healing skills but sensed the sorceress was worried about Abdelar. Aerindir had improved, his color returning, his breathing steady. Abdelar was pale as a ghost, his life signs barely present.

Ren feared Aerindir would wake to find his brother dead. More than brothers, Aerindir and Abdelar were like opposite parts of a whole.

Please, Mother Yu'an. Let Abdelar live.

Ren had never told anyone, certainly not Abdelar, but there had been a time when she thought herself in love with him. She might have pursued her feelings had it not been for her pride. Every girl in the kingdom imagined herself in love with Abdelar. Ren didn't want to be just another lovesick cow. And she was terrified that his code of honor would cause him to spurn her. A knight did not lie with his liege lady.

Yet she felt confused, for even as she bathed Abdelar's head, another emotion pulled at her. She thought of the strange knight who had arrived with Sianiave. From the first moment she saw him, galloping recklessly into the line of Uruk archers, she felt an attraction, almost frightening in its power—as though she knew him, did know him.

She saw him watching her from across the fire when she stood, yet he looked away. "Sianiave?" she asked suddenly, "The knight with Sir Osmodon, Sir Barrett?"

Sianiave had finished bathing the brothers, and was now applying the bandages. "Yes?"

"Who is he? Where does he come from?"

"He comes from far away. A soldier."

"Only a soldier?"

"Why do you ask?"

"I'm not sure. There is something about him."

"Oh?"

"I sense—."

"Yes?"

"Sadness, as if he does not know himself, as if he has never known his king or lady—if such a thing is possible."

Sianiave looked through the flames to where Barrett sat talking with Osmodon, the dog at his feet. Her face softened. Ren imagined an unusual tenderness in that look, but the moment was gone too quickly for her to be sure.

"Yes," said Sianiave finally, "the place he comes from is much the same."

CHAPTER 31

ABDELAR DIED DURING THE NIGHT, shortly before sunrise.

Sianiave knew, when she saw Abdelar's wounds, that even she couldn't repair such damage. One of the arrows had pierced his spleen, two others a lung. It was a miracle he had lived long enough to see Ren safe. He died peacefully and without pain. She made sure of it.

Despite a heroic effort to remain awake, Ren finally slept. Sianiave didn't have the heart to wake her, or anyone else, for that matter. They all needed as much rest as they could manage. They couldn't remain where they were, even with Aerindir injured as he was. One Uruk, at least, had escaped, perhaps others. If what she suspected was true, they would be back, this time in greater numbers.

She covered Abdelar with a blanket, placed another log on the dying fire, and sat back to smoke her pipe.

Things were not going well. Not well at all.

CHAPTER 32

A SOUND THAT WASN'T A SOUND woke Barrett. At first he wasn't sure what it was, only that it tore at his heart and he wanted it to go away.

Then it came to him—grief of a depth he had never known, worse than any physical pain he could imagine.

He sat up, rubbing tears from his eyes. A dream—or was it a dream, for it wasn't going away. He rubbed his eyes again and looked around. The fire had burned to embers and there was a comfortless chill in the air. A pale yellow light was breaking over the treetops.

Ren was seated cross-legged beside Abdelar. Her body was trembling, and silent tears ran down her face. The dog lay beside her, his head on her lap as if to console her. Sianiave was nowhere to be seen.

And then Barrett understood. Abdelar was dead. It was Ren's loss he felt. But her grief was no longer just for Abdelar. It was grief for all things, Abdelar, Aerindir, her family and friends now gone. It was grief for Barad'An and a vanished childhood. It was grief for life itself.

He wanted to put his arms around her, tell her everything would be fine, but he knew it would be a lie. He shook his head. *How did she bear it?*

Aerindir lay unconscious but still breathing. Osmodon was in the meadow, stacking logs into the shape of a rough rectangle. A shelter? Were they going to stay here?

Wanting to console the girl, but knowing anything he said would be inadequate, Barrett joined Osmodon in the meadow.

"Abdelar's dead. Princess Gwyndolyn, I don't know. Maybe someone should—."

Osmodon shook his head. "Best let her be."

Barrett studied the pile of Uruk bodies nearby. It seemed smaller than it had the evening before. There were pools of drying blood nearby, and drag marks leading into the woods opposite the camp. A paw print marked the soft earth; it was as big as a dinner plate, with six toes ending in long claws.

Osmodon walked over beside him. "Aye. Something's in the woods, right enough. It's watching us, and whatever it is, it has no qualms about what it eats. Must've dragged off four or more corpses during the night. If I'd known something that size was around, I wouldn't have slept so soundly."

"Where's Sianiave?"

Osmodon piled another log on the structure he was building, eyed it, then repositioned it. "She went for a walk, looking for herbs, I imagine, or to work things out. Things aren't going exactly how she planned, you may have noticed."

"She knew we'd find the princess here."

"A hope more than a knowing, I'd say. When she heard Princess Gwyndolyn and the brothers had left Barad'An, it wasn't hard to guess where they were headed. Gallian is the only place in a hundred leagues where the princess might be safe. They wouldn't take open roads, not with Uruks about. As it is, we were both lucky and unlucky. A bit sooner—." Osmodon shrugged, picked up another branch.

"Does she know about our friend with the big feet?"

"I may have mentioned it." Osmodon nodded toward a granite cliff perhaps a quarter mile distant and visible through the trees. "The trail leads toward that stony place. That's where it dens, I reckon. We can hope its stomach is full by now. Sianiave is safe enough. Whatever she decides, one thing's certain. We leave this place after the funeral."

Funeral? Barrett suddenly understood. Osmodon wasn't building a shelter. He was building a pyre. "I'll give you a hand," he said.

"Good. We'll need more of these larger limbs, and underbrush for fill. But keep your sword handy."

Barrett glanced around warily. He'd had enough of ravenous creatures.

Osmodon wanted a large pyre so nothing would be left to tempt predators. Much of the wood they found was damp, but Osmodon insisted this was not a problem, since he was mostly choosing maple wood, and another wood he called "ironbark," for their flammable sap. He also had faith in Sianiave's skill with fire, though so far Barrett had seen little to convince him of this.

Why hadn't she just blasted the Uruks with a fire bolt rather than risk their lives in a cavalry charge?

The sun was high over the trees when the pyre was ready. Sianiave had returned and Ren appeared calm, though Barrett could still sense the sadness behind her mask of quiet determination. She spoke little, helping Sianiave fashion a travois out of aspen logs and blankets. Osmodon had guessed right. They would leave as soon as the pyre was lit.

"We'll continue on to Gallian," Sianiave announced. "Ren told me it was Cuchulain's last wish, and I've no better plan at the moment. Ellohir should be informed in any event. And I must consult with Bronwyn."

Barrett and Osmodon laid Abdelar's body on the pyre. Ren placed his lyre in his hands, and his bow and dagger at his side. Sianiave kept Daemonsyr, wrapped in a blanket with Aerindir's sword.

Glaerindor, Abdelar's mount, had survived the battle, and Ren chose to ride him. They yoked the travois to Osmodon's pony who, as Osmodon remarked, was "better suited to that sort of work." Osmodon himself had taken a Uruk pony, a buckskin somewhat larger than the others. The rest they kept as pack animals, and for Aerindir when he could ride again.

After a meal they gathered in the meadow. Osmodon and Barrett stood silent as Sianiave and Ren spoke a prayer. Then Sianiave gave the blessing and, as tradition deemed, notified the doorkeeper of Velkela, the Hall of Heroes, that one of their greatest was arriving.

Ren lit the pyre with an ember from the campfire, and Abdelar's body was soon engulfed. Without further word they mounted their horses and started toward Gallian.

CHAPTER 33

THEY TRAVELED EAST for nearly a week, encountering no enemies, human or otherwise. Woods and grassy hills gave way to arid land, flat-topped mesas, and wide expanses of tough yellow grass. The few areas of green they encountered usually meant a spring or water hole where they would sometimes camp.

A massive herd of deerlike creatures passed to their left. Osmodon pointed out lions and packs of wild dogs stalking them. Occasionally they spotted a larger animal, but always too distant to identify.

The weather grew warmer, and rain more frequent. They could see a grey curtain of a storm coming from miles away in an otherwise cloudless blue sky. Osmodon called it "walking rain," and it often missed them completely. The showers were short-lived and left the land smelling fresh and sweet.

Aerindir still had not yet opened his eyes. His wounds had healed well enough, but it wasn't these wounds that concerned Sianiave.

One evening, as she and Ren bathed his body in a nearby stream, she said, "He may be valiant in battle, but there is a part of him afraid to face the world without his brother beside him."

Anger, along with a steel-edged resolve, had replaced Ren's grief. "Is there nothing we can do?"

"We must continue to tend to him."

It was a dark night, the moon not yet risen, the sky speckled with stars. Their campfire was barely large enough to boil water, but neither Sianiave nor Osmodon wanted to risk a larger flame. Along with the dangers that haunted the wilds, they considered it likely that Ren was still sought by the priest's men. That Uruk band had not happened upon her by chance, and Ren thought she recognized the Uruk Barrett had killed as the one whose arrow had murdered Cuchulain.

They made camp beside a stream in a grove of cottonwood beneath a low mesa. Conversation was muted, as it had been for much of the journey. Since

Abdelar's death Sianiave and Ren rarely spoke. That afternoon, before making camp, Ren rode alongside Barrett for a way, and thanked him for his help. There was little he could say in way of small talk so the conversation was brief. That night he drew the first watch. After the meal Osmodon and Bear joined him on a ledge above the camp.

"You should be resting," Barrett said, though he was glad for the company. Earlier the dog had growled at something in the shadows. There had been furtive movement, and a clicking sound, like claws scrabbling over stone. Bear lay with his head tilted toward the rocks, wary and alert.

"The less sleep I get, the harder it is to sleep," grumbled Osmodon, squatting beside Barrett. "It's a fair night. Didn't want to waste it tossing and turning in my blankets. And Sianiave asked me to warn you, there's something out there. The horses have been restless."

"I've heard something, a clicking sound."

"Rock beasts, perhaps—loathsome creatures, sharp teeth and claws."

"Wonderful. How big?"

"Like a cat, a bit larger. They travel in small packs and can strip a man to the bone, though a man armed and awake, with the dog here, shouldn't be troubled. They're cowardly creatures."

"All right. I get it. Stay awake if I want to avoid being eaten by rock beasts."

Osmodon chuckled. "I take it you don't have such things in Amra?"

"Our monsters are more of the human kind."

The clicking in the rocks had subsided since Osmodon's arrival. Barrett was grateful the big man didn't seem in any hurry to leave. "What do you know about this place—Gallian?"

"Never been there myself. Was a barony of a sort, but independent now. Ellohir rules with his wife Bronwyn. Both are well regarded by all accounts."

"How far is it—and why are we going there?"

"From Barad'An, on a fast horse by the Eastern Road, a man can reach Gallian in less than a week. Us, traveling overland, with Aerindir on a litter, difficult to say. Three or four more days. As to the why, I can only guess. Ellohir is known for his loyalty to the bloodline, and Gallian is said to be impregnable."

"Is there such a place?"

"Never seen one myself, though Barad'An comes close. More than one army has been broken on its walls. But I reckon these days even Barad'An can be taken. Its walls are forbidding, but with Artos gone, there aren't enough bodies to defend them properly."

Far off on the horizon lightning flashed. Seconds later came the dull rumble of thunder. Eastward a full moon, or nearly so, was rising over a distant mesa, its bright light casting sharp shadows among the rocks.

"Why me?" said Barrett after a long silence.

"You're still chewing on that bit of fat? A liege man has certain duties and obligations, mind you, and discretion is one of them."

"I understand if you can't talk about it."

"I can talk about it. She's never forbidden me that. But the truth is, I know little more than you, though I've certainly pondered on it."

"So, what do you think?"

"Well, first off, it doesn't take a soothsayer to see you're no common man. You proved it back there in the meadow, the way you fought. I've never seen the like."

"You held your own."

"I'm a good infighter, built for it, you might say. Gang like that, undisciplined and not prepared, can't bring their numbers to bear."

Barrett looked up—*numbers to bear*—the phrase struck a memory, then faded away.

"Wasn't much for us," Osmodon continued. "But the way you and that horse worked together was a thing of beauty. By the gods, busy as I was, I almost stopped to watch."

"But—Sianiave?"

"Aye. Sianiave. Why bring you here when Gwyndolyn has protectors aplenty in Barad'An? Could be chiromancy, her knowing you'd be needed at the meadow, and maybe later. Except, if she had foresight of that battle, she kept it well hidden. When that innkeeper let it drop that Cuchulain was no more, and Gwyndolyn gone from Barad'An, I could see it threw her mightily."

"So, if I'm not here as a bodyguard—?" Barrett grew exasperated.

Osmodon held up his hands. "Hold there. I'm not saying you aren't here to look after the girl. But Sianiave never does anything without having at least six reasons for it."

"One good one would do," Barrett mumbled.

Osmodon studied Barrett in the darkness, stroking his beard. "It's only a guess," he said finally, smiling. "An opinion, mind you. But I reckon she might be matchmaking."

"What!" Barrett straightened, almost dumping his sword from his lap. "That's crazy!"

"You asked."

Barrett took a deep breath, his mind spinning. "Tell me how you came to this—opinion?"

"First off, it's plain you're highborn. You can't hide something like that. It's obvious in your manner, in the way you speak and think. Besides, why else would Sianiave go to such lengths?"

Barrett shook his head. He felt threatened by the idea. "Ozzy, you're way off. I'm about as far from highborn as you can be. I'm an orphan, for God's sake!"

Osmodon nodded. "So, you never knew your parents?"

"I know what you're thinking. But believe me, it's impossible."

But even as Barrett objected, he wondered if Osmodon was right. It certainly would explain the loneliness he always felt in that other world, the uncanny familiarity he felt in this one.

What compelled you to engage in such martial pursuits as archery and fencing?

Worlds within worlds, puzzles within complexities, like an elaborate Chinese box—if any of it were true, it would mean Sianiave had known him beforehand, which led to the inevitable conclusion that Sianiave, or someone, had been keeping an eye on him, possibly for his entire life.

You are not alone in this—.

How dare they? How dare they play with his life like this!

He chose his next words carefully. "You're suggesting that I was spirited away from here as a baby? For what possible reason?"

Osmodon looked up at the night sky. "I'm not saying I know it for fact, but you could do worse than throw a rose or two the girl's way."

"Ozzy—."

"I know you favor her, lad. I've seen it in your eyes when she's near. She doesn't hold your liege—if that's what's troubling you."

"She's a child, not to mention a bloody princess!"

"Hardly a child. You saw the way she fought. As for being a princess, she's also a woman, and a randy one at that. I'd bet a good sword she hasn't been a virgin since her first moon—and she has eyes for you, lad."

"She hasn't spoken ten words to me since we met."

"She has other things on her mind, as you might expect. But she's interested, no doubt. You can't see it yourself, perhaps, but Sianiave's certainly noticed. Little gets by her."

Osmodon stood to leave. "Give it a go. What's to lose, after all? If nothing else, it'll make this journey a bit more pleasant. Now, don't forget the rock beasties."

Barrett was speechless.

Bear rumbled deep in his throat and lay his head in Barrett's lap. Absently, Barrett scratched his ears. Rock beasts were the last thing on his mind.

CHAPTER 34

THE VOICES WERE SOFT, soothing.

Sleep. Sleep is good. You are tired, so tired. Rest . . . Sleep . . . Sleep. . . .

Barrett's hand tightened on the pommel of his sword. He had almost dozed off and had no idea what time it was, but the moon was full overhead.

Waiting.

He shook his head. It had been no dream. He could still hear the voices, whispering, expectant. He looked about. A half-dozen pairs of jewel-like eyes peered down at him from the rocks, their movements accompanied by the sinister clicking of claws on stone.

One beast had slipped down from the rocks and was standing less than six feet away. In the moonlight it appeared to be a sort of monkey or ferret, with sharp, slender claws and a mouthful off needle-like teeth. When it saw he was awake, it chittered and disappeared into the rocks.

The voices stopped, the gleaming eyes vanished. Bear, who was now asleep at his feet, lifted his head. "It's all right, boy. They're gone."

"Congratulations. You've earned your first shield." Sianiave emerged from the shadows, sword in hand. "Get some rest. I'll keep watch. They won't be back," she added.

"The rock things? I heard their voices. Bear was asleep."

"Don't blame the dog. They work as a pack with a group mind. They can be more powerful than a grendel when their prey is tired. But the Enemy can't get at you that way again."

"Enemy? You speak as if there's only one."

"One and many. The morghul, the weir-beasts, the grendel, these creatures are real and dangerous in their ways, but we cannot name the One, not in the dark, with Its creatures still about."

"You mean the priest, Glays?"

"No, not Glays. He's just another creature under its thrall. Wait until we reach Gallian. For now get some sleep. We've still a way to go, and we enter the badlands tomorrow."

Badlands? Barrett wanted to question her more, but found the idea of sleep more attractive. He would wait until they reached Gallian. Maybe there he would get some clear answers. Bear followed him as he made his way back into camp.

"Sleep well," Sianiave called after him. "There's a binding on the camp. Not strong enough to attract the hunters, but enough to keep these little monsters at bay."

CHAPTER 35

THE FOLLOWING MORNING Aerindir opened his eyes and sat up. "Welcome back," said Sianiave matter-of-factly. "How are you feeling?"

The knight looked around and asked, "Where are we?"

"Two days out from Gallian, three at most."

"Gallian? How long have I—?"

"A week."

"A week." Aerindir closed his eyes again, then with an effort, he rolled to his side and attempted to stand. Ren moved to steady him. "Be still. You'll open your wounds."

"I'll manage." He looked down at the travois, then turned to Barrett, who was packing up his bedding. "Sir Osmodon I know, but forgive me. I do not know your name?"

"My name is Barrett," said Barrett.

"I owe you my life, Sir Barrett. Those archers overwhelmed us."

Barrett knew then he was aware of his brother's death. There was an awkward moment of silence.

"Come along," Ren said to Aerindir. "I'll fetch your clothes."

Barrett returned to his bedroll, watching from the corner of his eye as Ren helped the knight to dress. Intimate as the act was, neither expressed any self-consciousness—like family, Barrett thought.

"Cheer up, lad," said Osmodon, putting an arm over his shoulder. "Nothing strikes a woman's heart more than a sick puppy or a wounded knight. He's her friend, after all."

Barrett's feelings were more complex, however. It was hard to deny a certain jealousy, though he was pleased at the knight's recovery. There was something about the man he could not help but like, courtliness, an indefinable charisma. Behind Aerindir's forbidding looks and grim demeanor, Barrett recognized him to be a knight in the best sense of the word—the sort

he and Billy had imagined themselves to be only after many beers—courageous, honorable, ready to lay down their lives for something higher. Women
loved them, men admired them, minstrels sang songs about them. But with
the admiration also came envy.

Osmodon had described the arduous years of a knight's apprenticeship,
not only in the martial arts, but also in regard to honor and virtue. Few completed the training. Those who fell out often became mercenaries or sheriffs.

Barrett had confidence in his own martial abilities. It was virtue that
troubled him. Men like Aerindir lived in a world that understood such ideals,
venerated them. He, on the other hand, came from a place where such notions
were all but lost, considered quaint and romantic, suited to eccentrics and
sentimentalists, but of no value in the "real world."

Greywind shifted his legs, snorting as Barrett tied his bedroll to the saddle. They had been getting along better since the fight in the meadow.

What the hell. Give it time, like Osmodon said. He was still new at this.

Though still weak, Aerindir refused the travois, preferring to ride. Barrett
suspected he accepted the physical pain as a way of avoiding a greater one. The
others saw this as well, for no one argued with him, though at times it looked
as though he might fall from his saddle. By early the next afternoon he was
sitting upright, his strength much improved. Still he spoke little, and Ren often
rode beside him.

They made better time without the travois. Savannah grass, scattered
trees, and flowing streams gave way to sandy arroyos, desert sage. The days
had grown warm. Monsoon rains still arrived like clockwork, leaving rainwater in sinkholes, arroyos, and rocky depressions. Wildflowers of all colors
abounded, and cactus bloomed red, yellow, and blue.

Barrett was riding behind Osmodon when the big man reined in. A
troop of horsemen was visible in the distance, sixty or more, also riding east.
Sunlight gleamed off of their shields and the bronze tips of their lances. A line
of oxcarts followed behind, with people walking alongside.

"Uruks?"

"No. They carry lances. And their shields are metal, not leather. Besides,
Uruks would never ride in a column like that, or use oxcarts. It was difficult to

make out their colors, though."

Aerindir stood in his stirrups to get a better view. "Ellohir's men—I'm certain."

"Pick up the pace," said Sianiave, spurring her pony forward. "We'll be in Gallian before nightfall. I for one would greatly appreciate a hot bath tonight!"

Barrett looked over to see Ren beside him. "Have you been to Gallian before," he asked.

"I have," she replied, "twice—as a child. I visited there with my grandfather. He and Ellohir were great friends."

"And we can get a hot bath there?"

"More than a hot bath, I would say." Ren grinned impishly, then spurred her horse forward to join Sianiave.

Barrett gave a questioning glance at Osmodon, who shrugged. Aerindir was smiling. "Ellohir has nine daughters. Only two are married, so be warned."

Osmodon laughed as he rode after the knight. "Nine daughters? Aerindir, tell me more!"

Barrett was the last to follow. Nearing their destination cheered the others, but he was having the opposite reaction. It would be good to get back to civilization, to a real bath, clean clothes, fresh food instead of dried cheese, and stale jerky. But their arrival might also mean the end of his service.

Gwyndolyn would be safe. Aerindir would be there, not to mention Osmodon and Sianiave. Much as he would have liked to believe in Osmodon's notions about romance, deep down, it just didn't feel right.

He dreaded leaving this place, this world. What was back there for him—a life on the run, if he was lucky—or prison, even death? His memories of that other world were dim and nightmarish, endless war, worsening climate, ever-burgeoning population, meaningless technology, and all the while, people living with fear, laziness, and greed. Who in their right mind would choose to go back to such a place?

There was Billy, of course. He owed Billy. Maybe he could bring Billy to this world. It would suit him. He could bring Elyse. They could work as teachers, healers.

He would ask Sianiave about it.

CHAPTER 36

"HALT AND DECLARE YOURSELVES!"

The mounted warriors had appeared like ghosts out of the broken rocks, their lances at the ready. The challenge had come from their captain, a tall, lean man with the scowl of a lifelong soldier. His scrutiny passed from Osmodon to Barrett, lingering for a moment on Ren and Sianiave, as if to place them. Bear gave a low growl and bared his teeth.

"Greetings Beothyr," said Aerindir. "We saw your column from afar and thought to join you."

Recognition came slowly. "Aerindir? By the gods, man. I didn't recognize you under that beard!" The captain's scowl gave way to a wide grin as he signaled the other riders. "Raise lances! It's Aerindir of Caerlain!"

A ripple of relief passed through the riders. Aerindir was obviously known and well regarded by them, for which Barrett, at least, was grateful.

"We've heard rumors—." Beothyr turned to Ren. "Then you must be—. My deepest apologies, m'lady! I should have known you!"

"I would have been surprised if you had, Captain," replied Ren courteously. "I was a child when last we met."

"Ellohir told us to look for you. It was said Aerindir and Abdelar would be with you. But no one mentioned the Lady Sianiave, or your companions. And where is Abdelar?"

"He fell nine days ago," said Sianiave. "Uruks."

"Abdelar? Dead?" Beothyr looked stricken "This is sore news, sore news indeed. Aerindir, I am sorry."

Beothyr's men were covered in dust and weary, their dress stained with blood, their helms and shields battered. The news of Abdelar's death again darkened their mood. Aerindir remained silent.

"You've seen recent battle yourselves," said Sianiave.

"Aye. Uruks. They laid waste to Rumstock. We crossed the band responsible this morning, at Talisyr where the rivers meet."

"The oxcarts? The people on foot?"

"The lucky ones, I'm afraid, mostly women and children. We're escorting them to Gallian. No other place is safe. Not since the war started."

"War?"

"You haven't heard? Sabbat Khan, Kosha Khan's son, has taken power. He has rallied the tribes, promising land and booty—our land, if you will. He means to carry out his father's purpose, gathering an army in Nibur. Knowing our weakness, the Uruks have grown bolder. Rumstock was a slaughter."

Beothyr's lips tightened in anger, and he looked away. "Now is not the time to speak of it. We have a patrol to keep, by Lord Penthys' command," he added, as if to explain.

Aerindir frowned. "Penthys? I thought he retired to his estates years ago."

"You'll find many good men who thought they had seen the last of it back in battle dress. We can no longer count on Barad'An for support."

"We have some knowledge of this," said Sianiave. "But as you say, we'll speak of it later."

"Certainly, m'lady."

Beothyr motioned to a freckle-faced squire with blue eyes and a shock of red hair visible beneath a dented helm. "Miklos will have to accompany you. Battle protocol is in effect. Lord Penthys insists."

Sianiave gave a short laugh. "Say no more."

"Aerindir! We'll tip a cup in Gallian soon, gods willing." With that Beothyr swung his horse around and disappeared up the arroyo, his men close behind.

Barrett's party followed the squire through the cactus and up another arroyo. A dozen riders broke from the column as they approached, galloping out to confront them. "Halt!" shouted their captain. "Word of the day!"

"'Fortengyn,'" the squire shouted back. "Squire Miklos, Beothyr's scouts, escorting the Princess Gwyndolyn, the Lady Sianiave, and their company!"

The formal protocol made Osmodon roll his eyes and Aerindir shake his head.

"The princess and the Lady Sianiave can proceed!" answered the captain. "The others, to the rear!"

"We will stay together," said Ren.

"Captain," whispered Miklos uneasily. "It's Princess Gwyndolyn."

"I see that. But Penthys would have my head if I disobeyed an order, even for a princess. Even for you, m'lady," he added to Sianiave.

Sianiave nodded. She turned to the others. "You'll be better in the rear. Lord Penthys is a good field general, but you'd have better conversation with a brick. Who will take us to him, captain?"

"I will escort you. Miklos will return to the scouts."

The young squire looked disappointed, but saluted without complaint and rode off with only a glance back.

Ren was miffed. She felt like baggage. She respected Sianiave, emulating her in many ways. But princess or not, growing up in a city dominated by strong-willed men and equally strong-willed women, she had earned a place of respect among the knights of her realm.

The truth was, she preferred to remain with the three knights, men she considered friends, if not more. Aerindir was recovering nicely, but he still needed her ministrations. She was his liege lady, after all, with everything that implied. Osmodon was immensely capable, funny, wise in the ways of the world, and a wonderful storyteller. But it was Sir Barrett she was most taken with, and that confused her. It wasn't as if they were close. But she felt they knew each other already. Her feelings were deeper and far more complex than lust. The thought that it might be love had crossed her mind.

Who was he? She had given him every opportunity to talk about himself, but he always backed away. At first she wondered if it might be some fault of her own, but how could that be? She sensed the attraction was mutual. A vow of some sort, she decided—another woman? Chastity?

Men could be such fools! She would talk to Sianiave.

Lord Penthys was a hard-faced veteran whose frame, though stooped by age, was still formidable. He sat straight in the saddle, his dress as bloodied as any of his men. His helm bore the raven crest of his estate, several leagues to the north of Gallian.

"Princess Gwyndolyn," he said, addressing her formally, which annoyed her greatly. "I'm glad to see you safe, though your arrival was known to us."

"You expected us?"

Ren remembered the old knight from a visit to Barad'An, years before. He had been distant, even then. The years hadn't changed him overmuch. In his youth he'd been counted among the greatest of field commanders—abrasive, honest, hard on his men, and uncompromising in his sense of duty. In many ways he reminded her of her grandfather.

"Refugees from Barad'An brought accounts of the king's passing, and of your escape."

Penthys regarded Sianiave, his demeanor showing neither warmth nor welcome. "There was no mention of you, m'lady, or your two companions. And I understand Abdelar is absent?"

Penthys bore no unnecessary conversation, so Sianiave was brief. "Abdelar was killed in an Uruk ambush. Their purpose was to capture Ren. My companions and I came across the fight. We dispatched most of the attackers, though some escaped."

The old warrior frowned. Ren couldn't tell if he regretted Abdelar's death or disapproved of the Uruks' escape.

"Abdelar was a good fighter," Penthys remarked. "A league back, our scouts reported seeing a band of Uruks, but they ran before we could overtake them. The princess will be protected, of course. You and she will ride with me."

It was an order, not an invitation. Ren started to protest, for the last thing she wanted was to ride behind this harsh old man. But Sianiave stilled her with a look and said, "A gracious gesture, m'lord."

Either the old knight hadn't heard or he had chosen to ignore the slight edge of sarcasm in Sianiave's reply. Ren looked back, but could no longer see the rest of their party.

"Look's like we're baggage," grunted Osmodon as Sianiave and Ren rode off with the captain to the front of the column.

"Sianiave is right," said Aerindir. "Companionable—Penthys is not."

Barrett was preoccupied—appreciating Lord Penthys' guard and taking note of their formidable discipline—sitting straight in their saddles despite the recent battle. They rode in double column, with flankers on either side. There were also men riding point—and a rear guard. Add to that the scouting party they'd encountered earlier, and he figured the total strength of the company to be nearly a hundred.

The men carried long wooden lances tipped with bronze blades, capable of either piercing or slashing. Their helms and their shields appeared to be bronze, their armor—lacquered leather over quilted padding.

They joined the refugees at the rear of the column. Their blank faces Barrett had seen too often before—witness to the slaughter of family and friends, their fields and houses destroyed. In time, the grief would come. But now, they just struggled to survive.

Oxcarts were filled with whatever valuables they had salvaged. There were few wounded, which spoke both of the Uruk's cruelty and efficiency at killing. Penthys's soldiers had been even more efficient, for they appeared to have suffered few, if any, casualties.

A dreary procession in all—grim reality dampened conversation.

The road on which they traveled was very much like the road between Ardendell and Graylen Tor. Some sections were well preserved, others broken down or entirely washed away. Not a few times, the column was forced to slow when the carts became bogged down in sand.

They began a long, shallow ascent toward a solitary tableland that spread across the horizon for several miles. "Gallian," said Aerindir.

Osmodon looked skeptical. "That's Gallian? Where's the keep?"

"The mountain *is* the keep."

The road branched, one fork continuing east, the other, north toward the mesa. As Barrett studied the surrounding geography he began to suspect the nature of their destination. Imposing cliffs with watchtowers on the rim rose before them. It wasn't until they were in the shadow of the cliffs that he could make out an opening—little more than a seam in the red rock wall.

Horns sounded at their approach. Barrett sensed rather than saw soldiers posted among the rocks as the column proceeded through the opening.

The opening became a tunnel, high enough for a mounted man, but barely wide enough to accommodate the carts. The tunnel floor was paved with cobbles and deeply worn. Oil lamps bracketed the walls. The sound of hooves, creaking saddles, and cart wheels filled the tunnel. It was a quarter of a mile before they saw natural light again.

When they emerged, Barrett could only stare in wonder. His guess had been correct. The mesa was, in fact, the outer wall of a dormant volcano. But the vision before him was beyond anything he could have imagined.

CHAPTER 37

THEY WERE GREETED by a panorama of green surrounded by red rock cliffs. The valley was, perhaps, five miles across. A sizable river ran through its heart, fed by a half-dozen waterfalls. On the far horizon, seemingly carved into the cliff itself, was an imposing structure.

It was nearing sunset. The caramel light of the lowering sun bathed the cliffs, causing the palace—for such it was—to burn with a golden fire. "It's enough to make one forget Linsraden," murmured Osmodon.

A brick road curved through well-kept fields. The main column turned right, following a trail below the cliff. Riders dropped back to take the refugees on another trail to the left.

"The legion barracks are to the right," Aerindir explained, "hollowed out of the cliffs. The barracks on the left haven't seen use in half a century. I imagine that's where they're housing the refugees."

Ren and Sianiave galloped back down the column, accompanied by Sir Penthys. "You will continue on to High House!" barked the old man. "There will be a council in the morning. I trust you will be there."

Without further ado, he galloped off to rejoin his men.

"Pleasant fellow," remarked Osmodon.

Ren laughed. "You had the best of it in the rear, even with the dust."

"He is a great military commander," said Sianiave, though she was as relieved as was Ren to escape Penthys' stifling formality.

"His reputation is well earned," said Aerindir. He wasn't particularly fond of Penthys himself, but he recognized the man's martial skills.

Abdelar had often kidded Aerindir about his lack of warmth. Aerindir knew that it wasn't lack of feeling, but its overwhelming presence that challenged him so. But such thoughts were new and troubling to Aerindir. He had always left charm and poetry to his brother who had a more agile wit than he.

Barrett, rode through Gallian as if in a dream. How could such a place exist in the midst of a desert? A lake shimmered in the distance, or was it a mirage? Two dogs chased a herd of goat-like creatures toward a pasture gate. A large, tidy looking farmhouse stood nearby. To the left was a small village with houses, shops, corrals, barns, and a multistoried inn. But it was the palace that caught and kept his eye—its dazzling colors changing as the sun set, from white gold to burnished bronze—to glowing burgundy—High House, Penthys called it.

As they drew closer to the palace, Barrett saw signs of military activity—tents on a parade field, hastily-built corrals and barracks, and smithies tending to all manner of iron work. Soldiers quitting their drills as dusk settled, moved aside as the small group passed by—grim, battle-hardened veterans and fuzzy-cheeked boys, many who looked as if they would be more at home behind a plow. There were even a number of women among them, most carrying bows.

A stone causeway swept upward to the palace, wide at the bottom, and narrowing as it neared the gate. Its supports were slender and elegantly formed, giving the causeway a deceptively fragile appearance. But Barrett saw immediately that its graceful beauty belied a more practical purpose. It would be impossible for massed troops to storm.

"Can't starve 'em out," mused Osmodon. "There's plenty of water and they grow their own food. Can't dig under the mountain, and can't feed and water your own army in the meantime, not in that wasteland. It would have to be taken from within, by treason or sorcery."

Aerindir grunted. "You have a devious mind, Sir Osmodon."

"Habit of an old soldier, I'm afraid."

"In two thousand years, Gallian has been threatened but once," said Sianiave, "by the sorcerer king Paracelsor, in 1273. Gallian lay under siege for eight months."

"Saolin has told me something of this," said Ren. "A dreadful tale, and with a proper ending."

Sianiave nodded. "It was betrayal and sorcery. Banothyr was the younger brother of Baron Antoris, Ellohir's great-grandfather. Paracelsor promised him title for his betrayal. There were other reasons as well. Banothyr was said to be enamored of a certain concubine, who presented him the scheme.

"Banothyr slipped a potion into the evening meal, incapacitating Antoris, his wife, and seven of his children. But Arn, the eldest son, was late to dinner that night, having been in training to be a page. The boy arrived to find his uncle in the dining hall, covered in blood, the dagger he used to perform his grisly business still in hand. With his training sword as his only weapon, Arn managed to kill his traitorous uncle. He was not yet sixteen. He lost a hand in the fight, and became known as Arn One Hand, and he ruled well and wisely for over a hundred years."

"As great a baron as Gallian has ever had," remarked Aerindir. "Save perhaps for Ellohir."

"What happened to this sorcerer fellow and his army?" Osmodon asked.

"Barad'An sent knights to break the siege. Later Paracelsor was killed in a duel. His land now lies in waste."

"I thought he was a sorcerer," said Barrett. "Yet he was killed in a duel?"

"He dueled with another wizard, a Megidian. Neither man survived. When it was over, it's said there was nothing left but a shattered hall and two bloody puddles on the floor."

Osmodon grimaced in distaste. "Dangerous calling, sorcery. Give me a good horse and an honest sword any day."

Aerindir nodded agreement, but Barrett saw Ren exchange an amused glance with Sianiave as if to say. *"Men!"*

At dusk, lights came on in the palace above. Boys carrying burning wicks ran down the causeway, lighting its many lamps. Eastward, across the valley, a maroon sunset lowered into night. Lights winked on in farmhouses, barracks, and the village.

The wooden gate stood open as they rode into the courtyard. An old man came out to greet them as grooms hurried to take their horses. The old man was tall, nearly Barrett's height, with short white hair and kindly features. He wore a simple grey robe, but he carried himself with authority.

"Lady Sianiave!" he cried. "Princess Gwyndolyn! Such an honor! We're delighted to see you safe! Aerindir, my boy, we heard the news of Abdelar's passing. I am truly sorry. A great loss for us all."

Aerindir nodded shortly, but said nothing.

"Membrion is Ellohir's chamberlain," said Sianiave, "as he was to both Ellohir's father and grandfather. Membrion, this is Osmodon, my liege man."

The vizier took Osmodon's hand in a warm grip. "Sir Osmodon, delighted. You were in Nibur when last Sianiave visited, I recall. But we've certainly heard word of your exploits."

"The honor is mine," returned Osmodon politely. "Sianiave speaks highly of you."

The old man turned his attention on Barrett, and for several moments didn't speak. His grey eyes bore into Barrett's.

It was Sianiave who finally broke the silence, and with it the old man's gaze. "This is Barrett of Amra. A soldier, and our companion."

There was an odd inflection in the way she said this last, but it may well have been his imagination. Barrett felt a sense of relief when the old man turned away, a feeling of almost physical pressure was gone.

"Good, then. I'll see you to your apartments. Don't worry about your baggage. The house folk will see to it. You've had a long journey and baths are waiting. Ellohir is cleaning up after a day in the field. Dinner is at seven. You are all invited to attend. This way. Follow me, follow me."

CHAPTER 38

DESPITE ITS IMMENSE SIZE, there was an appealing homeliness to High House. As with Tor Eyrie, much of it had been tunneled out of rock, but there was artistry here that Sianiave's retreat lacked. High ceilings were set off by fluted columns and handsome arches. Tiled stairs led to many levels. Paintings and finely embroidered tapestries covered the walls. In sitting areas, fountains and fireplaces were encircled by luxurious divans—all lit by a multitude of lamps.

Barrett was the last of his companions to be shown to his apartment. There was a spacious sitting area with chairs, a table, and a fireplace. The massive oak bed was dressed with blankets and down pillows. An open window overlooked a garden where a curtain of water fell into a pool before passing again over the cliff.

The valley itself resembled a dark sea speckled with starlight. Village lamplight and campfires glowed in the distance. A slight breeze came through the window, carrying the scent of flowers and the sound of a woman singing. Barrett couldn't make out the words, but the melody was haunting.

"The baths are down the hall," Membrion said before leaving. "If you need anything, just ask one of the house folk. We hope to see you at the morning council. Your arrival has caused quite a stir."

The old chamberlain stood for a moment as if wanting to say more. Then, appearing to think better of it, he bowed and left.

Barrett stood by the window, captivated by the woman's song and the night breeze. From the moment they entered the valley his spirits had lifted. Gone was the weariness from days in the saddle. There was a sense of timelessness to the place that was strangely familiar, as though he should know it—had known it.

Fighting back a sudden and inexplicable urge to weep, he turned away from the window. Membrion had told them dinner was in an hour. That didn't leave much time.

Osmodon and Aerindir were already at the baths, soaking in separate tubs when he arrived. Four girls attended them, none appearing to be older than eighteen. Their hair was cut short and they wore simple blue linen shifts. The eldest of them helped Barrett with his clothes before escorting him to a waiting tub.

The water was pleasingly warm, almost hot. A second girl scrubbed his back with a long-handled brush while the first kneaded soap into his beard and matted hair. It was all done with gentle professionalism.

When the girls finished, they left the room. "Lovely lasses," sighed Osmodon. "Do you think they'll be around later?"

Aerindir laughed. It was first time Barrett had heard him do so. "They're Sister initiates. This service is part of their training, so don't get any ideas. They're sworn to celibacy, leastwise 'til they've earned their robes."

"Sisters?" Osmodon frowned. "How unfortunate."

"Working in a men's bathhouse seems an odd sort of training for young girls," Barrett commented.

Aerindir smiled again—a strange smile, amused, yet rueful, and conveying deep sadness. "What better way to learn about men? Women are not allowed into the mysteries of the Right Temple, any more than men are allowed into the mysteries of the Left Temple, though there are exceptions for those who show great capacity. Abdelar was one such, though he never completed his training. Sianiave knows both, as does Lady Bronwyn."

Osmodon looked up in surprise. "Lady Bronwyn is a sorceress, you say?"

Aerindir replied, "Of high degree—surely you've felt it in the energy of this place. It's not in small part due to her presence."

Before Osmodon could respond, the initiates returned with clean towels.

"You'd best finish your baths," said the senior girl. "You still have your massages, and dinner will be served shortly thereafter."

They were toweled off and led to narrow tables in an adjoining room where the girls rubbed them down with scented oil. When the girls finished, they gave the men clean robes and lambskin sandals to replace the travel-worn garments which had mysteriously vanished.

"That was a bit of all right," sighed Osmodon as they stepped back into the passageway and closed the door to the baths behind them. "Have to visit here more often."

A number of other guests were already in the dining hall when they arrived. Barrett immediately sensed tension in the room—not the fear he'd experienced in Ardendell, but a common, unspoken concern. He stood beside Aerindir as they surveyed the gathering.

There were more women present than men, a surprising number of them exceedingly attractive. Bronwyn and Ellohir's daughters were there, Griselda, Katrina, Gwenyth, Niobe, their names came too fast for Barrett to remember. A dark-haired beauty with lavender eyes stood back, her attention on Aerindir alone. A burly, red-bearded man stepped between the two men. "Aerindir! We've heard about Abdelar. Terrible loss. Terrible."

"Lord Crespin. What are you doing in Gallian?"

"Bran's Well was sacked—Uruk raid. The sheriff was killed. The south holding is in a frenzy. I came with a troop to help sort things out and met one of Ellohir's Scouts. He told us he had seen you with the Princess Gwyndolyn and the sorceress. We arrived ahead of you by several hours, I would guess. What happened in Barad'An? We've heard only rumors so far. Has the king really passed?"

"He has. But we'd best leave the telling until tomorrow, at the council. You'll be there?"

"Yes. Of course. War is upon us, like it or not. Without Barad'An, how can we—?"

"Tomorrow. We'll speak about it tomorrow."

Crespin left. Aerindir started again toward the dark-haired girl, only to be interrupted by a matronly woman in a flowing gown. "Aerindir, my dear boy. We're so sorry to hear about your brother."

The woman kept glancing at Barrett as she talked, and Aerindir introduced them. "Lady Conseltrane, Sir Barrett of Amra. Lady Conseltrane is Lady Bronwyn's aunt," he added.

Barrett had given up denying his knighthood. Apparently if you carried a sword and rode in such company as he, everyone assumed you were a knight. "A pleasure, m'lady," he murmured politely.

"The pleasure is mine," gushed the woman. "We all have so many questions. It's said you're Sianiave's new liege?"

"No."

"Oh, but you must tell me."

"At the council," said Barrett, following Aerindir's example and pulling himself away. He looked around for Osmodon, finding him in animated conversation with one of the daughters, a buxom blonde, Griselda, Barrett thought.

"They'll bore you to death," said a small voice beside him.

"Excuse me?"

He looked down to see a young girl staring up at him. Her large brown eyes were disturbingly straightforward. He guessed her age about ten. "They're good folk," the girl said. "As you can no doubt see, since you have the Sight."

"The sight?"

Barrett guessed immediately she was referring to his inconstant ability to see into people, to read their character. Since arriving in Gallian his ability had been improving. So far he felt none of the greed, fear, and envy he felt in Ardendell. The people he'd so far met here were who they appeared to be, strong, self-reliant and good-hearted, even the overly curious Lady Conseltrane.

"Don't bother to deny it," the girl continued firmly. "I won't tell anyone. I have it myself. It's my speciality, you might say. And I do love my sisters, but unless you enjoy talking only of men and their deeds, they'll bore you to death. Only two are married, you know."

She nodded at the dark-haired girl who had been watching Aerindir so intently. "Yseult is the only one besides myself who qualified for training, and she has her heart set on Aerindir."

Barrett was at a loss. "Qualified for training? You mean for the Sisterhood?"

The girl sniffed. "Only if we don't measure up."

"Measure up?"

"To the standards."

He shook his head, standards for what? The child's mother was a sorceress. It might be expected that one or more of her daughters would follow in her footsteps. Apparently the Sisterhood was only a stage in women's initiations.

"No doubt you're wondering," continued the girl seriously, "if I can read you, which obviously I can't, just as you can't read me, or Sianiave, or my mother. Everyone's been very curious about you since hearing of the mysterious knight accompanying Sianiave. Sir Osmodon has never been to Gallian before, but we've heard the songs. He is as great a knight as any, it's said. Without a king or even a holding of his own, he is Sianiave's perfect liege man.

"But I overheard you with my auntie, Lady Conseltrane, and if you aren't Sianiave's new liegeman, then who are you, and why are you here? And why, if you're of any importance at all, which I assume you to be since you do have the sight and you came with Sianiave, are there no songs about you?"

Barrett stared down at her, speechless. This precocious child had cut to the heart of his being. Who was he? Why was he here? She showed such clearheaded awareness, he wondered if he might not be talking to a midget. The girl looked up at him, eyes wide and guileless, waiting for an answer.

"Who did you say you are?"

"Oh, I'm sorry. I should remember my manners. I'm Kaitlyn, the youngest daughter. Kate, if you please. I thought you knew. But then, how could you, since this is your first time here."

A rustling among the guests saved Barrett. Ren and Sianiave had entered the hall. They were dressed in identical sleeveless gowns of ivory white silk, and looked like sisters. Their hair, bleached almost white by the sun, had been washed and woven into flaxen braids and set with jeweled pins. An aura of light seemed to surround them.

Another woman accompanied them, more petite than Ren, but just as striking. Her short cropped silvery hair was covered with a silver mantle adorned with tiny blue stones. It was impossible to guess her age. Her face was both young and old. Her eyes were silver grey, the color of dawn just before sunrise, her skin flawless alabaster. She wore a pale yellow gown, embroidered with blue and silver filigree. Despite her diminutive size she carried an air of command. Barrett knew at once this was Bronwyn, Baron Ellohir's wife, and mistress of High House.

"Please take your seats," she announced. Her soft voice was easily heard throughout the large hall. "My husband sends regrets he will miss this evening's dinner. There is a matter he must attend to. All of you know Lady Sianiave, and her beautiful young companion is the Princess Gwyndolyn Ambergin, who visited us years ago as a child."

All conversation ceased. The guests took their seats. Barrett held back, uncertain of his place. It appeared as though the seating was determined by some etiquette about which he knew nothing.

Soon he was the only one still standing, and aware that all eyes in the room were on him. Other than Ellohir's empty chair at the head of the table, only one other seat was vacant, immediately to the right of Bronwyn, and facing Ren and Sianiave. Clearly it was a seat of honor. Osmodon, and even Aerindir, were seated further down the table. Having little choice, Barrett took the vacant chair.

Bronwyn acknowledged him with a nod and tapped a silver bell. Immediately boys and girls dressed as pages entered, carrying decanters of red wine which they poured into ceramic goblets placed around the table.

"To Abdelar," said Bronwyn, raising her cup. "A great and good knight, and a friend to us all. He will be sorely missed. May he find peace in Velkela."

"To Abdelar!" Solemnly everyone raised their cup and drank, even little Kate, Barrett noted.

The wine was heavy with a sweet taste akin to honey. Glancing around the table, Barrett saw that many of those seated had tears in their eyes, and some were openly weeping.

The cups were refilled. Bronwyn raised her glass again in a toast. "To our guests, Lady Sianiave, Princess Gwyndolyn, Sir Aerindir, Sir Osmodon, and Sir Barrett of Amra. They have survived a terrible journey. May they find safety and rest during their stay with us in Gallian."

"Here, here!"

Again the cups were raised and emptied. More wine was poured. A second group of servers arrived carrying trays of food, greens and game hens, sweetmeats and fruits, breads, cheeses, olives and vegetables. The dinner had begun.

Belying her small stature, Bronwyn had drained her second cup with one swallow, pouring herself a third as she turned to Barrett. "So how do you find this land of ours, Sir Barrett? Not too strange, I trust?"

She smiled, her eyes twinkling in amusement. Across the table Sianiave was watching with an equally mischievous grin.

She knows! Barrett realized with a shock. Sianiave must have told her. Not Sir Barrett of Amra, but Barrett O'Byrne, a disgraced soldier from another world.

The idea left him feeling exposed, and not a little intimidated, though the wine helped. He was already feeling a pleasant buzz. It had come on quickly. He'd never been particularly susceptible to alcohol. Then it occurred to him that it might not be wine at all. He only assumed it was wine. "It's been . . . interesting," he said in response to Bronwyn's question.

"I imagine so. I travel only rarely, myself. Sianiave has told me of your land. By description, it sounds rather horrifying."

"Don't tease him," said Sianiave. "He's come a long way."

"Has he? Well, we'll see."

Barrett knew there was more to the short conversation than the obvious, but what that was he could only guess.

A warm glow settled over him. He raised his cup again only to find it empty. Bronwyn refilled it herself. "Thank you, m'lady."

M'lady. He liked that, liked the formal courtesy here.

The mistress of High House laid a small hand gently on his and leaned forward. Her lips were so close to his right ear he could almost feel their soft touch. "Tonight is a night for enjoyment, Sir Barrett," she whispered, "not for pondering."

Surprised, Barrett looked at her, but she had already turned away to speak with a server. He glanced across the table, first at Sianiave, then at Ren. Both were astonishingly beautiful, radiant. But it was Ren who captured his attention. She looked back at him, a questioning smile on her lips. He forced himself to meet her eyes, unsure of what he would find.

That moment, when their eyes met, was so intimate, it shocked him to his core.

So far as he knew he had never been in love. The feeling was unknown to him. The fact of it was as unexpected as it was unmistakable. It came as a wave of joy, and he saw it mirrored in Ren's eyes.

He looked quickly away. The wine. It had to be the wine. He was being too bold.

No! It was true. He was in love!

He'd known when he'd first set eyes on her across the meadow. He'd just been unwilling to admit it. It was far too frightening, beyond reason. It was life changing.

He looked again, but Ren was caught up in conversation with the man next to her, the red-bearded fellow who'd spoken with Aerindir earlier, Lord something-or-other.

Was Osmodon right? Were he and Ren meant for one another? Was that why Sianiave had brought him here? Why else were they seated so close?

Tonight is a night for enjoyment, not pondering.

Bronwyn's words were prophetic. Never had food tasted better, nor conversation been brighter. He lost count of how many times his cup was filled. Musicians arrived, a man playing a flute and another a harmonium. An assortment of drummers were joined by a singer, a woman whose voice was undoubtedly the one he'd heard earlier from the window of his room.

The music washed over him like warm honey. The night seemed to go on forever. At one point he looked up from his wine cup to see Sianiave, Ren, and Bronwyn watching him with the same knowing smiles he'd seen earlier. For a brief moment he imagined every woman in the room was staring at him with smiles in their eyes and on their lips.

The drumming grew louder, the wild strains of the flute more intense. Guests swayed to the rhythm of the drums. A man began calling out, the women responding with a chorale so haunting and beautiful, the sound penetrated to Barrett's very soul.

And then a green light engulfed the hall.

❖ ❖ ❖

Later, much later, at sunrise, Barrett found himself alone in his bed, remembering little about how he'd gotten there. He fell fast asleep, a wide smile on his face.

CHAPTER 39

"So," growled Ellohir, "it's true. Barad'An has fallen to this pig's ass of a priest, and Cuchulain never suspected?"

"His sight was always on external threats," said Aerindir.

"He fooled everyone," said Ren, "even the Sisters. A petty man spouting nonsense—no one took him seriously."

In appearance the lord of Gallian was the exact opposite of his wife, bear-like in stature, with flaming auburn hair and piercing blue eyes. He looked at Ren seated across the table from him and smiled. *She's a fighter, by the gods, despite her youth. And will be a good queen, if she lives that long.*

"Cuchulain may have been shortsighted," he said with a gentleness that belied his formidable appearance, "but his last act was to see you safe, child, and that is no small thing."

Bronwyn nodded.

Barrett, fighting a dulling headache, listened with only half an ear. What was he doing there? A page had woken him from a deep sleep early that afternoon. Everyone else was already seated when he arrived. He felt like an interloper.

Relative to the rest of the palace, the council room was small, no more than twenty feet across, with three tall, lead paned windows facing east. The table at which they all sat was circular, inlaid with multicolored wood set in a nine-sided geometric pattern. Each of the nine points matched a chair, one each for Ellohir, Bronwyn, Membrion, Penthys, Aerindir, Lord Crespin, Ren, Sianiave and himself.

Barrett was seated more or less opposite the baron. Aerindir was to his right, Crespin to his left. Ren sat to the left of Crespin, away from his direct line of sight, for which he was grateful. He couldn't remember what happened at dinner, but he was sure he'd made a fool of himself.

God, what must she think of him? Wine had never affected him that way before. He'd apologized when he'd arrived, only to be met with an amused smile. Ellohir's reaction baffled him.

"Sorry I missed it," the baron said, his eyes sparkling with humor. "I've always enjoyed Bronwyn's dinners. I tend to forget sometimes, what it is we fight for, us men."

Barrett nodded. Maybe he'd missed something. The headache made it hard to think clearly.

Across the table Crespin was fidgeting with a button on his tunic. "We've always been able to count on Barad'An's help. With these Uruk tribes marauding, and this new Sirdar in Nibur with an army ten times the size of ours, what hope have we?"

"Barad'An was in no position to come to Gallian's aide even before the priest's treachery," said Sianiave. "Or am I wrong in that? What say you, Aerindir?"

Aerindir nodded. "It's true. This year we have been at battle constantly, yet barely managed to keep the borders to our own shire protected."

"I find it difficult to understand," said Sir Penthys. "How Cuchulain allowed things to come to such a state."

"We know your mind on this, Penthys," said Ellohir irritably. "Whether we agreed with him or not, he was our king. I'll not hear him belittled."

"I'm sure Lord Penthys meant no disrespect, my husband," said Bronwyn calmly. "If discussion of a man's missteps can help us better understand our situation, it is only wisdom to listen."

Ellohir opened his mouth as if to reply, then sighed. "You're right of course, my dear. My apologies, Penthys. Cuchulain's death sits poorly with me. Can we at least agree we've lost an ally?"

Penthys gave a short nod. "Of course."

The exchange, brief as it was, gave Barrett an insight into the political dynamics in Gallian. Ellohir and Bronwyn were as different as two people could be, yet they functioned as one. Ellohir was the protector and strongman, Bronwyn the conciliator, the voice of practical wisdom.

"Good," said Ellohir. "Our scouts report that the Sirdar's army plans to march in no more than ten days."

"Ten days!" cried Crespin. "So soon?"

"It was to be expected," said Penthys, unperturbed. "Later and he would have to contend with the full heat of summer."

"Yes. Certainly. But ten days! He will be at our gates in a matter of weeks! We've hardly time to call in the outliers."

"That's already been done," said Membrion. "But there's another matter. It seems the Sirdar has found a morghul to lead his army."

Crespin paled. "A morghul!"

"Posh," sniffed Penthys. "Morghuls have never aligned with men. But even if true, the creatures are hardly known as strategists."

"What need of strategy when one has an army seventy thousand strong?"

"Someone's thinking for them both," said Ellohir. "Barad'An is their objective. They will bypass Gallian."

"And leave an enemy in their rear?"

"Hardly a threat," said Penthys. "Why waste resources when a single brigade could close Gallian off like a cork in a bottle? It's what I would do."

Barrett's headache had subsided, and he found himself listening with interest. At the word morghul a sharp pain cramped his left shoulder.

"Something troubles you, Sir Barrett?" asked Bronwyn.

"Nothing. An old injury."

"Sianiave told us of your own encounter with a morghul."

"You did battle with a morghul!" Aerindir regarded Barrett in amazement.

"Hardly a battle, it nearly killed me."

"Yet you survived. I wouldn't have thought it possible!"

"Yes! Tell us about it." cried Crespin eagerly, as though Barrett's encounter somehow offered hope. Even the aloof Sir Penthys showed interest.

Sianiave came to his rescue. "Whether the morghul Sir Barrett fought is the same creature who leads the Sirdar's army is irrelevant. The Uruks, the morghul, even the Sirdar, are pawns. Another force moves them."

"The priest?" Crespin asked.

Sianiave dismissed the thought with a wave. "Hardly. As Ren said, a trivial man, barely capable of seeing past his own nose. Whoever or whatever lies behind our travails is far more of a threat than the priest."

Penthys looked unimpressed. "Any thoughts as to whom this other—force —might be?"

"I've suspicions, but I'd rather not voice them until I know more."

"But, surely—."

"First things first," interrupted Ellohir. "The Sirdar's army will be on us in less than six weeks. We have to decide on a plan. Sianiave has told us you have some knowledge of warfare, Sir Barrett? What are your thoughts?"

Barrett looked up, startled to have the question directed at him. In the past few weeks he had, unwittingly perhaps, absorbed a great deal of knowledge about this world. Something about the political situation was familiar, though he had yet to place it.

"Six weeks to prepare? How many men can you muster in that time?"

"We can gather a hundred knights, perhaps. Two hundred mounted soldiers, a thousand trained foot soldiers, another thousand untrained, farmers and shopkeepers for the most. But they'll fight."

"Allies?"

"Expect less than twenty knights from the outliers," said Penthys, "though it might be possible to raise another thousand soldiers, mounted and foot."

There was a long silence. "Have we forgotten the desert people?" asked Membrion. "They've no love for the Sirdar."

Crespin snorted. "Their politics are a madhouse. We could never get them to join us."

"They're good fighters," said Osmodon. "There's a saying among them, '*Me against my brother, my brother and I against our cousins, our cousins and us against the world.*'"

"Meaning?"

"Meaning, Sir Crespin, that if they can be convinced the Sirdar is a bigger threat than the other tribes, they will join us."

Barrett was thoughtful. "Saying it's possible, how many can we count on?"

"If their *madhias*, their wise women, declare for it? Three thousand mounted, at least."

"We are also forgetting Artos," said Sianiave.

"Artos?" scoffed Penthys. "There's been no word in a decade. Even if he lives, what makes you think he would ally with us? He made his loyalties clear."

"His argument was with Cuchulain, not Barad'An."

Sianiave turned to Barrett, who appeared lost in thought. "Sir Barrett?"

He looked up to see all eyes upon him. "So," he said, "if my numbers are right, even if the desert people join the fight, Artos is found, and this priest dealt with, we're still talking less than seven thousand men. This against an army ten times that number?"

Ellohir nodded. Crespin shifted in his seat. Even Penthys looked subdued as he absorbed the bleak prospects.

Barrett smiled. His headache was gone and he was suddenly feeling much better. "Well, others have triumphed against worse odds, much worse, really."

CHAPTER 40

DINNER THAT NIGHT WAS a very different affair from that of the previous evening. Ale replaced the honey tasting "wine." The atmosphere was quiet and sober. Bronwyn and Ellohir did their best to keep the conversation light, but the topic of war was on everyone's mind. Beothyr, the Scout captain, attended as did the ruddy-faced mayor of the local village. All nine of the daughters were absent.

Penthys and Crespin left immediately after the council meeting, as both had long rides back to their own estates. Aerindir was also absent, as was Yseult, the dark-haired daughter. The coincidence did not go unnoticed.

"Abdelar would certainly have approved," said Ellohir, cutting into his steak. "He encouraged Aerindir to show more interest in women."

"Yseult is often said to be the fairest of our daughters," explained Bronwyn. "Certainly the most gentle."

"Does she really fancy him?" asked Ren.

The question might have come from a curious and protective sister. Still, Barrett wondered if there might not be a note of jealousy behind the concern.

Bronwyn sighed and shook her head. "Since they first met, she was twelve, I think, Yseult has thought only of Aerindir."

"They're kindred souls," said Sianiave. "Pure and giving."

"You know my opinion," growled Ellohir. "Hers is a gentle nature. The training would do her good."

"You would have our daughter spend her life in a cloister?"

"I would not see our daughter disappointed. These are dark times. Too many knights do not return to their wives."

"Yet, here you sit," said Bronwyn, patting Ellohir's hand affectionately. "In any case, it's moot. Yseult has made her decision. I do not think we need worry about it overmuch. And I do not think Aerindir will be easily killed."

"Yesterday I would have said the same about Abdelar," Ellohir muttered gloomily. He took a long draft of ale and was silent.

Barrett was fascinated by the conversation. He glanced at Ren, their eyes briefly meeting before he looked away.

Kindred souls?

The council meeting had gone on most of the day. Barrett had been surprised by the weight they'd given his views. Even Sir Penthys had listened without interrupting, afterward asking some pointed questions.

Why? This was always the question. Why was he here in this world? Why was he at the council meeting? Why was he, a simple soldier, being treated with such respect? Sianiave must have said something, but what? What were her real reasons for bringing him to this world? Had she made a mistake?

During the meeting he'd felt more self-assured. He did have something to offer. His years in that other world, many spent studying military strategy, had given him understanding, expertise, knowledge they lacked here. His memory of that place may have diminished, but the knowledge was still there

He also learned that his job here was not yet done.

After dinner Barrett returned to his room to pack. He and Osmodon were leaving before dawn. Another long journey lay ahead, and he wanted to sleep.

He was almost finished when there was a knock at the door. He opened it, startled to find Ren, changed into a thin shift of light green silk, standing there. Her hair was loose about her head, and there was a determined set to her jaw that gave him the mistaken impression she was angry. He half expected her to stamp her foot while pointing an accusatory finger.

But she surprised him. "It would appear you were going to leave without speaking to me," she said. "So I decided to come to you."

Barrett was at a loss. "Would you like to come in? I've got nothing to offer you, some water. There's a cup—." He stopped, embarrassed.

Her laughter, sweet and genuine, broke the tension. "I came to ask if you would join me for a walk?"

Barrett, startled, glanced at his kit on the bed. There wasn't much left to pack.

What was he thinking?

"I would like that very much," he said, surprised at his own boldness, but also pleased with himself. It was a relief to speak honestly for a change.

"Good," she said, taking his hand. "It's a beautiful evening."

They walked together down the curving stairway that led to the garden below. Whether by design or chance the falling waters caught the lamplight in such a way as to create a rainbow. The faint sound of a lyre drifted on the breeze.

"It's a courageous thing," said Ren as they stood, watching the play of light. "To volunteer as an emissary to the desert people. The dangers are legend."

"Osmodon has traveled there before."

"Aye. A doughty warrior and a good traveling companion, though I find it curious he is not going with Sianiave."

"I think Sianiave wants to go it alone for a bit. Osmodon guesses she's planning to use sorcery to locate Artos."

It was difficult to keep the skepticism from his voice at the mention of sorcery, but clearly Ren had no problem with the idea. "In any event, I'm glad you're traveling together. I wouldn't want harm to come to you."

"You wouldn't —?" Barrett stopped. A sudden understanding came over him. "That night? It was real."

"Of course. I'm surprised you doubted. When you didn't speak with me afterward, I was quite disappointed."

"I thought I was imagining things, that it was the wine."

Her smile was gone, her eyes locked onto his. "That was not wine. That was the sacred *haoma*. Unlike wine, *haoma* does not lie. It opens the heart. You experienced the unveiling, a vision of all that is real. Did not you feel it?"

"I didn't realize."

She's shaking, Barrett thought, then realized it was he who was shaking. They stared into one another's eyes, then came together as their lips met.

They backed away, as if in surprise, then laughed, and kissed again. Sweetness, joy, and a growing excitement took them both.

Time seemed to stop. A maidservant saw the couple. She smiled to herself and did not interrupt.

Before the sun was up, Barrett kissed Ren gently on the forehead, rolled out of bed, and dressed. She appeared to be asleep, and he hadn't the heart to waken her.

In the light of the waning moon he gazed down at her body, naked beneath the sheet. Her knew he would give his life for her. Nothing was more important or more precious. Their lovemaking had been unlike anything he had ever experienced, bringing him ecstasy he hadn't known to exist. The soft mounds of her flesh, her breasts, the curve of her thighs and the secrets between them, her smell, her taste, everything was perfect.

It took an effort of will to turn away.

Ren, only pretending to sleep, watched as he took up his kit and closed the door quietly behind him. She struggled with her feelings. He was a good and kind man, with greatness in him. Of that she had no doubt. She also knew that she loved him, as if she'd been waiting for him her entire life. But there was a void she sensed at the center of his being, some terrible wound that terrified her. She wanted to help heal it, but had no idea where to begin, or what might have caused such horrendous pain.

What if he never returned? The thought was unbearable.

A great ache rose in her heart. Yet painful as it was, she knew it was only a fraction of the pain that Sir Barrett must always feel. She wanted to run from it, from him, avoid that pain at any cost. But she also knew that at the center of that emptiness lay a great and valuable secret.

The pitiless voice of her ancestors, the bloodline, rose up in her. *"To be a true queen, you must know this!"*

"No!" She cried the word out loud, clutching at her pillow as tears streamed from her eyes. "I'm not ready. Not yet. Please!"

But the voice was relentless. *"It is your destiny, Ren. You will know!"*

CHAPTER 41

Barad'An
May 17

MILFORD ANASTIS GLAYS, lord steward of Barad'An, archon of Anor, and guardian to the crown princess, was in a rage. "You imbecile! How did you allow her to reach Gallian?"

Gothmog cringed under his glare, though inwardly the little magician was seething. He'd had enough of the priest. If the fool had listened to his advice the girl wouldn't be a problem. But the priest wanted to wed her, to give him the legitimacy he imagined he still lacked. As if real legitimacy was based on anything but power.

There was more than politics behind Glays' desire, Gothmog knew. The man's lust for the child sickened him. Nothing compared to the ecstasy he himself knew, complete release, without the disgusting taint of animal rutting.

The cleansing was nearly complete. The last of the knights were either dead, imprisoned, or in exile. The Sisters were gone, their tower turned into barracks. What resistance remained was scattered and weak. So many bodies were hanging from the oaks bordering the Great Way that crosses had to be erected on which to hang more victims. The crows had feasted for weeks.

The smell of their decay blanketed the city, making its way even into Glays' chamber. It excited Gothmog, nourished him. "All is not lost, m'lord," he murmured. "The princess can be retrieved."

"Retrieved!" The priest swung his scepter, shattering a vase. "She's in Gallian, you dolt! You imagine your Uruk hirelings can take Gallian when an entire band was undone by three warriors?"

Gothmog shifted uneasily. The arrival of three unknown warriors at such a moment could not have been coincidence. Descriptions provided by the two Uruks who'd survived the rout left no doubt in his mind as to their identities, at least two of them. When years ago the witch had vanished, he'd thought her gone for good. Now she was back. As with Prince Corwin, Sianiave was one of the few people he truly feared.

Glays studied the red jewel atop his scepter. Gothmog suppressed a smirk. The scepter once belonged to the imperial herald, an office vacant for over a century. The priest had found it in the treasury and, thinking it kingly, claimed it as his own.

"So," said Glays. "Capture her, you say. From Gallian."

The scepter swung again, shattering another vase and missing the magician's head by inches. "And how will you accomplish this, may we ask?"

Gothmog cowered at the close call. "M'lord, we have her nanny, and others beloved by her. She will be concerned about their welfare."

"Welfare?" Glays weighed the idea, and a slow smile spread across his thick features. "Yes! Of course! Pen an invitation. Be sure she understands the consequences of refusal. Send a messenger, someone with flair, and provide him with a fast steed. It's a long ride to Gallian. We'll hold the wedding immediately upon her return."

"Wedding? M'lord, isn't that a bit precipitous?"

Glays almost appeared to gloat. "The sooner the better. It will help to still the rabble." He waved at the broken pottery. "Have someone clean this up."

"Yes, m'lord."

Gothmog bowed and left the room. Since taking office the smallest slight sent the priest into a rage. His sermons, now attended by mandate, had become rants, but it was his fixation on the girl that was most worrisome.

A stairway behind a bolted door in the administrative wing of the palace led to the dungeon, one hundred and forty-eight stairs. Gothmog knew every stair by heart, counting them in his head as they spiraled into a darkness lit only occasionally by wax torches. In the past the dungeon held only the most dangerous offenders. Common criminals were kept in the citizen's jail, beyond the palace walls.

When Gothmog had been given the position of "holy inquisitor," he'd changed all that. He wasn't interested in pickpockets, thieves, and drunks. Even murderers were of little concern. Let the templars deal with them, sever a hand or foot, hang them, as they saw fit. But the dungeons were his domain. Where once they housed fewer than half a dozen prisoners at any given time, they now held well over a hundred. Individuals that might have useful information, recalcitrants, traitors to the regime, it hardly mattered. They were his playthings now, to do with as he pleased.

The winding stairway ended at a large door, fastened with an iron lock. A bell hung nearby. Gothmog rang twice in quick succession. There was a grinding sound as the lock turned. A huge, lumbering brute holding a lantern and a ring of keys acknowledged Gothmog with a grunt.

Radlik, the keeper of Barad'An's dungeon, had been taunted in his childhood by other children. They called him goblin, or troll's bastard, for even then he looked more troll than man. And, like trolls, Radlik had a taste for human flesh.

Gothmog had discovered him in a dungeon cell, awaiting execution for the rape and murder of a farm girl. Gothmog appointed him keeper, and, as a safeguard against indiscretion, he had Radlik's tongue cut out. Radlik didn't mind greatly. He rarely spoke as it was, and he enjoyed his new status. He took up residence in a large cell in the rear of the dungeon. The dank atmosphere had turned his skin a maggoty white, and his hair was falling out in patches.

Save for the occasional moan, the shifting of chains, and the unrelenting drip, drip of water, the dungeon was as silent as a tomb. Prisoners had learned to expect the worst if they attracted the keeper's attention. Occasionally one would go missing. A nuisance at times, but Radlik was clever enough to avoid the more useful inmates.

"Is it ready?" Gothmog asked.

Radlik grunted affirmatively. He led the magician past rows of cells inhabited with emaciated prisoners who looked quickly away when Radlik cast his baleful eyes in their direction.

They turned a corner into another vaulted passageway, following it for a distance before stopping at the door to a large room Gothmog called his "workshop." Inside were shelves of manuscripts and leather bound books, cabinets and drawers containing poisons, thumbscrews, needles, and other implements of torture.

A boy, no older than fifteen, was chained spread-eagle to a wall. His shirt had been torn from his chest, and his face was bloodied. The drain beneath him and the wall to which he was chained were mottled with rust-colored accretions.

"Please!" he screamed, his voice hoarse with terror. "I didn't do anything! Please!"

The boy had been arrested for speaking ill of one of the priest's men, though he pleaded innocence. His guilt or innocence was irrelevant to Gothmog, who preferred just such a young specimen for his practice. In the past he'd dealt mainly with runaways and orphans, nonentities who wouldn't be missed. This was of little consequence now. It was an aspect of the art he studied alone, for the practice had been banned for over a thousand years. It was the cause of his banishment from the academy at Megida.

He checked the boy's chains, then looked to see that the proper ingredients had been placed in the brazier. He retraced the containment circle Radlik had drawn on the floor with chalk, leaving the pentagram intact. He'd taught Radlik well, but in this work, one impure ingredient, a mispronounced word, could be disastrous. His failure with Corwin had undoubtedly been due to such an error, or so he'd convinced himself. Since then he had been even more rigorous in his procedures.

Satisfied that all was in order, he donned his robe and, with a wave of his hand, lit the brazier. The robe was woven of black silk, with red embroidery that gleamed in the torchlight. Though it had been soaked in the blood of a thousand victims, it never needed cleaning.

He removed a stone from a felt-lined drawer. The death stone was black obsidian, ancient beyond reckoning, and said to hold the souls of the people it murdered. Its cutting edge was so fine it was translucent when held against the light.

Radlik left the room to stand guard in the hall outside. The boy was babbling now, repeating himself over and over. "Please don't! Please don't! Please —!"

Gothmog ignored the entreaties, emptying his mind of thought. A minute passed, then another. Then the moment came and he began the invocation. *"Nazghat'ul ishka'mar kh'en, nazghat'sul, ishka'mar ch'en, nazghat'ul esha'mar sya'nif."*

The words echoed against the stone walls. The torches flared and dimmed. The room grew dark, illuminated solely by coals glowing in the brazier.

A corona of black light began to form above the boy's head, pulsing like a living thing. Gothmog traced the requisite pattern in the air, watching it hang fluorescent in the darkness for a moment before vanishing. The acrid smell of sulphur filled the room. *"Nazghat'ul esha'mar gha'anif, nazghat'asul, esha'mar atua'hul. SHAMMAT!"*

The boy moaned and spittle flew from his mouth. The pungent smell of urine filled the room as he vented himself.

With the skill of long practice, Gothmog brought the stone down in a vicious arc, slashing open the boy's chest. The boy stared at him in reproachful disbelief as the magician reached into the open cavity and removed his heart.

Gothmog placed the still beating heart in the brazier. "Come, my master. The way is open. *Nazghat'ul esha'sul, nazghat'ul sensa'nul—.*"

The black circle of light expanded, shaping itself into a globe. For a brief moment the globe floated in the darkness, black and shimmering. Then, with a terrible urgency, it poured itself into the boy's open body.

The head jerked erect. The eyes, no longer blue, were filled with an alien blackness. The lips formed into a grotesque grin. "Servant, what have you for me?"

Gothmog could not stop a small moan. The ecstasy was close now. "Princess Gwyndolyn escaped, master," he rasped. "I believe the witch Sianiave is responsible. They are in Gallian."

"I know this." The voice coming from the boy's mouth was hoarse as it fought to control unwilling vocal chords. "A small matter. A fortress can also serve as a prison. When Barad'An has fallen the Sirdar's general will install a permanent garrison outside Gallian."

"The army is on the march?"

"They will pass by Gallian in eighteen days." There was a brief pause. "I am concerned with the witch. She has companions?"

"My scouts reported two," replied Gothmog. "The Linsraden mercenary, and one other, whom I know not. He is tall, dark-haired, and uncommonly skilled with a sword."

"Mark him well, servant. This one may be more dangerous than all the rest."

"A warlock, master?"

"The witch has gone to great efforts to bring him here."

The boy/thing gagged, spitting out blood. It licked its lips. "How goes it with the priest?"

"Poorly. His self-importance grows daily. He refuses the steward's seat, instead taking the throne. He uses the royal 'We' when he speaks. I fear he will not honor the agreement. He is obsessed with the girl."

There was a long silence. The boy-thing spat out more gore.

"Master?"

A loud gurgle escaped the body. The gollum's eyes bulged as if any second they might burst from its head.

"This body grows unstable."

"Master, it was healthy . . ." But the black light was already gone from the dead boy's eyes, the head once again collapsing on to his chest.

Gothmog stepped back in frustration. He hadn't achieved his usual release. In fact he felt unaccountably drained and exhausted. The boy must have had health problems he was unaware of.

He replaced the stone in its case and doffed his robe. Radlik would clean up the room, as he always did. The dungeon baths emptied into the city sewers, which in turn emptied into an underground river. Where that river flowed Gothmog had no idea, and didn't care. All he knew was that it was a good way to dispose of garbage.

Radlik refused to eat the corpses, considering them tainted in some way.

CHAPTER 42

Gallian, May 27

REN FINISHED READING the letter brought by the "emissary" from Barad'An and handed it to Bronwyn who held the letter up and read the words aloud:

Felicitations to Crown Princess, Gwyndolyn Ambergin

My Dearest Child;

With the lamentable passing of your grandfather, King Cuchulain Ambergin, and the recent finding by the Court that your Uncle, Prince Artos Ambergin, now ten years absent, is to be stricken from the Roll of Ascension, it stands now that you are the sole heir of the line of Ambergin.

Furthermore, upon your maturity at the age of 33 years, you will ascend to the throne as Queen, ruling over the Kingdom of Anor and the Imperial City of Barad'An. Until the time of your ascension, and in the absence of any relations of sufficient means and standing as to be able to care for you in the manner befitting your Station, the Court has ordered you to be placed under the guardianship of the Lord Steward of Barad'An. We urge you take return to Barad'An and take up your rightful duties. But, should you choose to deny this request, We cannot assure the safety of your Property, or those citizens in Barad'An to whom you owe allegiance. Your immediate return will do much to forestall Havoc and distress upon these good persons.

Your Servant,

Milford Anastis Glays, Lord Steward of Barad'An and Archon of Anor

Bronwyn lowered the letter. Sianiave, seated nearby, said nothing. Ellohir regarded the messenger with a careful eye. "You said your name was Gaskel. Were you privy to the contents of this letter?"

"Of course," said Gaskel, ignoring the frown that darkened Ellohir's features. "It's plain enough. I assume the princess will wish to leave immediately. You may provide a reasonable escort, though as personal representative of Lord Glays, it will of course be under my command."

Captain Gaskel of the temple guards had been raised a privileged son of a wealthy Meridorian merchant, and knew something of court protocol. It was why he had been chosen for such an important mission—that, and his appearance, about which he had little false modesty. He was tall and well set up, with a long mustache and curly locks of brown hair. He'd joined the temple guards early on, seeing it as a way back to the station he considered his due. As emissary to the Barony of Gallian, he represented Barad'An's highest seat. He intended to make it clear that Ellohir had no say in this matter.

He gave Ren a slight bow and a roguish smile. A princess, yet still a woman. He knew Lord Glays planned to marry her, but she would be in his keeping for nearly a fortnight. The prospects were intriguing.

Bronwyn handed the letter back to Gaskel. "A bit presumptuous, Emissary Gaskel."

"Excuse me?" said Gaskel, surprised. "Presumptuous?"

"Exactly so," agreed Sianiave. "It seems more the sort of thing a petulant boy might pen. Why not just say what he meant: return immediately or he will have every man, woman, and child Ren ever loved put to death. Straightforward. No temporizing."

Gaskel flushed with indignation. In Barad'An such disrespect would mean death.

He had arrived at Gallian the night before after eighteen hours in the saddle, very nearly killing the horse. He may very well have killed it, for all he knew. Despite his fatigue and the comfort of the bed, he'd managed little sleep. He sensed immediately that something malignant lay behind Gallian's deceptive beauty, something that threatened to undo his very manhood.

Now he knew the source of the threat. These women, the one called

Bronwyn in particular, ruling side by side with her husband. Intolerable.

Without thinking his right hand moved to the pommel of his sword. "I would not treat this matter so lightly, m'lord," he said, ignoring the women.

"No?" asked Bronwyn prettily. "And how should we treat it, Emissary Gaskel?"

"Yes," said Sianiave. "Tell us, Emissary Gaskel. What is the proper way to treat such threats?"

It was their scorn that did it, condescending, as if amused. Amused by him!

"Enough!" he cried. "Gallian is a vassal holding! You have read the letter and seen the seal. I'm taking the girl back to Barad'An! Escorted or not, she leaves with me! Now!"

He lunged forward to grab Ren from her seat, but Ellohir stepped between them. Enraged at the man's temerity, Gaskel drew his sword. "You dare to interfere?"

Too late he realized his mistake. With a speed that belied his girth, Ellohir swatted the sword from his hand, sending the weapon flying across the room.

"We do not deal with regicides and traitors," said Ellohir evenly. A twitch under his left eye was the only sign that he was struggling to control his anger. "Nor with their lackeys."

Gaskel stared, unbelieving. Ellohir had disarmed him with the casualness of a father taking a spoon from a child. His hand was broken, he was certain. He looked for a way out of what was fast becoming a dangerous situation. His sword lay some ten feet away, on the floor where it had landed.

His hand! Even if he managed to get to the sword he would never be able to use it.

"Well," said Bronwyn, unperturbed. "It's Ren's decision, of course."

Ren nodded matter-of-factly. "I'll return, of course."

"Return?" Ellohir turned in amazement. "To Barad'An, to that weasel of a priest? Even if he doesn't have you throttled the moment you enter the gate he'll lock you in a cell and parade you around like a pet!"

"The priest has other plans for Ren," said Sianiave.

"Other plans? She's all that stands between Glays and the throne!"

"He plans to marry her."

"Marry her?" Ellohir was dumbstruck.

Bronwyn nodded in agreement. "Ren is nearly eighteen. As her guardian that only gives him fifteen years until her maturity. But were he to marry her and father a child—."

Ellohir nodded as he began to understand. "Of course. I'm a fool. But that still leaves the question of—."

They were speaking as though he were invisible. Holding his broken right hand with his left, Gaskel began to hope. The girl would return. He just needed to be patient.

"It's decided," Ren said firmly.

"It will be a grand wedding," said Sianiave, nodding. "As befits the Archon of Barad'An."

"Difficult to find time alone with the groom," suggested Bronwyn.

"It will need only a moment," said Ren. "The blade must be poisoned, to be certain, as it was how grandfather died."

Gaskel's hope turned to dismay. Bantering as they might at a quilting, these women were plotting to murder the Lord Steward of Barad'An!

There was still time. He could get away, warn —.

"What about this worm?"

Startled, Gaskel realized the girl was speaking about him.

"Oh, him?" Ellohir waved negligently. "I'd almost forgotten. Gaelin! Robby!"

At Ellohir's command the door flew open. Two men, dressed in a sheriff's garb and carrying long daggers, entered. A third man stood quietly in the background. Gaskel had seen him before, the knight Aerindir!

They'd been waiting, he realized with a shock. He thought the royal seal would protect him. He'd been a fool. "Wait!" he cried, his pride forgotten. "I can help you!"

"As I mentioned earlier," said Ellohir dismissively. "We don't deal with traitors." Then, to the two men, "Squeeze what information you can from him, then toss him off a cliff."

"With pleasure," said the larger of the two.

Gaskel hollered as the deputies grabbed his arms. "You can't do this! I'm an emissary. The covenants!"

"You broke the covenants when you drew your sword," said Bronwyn.

"You bloody witch! You did this!"

"Take him away," said Ellohir, disgusted.

"Get your hands off me, you oafs! You'll see! You'll be hanging from the trees! All of you! Scum! Witches!" His curses echoed down the hall even after the door had closed.

"Pleasant fellow," murmured Ellohir dryly. He turned to Aerindir. "You heard, of course."

"It's as expected."

"You'll accompany Ren?"

"I will."

Ellohir stroked his beard and sighed. "I envy you. Sir Barrett and Sir Osmodon face unknown dangers in the Great Desert, Lady Sianiave travels alone in search of Artos, and you return to Barad'An and possible death, while I have to remain here, like a rabbit in a trap."

Bronwyn put her hand on Ellohir's. "You will not be alone, my husband."

CHAPTER 43

BARRETT STIFFLED A CURSE. The oasis, which had been both their destination and their hope, was a blackened charnel house.

"We won't quench our thirst here," remarked Osmodon, his voice dry from the heat and thirst. "The water appears tainted."

An understatement, Barrett thought, as he studied the bleached skeletons and rotting carcasses that surrounded the pool. He recognized camels, hyenas, and what he took to be lions, though larger than those he knew. Other remains could have been cattle of some sort. There was the horned skull and bleached rib cage of some huge beast whose identity he couldn't even begin to imagine.

He passed his tongue over cracked lips, recalling what he had learned in survival training, how to make use of succulent plants, condensation pits, even drinking the blood of their horses. The desert was an oven, easily a hundred and ten degrees in the late afternoon.

"Who would have been so cruel as to poison a *wadi*?" Osmodon sounded genuinely aggrieved. "*Wadis* are sacred to the nomads; politics and fighting are *haram* there, forbidden."

"Could it have happened naturally?"

"Not likely. Wadi Nuri was known for the purity of its water. Now even the sand looks afflicted."

Osmodon was right. A black stain circled the pool, and everything within its circumference was dead.

Greywind fought his bit as Barrett backed the horse away from the tainted pool. Whatever had poisoned the oasis was virulent and quick to kill. He was glad they'd left Bear back in Gallian.

"What now?"

"Abu Mesina is still four days off. We won't make it without water." Osmodon was thoughtful. "I remember the nomads talking of another *wadi*, a small one half a league east of here. Bistami, it's called."

"Do we have a choice?"

"We can go back."

"The last water we passed was three days ago."

"Aye. But I'm not sure Wadi Bistami even exists. And it also may be tainted."

Barrett looked at the water skin sagging against his saddle. There was barely enough to last a day, much less three. However bad it got, he would not slaughter Greywind for his blood.

He pulled off his makeshift headdress, shaking out the dust and sand. They were surrounded by a desert the like of which he'd never seen: blasted earth and scorched salt flats, sand dunes as high as small mountains. The sun seemed to take up half the sky.

Ren had called him brave. When he agreed to travel to Abu Mesina as Ellohir's envoy to the desert people, he had no idea what lay ahead. Volunteering had been a way to extend his service, to remain in this world, and near Ren, for he knew now she was the center, the very heart of it. The thought of leaving her, of returning to the dreary place of his past, still troubled his sleep.

"I'm going on," he said, replacing the headdress. "You coming?"

Osmodon sighed and nodded. "You're decision, lad. I do my liege lady's business, and looking after you is that business."

"I appreciate that."

"Man's oath and all, you know."

Laughing, though with little enough reason, they turned their reluctant horses and headed into the desert. After the desolation of the oasis, the desert seemed absolutely cheerful.

They rode on the rest of that evening and through the night. The following day, when it again became too hot to travel, they stopped, setting up camp under the cornice of a windswept dune. There they ate a meal of hard bread, dates, and dried meat, drinking only a mouthful of water each to wash it down. They saved what remained for the horses. They spoke little, their mouths dry, and their lips chapped and bleeding. Eventually both men lay back in the thin shade of the cornice and slept.

Barrett was awakened by a thumping sound. He opened his eyes to find

Greywind pawing at the sand by his head. He dusted himself off and sat up. The sun was low in the west and Osmodon was nowhere to be seen. A line of footprints led from their small camp up the slope of the dune. He found Osmodon lying prone on the sand, staring intently at something in the distance.

Osmodon cautioned him with a wave. "Keep down. Their scouts have eyes like hawks."

Barrett dropped to his elbows and shimmied forward. Perhaps a mile off, silhouetted against the dying sun, marched a long line of camels, with some people herding goats alongside.

Osmodon spoke quietly. "The camel bells woke me. Thought it my imagination, but there it is. Must be over a hundred animals. See how they circle? They're setting up camp for the night."

"Why are we hiding? They'll have water, won't they?"

"Aye. They'll have water, and food as well. Trouble is, they're as likely to murder you as give us a meal. No telling with them."

"How long did you live with them?"

"Six months, and that was in Abu Mesina. A rich sheik hired me to train his sons with the sword. If these are Bani Faisal, or from a tribe allied with the Bani Faisal, it's our good fortune."

"And if not?"

"Could mean our heads unless we do some fast talking. Alliances between tribes shift about more than this sand."

"And we're asking them to be allies?"

"The nomads have a saying, 'Me against my brother, my brother and I against our cousins, our cousins and us against the world.' Terrific fighters. They're honorable, in their way, not like the Uruks. Give 'em a common cause and they could conquer the world. Almost did once, or so the stories go. And they hate the Sirdar. They still remember when raiders from Nibur stalked the trade routes and ravaged their caravans. Gallian protects their western border, and if Barad'An falls, so will Gallian. Leastways that's the argument we'll give."

"Why wait? Let's give it to them now."

"Abu Mesina welcomes travelers, caravans in the open desert tend to be more suspicious. They may think us spies or bandits."

"I'd rather trust desert hospitality than our chances of surviving two more days without water."

Barrett moved to stand, but Osmodon grabbed him. "Wait until they set up their tents. They'll feel safer then, less apt to spike us on sight."

The sun vanished behind the horizon when Osmodon finally deemed it safe to move. On their approach they were immediately surrounded by riders, young men robed in black and wielding scimitars.

"We've gotten into something," whispered Osmodon as the riders surrounded them. "Caravan masters use mercenaries as guards. These fellows are house guards."

"House guards?"

Before Osmodon could answer the leader of the riders called out. "*Estopa haena! Min! Min wa'en!*"

Surprisingly, Barrett understood the command. He'd been fluent in both Pashto and Arabic in that other world. The same concurrencies in language must hold, he decided.

"Stop here!" the troop's captain had said. "Who are you? From where do you come?"

"Greetings!" Osmodon called out in a halting version of the same language. "Peace be upon you. I am Osmodon of Linsraden and this be Barrett of Amra. We travel to Abu Mesina with a message for the *loya jirga* from Lord Ellohir of Gallian. We claim the right of travelers! Whose caravan is this?"

The man who had hailed them was a handsome, dark-skinned youth. He prodded his horse forward. "From Gallian? This is true?"

His dark eyes had a look of fierce intelligence, but Barrett sensed Osmodon had caught him by surprise.

"By the gods and my honor, it is so. Can you take us to the caravan master?"

"This is no merchant caravan," the man said, smiling for the first time. "Emir Malik bin Abdulafaiz al Shah is lord here. I am his son, Bandar bin Malik al Shah."

Barrett started. A memory surfaced, Bandar. It was a common enough name in the east, and the man before them bore little resemblance to the Nuristani chieftain he had met that terrible night in the Pamirs. Still the name had shaken him. That Bandar had been older, with grey eyes. Although of a great size, this fellow was younger and bearded, his eyes the color of night. What the two did share was an almost mocking sense of self-awareness.

Osmodon bowed. "Beg pardon, your highness. We saw your caravan and assumed—."

"Apologies are unnecessary. I will take you to my father. If you are who you say you are, you will be welcome. Follow me."

The caravan was larger than they had first thought. Barrett guessed there were over a hundred tents, with twice that many camels. It was well protected, with numerous armed men about. Their guide's father was obviously a man of some stature.

The camp had been set up with military efficiency, the livestock herded into rope *kraals*, the camels tethered, the cook fires fueled by camel dung. Women and children turned from their tasks and called out, "O Bandar? Who are these prisoners? Are we in for an execution?"

"They aren't prisoners," responded Bandar, laughing. "They are guests, and I'm taking them to meet my father."

The easy informality with which their guide was met made it clear the young man was well regarded among his people.

Bandar led them to the center of the encampment where a large tent, made of a pale orange canvas, stood. A boy took the reins from the prince as he dismounted. "A moment, please."

Bandar pushed open the tent flap and vanished inside. Several minutes later he reappeared. "My father will see you. It is customary for guests to leave their shoes and weapons outside."

"Your horses will be well cared for," he added, seeing Barrett's hesitation.

Barrett and Osmodon left their boots with their swords and daggers by the entrance. Inside the air seemed cooler, the tent insulated from the heat by thick cotton panels tied to the walls. The interior was lit with brass oil lamps. Richly woven carpets covered the floor. A portly man with a trim white beard and a purple and gold headdress sat cross-legged in a circle with six other men near the back. The mouthpiece of a large hookah was being passed between them.

An old woman in a black *chador* sat cross-legged to the right of the entrance flap. She wore no veil and appeared to be studying a pattern of cards on the rug. It was impossible to guess her age. She looked as old as the desert. Her thin hair was dyed black with kohl, her face burnt brown by the sun, her wrinkled hands little more than claws.

Oblivious to both the men in the circle and the new arrivals, she took another card from the deck, placing it carefully with the others.

Something about the old woman bothered Barrett. And then he saw.

She was blind! Her eyes were solid white, the disturbing milky white of a boiled egg. How could she read the cards? Yet read them she did, studying the patterns emerging before her with a peculiar intensity.

Ignoring the woman, Bandar bowed toward the white bearded man seated across from him in the circle. "My father, these are the travelers of whom I spoke. They bring a message from the Lord of Gallian to the council of tribes in Abu Mesina."

"Peace be upon you, o' travelers," murmured the Emir, bowing his head in formal greeting. "You have come a long way. Join us."

The men moved aside to create room for them. Bandar bowed again to his father, nodded at the two travelers, and left.

The hookah's mouthpiece was passed to Barrett. It was carved in the shape of a dragon's head, from bone or ivory, he guessed. It was yellowed with age, attached to the pipe by a tube of woven silk. He nodded thanks to the man who handed him the mouthpiece and took an experimental puff.

The smoke was surprisingly mild and pleasant, even familiar. If not the same herb Sianiave was fond of smoking, it was certainly related. Rather than making him feel light-headed like some other leaf he had once smoked, it produced a sense of clarity and calm. He took another puff, deeper, and then passed the mouthpiece to Osmodon.

"My son is unable sit with us," explained the Emir. "As a captain of my soldiers he is quite busy. These are troublesome times. The desert has grown more dangerous for everyone."

"We are grateful for your hospitality, Emir," said Osmodon, exhaling a cloud of the mild smoke. "Two days ago we arrived at Wadi Nuri to find it poisoned. This afternoon we gave the last of our water to our horses."

Barrett admired his friend's tact. In one brief sentence he had described their plight, alerted the Emir to the poisoned oasis, and demonstrated their good character.

A murmur of dismay passed among those seated. "Forgive me!" cried their host, motioning to a servant. "Sabry! *Gibli moiya! Bisora!* Bring water for our guests!"

"We are in your debt," said Osmodon.

"It is we who are in your debt for bringing us news of Wadi Nuri, for it was to be our next stop. Those who would poison a *wadi*, may their souls wander the desert without respite."

There were nods of agreement from the men in the circle. A boy hurried over with two cups and a pitcher of water. Trying not to appear greedy, Barrett drained his cup in one swallow. After the third refill his thirst began to slake.

"The people of the desert have always been on good terms with the people of Gallian," observed the man next to Barrett, smiling.

"Indeed," agreed the Emir. "They were once *Saharim* themselves, before they chose to settle, it is written. My son tells me you bring a message."

"We wish to present it in Abu Mesina," said Osmodon. "It concerns all the tribes."

"Come. All here have seats on the council. Emir Abu Salim, my uncle, sits at its head. Can you not tell us something?"

Osmodon considered for a moment, then nodded. "I don't see why not." He paused for a moment. "The Sirdar's army prepares to move against Barad'An. It is said a morghul commands."

"Of this we already know," said the Emir. "They are already on the march."

Osmodon leaned forward in alarm. "This is troublesome news indeed. When, may I ask?"

"Five days ago. We've just received word ourselves. It is why we are here, to discuss the matter. We have known of the Sirdar's plans for some time. We are moving our people south, to the safety of Abu Mesina. The Sirdar's agents must have poisoned the wells. Wadi Nuri is not the first such atrocity to be committed."

"If their goal is Barad'An," snapped a sharp-faced man across from Barrett, "what matters it to Gallian, or to the desert people, for that matter?"

Osmodon barely glanced at the man, his attention on the Emir. "If Barad'An falls, where will this army go next? Gallian will be surrounded, a prison to those within, unable to protect its borders, or yours."

"What need have we of Gallian?" said the man. "The desert will protect us, as it has always done." There were nods of agreement.

This time Osmodon did face the man who spoke. "A desert with poisoned wells will not protect you. Once this army has taken Barad'An, it will turn to Abu Mesina, whose walls are not nearly so strong."

Silence greeted this announcement, and Osmodon pressed his point. "The Sirdars have always been jealous of the desert people's hold on the caravan trade and your seaports to the south. The son of the one they called 'The Butcher of Megida' has openly declared his intent to succeed where his father has failed, to build an empire that will stretch from the sea to the mountains."

"Other men have had this dream," said a white-haired man quietly. "All have failed. Only the desert abides."

"They've failed because people rose to fight them."

"Is this the message you bring!" cried the sharp-faced man. "You wish us to join with this mad priest who rules Barad'An, to fight against an army that, with all the tribes together, we cannot hope to equal? Why do you think we go south? If we thought there was any chance of defeating the Sirdar, I would offer my sword gladly. But I say, to ride to Barad'An is foolishness!"

There were nods and murmurs of agreement. To Barrett the sentiment of the group was clear. They knew about the coup in Barad'An. It wasn't a surprise. To their way of thinking the priest must pose as great a threat as the Sirdar's army.

If he and Osmodon couldn't convince the men seated here, Barrett knew they would have little success in Abu Mesina. But what argument could convince them to disregard the safe course, and agree to ride to possible death in a land not their own?

Osmodon was having difficulty coming up with another approach. "When they attack Abu Mesina? What—?"

Barrett put out a restraining hand. Osmodon stopped in mid-sentence. Barrett handed his cup to the boy and stood. "How many times in the past has a large force been defeated by a smaller one? With your people and ours allied, we can defeat this army. As for the priest, he will be gone. This I promise you."

He sat down to silence. He didn't know why he mentioned the priest, but it felt right. Unfortunately, with the Sirdar's army already on the move, he knew it might already be too late.

One of the men confronted him. "How can you promise such a thing? Are we to risk our lives and the lives of our families on the desperate promise of a *ferengi*? A stranger? A man we know nothing about?"

"Abdul asks a fair question," said the Emir, frowning. "Who are you to make such a promise?"

He'd gone too far, Barrett thought. What had caused him to promise such a thing? Even Osmodon was giving him a questioning look. Before he could think of an answer he was interrupted by a shriek from the old woman sitting in the corner. "Malik! Listen to this man!"

"But *dol amrick* — ? Your highness?"

With astonishing agility, the old woman leapt to her feet, pointing at Barrett with a bony finger. Her glaucous eyes, sightless as porcelain, seemed to bore into his soul.

"Listen to this one! He speaks the truth! Listen to him, for he has been sent to us!"

No one argued. Even Osmodon nodded, as though her cries were irrefutable.

Only Barrett questioned the old woman's words. The rest of the company was staring at Barrett, their faces displaying wonder, even awe.

"The *mahdi*?" whispered one, half question, half hope. But the question went unanswered, and the name was not repeated.

CHAPTER 44

It was late afternoon when the caravan moved off. A light breeze, hot enough to have come from an oven, blew in from the east. Nearby, rising out of the sands, stood a great stone obelisk, its bleached and pitted face inscribed with lines of cuneiform that neither Barrett nor Osmodon could decipher.

"Go west from the stone," the old woman had said. "You will come to a road that will lead you to the ruins of a city. Khagad'Oth it is called, though once it had a different name. Do not remain there after nightfall!"

Her sightless eyes held Barrett with a singular avidity. He gave his word they would leave the place before dark, though Osmodon appeared reluctant. They would save two days by taking this route, the old woman told them.

"Mad as a mud hen," grunted Osmodon, shaking his head.

Barrett studied the obelisk. The stone was unnaturally cool. He imagined he could hear voices emanating from it, and the horses shied away. Osmodon liked the stone no better than the horses, but was more concerned about the promise Barrett had made.

"You seemed to agree with her readily enough yesterday," Barrett said.

Osmodon shrugged. "Why not, if her delusions gain us an alliance. But this road and Khagad'Oth are both steeped in evil. They say effretes abide there."

"You're afraid of an old wives' tale?"

"And if I am?"

Barrett looked at Osmodon in surprise. The big man was truly worried.

"Makes my skin crawl," Osmodon admitted. "The old woman, those eyes, like milk left too long in the sun, staring like she can see right through you. Now we're on some cursed road heading to a cursed city, for what, to save a day's travel?"

He pointed at the obelisk. "You noticed how the caravan kept shy of it?

Have you touched it? How can stone remain cold in this heat?"

He's right, Barrett thought. The stone was cold when it should have been scorching. And the shadows it cast, they seemed to move.

"Too late to back out now. I gave my word."

"What's a promise to a crazy woman? Wait 'til they're the other side of that dune. We can head back the way we came."

Barrett was tempted. A sense of anxiety had been growing in him ever since the old woman had spoken the name Khagad'Oth. The whole matter disturbed him in ways he couldn't put words to.

A commotion at the rear of the caravan caught his attention. A lone figure on a white horse was riding toward them at full gallop.

"The Emir's son," observed Osmodon, squinting against the glare.

Reining in his rearing horse, Prince Bandar greeted them. "*Uma o'rabia* asked me to tell you that the Bani Attar will be with you at Barad'An in one month. She said you must hold until then, by any means. She said others will come, that you are not alone. May Ahriman be with you."

Without waiting for a response, the young prince spun his horse around and galloped back to the caravan.

"A month," muttered Osmodon darkly. "The Bani Attar can muster at most five hundred men. And we're supposed to hold? Hold what? I told you the old woman was mad."

"You are not alone —."

Barrett, remembering similar words from a man in another world, shrugged. Yet the old woman's message did little to allay his concern.

Without further talk, they mounted their horses and rode west from the obelisk, in the direction of the lowering sun and a line of low chalk hills. For a time they rode in silence, until the sky began to darken. Osmodon had turned uncharacteristically pensive.

"What do you really know about this place?" Barrett asked, trying to lighten the mood.

"Enough to avoid it."

A glum silence followed. Stars appeared in the east.

"It's said that Khagad'Oth was once a center of great learning," said

Osmodon suddenly, as though he had been turning the thought over in his mind. "It was known as *Ain al Arif* then, The Magnet of Wisdom, a place of sorcerers and healers. There was good in their knowledge, but even greater evil."

"Anything to the stories?"

"When I worked for the sheik in Abu Mesina, a rich merchant visited. He told us that once, as a boy, while searching for a goat that had escaped from his father's herd, he'd stumbled upon the place. I still remember the way his hands shook when he spoke of it.

"'Don't leave the road at night,' he said. 'To leave the road at night is death.' Should we ever have the misfortune to visit the place, under no circumstances should we remain after dusk, for it is then that the horror awakens."

"That's what the old woman said."

"Aye. Last night the Emir called her *dol amrick*, your highness. Bandar called her *uma o'rabia*, which means mother number four. Whoever she is, she certainly had them under her thumb."

At first the road was little more than a vague suggestion in the sand. But as they continued forward they began to make out cracked and pitted paving stones. The breeze had picked up, and sheets of sand swirled across the stones, but even in the dimming light the road's outline had become remarkably clear.

Barrett felt a tingling sensation down his back as he urged Greywind forward. It was a strange mix of dread and anticipation. The horse must have felt it as well, for he had begun to shudder, not stopping until all four of his hooves were set firmly on the paving stones.

Osmodon looked down, studying the stones. He opened his mouth as if to speak, then closed it. He might treat werewolves and Uruk war parties with equal aplomb, but talk of anything that smacked of the supernatural clearly made him edgy.

The sun settled behind the chalk hills, only its glow remaining. The wind changed directions, bringing with it an unusual chill. At first it was a welcome relief from the stifling heat, but it soon grew uncomfortable and they donned heavier clothes.

They continued on until the moon was full overhead. The road reflected its light, a white ribbon in a timeless sea. They stopped, dismounting near the remains of a weathered oxcart half buried in sand. Osmodon made quick work of the cart with his axe, using it to build a fire in the center of the road.

They ate a quiet meal, each caught in his own thoughts. The wind had settled into a steady breeze, blowing the smoke from the small fire eastward, away from the hills. The horses chewed on a sparse meal of grain and tribulus. Barrett lay close to the fire, his back to his saddle, his clothes wrapped tightly around him.

Khagad'Oth lay in a shallow canyon just beyond the hills. Osmodon sat, his eyes intent on the desert, sword in hand and axe nearby as if he expected attack at any moment.

Just before he fell asleep Barrett imagined he could hear voices in the soft whisper of the wind, calling him into the desert. But he'd heard such voices before, and they no longer had power over him.

CHAPTER 45

HE WAS AWAKENED BY VOICES.

The fire was little more than embers. A low fog covered the desert in thick patches. The horses stood quietly, their eyes closed as if asleep.

Osmodon stood at the edge of the road. He appeared to be arguing with someone or something further out in the sand. Barrett could almost imagine another figure, shrouded in mist.

Alarmed, he started to call out, but some sixth sense warned him to keep silent. A battle was raging, though of what kind he had no idea. But he was certain that to call out would be his friend's undoing.

Osmodon's face was a mask of anger and pain. "You wasted the best of us in a goose chase!" he cried out. "You gave us to our enemies!"

The shape in the mist seemed to answer, a low whisper, like silk pulled over sand.

Osmodon leaned forward as if to answer, his fists raised in defiance. "You have no right to accuse me! I kept faith! It was you who failed! You who betrayed your people! Your greed, your arrogance! You led your people to their doom, and I'll hear no more!"

With obvious effort he pulled away from the desert, turned his back on whatever was hidden in the mist. For a time the ghostly voice continued to speak, softly, soothingly, then with increasing anger. Osmodon ignored it and returned to the fire.

With a shriek of rage, the mist-thing dissolved, and there was silence.

Osmodon let out a great sigh and his body slumped. Perspiration dripped down his broad brow, droplets glistening in the moonlight. He looked up to see Barrett watching him. "Terrible things," he said. "These ghosts."

"You OK?" Barrett asked.

Osmodon thought for a moment, then nodded. "Never stood up to my father when he was alive. Perhaps if I had things would be different now."

CHAPTER 46

THE MIST AND COLD WERE GONE with the first glimmer of dawn. Osmodon did not speak of his encounter, and Barrett didn't ask, but the big man seemed calm, as though a great tension had left him.

"They attack you where you're weakest." Sianiave had said. Why had the ghost singled out Osmodon? Barrett wondered. Was it simply that he slept too near the edge of the road?

They ate a quick meal and broke camp, anxious to leave the haunted desert behind. The sky was cloudless, the air hot and still. An hour passed, then another, when suddenly the road ended at a high cliff. Below lay the fabled ruins of Khagad'Oth.

From their viewpoint most of Khagad'Oth appeared little more than a series of broken walls and featureless piles of stone. Much was covered in sand, and the mounds that remained revealed only a hint of human design.

Near the center of the canyon, though, a number of larger buildings still held their form. Barrett tried to envision the city as it once had been, not large, for the canyon itself was not large, less than five kilometers long, and narrow. Khagad'Oth existed in striking contrast to the natural forms of the landscape, its man-made structures had been laid out in geometric patterns. He sensed a purpose to the design that went beyond aesthetics.

The road had almost completely eroded where it dropped into the canyon. What remained was little more than a goat track etched into the side of the cliff. Any other time Barrett would have turned back, but to do so now would add days to their journey, days he knew they didn't have.

"Have to walk the horses," said Osmodon. He looked as unhappy at the prospect of descending that broken path as did Barrett.

They started down in single file, Barrett in the lead. Stones dislodged by their passage fell several hundred feet before hitting the valley floor.

Pictographs marked the cliff walls, pecked into the stone. They reminded

Barrett of the carvings at the ferryman's cottage at Ostengarth and the patterns he'd seen in the tile work and tapestries at High House.

Near the bottom the trail passed between the cliff and a large slab that had broken away from the main wall. As he entered the gap between them, Barrett felt the same frisson as he had experienced when Greywind had first stepped foot onto the ancient road.

This time Osmodon felt it too. "A binding," he announced. "There are places that have them naturally. This is no human sorcery."

Unlike Gallian, the canyon was not enclosed. Its western wall was a series of tablelands with openings between them. A shallow riverbed ran through the canyon's center. In ages past it might have been a running stream, but now its bed was choked with thorn bushes and stunted trees.

They rested in the shade at the bottom of the cliff where the road was in better repair. A pair of ravens passed overhead, their glossy black heads cocked toward the intruders. Their caws sounded both welcome and warning.

The horses drank a small amount of water, cupped in Barrett's and Osmodson's hands, then Barrett and Osmodon drank some themselves. When they were refreshed, they mounted again and continued on.

As they approached Khagad'Oth, the structures appeared to be in better condition than they imagined from a distance. Streets and alleyways could be made out. Walls protected from the elements still displayed much of their original plaster, though any color had long ago been bleached white by the sun.

Barrett felt a rightness and harmony about the place completely at odds with its evil reputation. He doubted its architects were the sinister magicians of legend, or that evil brought the city to its end. More likely it was the changing weather and the encroaching desert, though some might argue evil and man-made decay went hand in hand. It wouldn't have been the first civilization to end that way.

"This is something," remarked Osmodon.

They had come to a central square, a five-sided obelisk at its center, its top half laying broken at its base. Fallen walls surrounded the square, though one structure, larger than the rest, appeared almost intact. Its domed roof was at least thirty feet high. The facade was wide and windowless. Marble steps led to a broad gallery lined with broken columns. Two massive metal doors, one partially open, guarded its entrance.

The building was so large that Barrett wondered why they hadn't noticed it from above. "A temple of some sort," he mused.

Osmodon nodded. "Likely. Those doors, bronze, must be worth a king's ransom. Wonder why no one's carted them off."

"They must weigh tons." Barrett wiped a sleeve across his forehead. The heat was intense, reflecting off the sand and bleached stones with the ferocity of a forge. The sun was directly overhead. Even the ravens had sought shelter from its pitiless glare.

The open door of the building looked inviting. It would be cooler inside. They could rest until the stifling heat had subsided.

"We've guests," said Osmodon suddenly. He nodded toward a series of indentations in the sand. They were clearly footprints.

Barrett felt it now, eyes watching them. The horses had grown skittish, their ears cocked. The road was the main access to the square, east and west. If someone was hiding behind those walls, then they had been observing them for some time.

"Through that arch looks clear," suggested Osmodon.

Barrett hesitated. *If they had to flee, west through the arch would be the obvious direction to take. Too obvious. But what were the options? They couldn't go back. Maybe no one was out there. Maybe the feeling of being watched was nothing more than the affect of the heat. Maybe those dimples in the sand had been left by a wandering mountain lion.*

A bloodcurdling cry came from somewhere within the ruins, cutting off Barrett's thoughts, and any hope that they were alone.

Osmodon drew his sword.

The cry was followed by a second, then more and more, until Barrett could no longer count the voices.

They appeared like ghosts, men in ragged robes and blue headdresses, standing on walls and in alleyways. Ten, at least, blocked the way to the arch. Their faces were strangely distorted, scarred by disease and marked with tattoos. Their teeth were filed to sharp points.

Behind them, atop a high wall, stood an old man, his face so corroded it was difficult to make out his features. Only his eyes stood out, gleaming black and malevolent.

The ululating cries became a cacophony. Then, at a gesture from the old man, the men abruptly fell silent.

The old man raised both arms over his head. *"YALA AL FEHUDIN! AL FERENGI AL MAT!"*

"The temple!" cried Barrett, drawing his own sword as he spurred Greywind toward the steps. He felt a sudden sharp pain in his side but was too busy staying in the saddle to worry about it.

The opening between the bronze doors was just wide enough for a horse. Spears, arrows, and rocks followed them like a hailstorm.

Barrett was first through, followed closely by Osmodon. He leapt from his saddle, slapping Greywind on the rump to move him away from the deadly rain of missiles.

They were in a large antechamber, its recesses shrouded in darkness, the floor covered in mounds of grit. A rock skinned Barrett's ear, and he ducked behind one of the doors. The door moved as his shoulder fell against it.

"Ozzy! Give me a hand!"

Immediately Osmodon ran to his aid. With both their weights against it the massive door gave way, swinging shut with an echoing boom. The room was pitched into darkness, the impenetrable dark of a tomb.

"Too easy," said Osmodon. "You'd think someone oiled the hinges."

Then they heard a strange rustling sound above them. Barrett looked up, but in the darkness could see nothing. The air was bitter with the caustic odor of ammonia mixed with the smell of sheared copper. Outside they could hear the muffled cries of their attackers, the ringing thumps of their weapons hitting the metal doors.

There was one last, trilling cry, then silence.

"They're leaving," said Barrett, with more hope than confidence.

"Probably the smell," muttered Osmodon dryly.

Barrett had his own thoughts. *Was there another entrance? Were their attackers even now stalking them in the dark?*

The horses were shifting about, nervously. Barrett put his hand on Greywind's shoulder. *They're frightened of something. Not the men outside. Both are trained warhorses. What are they afraid of? What is that eerie rustling?*

There was a spark and a metallic snap as Osmodon struck his flint. With the third spark his traveling lamp came to life. "A little light on the subject does wonders, as my nanny used to say."

The first thing Barrett noticed was the floor. The mounds of grit weren't sand. The substance was damp and stuck to his boots. It was also the color of dried blood.

He suddenly remembered where he'd encountered that smell before. *A cave, somewhere, a training mission.*

"Bats!"

"These aren't bats," said Osmodon grimly. He held the lamp higher. Above, clustered against the dome of the ceiling, were hundreds of huge, tick-like creatures. Birds or animals, Barrett couldn't tell. Whatever they were, they made the hair on the back of his neck stand up.

"Blood kites," said Osmodon.

"Are they dangerous?" Barrett knew it was a foolish question even as he asked.

"If a thing that flies in swarms large enough to blacken the sky and can pick a camel down to bone in a matter of minutes isn't dangerous, then I don't know what is."

Osmodon lowered the lamp. "Kites only feed at night. Explains why our friends outside aren't trying harder. Probably figure us as good as dead."

Every now and then one of the kites would lose its hold and drop, floating in the air for a brief moment before fluttering upward to find another hold.

Osmodon handed Barrett the lamp. "Let's get that arrow out of you. Makes me uneasy."

"Arrow?" Startled, Barrett looked down to see the shaft of an arrow sticking just below his rib cage.

Osmodon studied the arrow for a moment, then, with a single quick movement, grabbed hold of the shaft and yanked it out.

"Ow! You might have warned me!"

"Don't be a goose. It wasn't deep. See. Clean. No poison." Osmodon held the arrow up. The head was chipped obsidian. Blood covered no more than an inch.

He tossed the arrow aside and rummaged through to his saddlebag, bringing out a small jar and some strips of bandages. "Beeswax and goat grease, with some of Sianiave's powders thrown in. Lift that shirt up."

As Barrett held his shirt up, Osmodon rubbed a sticky green salve on the wound. "Not much bleeding. I've patched worse with this stuff. Be right as rain in a day or two."

When he finished he put the jar back in his saddlebag and retrieved his lamp. Barrett lowered his shirt. The salve had stopped the bleeding, and what little pain there had been was gone.

The kites were becoming more active. Ray-like, with barbed tails, their eyes and eel-like mouths were on the underside of flat, heavily veined bodies. For the moment at least, they took no notice of the men.

"Our friends outside will want to be in their caves before nightfall," said Osmodon, thinking out loud. "Kites hunt by scent. It's been windy the past few evenings. If we ride with the wind we should be safe enough. We'll have to wait 'til dusk."

"Maybe there's another way out. There's a passage."

"Fair enough."

The horses in tow, they crossed the room and entered a long corridor. Once out of the kite chamber the horses seemed to calm. Barrett saw that the floor of the passageway, though dusty, was free of dung.

Out of habit he counted his steps; forty, sixty, at eighty the passage ended at the top of a narrow flight of steps leading down into more darkness.

"Doesn't likely lead to a back door," commented Osmodon doubtfully.

"Can't hurt to look. Besides, we've got a few hours 'til dusk. It's better than sitting in a pile of kite dung, waiting for them to attack."

"You have a point."

They left the horses at the top of the stairs. Barrett counted twenty-nine, set with black marble. He smelled the improbable, though not unpleasing, scent of lemon, a relief from the dung heaps. The silence was almost total.

They entered another vaulted room. As Osmodon raised his lamp to get a better look, Barrett had a sickening impulse to bolt and run.

"Hold there, lad," said Osmodon, grabbing his arm. "What's wrong? You look like you've seen a ghost."

Barrett took a breath and let it out. "No. No . . . it's OK. I'm fine."

But he wasn't fine. He was as close to panic as he'd ever been.

The room was perhaps thirty feet in diameter, with no other way in or out, and no place for an enemy to hide. Like the kite chamber it had a domed ceiling, though this one was tiled a vibrant blue. The marble floor tiles formed a large enneagon identical to the one on the council table at High House. The figure was enclosed in a border of alternating black-and-white tiles.

Barrett's panic began to ease, though he had to force himself to take a step forward. Each step took increasing effort as he neared the center of the room, as if an actual physical force was attempting to hold him back. But with each step came an increasing sense of expectancy, of something momentous about to happen.

He put a foot on the green tile marking both the center of the room and the center of the enneagon. Relaxing, he took another deep breath and turned back to Osmodon.

But Osmodon wasn't there. Instead he faced a blinding pillar of light, so ferociously bright the pain it caused drove him to his knees.

"NO! NO! IT ISN'T TIME! I'M NOT READY!"

The light had vanished, the pain with it.

He opened his eyes. *Had they been closed?*

He floated weightless in an ink black sea under a dark sky littered with stars. It was impossible to tell where the sea ended and the sky began.

A small constellation, set at the apex of the dome, drew his attention. The stars drew together, merged into a lattice, a tetrahedron pulsing with color. It descended, engulfed him with light, and lifted him up.

This was death, and yet, not death. He felt no fear. He was on a craft, a chariot that was carrying him through time and space.

He saw terrible things, battles through all of time, visions of death and destruction, men killing with stone axes, mobs fleeing burning cities, sailors throwing themselves into the sea as fleets of ships were destroyed by cannon fire, squadrons of flying machines using beams of light to boil the oceans and turn the Earth into molten slag.

And just as the images became too much to bare, the landscape altered once again. Barrett looked down on Khagad'Oth, seeing it no longer as a ruin, but as it had been, a timeless place, hidden and protected from the world, perfect and eternal. He saw himself at the center of a great pattern, a labyrinth whose luminous lines reached out into the infinite.

And as he followed these lines back to the stars, the stars merged into a singular point of radiance that took the form of a woman.

But before she revealed her face, a shadow descended.

CHAPTER 47

West Arden Forest, May 29

SIANIAVE WAS TROUBLED. Things had been going amiss ever since the morghul had appeared at Langton Manor, and she wasn't sure why. She was aware that she and her companions were moving through an amorphous cusp. She was old enough to have experienced the previous one—when reason had become the predominant mode of thought. There had been unrest then as well, but nothing to equal the difficulties that now faced them.

The ethereal world was out of balance. Reason and logic seemed to be stuck on the same narrow path, at the risk of losing it all. But Sianiave suspected a deeper and darker cause, a shadow player using reason for its own purposes, manipulating reason's weaknesses of arrogance and gullibility.

Waning sunlight cast amber beams through the forest. She'd been nineteen hours in the saddle, twenty the day before. Her recuperative powers were far beyond those of most men, but even she had her limits, as did Phaeton, the white stallion Bronwyn had provided for her journey.

Marduk was still two days off, the only place on the continent where the dragon lines met in the appropriate configuration. She found herself thinking of that other Earth and how its technological marvels could have whisked her to Marduk in an hour.

Such clever technology was, of course, impossible here. And she was concerned with the rapid and unexpected advancement she'd witnessed on her last visit to the other Earth. She'd had the distinct impression the science was being seeded. If so, who was doing the seeding, and for what purpose? Better to give a five-year-old child a bucket of gunpowder and a box of matches.

She doubted it was the lizards. They were evil brutes. Just the thought of them turned her stomach. But they were also slow to change and relatively crude in their thinking. Such a refined strategy as she sensed here was beyond them. In this they were a great deal like the morghul.

Shared patrimony? She'd heard stories, of course, the legends and myths, had read many of the ancient writings. When she had more time, she would look into that.

Should she fail here, that other Earth might have to be written off. The thought saddened her. Despite the growing foulness that engulfed it, there was much about it she would miss.

The ancient track she'd been following passed through a meadow where a small stream ran. She dismounted, allowing the stallion a long drink before tethering him to a tree near some long grass. She removed the saddle and travel bags, then rubbed him down with the saddle blanket.

Phaeton was an extraordinary horse, fire in his grey-green eyes. Even in her long life she'd seen few to match him. Bronwyn had been generous in offering him, but then Bronwyn was as aware of the stakes as she. Gallian couldn't stand alone.

She built a small fire, cooking a wild hen she'd killed earlier. When she finished eating she set out her blankets, stuck her sword and dagger in the soft earth within easy reach, and lay down. This night she was determined to get a good night's sleep.

Time passed, yet sleep eluded her. None of the mind quieting techniques she knew helped, even her personal favorite of matching names to the stars overhead. Eventually she gave up.

She withdrew her pipe, tamped the dried *suph* into the bowl, and lit it.

A wolf howled in the distance. The cry held no menace, for it was not one of the shape-shifting kind. Moments later its call was answered by its mate.

Pebbles rattled in the stream. A brace of rabbits hopped past, searching for cover. Moments later the dark shape of an owl passed overhead. Nearby, Phaeton continued to munch quietly on the grass.

An omen, owls. Psychopomps, like ravens and coyotes. Messengers from the nether world, worshipped in some cultures, considered evil in others, a harbinger of death.

So many years she'd been at this. And now it appeared all was drawing to a climax. Did this include her own life as well?

It was worth considering. Part of her early training had been to travel to the moment of her own death. She'd forgotten much of what she'd seen that night, so long ago, though she knew when it was time the memory would be there. At this moment death did not feel particularly imminent. The way things were changing there wasn't much you could count on anymore, even mystical visions.

Sianiave rarely dwelt on the past. There was too much pain, too many people, places, and times once loved, now gone. Yet the memories were there, many of that other Earth. Sitting on the steps of the Parthenon, debating virtue with that wise little man Socrates, that year in old Jerusalem, learning the secrets of the *merkaba* from the Brothers of the Chariot, the warm evenings in Baghdad's House of Wisdom, smoking hashish and discussing the nature of reality with the savants of Haroun al-Rashid. In Toledo she recalled the ecstasy of the Mirror Dance; years later in the orient the satisfaction of studying with such incomparable masters as Hodo-kai, Dr. Shei, and Sensei Ueshiba.

Some of her most prized memories, however, were of more commonplace things. Lunch on Paris' Left Bank, drinking the good house red and watching the throng pass by, late nights at the old Blue Note, listening to Charlie Parker practice his rifts.

It had always surprised her how very little she had changed over time. Her essence hardly seemed to have changed at all.

She still enjoyed life's pleasures. And she still loved, which was perhaps the greatest surprise of all. She'd had countless lovers, most were gone from memory. But she'd been in love only three times, and those loves were etched deep in her soul.

She leaned back against the oak to which Phaeton was tethered, inhaling a lungful of smoke. A meteor arced overhead, its blue and gold trail vivid against the onyx sky.

Another omen?

A fish jumped in the stream. A warm breeze, smelling of pine, tickled the tree leaves. Phaeton snorted contentedly.

For a moment, all seemed at peace, a feeling all too rare these days. The binding on the other Earth was broken. Chaos was in the shifting winds.

She found herself mouthing the words to a poem by Yeats,

Turning and turning in the widening gyre
The Falcon cannot hear the falconer;
Things fall apart; the centre cannot hold;
Mere anarchy is loosed upon the world,
The blood-dimmed tide is loosed, and everywhere
The ceremony of innocence is drowned;
The best lack all convictions, while the worst
Are full of passionate intensity . . .
The darkness drops again; but now I know
That twenty centuries of stony sleep
Were vexed to nightmare by a rocking cradle,
And what rough beast, its hour come round at last,
Slouches toward Bethlehem to be born?

Was she right in this pursuit? Artos had left Barad'An with a formidable force. Such a large company did not just vanish without word or sign.

She'd known him in his youth, knew of his dream, a new city, a new kingdom, safe from the encroaching storm.

Cuchulain had ridiculed him, calling his dream unmanly, even treasonous. Because of her close relationship with his grandfather, Artos had distanced himself from her as well.

She missed Osmodon, and she was anxious about Barrett, but Barrett had to face his challenge alone, without her support. The ordeal that awaited him was beyond the capacity of most to understand.

Had there been time, had she taken time, the shock could have been lessened. But the depth to which that Earth had fallen in just twenty years had caught her off guard, its tools of mind control grown unbelievably more subtle and efficient.

Phaeton snorted again, stamping his hoof as if to distract her. Even from so distant a place as this, she knew her thoughts could reach Barrett, and interfere.

She took another puff of the calming smoke and began naming stars.

CHAPTER 48

"BREATHE!"

The word was simple, primal in its power. Barrett took a deep breath, choked, and opened his eyes. A face formed amid the emptiness of space, and with it recognition.

Osmodon!

"Thank you," was all he could say, or perhaps he didn't say it, only felt it, immense gratitude, gratitude to Osmodon for bringing him back from the desperate loneliness of nonbeing.

"You had me worried, lad. You stopped breathing there for a time."

They were in the kite chamber. Osmodon must have carried him there. The rustling of the kites had grown noticeably louder, and the light through the now open door was grey and dim. Nearby the horses were saddled and wary, anxious to be gone from that place.

"We haven't much time," said Osmodon, helping him stand. "Our friends outside have gone."

The world still did not seem quite real. Looking about he imagined he could actually see through the building's stone walls. Dusk was settling outside, and the ancient streets were empty. A hot breeze blew sand across the cobblestones. Greywind nudged Barrett with his head, as if to hurry him up.

"The kites are waking! Can you ride?"

Barrett hesitated. Could he ride? His body seemed to be functioning well enough. "Yeah. I can ride, little woozy is all."

He took the reins. Osmodon caught him when his foot slipped in the stirrup, helping him into the saddle. "The wind is right, out of the east. If we survive this I'll give a year's tithe to Asgar!"

Even as Osmodon spoke a kite dropped from the ceiling with a blood-chilling screech and landed on his back. He ripped it off before it could sink its fangs, slicing it in two with his sword, then quickly swung into his own saddle.

"Time to go!"

Another kite dropped from above, fastening its claws into Greywind's neck. Greywind screamed and Barrett tore it free, slamming its squirming form against the doorway as the big horse bolted through.

Greywind took the lead with Osmodon's mount close behind. They passed down the steps and through the ruined city at full gallop. Dusk was lowering into night, and overhead stars were appearing. Behind them came a sound like a great wind, but Barrett didn't look back. It took all of his effort just to stay in the saddle.

They rode until the horses began to tire. Only then did they slow their pace. When Barrett did look back it appeared as if a dark cloud was rising out of the ruins. But it headed northeast, and away from them.

Osmodon straightened in his saddle. "Asgar will get that tithe I promised."

The horses were heaving, and their mouths foaming. "What now?" asked Barrett. "The horses are done in."

"I suggest we keep on, riding easy. I would be quit of this canyon. I reckon if the horses could talk, they'd agree."

"You'll get no argument from me, not if it gets us to Barad'An sooner."

"Barad'An? Not Gallian?" Osmodon looked over in surprise.

"Barad'An. Ren's there."

"Ren? Why would she go back? How could—?" Osmodon studied Barrett's face a long moment, then nodded. "Barad'An it is."

CHAPTER 49

Men'leth Hills,
South Arden Forest
June 3

BARRETT NEEDED REST. It had been over a week since they'd fled Khagad'Oth, riding hard, with little sleep. He said little about his experience there. Much of it was beyond words.

Five days ago they'd seen a dust cloud rising in the north. Osmodon guessed it to be the Sirdar's army, already nearing Gallian. He estimated it would be no more than three weeks before Barad'An itself was under siege.

The Great Eastern Road lay to the north of them. To save time and to avoid the Sirdar's army they'd ridden directly west from the ruined city, following a little used trail the old woman had described. That morning they'd entered the Men'leth Hills, marking Arden Forest's southern border. There the trail had grown vague and steep, often forcing them to walk the horses.

"You know," said Barrett after a difficult incline, "I never asked what *you* saw back there, before you woke me up."

"You screamed. You were tearing at your face like the kites had you. I started to help and—."

Osmodon looked puzzled. "That's all I remember. I must have fallen asleep. When I awoke you were on your knees, staring at what I couldn't say, but no longer fearful, more in wonderment. I hauled you up the stairs, threw you across Greywind, and hurried back to the kite chamber. By that time the kites were waking, and the horses were going mad. I had to wrap their eyes so they would mind me."

"I saw things, Ozzy, terrible things—."

Barrett stopped. The trail had suddenly veered to the left, then leveled off. They had reached the summit.

"Barad'An?"

"Aye," said Osmodon quietly. "The old lady herself."

They stood for a long moment, not speaking, for the sight was breathtaking. Beyond the mountains and forest, circled by a plain of emerald grass, stood Barad'An, once empress of the world. Her massive walls appeared to be seamless and sloped slightly inward, with battlements at the top and watchtowers at regular intervals. The outer wall stretched six miles in either direction from a central gate, which stood open.

The sun was setting in the west, and high clouds cast a glow on the city. Barrett could imagine her walls to be made of pure gold. Beyond he could see the towers and tiled roofs of palaces and temples, hostelries, and public halls.

The Great North Road had been laid straight as an arrow to the great gate. It was bordered with oaks, and paved with multicolored stones.

Osmodon sighed. "She's still beautiful, but don't be taken in by her looks. That field that surrounds her was once a town in itself, destroyed by raids, warfare, and dwindling trade. Her walls are still high and strong, but not as they once were. A keen eye can find many faults.

"Skilled masons are in short supply, repairs costly. But her greatest weakness is the lack of defenders. Forty-eight towers once housed a hundred and eight men each. Now they're empty, or mostly so."

"How do you suggest we get in?"

Osmodon grinned. "The gate's open, lad. Should anyone ask, we've come to offer our services. I assume the priest will welcome new recruits, especially two good fighting men such as ourselves."

They mounted their horses and started down the trail. "There's an inn," Osmodon reflected, "the Golden Dawn. Strongest ale and prettiest wenches in Anor, and the best gossip. If you're right, and Ren is here, we'll find out soon enough."

It was late afternoon by the time they reached the road. The air stank of decay. "I've no good feeling about this," muttered Osmodon. "I know that smell."

Barrett too recognized the smell, the cloying stench of death. Its source soon became all too apparent. The great oaks that lined the road were filled with corpses, some spiked to the trunks, others hanging from the limbs like some hideous fruit. Many appeared recent, while others were clearly weeks old, their skulls stripped of flesh by the swarms of crows. What from a distance Barrett saw as multicolored paving stones, he now saw to be stains of blood and offal.

Osmodon's face was a mask. "I can't abide this stench. Let's ride in the field."

The air was still. Even in the open field the smell followed them. Grim purpose had settled over both men. For Barrett the walls before them no longer looked golden, but red and bloody.

No trumpets sounded their approach as they neared the gate. No soldiers came out to greet them. They were halfway through the gate tunnel when the first challenge came. "Halt! State your allegiance and your business!"

An aged pikeman in a tattered white cloak blocked the tunnel. A red cross decorated his breast. Half a dozen white-cloaked ruffians lolled against the walls, their garments hastily fashioned of dirty cloth. Several carried tankards, which they passed back and forth with ill-natured humor.

"We've come for employment," said Osmodon. "We've heard you're in need of good fighting men."

"Pike, 'em, Willy," cried a sallow-faced drunk. "Send 'em to hell with the rest of the heathen trash!"

"Yeah, Willy," cried another. "Show 'em that pike you're always bragging about."

"Mercenaries, are ye?" growled the old man, ignoring the taunts. "Be ye heathens or believers?"

"Oh, believers, most certainly," said Osmodon.

The old man squinted, clearly skeptical. "Be ye heathens, you will burn in hell. If ye speak the truth, there'll be a place for ye. But ye won't get an audience until after the occasion."

"Occasion? And what occasion would that be?"

"Why the wedding, of course. Ye haven't heard?"

"Not a wit."

"Ye haven't come for the drink, then? Perhaps ye'r true after all."

"Aye, true we are. But this wedding—someone highborn?"

"The highest." The old man squared his shoulders. "The Lord Glays will wed Princess Gwyndolyn come morning."

Barrett blanched. "Wed? Ren? That's impos—!"

"A great occasion, indeed!" interrupted Osmodon quickly, shooting Barrett a dark look.

"Aye. Lord Glays has ordered three days of festivities, free drink to all off-duty templars." The old man cast a frown of disapproval at the soldiers lining the walls. "Though it's become impossible to say who's off duty and who's on.

Then, to Osmodon, "Perhaps you know something of soldiering yourself, sirrah," he added quietly. Then louder. "Enter, if you will. We've orders to be lenient to travelers during the festivities."

Barrett, still choking down his outrage, followed Osmodon into the city. "It can't be true! Ren would never—."

"Enough!" grunted Osmodon without turning his head. "We aren't out of it yet. Look around you."

They had entered a large plaza. Cobbled streets branched off it in six directions. Templars were everywhere, drinking in doorways, leaned against walls, seated on fountains where no water ran but their own.

Coarse laughter echoed from the taverns and alleyways. A few of the more sober men regarded the pair with narrowed eyes. Others gave them an incurious glance before continuing with their drinking. Most were armed with daggers or pikes, though many carried nothing more than clubs or rude spears.

The cobbles were littered with trash and offal. The windows in dozens of shops were shattered, the shops looted of wares. Feral dogs pawed through garbage, occasionally breaking into fights over a piece of trash. What few of the citizenry they saw were either old women or men too stooped with age to be of use as soldiers.

"Look at the bright side," whispered Osmodon. "We've made it into the city, and we know for certain she's here. Not that I doubted, mind you."

"But I tell you, Ren would not . . ."

"Don't speak her name! Of course she wouldn't, not willingly. There's something we're missing. In any case it seems we've arrived just in time."

Osmodon was thoughtful. "Look at them. Undisciplined, untrained, and ill armed. Do you see preparations for a siege? The priest must know the Sirdar's army is headed his way. Does he think the walls enough to save him?"

Barrett was forced to agree. There was a commotion as a fight broke out among the soldiers gathered around a chandlery. It ended quickly when one smashed his tankard over the other man's head, knocking him unconscious.

They turned off the main street and down an alley so narrow the opposite walls could be touched with outstretched arms. A block later the alley opened up on another plaza. Judging by the wooden booths at its center Barrett guessed it had once been a market square. Now the booths were as empty as the streets, not a soul in sight, not even a drunken soldier.

Streetlamps remained dark. With lengthening shadows the streets had become sinister. What few lights there were shone from behind closed shutters and curtains. It reminded Barrett too much of Ardendell.

They came to a five-storied building just off the square. Wooden balconies hung below the upper windows. The sign over the front door showed a sunburst, its face and rays painted in gold leaf against a maroon field. They had arrived at the Golden Dawn.

A smaller sign, handwritten and tacked to the door read: *Closed. No provisions. The Management.*

Swearing, Osmodon dismounted. "Hells! Probably the first time in a thousand years they've closed their doors."

Barrett had been looking forward to a good meal and a night's rest. "What now?"

"There are other inns, though none so hospitable as the Dawn. It's where I met Sianiave, you know. I still remember—."

"Who speaks of the Lady Sianiave?!"

The hoarse whisper startled them, coming out of the darkness as it did. Barrett drew his sword, turning to see a man standing in the shadows. There was a long sword in his hand, which he carried with an easy familiarity.

Osmodon drew his own sword and dismounted. "Who asks?"

The man gave a sudden laugh and stepped forward into the light. "Osmodon of Linsraden! With that block of a body, it can be no one else!"

"Bors?"

Bors sheathed his sword and grabbed up Osmodon in a great hug. "Gods, it's good to see you, Osmodon. Of all of us, you were the last I expected to come."

"Bors, why are you here? We'd assumed every knight worthy of the name had left this place, or is on the oaks yonder."

"You're not far wrong. But first things first, the priest's spies are everywhere. We're lucky tonight that most of them are drunk." The knight eyed Barrett. "Your companion? He can be trusted?"

"With your life."

"It is with my life, and many others. Come with me. We'll attend to introductions later. Quickly."

The knight led them to a small door near the larger stable doors. He knocked three times, the knocks evenly spaced. The door opened immediately, and they were quickly ushered in by several hands. Someone struck a flint, and a lantern flared to life.

They found themselves in a large enclosed courtyard with a stack of hay in the center. Stalls made up three of the four walls. Three other men were present, a stoop shouldered man who carried the lantern and two teenage boys who took the reins of their horses.

"Andy and Adelph will see to your horses. Grab your kits. We can talk inside. By your looks you could use could use a drink and a bite to eat."

"The sign said the inn was closed."

"To keep the soldiers away. Buffoons they may be, but they're raiding the city. Gastain was taken. He refused service to anyone wearing the white cloak. Giselle hung the sign the same day."

"Gastain taken? Dead?"

"We don't know. Many are hanging on the oaks. Others are taken to the dungeon. I'm not at all certain which is worse."

They followed Bors and the old man through a door, then down a hall and into the common room. There were two lamps lit and much of the room was in shadows. There was a bar and numerous tables, all empty.

Bors seated them at a circular table under one of the lamps. The old man hung his lantern on a nearby hook and vanished, returning moments later with three tankards of ale.

"Gregory has worked at the Dawn for ninety-three years," Bors explained once the old man had vanished again. "He'll bring food. In the meantime we'd best trade tales. Your friend here, to start."

"Barrett of Amra, meet Sir Bors Graalwyth, one of the greatest knights of Barad'An and a good friend."

"Honored," said Barrett.

"I've not heard of . . . Amra, did you say? A land to the south?"

Osmodon took a long drink of ale, wiping his beard with the back of his hand. "Sir Barrett is from beyond the White Mountains."

Bors looked at Barrett in surprise. "Beyond the White Mountains? A long way to travel, indeed."

"Indeed," said Barrett. He drank. The ale was good, delicious after the long journey.

The knight regarded him for a long moment, opened his mouth as if to say something, then, thinking better of it, turned back to Osmodon. "You received the word, no doubt. Tell me, is Sianiave with you?"

"She is elsewhere. The lad and I've been traveling. It's been weeks since we've heard word of anything."

"Then why did you come here, to the Dawn, on this day and at this time?"

"Happenstance, it would appear. Though I suspect your waiting outside in the dark has something to do with it."

"Aye. Though I was not waiting outside. The boys saw you and summoned me."

"You were expecting someone?"

"Hoping is the better word. You have heard of the marriage the priest has planned for the morrow?"

Barrett tensed, but held his tongue.

"Only this evening," said Osmodon, nodding. "When we entered the city. It seemed unlikely, to say the least."

"Ren arrived last week with Aerindir. He was arrested immediately and taken to the dungeon. We've heard nothing of him since, though I suspect he's still alive, at least until the wedding. That rat-faced magician of Glays' runs the dungeon now. What tales we hear would give nightmares to a crow."

"She came willingly? Ren, I mean?"

Bors gave Barrett a curious look. "Willingly enough, though when Aerindir was dragged off she fought. It's said the priest threatened to kill her loved ones unless she returned."

Osmodon nodded. "It's as we thought."

"We can't let it happen, of course. I sent word that all knights still loyal and free should meet here tonight, at the Golden Dawn."

"How many have arrived?"

Bors hesitated, then clapped Osmodon on the arm and said, "So far? Two."

CHAPTER 50

"AERINDIR'S DONE NOTHING WRONG," said Ren, struggling to keep her voice even. "Release him and I'll give you no more trouble. At least allow him to attend the wedding."

Glays lowered the scroll he'd been reading and looked at her in surprise. "Done nothing wrong? My dear, he's a traitor. How would it look if he were to go free?"

His puzzlement appeared so sincere Ren wondered if he'd actually begun to believe his own lies.

She knew it was hopeless when she came to him, but she had to make the effort. She heard the rumors about the dungeons, and suspected she was meant to hear them, to keep her in line. Aerindir wasn't the only one of her friends being held in that foul pit.

"It can do you no harm. He's faithful to me, and I'll keep my word."

She hated lying, but it was a small matter considering her intent to kill the man. She remembered one of the Sister's aphorisms. *"The definition of a fool is someone who tells the truth to a liar."*

Glays appeared to lose interest in her pleas and set the scroll on a table. "If he's found innocent, the proceedings will have a favorable outcome. When you commence your wifely duties, we can discuss the matter further."

Wifely duties! That was it. Ren's control broke. "You arrogant, evil pig!"

She struck at him, but Glays caught her hand inches before it reached his face. He twisted her arm, forcing her to her knees. As she struggled to free herself he landed a blow that sent her sprawling backward to the floor.

"Speak to me again like that and Gothmog will cut off Aerindir's feet. You both can watch while the dogs have them for play."

He'd spoken equably, without apparent anger, but Ren did not doubt he would do exactly as he said.

"Spare her face, m'lord," remarked Gothmog dryly. "There is a wedding in the morning, if you recall."

The magician had been watching from the doorway. It mattered not to him if the fool cut the girl's throat, but there was more involved. If this farce of a wedding was to play out correctly it wouldn't do to have the bride's face looking like stew meat. Nor did he think Belliol would appreciate it. For some reason the master wanted the girl delivered unscathed.

Ren remained still. It wasn't the blow that had shaken her as much as her lack of self-control. Letting her anger show was a weakness.

He'd provoked her, of course. The question was, had he done so deliberately? Was his insouciant manner an act designed to force her off balance? Was he that clever?

She took a trembling breath. So much depended on her. If she'd known what she knew now she would not have returned.

Tomorrow. Tomorrow it would be ended—one way or another.

The thought gave her strength. She wiped blood from her bruised lip and struggled to her feet. She lowered her head so he wouldn't see the hatred in her eyes.

"Apologies, my—lord—." The words choked in her throat. "It's only that Aerindir has been my good friend, and I wish no harm to come to him."

Glays stared at her as if trying to gauge the truth of her words. He pursed his lips, and with some hesitation said, "Good."

He adjusted the heavy gold cross around his neck. "You'll make new friends, my dear. Be a good girl and we'll consider your friend's release. It would not be seemly for you to visit him on the oaks."

Ren had seen the bodies of the poor wretches along the road. She hadn't looked too closely for fear she would recognize someone she knew.

She swore to kill this man, or die in the attempt. But her confidence was shaken. They'd taken her dagger when she arrived, but the poison meant for its tip was hidden with her toiletries.

A knife, a needle, anything with a point or an edge would do. That was her task now, to find a weapon.

Glays clapped his hands. A woman appeared and bowed. "My lord?"

Her name was Nadwyn. She was introduced as Ren's new handmaiden but was, in truth, her jailer. Meg, her handmaiden since birth, was being held in the dungeon. This woman was as tall as a man, with short cropped hair. She wore a stern grey dress with a black stitching. Her narrow black eyes regarded Ren's bruised face without comment.

"Take the Princess Gwyndolyn back to her chamber. She's had a fall."

The priest picked up the scroll, as if his mind were already on other matters. The woman took Ren's arm, her strong fingers digging painfully into the muscle. "Come with me, Princess."

Ren detested her. She had no doubt she could best her in a fight, despite the woman's formidable appearance, but now was not the time. Feigning weakness, she allowed herself to be led from the room.

After the girl had gone, Gothmog stepped forward. "She'll murder you first chance she gets," he said.

Glays seemed honestly amused. "Oh, come now. You don't understand women. Their deepest need is to subjugate themselves to a man's power. She fights it now, like a young mare fighting the bridle. But she'll learn."

"If you say so, M'lord."

The magician kept his thoughts from showing. The priest was oblivious to the real danger the girl presented. His assumptions, his ideology, made it impossible for him to take any woman seriously.

But counseling the priest was no longer Gothmog's concern. In three weeks' time, fewer if the stars were favorable, he would no longer have to put up with the preening dolt. Barad'An was damaged beyond redemption. His own success was at hand. In a very short time the priest would be irrelevant.

"The preparations are coming along, I trust?" Glays asked, picking up another scroll. A list of wedding guests, Gothmog saw.

Since Cuchulain's death the priest had grown more aloof, more self-involved. Other than the wedding, little interested him. He made no effort to attend to affairs of the city, leaving those matters in the hands of lesser clerics. With his talk of an alliance, rather than the agreed-upon vassal-ship, it was unlikely he planned to honor the bargain with the Sirdar, yet he'd done nothing to prepare for the city's defense. Maybe he truly believed this god of his would save him, but it was more likely the man was slipping into madness.

For Gothmog, either way would end the same. If Glays honored the bargain to turn the city over to the Sirdar's general, so be it. If he chose defiance, what matter? With Barad'An so weakened it would be impossible to mount a serious defense.

"Preparations for the wedding are well in hand," Gothmog said out loud. "The hall is ready, as you ordered."

"Musicians?"

"Yes, m'lord."

"Excellent. Come with us, then. We wish your opinion on a new robe I've acquired for the wedding. It is from the east."

Gothmog dutifully followed Glays to his dressing chamber, though in his mind he was already anticipating nightfall. Guardsmen patrolling the forest had brought in a young man, a stable boy from the north. He was strong, naive and, most importantly, in excellent health.

Gothmog decided his last subject must have been tainted. This new one should be perfect.

CHAPTER 51

THE GOLDEN DAWN'S COMMON ROOM was easily twice the size as that of the Lion and Unicorn's, though much of it was now lost in shadow. Light shone from behind the kitchen doors, but Gregory had not yet returned.

"It began the day the king was murdered," said Bors, glancing over his shoulder toward the kitchen doors. Barrett couldn't tell if Bors was concerned that they might be overheard or impatient that the food was taking so long.

"They call it the 'cleansing,' a nasty name for butchery. Those unwilling to pledge their allegiance to the priest and his god are either imprisoned, or—."

Bors stopped, his jaw tight. "You've seen the oaks."

"How many knights still live?" asked Osmodon.

"Difficult to say. Some survived the assassins and escaped into the forest. Squire Belarane, Lord Claymore, Yvon Branch and his sons, Dorset and Banks, all are dead. You tell me Abdelar is also passed, a grievous loss. He was the best of us."

"You say some are held captive."

"It's impossible to know how many rot down there. Parsifal, Pelidon, and others were taken—and a dozen captains, most recently Aerindir."

Barrett looked up in concern. "Where is she now? Ren, I mean?" Barrett tried not to let his worry show.

"Prisoner in her own chambers, by accounts." Bors slammed his fist on the table. "Dammit! You know she's our last, best hope!"

Barrett and Osmodon exchanged glances. "You hinted you've a plan," said Osmodon.

Bors picked up his flagon, then set it down again without drinking. "Aye. Such as it is. We were hoping for more than the two of you to show tonight."

"There's time yet. How many men does the priest command?"

"Three thousand, at least, with more arriving every day, greedy for spoils. Some few even believe his fairy tales."

"How many can we count on?"

Bors looked at the two men, then smiled. It was not a pleasant smile. "Let's just say your arrival has more than doubled our current complement of knights."

There was a moment while this sunk in. Then Osmodon laughed. "We're it? We three?"

"Bleak odds, admittedly. But not so bad as it appears. There is support among the common folk, like those you've met tonight."

Bors' hand clenched the handle to his tankard, and he drank.

The kitchen door flew open and Gregory arrived with a platter of food—a pot of dense beef stew, bread, and cored apples. A boy carried bowls, napkins, and spoons. For a moment conversation abated as the bowls were filled.

Three against three thousand.

Barrett sorted his thoughts. Bors was neither as tall as himself nor as broad as Osmodon, still the man exuded strength. Balding and sunburnt, with a large, ragged cicatrix down the right side of his muscular neck, Barrett guessed him to be in his late forties, though from recent experience he knew better than to make assumptions.

Bors tore off a piece of bread, passing the loaf to Osmodon. "Few of the templars are real fighting men, farmers, dandies from Meridor, brigands, and freebooters alike. With this holiday the priests declared, half are drunk, the other half doing their best to get drunk."

"What of the Sirdar's army?" Osmodon asked. "It will be at the gate within a month. They aren't prepared. The wall is unmanned, the soldiers are poorly armed. Is the priest unaware of this?"

"He speaks of the Sirdar's approach with disregard. He says his god will protect him."

Osmodon dipped his bread into his stew and chewed. "Sounds like Megida to me."

"Who's Megida?" Barrett asked. The name seemed familiar, but he couldn't place it.

"Not who, lad, what. Megida's a city, or was. Its walls were not nearly so great as Barad'An's, yet still it was thought to be impregnable. It was the seat of the House of Seven Worlds, where the sorcerers of the Brotherhood were taught. Yet this current Sirdar's father took it as easily as picking ripe fruit."

"It's always been suspected it fell to treachery," said Bors.

"The priest's magician, Gothmog, was an acolyte then," said Osmodon, taking another bite of bread. "Sianiave said he was excommunicated for practicing necromancy. It's why she holds him in such contempt. He's an evil little worm."

Bors nodded thoughtfully. "Necromancy? That puts a new light on it. If the magician is allied against humankind, and with some morbid demon, it's possible the priest isn't our biggest worry."

"Does this affect your plans?"

"Let me ask you this, when you arrived, did you notice any blue robes among the oaks?"

"Sisters?" Osmodon stared at Bors in surprise. "I don't recall, though I wasn't looking too closely."

"There are none. The priest declared them traitors, and Saolin herself the architect of the plot to kill Cuchulain, as if the Sisterhood hasn't protected the Ambergin line for over two thousand years. Yet when Glays' soldiers arrived to arrest them, they found the tower empty, all two hundred and sixteen Sisters vanished. It's said Glays was beside himself for days, for he hates women, the Sisters most of all. He turned their tower into barracks for his guards."

"Interesting. But how does this apply?"

"Like Abdelar, I was once chosen by the Sisters, though I never completed my training. A vow was required, never to reveal what we learned, but there are vows and Vows. And a vow, after all, is only words, is it not?"

He stopped, waiting for an answer.

Osmodon nodded, closing his eyes as if searching his memory. "Men are made of words, and stories give meaning to those words."

Bors smiled, obviously pleased. "Good. I am released, then." He leaned forward, his voice dropping. "One story I heard, long forgotten, is that Barad'An was originally built over a series of granite caves. As the city grew, the caves were used, in part, for sewers, for a river flows through them."

"The Sisters escaped through the caves?"

"So I believe. The Left Tower is the oldest structure in the city. A door must still exist."

Osmodon dipped into his stew. "But we're not trying to escape."

"Think on it, my friend. The dungeon was also once part of the cave system."

There was a moment of silence as the men exchanged glances, then Osmodon slapped the table. "Forgive me for a dunce. Of course!"

Barrett stared at the two men, uncomprehending, then he caught their meaning.

CHAPTER 52

"OPEN! OPEN IN THE NAME of the Prophet Glays, or we'll break the door down!" A loud banging shook the inn's front door.

The boy who'd helped them in the stables came running in. "Sir Bors! Guardsmen!"

Bors was already on his feet. "We heard! How many?!"

"Ten by count."

"Warn Gregory and the others, then hide yourselves. Hurry!"

"We can fight!"

"Let them have the tavern tonight. You can have them in the morning, when they're too drunk to stand. Remember, first light in the old *stadia*! Tell the others. Go!"

The boy ran off toward the kitchen. Outside the clamor grew. "In the name of the prophet! Open or die!"

Osmodon stood, sword drawn. "Only ten? Why wait?"

"No!" Bors was already moving toward the back of the room. "Follow me."

Reluctantly, Osmodon sheathed his sword and did as the knight asked. Barrett was close behind. There was more cursing, then a loud crash. The soldiers had a battering ram.

Bors led them through a door at the rear of the common room, which he barred behind them. "They're looking for ale, not us. This way!"

They hurried down a narrow hall to a door behind which were crates and shelves full of plates, mugs, and utensils. Bors pushed aside a rack of wooden bowls, revealing the narrow opening to a tunnel. A lamp hung from a spike on the wall. He lit it with a flint, and motioned them to follow.

Heads bowed, holding their scabbards to keep them from clattering against the walls, they continued for several hundred feet before the tunnel came to an abrupt end at a stone wall. At the bottom of the wall was a drainage hole, barely large enough for a man to crawl through.

"Every city has its underworld," Bors observed.

He unhitched his scabbard and dropped to his knees. "No talking from here on out. The last one blow out the lamp." With that he disappeared into the hole.

Osmodon looked doubtful. "I'll plug it like a cork in a bottle."

"I'll go first," Barrett offered.

"No. I may need a push from behind."

Sighing, Osmodon removed his sword and dagger, his belt and his leather vest, pushing these before him as he squeezed his bulk into the hole and crawled forward.

Barrett waited until he could no longer see Osmodon's feet, then he blew out the lamp and followed.

The tunnel was at least twenty feet long, its walls slick with mold. He reached a cistern and Osmodon hoisted him into open air.

They stood in a deserted alleyway that stank of urine and things rotting. The only light came from behind the shutters of a nearby second-story window.

They buckled on their weapons. Bors replaced an iron grate over the hole. "This way," he whispered, motioning to their right.

Osmodon hesitated. "Isn't the Left Tower the other direction?"

"You forget. The tower is a barracks now. Besides, it might take us days to find that door. Trust me."

They followed Bors down a wider street lit by bonfires fueled by broken furniture and wood torn from market stalls. The city, which had appeared so wondrous from a distance, had now become dark and alien. Harsh laughter echoed from a distance. A woman screamed. A soldier with a tankard in his hand glanced in their direction, but said nothing.

From alleyway to open street to yet another alleyway, they traveled for what seemed to Barrett like miles before Bors finally stopped. They had come to the center of the city, a park that was now little more than a wild patch, a dense and dark forest in which one man or many could easily be lost.

A path led into the trees. "This way," Bors whispered.

Barrett followed, using his sense of hearing more than sight. Once deep into the park Bors stopped, lighting an oil lamp he'd removed from behind a bush. Before them was a large fountain, easily twenty feet high. It was crowned by a marble statue of a lion and a unicorn, rampant. The fountain was in disrepair, empty of all but rainwater.

Bors led them to the far side of the fountain where he revealed a grate hidden beneath a cloak of branches. He kicked the branches aside and lifted the metal frame.

"Down there you'll come to the main tunnel. Follow it to your left. Continue to follow it left whenever it branches. The way is marked with the rune for 'forward,' a trident, like this."

The knight held up three fingers, then turned to leave.

"Wait! Aren't you coming with us?"

"No. I'm to join the citifolk gathering in the *stadia*. They need one of us to lead them. Have faith. Keep to the left and follow the runes. You'll come to a wall. In this wall you'll find a stone door with an iron ring. Pull on the ring. The door should take you into the dungeon."

"Should?" Osmodon shook his head in disbelief. "By the gods, Bors! You haven't tried it, have you?"

"An old man who worked in the sewers told me about it. I trust him."

"An old man! Bors, this is no plan! It's a wild hope!"

Bors grinned. "Come, my friend. You're famous for your courage, and your friend certainly doesn't appear shy. If you're unable to locate the door, return the way you came. We'll meet at the *stadia*. The wedding begins at dawn, at the Ceremonial Hall. We have men inside who will see the doors are opened when needed."

Osmodon peered into the dark hole. "Well and good, but—."

"Take this lamp. There are torches at the bottom of the shaft when the oil runs out. If you should meet with the magician, dispatch him quickly. His helper is a half-breed troll by accounts, immensely strong but dumb as a brick. You should have no trouble."

"Just the two of them?"

"Aye, though there may be guards at the top of the stairs. Good luck." With that Bors turned and vanished into the darkness.

Osmodon stood, holding the lamp. "Well, damn my eyes. What do you make of that?"

"You don't really mean to go down there, do you?" asked Barrett.

"Not my first choice," replied Osmodon glumly. "But like the man said, if we can't find the door, we can always come back."

Barrett stared down into the black hole and sighed. "Right."

CHAPTER 53

Gallian, June 3

BRONWYN FOUND ELLOHIR sitting on a verandah, gazing at the valley below. There had been no word from Sir Osmodon and Sir Barrett, nor from Sianiave.

The night was warm, and there was the smell of frangipani and roses in the air, flowers she'd cultivated herself. She took a seat beside her husband, enjoying for a moment the peace, which she knew was so achingly ephemeral.

The Sirdar's army had passed by Gallian three days before, leaving behind three brigades to guard the entrance. The army was larger than first reported, at least eighty thousand strong. There was no doubt that a morghul commanded. Bronwyn had sensed its poisonous thoughts even as it approached.

After a long silence, Ellohir spoke. "Ren is the key," he said slowly, as if the thought was new to him. "Without her Barad'An is nothing but an empty fortress, without heart or soul, not worth the life of one of our folk."

Bronwyn remained silent. She knew this was hard for her husband.

"Do you the think the priest knows this of her?"

"He has no understanding at that level."

"If she were not at this moment in Barad'An, we would remain here, in Gallian."

"But she is there."

"Aye. But—."

He stopped, unable to continue with the thought, for it was deep, and he had not yet thought it through. Bronwyn could see this, and was proud of him for understanding as much as he did.

"We must go to Barad'An," he said finally. It was a half question.

"Yes," she said.

Ellohir stood, and a great weight seemed to have lifted from his shoulders. "Good. I'll give the word."

"And the brigades outside?"

"We'll leave through the caves. A messenger can advise Penthys and the others. We'll meet at Graylen Tor. Perhaps we can surprise even this morghul general."

CHAPTER 54

Western Coast, June 3

WHEN SIANIAVE SAW THE OCEAN, tears came unexpectedly. It was not because her long search was almost ended, though it was a clear day and there, less than thirty miles distant, she could make out the island that was her destination.

No, not the island, but the sea itself, for it touched something deep within her soul, the waves crashing restlessly against the sandy beach, the moist touch of the salt air, the cry of the seabirds in their ceaseless search for food. The Mother—patient, eternal, healing.

The tears caught her by surprise. She promised that when she completed this task, she would find a place in that other Earth, by the sea. She would remove her amulets, the stones and crystals, and embrace the forgetfulness, erase her long past.

They would return, of course, the memories, when she was needed.

It had been too long since she'd let go. Her emotions upon seeing the ocean told her it was time again. Her body could replenish itself endlessly, but her soul needed care. She had known others who had not taken such precautions. Eventually, over time, they had simply faded from existence.

She spurred Phaeton down onto the sand, in the direction of the little village that nestled under the cliffs at the far end of the beach. They would have boats to take her to the island.

CHAPTER 55

Barad'An, June 3

OSMODON LACED THE LAMP to a belt loop, then tested a handhold with his weight. Muttering imprecations, he slowly began to descend. Barrett counted to twenty and followed, pulling the grate over the opening as he did so.

The shaft dropped straight down, how far was impossible to tell. Even with Osmodon's lamp to light the way, they couldn't see the bottom. Some of the handholds were so worn they offered no grip at all. These they inched past by pressing their backs against the opposite wall.

It seemed like an eternity, though it had probably been no more than fifteen minutes, when Barrett finally heard Osmodon's whisper. "Watch it here. Don't lean back. The shaft opens into the main sewer."

Then, "I see the bottom. Pile of torches there. Almost down."

There was a muffled thump as Osmodon dropped to the floor, followed by the sound of breaking glass at the same moment the light went out.

Osmodon swore. "Damn. Broke the lamp. Hold on."

Barrett had an anxious moment while Osmodon fumbled in his pocket for a flint. There was a spark, and a torch burst into flame. Barrett quickly let himself down, falling the last few feet.

They were in a vaulted chamber. Arched tunnels opened in all directions. Filthy water flowed down the center of each tunnel. The air was dank but smelled more of moldy leaves than sewage, for which they were grateful.

The floor was covered in a black, grainy silt and littered with debris. There were eight torches there, nine counting the one in Osmodon's hand.

"Bors said left," said Osmodon, turning in a circle. "But left of what?"

Six tunnels led off the chamber, each of similar size. Barrett pointed to a trident shaped rune caved on the right side of the nearest tunnel. "That way."

Conversation was short. They turned left whenever a new tunnel branched. In the rocky warren even their whispers seemed to echo. Osmodon's torch cast shadows on the stone. At times they were knee-deep in piles of debris, leaves, branches, and other unwholesome things.

When they stopped to get their bearings, they heard other sounds, the rustle of some small creature scurrying for cover, the quick slithering of a snake as it disappeared into a tangle of dead leaves. Most disturbing was the dry, ominous chitter of rats.

More than once Barrett had glimpsed the sharp face of a gigantic rat as it glared out at them from the darkness, its feral red eyes a bright menace.

He mentioned this to Osmodon, for he had the unmistakable feeling it had been following them. He imagined he could hear its thin malignant thoughts: *Patience, brothers. They're strong now, and armed. But we'll have them soon. Patience.*

The darkness became more oppressive the further they went. One rat, the one that had been following, leapt ahead of them and refused to move, scurrying away only after Osmodon threatened it with the torch.

It sat out of range, watching them from a few yards away.

They had burned through all but two of the torches and had not found the door to the dungeon when they arrived at another chamber from which three new tunnels branched.

Osmodon's torch was almost down to his hand. He touched the dying flame to a torch Barrett carried. "We'd best find that door soon."

It was an unpleasant thought. "We can burn driftwood," said Barrett.

"Aye. Though it burns too quickly. I don't fancy being caught down here in the dark." Osmodon gave a nod over his shoulder to where rows of red eyes peered out at them from the darkness. "They've been gathering."

"I've noticed."

Barrett studied the three tunnels. He could find no rune to point the way. Bors had said keep left, but that tunnel held little appeal. Smaller than the others, its entrance was completely covered by an enormous web. Bones and carcasses of a dozen animals were caught in its weave.

Osmodon sliced through web with his dagger, but the blade stuck, and he pulled it free with difficulty. "It's like pitch! Try the torch."

Barrett held out the torch. The web resisted momentarily, then quickly flamed into ash. On the wall behind the web they found the rune.

The sinister chittering of the rats had grown louder. Dozens of vermin were now gathered behind them.

Almost time. Almost time—.

Osmodon's sleeve caught on a strand of web. As he pulled free a spider the size and shape of an orange dropped onto his shoulder. Its eight segmented legs were as long as Barrett's forearm, and the bloated body was black as polished ebony. Startled, Osmodon turned his head to see six opaline eyes staring back into his own.

He shrieked, trying to shake it off.

"Hold still!" cried Barrett. He swung the torch, knocking the thing from its hold. As if made of the same flammable stuff as its web, the spider caught fire. It emitted a high-pitched scream and scuttled like a living torch back into the tunnel. The agonized cries echoed for a moment, then stopped.

The rats paused, breaking ranks as they fled back from where they'd come.

"Gods," muttered Osmodon, brushing his shoulder repeatedly, "the size of that thing."

"We'd better go. The rats might regain their courage."

They moved off at a rapid pace down the tunnel, Barrett in the lead.

Unlike the tunnels they'd come through, this one had no center channel. Even the walls were different, more natural and cave-like.

"Listen," said Barrett, pausing. "You hear it? Water."

"The river, you reckon?"

The tunnel curved to the right, coming to an abrupt end at a deep fissure, the other side of which was a smooth stone wall. The fissure was at least four meters across, and out of the crack came the sound of rushing water. At one time a wooden bridge had spanned it, but the bridge had long ago fallen away, and now only the support posts remained.

On the far wall, Barrett could make out an iron ring embedded in the stone and the thin outline of a door marked with a trident-shaped rune.

"By Asgar!" muttered Osmodon. "I was beginning to lose hope."

"Just in time. We're on our last torch."

Barrett lit it with the torch he'd been carrying, which was almost out. He dropped the stub into the fissure, counting the seconds before the flame was extinguished in the torrent below.

"Fifty feet, at least," he observed.

Osmodon unbuckled his sword and dagger. "I'm more concerned about this crack here. Never been much of a jumper. Need a running start. Once over, we won't be able to get back. Not with so little room on the other side."

"I'll go first."

"I'm the eldest. Toss these over."

Before Barrett could object, Osmodon grunted and sprinted forward. His leap was poorly executed, and he came up short, barely managing to catch the ledge with his hands. Barrett held his breath as the big man struggled to pull onto solid ground.

"Nothing to it," Osmodon declared, dusting himself off. "Hold on there a minute. No use us both ending up here if we can't get this door open."

He took hold of the ring and pulled. The door gave several inches, but held. "It'll open, but I reckon it'll need both of us."

"I wasn't going back in any case," said Barrett. "Not alone. Not with those rats waiting."

He tossed the weapons to Osmodon, then the torch. Osmodon set them against the wall, ready to catch Barrett if need be.

Barrett took a running jump, landing well on the ledge, but something slick underfoot left him skidding across the ledge into the wall.

"Serves you right for trying to show me up," grinned Osmodon, helping him to his feet.

"Like you said," said Barrett. "Nothing to it."

They buckled on their weapons and faced the door. Both took hold of the ring. Osmodon counted. "One—two—three—."

With the grinding of stone against stone, the heavy door inched slowly forward. Then, suddenly, it broke free, swinging open with such speed Barrett barely managed to avoid being slammed backward into the chasm. As he scrambled to save himself, his foot caught the torch, sending it spinning across the floor. It teetered at the edge of the chasm for a brief moment, then disappeared over the side.

CHAPTER 56

REN WAS NEAR EXHAUSTION, but sleep was out of the question. Morning was only a few hours away, and she had yet to find a weapon. A long needle would do, or a shard of glass.

The problem wasn't the lack of such implements. The problem was the woman, Nadwyn, and her two helpers. They never left her alone.

She originally planned to kill the priest soon after the ceremony, when they were alone. But now she knew she could not wait that long. She would never take the marriage vows.

Bronwyn had hinted at this before she'd left Gallian, reminding her that marriage was a sacred pact, particularly for one of the high born, symbolizing the divine balance. The power and potency of symbols and ritual, of sworn word, had been drummed into Ren since childhood.

 She had to strike before the vows were exchanged. That left only a short time in which to act. She never would have thought herself capable of killing with such cold conviction, but her duty lay heavy on her, and, after the horrors she'd witnessed since her return, her compassion was in short supply.

Nadwyn reached out to touch her swollen cheek. "That bruise is healing nicely. A little powder and no one will notice. Now you must get some rest."

Ren started at the touch, but something in the woman's eyes, a subtlety in her voice, gave her pause.

Desire—.

Nadwyn had hidden it well.

Ren knew there were certain individuals, a few in the Sisterhood itself, who were known as the third sex. Such people were rare and generally revered. By their natures they intuitively understood the nature of balance. They made excellent magisters and healers.

But there was another sort, like Nadwyn, who knew little of balance. They identified themselves with only one side of the great scale, and in doing so allowed themselves to become agents of corruption.

Ren knew what she must do.

Smiling shyly, she placed her hand on the woman's. "Your hand is cool," she murmured, using the voice to mirror the woman's own desire.

Nadwyn was cruel, and naturally suspicious. Ren knew she would have to use every device the Sisters had ever taught her about seduction.

"I can't sleep," she said.

"You need your rest. You are to marry the most powerful man in the kingdom in the morning."

"Men do not interest me." Ren's voice was low as she looked directly into Nadwyn's eyes. "Not in that way."

Her fingers touched lightly at Nadwyn's wrist. She felt the pulse quicken.

There was a long moment of silence, Nadwyn's instinctive caution fighting a growing desire. "Leanna, Portia!" she barked suddenly. "You are free to go!"

"But Nadwyn—!"

"I will attend to the princess. She needs her sleep, and she won't get any with you two lurking about! Go!"

"Of course, m'lady."

The one called Leanna bowed and left. Portia, a stout girl with sallow skin and a distinct pout, stood her ground. She glared at Ren, her resentment obvious.

Jealousy, Ren saw.

"Nadwyn—."

"Go!" snapped Nadwyn.

The girl opened her mouth as if to retort, then abruptly closed it, and with a venomous glare at Ren, stomped off.

Nadwyn's mouth came close to Ren's cheek. "If I had known—."

"There's time."

It was the only encouragement Nadwyn needed. She drew Ren to her in a powerful embrace, forcing their lips together. Ren's hand fell to Nadwyn's thigh. A dagger was hidden there under the woman's dress, as she suspected. This made it easier.

Nadwyn carried Ren to the bed and began disrobing her as if she were undressing a doll. When Ren was naked, she removed her own clothing, letting the dagger drop to the floor. Ren lay waiting, picturing what she must do.

Nadwyn fell on top of her, kissing her mouth and neck, her hand stroking Ren's thigh. Ren allowed her right arm to fall backward, as if in pleasure, near where the dagger lay.

Almost.

Nadwyn raised her head.

Now!

In a movement so quick Nadwyn had no time to react, Ren loosed the dagger from its sheath and drove it straight into Nadwyn's eye. The woman shuddered once and then laid still.

Ren shoved the body away and staggered from the bed, her breathing coming in great gulps. Shaking, she took hold of the dagger's hilt and pulled it free.

She had a weapon now. She must calm herself. There were things to do, hide the corpse, get rid of the bloody sheets, wash herself, come up with a story to explain Nadwyn's absence.

Slowly her breathing returned to normal; the trembling grew less.

CHAPTER 57

Barrett swore. "What now?"

"Give me your sleeve," said Osmodon. "The linen will burn easier than my leather. Steady now."

Osmodon used his dagger to cut a length off Barrett's right sleeve, then wrapped it around the blade. Barrett heard the sound of Osmodon's flint, and for a brief second the tunnel was ablaze with light as the makeshift torch almost exploded into flame.

"Damn," cried Barrett, jumping back. "What did you put on that?"

"Polishing oil. Let's go. It won't last long!"

The door opened on a narrow passageway. The stench was overpowering. They had entered a charnel house. A stream of blood ran down center of passageway, the same awful ooze that had caused Barrett to lose his footing earlier.

Swords in hand, they moved quickly down. Within a hundred yards their torch began to sputter.

"Your other sleeve," said Osmodon.

As Barrett looked at his sleeve, some sixth sense caused him to lower his head. There was a whooshing sound as a spiked club the size of a fence post smashed into the wall behind him, missing his ear by less than an inch.

A nightmare stepped out from the gloom, its face a bloated mockery of a human. A bloodstained apron girdled its waist, and a large ring hung from its belt, rattling with iron keys.

"Gods," muttered Osmodon. "A bloody troll. What next?"

The creature belched. Its teeth were stained and rotten, and its tongue was missing.

Barrett moved away from Osmodon. The monster appeared not to notice. Its attention was on Osmodon, who still held the faltering torch. Barrett wondered if it could see in the dark.

"I take it you're the one responsible for this mess," said Osmodon.

Bellowing in rage, the monster swung. Osmodon jumped backward, barely avoiding the club. Barrett saw his opening, and shoved his dagger into the creature's side. Radlik grunted and jerked away with the dagger stuck in his bulk.

Radlik stepped back, his slow mind just beginning to grasp the precariousness of its situation.

Who were these men? Do they work for the priest?

"By Asgar, you're an ugly one," said Osmodon, stepping forward.

Still Radlik hesitated. *He must warn Master Gothmog.*

Osmodon thrust his sword, piercing Radlik between the ribs. The monster wailed, bringing his club down, but Osmodon had already moved out of reach.

Blood poured from Radlik's wounds. He lashed out again with the club. Barrett swung his own sword, severing the creature's left wrist. Radlik bellowed in pain as the warted hand fell to the floor.

"Find the magician, lad!" cried Osmodon. "I'll finish this fellow!"

Barrett recalled Bor's warning: if they encounter the magician, kill him quickly. The fight here would soon be over.

"Go!" cried Osmodon.

Barrett slid past the creature's flailing club. The beast's grunts had become a pitiful mewling. It would be over before the torch died.

There was light ahead where an iron door stood open. A voice echoed down the corridor, a chant of some sort. "*N'ash ash iskan gashsa. N'ash ash iskan hasha—.*"

They seemed somehow familiar.

Not the words, he realized. It was the feeling they invoked. Cruelty, hatred—.

There was no time left. He did not know why, only that he had to end that awful chant before it reached its conclusion.

He burst into the chamber. A small, ferret-faced man stood near an open brazier. He was dressed in a dark robe and held a black stone above his head. A boy, stripped above the waist, was chained spread-eagle to the wall.

Barrett took this in at a glance. What held his attention, however, was not the magician turning toward him in rage, nor was it the look of abject terror on the boy's face. Rather it was the small circle of blackness above the boy's head, an anomaly in the air, vivid against the stone wall, not just black, but the utter and complete absence of light.

Barrett had known evil in his life, had even lived with it as a foster child. He knew the black void that can engulf a person when life is bereft of meaning and hope. But never had he encountered a thing so profoundly evil as what hovered in that black circle.

"GET OUT!" screamed Gothmog, lunging.

The stone in Gothmog's hand cut through Barrett's leather jerkin as cleanly as a razor, but drew only a thin line of blood. Barrett pivoted, his own blade sweeping downward, skinning the left side of the magician's face, and lopping off an ear.

Snarling in rage, Gothmog threw himself forward, his teeth sinking into Barrett's sword arm. Barrett smashed a fist into the mess he'd made of the magician's face, sending him sprawling across the room. With a shriek that sounded much like the spider he'd flamed in the sewer, Gothmog disappeared through the open door.

"Sir—please—Sir Barrett—help me."

Hearing his name, Barrett turned in surprise. The foul halo had vanished. He peered closer and recognized the stable boy from Ardendell.

"Will? How in hell—?"

As he searched the room for a way to release the boy from his chains, Osmodon appeared in the doorway.

"Try these," said Osmodon, holding out Radlik's key ring. "Where's the magician?"

"He ran. Be careful. He's quick."

The lock on the boy's shackles was small, and the smallest key on the ring opened it. Barrett caught Will in his arms as he collapsed.

"Let's get you out of here."

He carried the boy into the corridor and set him down.

"Please, sir. Don't leave me here."

"You'll be alright. I'll be back."

Barrett hoped he sounded reassuring, but he could already hear the distant clangor of alarm bells.

He caught up with Osmodon in the main dungeon. It was lined on both sides with cells filled to capacity with hollow-eyed prisoners.

"The keys!" cried Osmodon. "Open the cells! The bloody magician got away! There'll be guards here any minute!"

Aerindir was in the first cell Barrett opened.

CHAPTER 58

AERINDIR HAD LOST WEIGHT, but his eyes blazed with a fierce energy when Barrett unlocked his chains. "Well met, Sir Barrett. How many are you?"

"Just two. Bors is with a contingent above. We came in the back door."

Aerindir staggered slightly as he stood, but soon found his footing. "The magician ran past as though the hounds of the hell were after him. He sounded the alarm."

"Here! Help us! Let us out!"

The clamor from the other prisoners was growing. Fingers fumbling through the keys, Barrett unlocked cell after cell, men, women, even small children, perhaps a hundred in all. Many were barely able to stand, or even speak.

Barrett sorted those who looked fit enough to fight from those too weak, sickly, or young. There were fifteen or twenty of the former, at most, and no way to avoid a fight. Retreating through the sewers was out of the question. He wondered how many soldiers would be waiting for them.

"Weapons," cried a grizzled veteran. "Have you weapons for us?"

"Fletcher!" cried Aerindir, grabbing the old man in a bear hug. "All this time you were here? By the gods, after your stand on the wall we thought you done for."

"Hello, Aerindir."

Fletcher held up his right arm. A dirty bandage covered the stump where his wrist used to be. "I'll never pull a yew again, but my left hand can still wield a sword."

"There's an armory by the door."

Aerindir led them to the main door, which hung open. To its right was a smaller door, made of oak, which Barrett opened with a key. Pikes, daggers, tri-flects, swords, and other weapons lined the walls in orderly racks. Aerindir drew a sword, balancing it in his hand. "It's not Drakulsyr, but it will do."

"Hurry!" someone whispered. "They're coming!"

Prisoners quickly found their weapons. Close now, they heard the heavy clatter of hobnailed boots. Those unable to fight were ushered aside.

"I can fight," cried a woman. "Give me a weapon!"

Her face was filthy and emaciated, but her blue eyes were clear, and her hand steady. "Maewyn!" cried Osmodon in recognition. "The wench from the Dawn."

"Was a wench, until I slapped one of their kind and blasphemed their prophet. Do you not want the help of an honest serving maid?"

Osmodon laughed and tossed her a sword. "On the contrary. I'm glad it's them you're facing, and not us."

The soldiers had reached the bottom of the stairs, eight of them, Barrett counted. Their leader was a red-eyed sergeant, angry at having to cut short his drinking. "What the hell goes on here!? Get back in your cells you bloody scum! By the prophet, you'll suffer for this!"

At first the sergeant seemed unable to take in the situation. He strode forward, his pike lowered. He stopped when he saw Barrett. "Who the bloody hell are you?"

The words were hardly out of his mouth when Barrett's sword flashed and the sergeant's head tumbled to the stone floor. "Good answer," remarked Osmodon.

The fight that followed was brief. Barrett's fury had been growing ever since he'd entered the magician's workshop and found Will chained to the wall. In necromancy, the sorcery of death, he recognized the embodiment of everything he despised.

Three of the soldiers he killed himself. Others killed the remaining five, including Maewyn, who took her toll.

Now more guardsmen were coming. Barrett stormed up to meet them, cutting down the first man he met, then two more. How many died under his blade he never knew, for a blood rage was upon him. The priest's ill-trained soldiers stood no chance.

His boot slipped, and he almost went down. Blood, the stairs were covered in it. Osmodon's strong arm steadied him. "Take a breather, lad. Let us have some of the fun!"

Ignoring him, Barrett continued up the stairs. He parried a pike thrust and took off a leg. The man toppled and fell screaming down the stairwell to join the bodies piling up below.

And then it was over.

Barrett looked around, but he was alone on the landing at the top of the stairwell. He stepped unchallenged into a large room.

An old man with long white hair and wearing a high-collared coat was stooped over a tall desk. He must be a scrivener or a clerk, Barrett thought. He was writing on a scroll by candlelight.

The old man lowered his spectacles over his beak of a nose and frowned. Or perhaps the frown was only an illusion of his craggy features, for his eyes actually appeared to twinkle. "You'd best hurry. It's almost dawn, you know."

Dawn? Already?

Barrett ran to the door. The chill caught his breath. In the east one large structure stood out, its walkways and windows ablaze with lights. Behind it the first light of morning cast its rays. Somewhere a cock crowed.

He turned to speak, but the old man was gone, and so were the desk, ink pot, and candle. Osmodon, Aerindir, and Fletcher stood where the desk had been.

Barrett shook his head, as though waking from a trance. Why was everyone staring at him? His head throbbed painfully, and his sword arm burned with a fever. He remembered the magician's bite. It had seemed inconsequential at the time. He would deal with it later.

His rage had diminished, but not his sense of purpose. He was covered head to foot in blood. No wonder they stared.

The blare of trumpets sounded through the city. Barrett leapt down the steps in the direction of the Ceremonial Hall.

"Hold up!" shouted Osmodon. "The *stadia*'s the other direction!"

"There's no time!" cried Barrett over his shoulder.

"He's right," said Aerindir, starting after Barrett. "The wedding has already begun."

CHAPTER 59

"THERE IS NO NOW but Now. All is part of the Whole. Even at the center of a whirlwind there is silence—."

A small hand tugged at Ren's sleeve. "M'lady. The horns—."

"I have ears," she snapped.

Ren looked down to see a flower girl staring up at her, a look of hurt surprise on her small face. She held a basket of bright colored impatiens.

"I'm sorry," said Ren, immediately contrite. "You're Semy, aren't you?"

"Yes, m'lady."

The girl's voice quavered. Ren stooped until their eyes were level. "Well, Semy," she whispered, "I didn't mean to bark."

Semy brightened. "It's alright. It's sad for you to marry that hateful man."

Ren blinked. She wanted to hug the child, but the wedding mistress intervened, grabbing Semy's arm. "Hush child! What makes you speak such nonsense?"

"But, ma'am," said Semy earnestly. "Everybody says—."

"Everybody says nothing, if they do, they're fools. You don't listen to fools."

As the mistress dragged Semy off to her place in the procession Ren caught her eye and winked.

There were at least two dozen women with her in the hallway, though only eight would accompany her into the hall.

The seamstress, a prune-faced harridan, stood glowering at a distance. Ren had ordered her away. It was hard enough to hide the dagger in her garments without the seamstress fussing about.

Breathe.

Ren thought of Nadwyn, hidden in a clothes hamper in the bedchamber. Portia was the only one who questioned her absence. Ren had sent her searching for her mistress in a distant part of the palace.

The thick makeup Ren had applied to hide her bruises itched. She lifted a hand to scratch her nose, then stopped.

The horns sounded again, this time joined by the steady rhythm of drums. Ren inhaled deeply, and let it out.

Bronwyn had said any wound that drew blood would be enough to kill, but she had to be sure. She pictured the priest's hulking body, with its small mouth and fleshy lips, his repellent touch. She thought of her grandfather, of Abdelar, or the corpses along the Great North Road.

I will not fail!

The wedding mistress straightened a last hair on Ren's head and stood back admiringly. "It's time, my dear."

Ren nodded. Semy led off the procession with her basket of flowers. A chorus of young girls followed, chanting a wedding song.

The priest had made changes to the ceremony. Once the flower girls had carried white lilies and golden adelentiums in their baskets, symbolizing the merging of the sun and the moon. Glays did not approve of such concepts. To him the moon was but a pale reflection of the sun, women no more than ancillary appendages of men.

But one thing he hadn't changed was the routes by which bride and groom entered the Hall. Traditionally the bride rose from below, through the underground hallway, the groom descending from above, down stairs that led to the wedding dais. In this way the groom was seen as spirit, descending from the sky, the bride as soul, rising from the earth. Glays imagined his descent from above as no more than his due.

Despite the changes, the ritual still carried tremendous power. Ren felt it even before she emerged from the passageway. The Great Hall, large enough to seat a thousand souls, was filled to capacity. A collective sigh greeted her as she entered.

Could she count on their help?

She saw that there was sympathy in their faces, and fear. She scanned the hall, noting the priest's archers in the balconies above. Templars lined the aisles, ready to quell dissent.

"Go ahead, dear," whispered the mistress, mistaking Ren's hesitation for fear. "This is a day you'll remember always."

If only you knew.

The priest was already on the dais as Ren approached. Her small entourage had dropped back, nearly out of sight of the audience. Anything that might have reminded people of the Mother had been removed from the hall. Glays wore robes of golden silk, trimmed in burgundy and spangled with jewels.

Templars surrounded the stage. Ren noted their positions, discounting them as threats. They would never reach her in time, though afterward they would have to be dealt with. She couldn't run, not in her absurd dress. It made her feel clumsy, the dagger hidden in her sleeve an awkward weight.

She turned to face Glays, noting with satisfaction his look of irritation when she didn't kneel, as she'd been instructed. The drum sounded once and fell silent.

The magister appeared. Instead of the traditional three-chambered reed staff he carried a gilded cross. "Our Lord God Almighty has ordained the union of the Crown Princess Gwyndolyn Ambergin and Lord Milford Anastis Glays, prophet of God, steward of Barad'An, and protector of Anor."

The magister had been chosen less for his spiritual knowledge than for the quality of his lungs, for his voice boomed like a herald's. "We are gathered here to bear witness to the joining . . ."

Ren was fully alert now, ready for the moment when the chalice would be brought and the magister would hand it to Glays. Glays would drink of the sacred *haoma* and, in turn, offer it to Ren.

It was then that she would strike, his hands busy with the large cup.

For her to accept the chalice would be to accept the marriage. That she must not do, whatever the consequences.

The magister droned on, his voice almost hypnotic in its effect. "—agrees to obey her lord and husband in all matters, including those of bed and household—."

Guardsmen shifted nervously at their posts. For a brief moment even the magister's confident voice faltered. Glays himself was either oblivious to the darkening mood of the crowd, or was pointedly ignoring it.

". . . brought together in the eyes of God, Princess Gwyndolyn Ambergin, do you take this man, Lord Glays, prophet of God and steward of Barad'An, as your lawfully wedded husband?"

The words, when they came, caught Ren by surprise. The vows! No chalice, no offering of *haoma*!

The hall was deathly silent. It was as if the walls themselves were waiting for her answer. "Don't!" screamed a woman from the back row. "Don't do it, Gwyndolyn! Don't betray us!"

The priest's mouth twitched in irritation. Two guardsmen grabbed the woman and dragged her away. It was the distraction Ren needed.

One continuous motion—.

She pulled the dagger free and turned. The blade was razor sharp, slicing through the magister's neck as easily as cutting parchment. But as she planted her right foot for the crucial thrust into the priest's midsection, her slipper caught in the hem of the dress.

"You traitorous bitch!" shrieked Glays.

Slight as the stumble had been, it gave the priest enough time to step clear. His hand shot out, grabbing her wrist and nearly breaking it. The knife dropped, and he struck her in the face, knocking her to the floor.

The magister clutched his throat, the blood leaking between his fingers turned a ghastly black. He gave a last gurgle and fell forward onto the dais.

Glays blanched. "You poisoned the blade? You'll pay for this! You'll pay dearly!"

Ren lay stunned. She felt no fear, only great sadness. She had failed, failed her people.

Guards started to drag her to her feet.

"Leave her there!" snarled Glays. "I want the bitch alive!"

He lashed out with his leg, the kick landing squarely on her ribs. Instinctively she pulled herself into fetal position, the thick folds of the dress the only thing between her and Glays' brutal attack.

"Watching your friends die will be the last thing you ever see!" he screamed. "I'll carve out your eyes myself! When you're dead I'll give your heart to Gothmog!"

"Stop!" a man in the front row shouted. "You're killing her!"

Others in the audience picked up the cry. "Stop it! Let her go! Let Gwyndolyn go!"

Glays stopped, his face flushed with fury. For the first time he remembered where he was. His small, mean eyes looked out on the sea of faces. He'd staged this event to make clear to them who was their ruler, but now—!

The crowd was on its feet, threatening, "Down with the priest! Let Gwyndolyn go! Beast! Murderer!"

"Kill them all," screamed Glays. "Any who resist!"

Templars waded into the crowd, cutting down any who stood in their way. Arrows rained down from the mezzanine. The mobs angry cries turned to screams of pain and terror.

At the height of the panic the great doors at the front of the hall swung open with a thunderous boom. Guardsmen and citizens alike turned to see a man framed in the doorway. He was drenched head to foot in blood. In his right hand he held a sword, in his left a long dagger.

"*Eanor—.*"

The name had been whispered, almost as a question. But others heard it, picking up the name and shouting it aloud. "Eanor! Eanor has come!"

Glays stood rooted. Eanor? Impossible. Then he remembered the squire's last words, and for the first time felt the chill of fear.

A knight covered in blood—.

"Stop that man! A hundred empresses to the man that kills him!"

Men greedy or foolish enough to take up the challenge were cut down. An arrow flew from the mezzanine, then another. The man's sword moved as though it had a will of its own, easily deflecting them. Swarming in behind him came dozens of armed men.

The priest's slight hope was quickly dashed, for these men were not wearing the white robe. They were dressed in rags, commoner's clothes, bits and pieces of armor.

"Best leave, m'lord," urged a guard.

Suddenly Glays remembered Ren. He'd kill her now. That would end it. He looked around, expecting to find her broken, cowering at his feet. Instead the bitch was crawling toward her dagger!

He grabbed at her dress, too late.

An excruciating pain buckled his left leg. Shocked, he looked down. She'd stabbed him.

"You bloody—!" Even as he faced the certainty of his own death, Glays was unable to keep the arrogance from his voice.

They were the last words he spoke before Barrett took off his head.

CHAPTER 60

THE FOG SEEPED OUT OF THE FOREST, thick and damp, spreading in great billowing rolls. Some swore it was the work of the morghul who now commanded the Sirdar's army. Such creatures could influence the weather, as well as men's thoughts.

Captain Fletcher had managed to bring together what remained of his wall guard. A scarce eighty men now stood watch where once might have been a thousand. "Post three, all's well," "Post nine, all's well," the calls came along the wall.

Barrett felt drained. The madness that had come on him in the dungeon was gone, replaced by aimless lethargy. When he'd tried to sleep his dreams were full of nightmarish images. His right arm ached with a deepening chill. The pain had lessened during the past hour, but the numbness that had replaced it was worse.

How many men had he killed that day? Fifteen? Twenty?

He'd called himself a soldier once. But now he felt the weight of eternity pressing down on him, as if he'd been fighting through countless lifetimes. He was tired of it, the fighting, men killing men, the pointlessness of it all.

Forcing his arm to move, he drew his sword, running the fingers of his good hand along the once keen blade, now scaled with dried blood, notched in so many places it could be used to saw wood.

It deserved better. He should have cleaned it, but to what purpose. He'd done his job. What now? Duty? Honor? This wasn't his city. Barad'An was a hollow, decaying fortress, fit for little more than the rats in the sewers. He wanted nothing more to do with it.

The priest's death had ended resistance within the city. Glays' men had fled like rodents. Those who fought had easily been dispatched. Others had been killed by mobs holding little sympathy for the men who had filled the oaks with their loved ones.

Bors had been appointed temporary steward. His first act had been to call a council of the remaining knights and captains. There was still the Sirdar's army to be dealt with.

The council meeting had gone on for much of that afternoon. Many of those present favored abandoning the city, and retreating to the keeps in the south. There was no time left to prepare, and too few able-bodied men to hold the great walls.

Barrett agreed with this assessment, though he kept his thoughts to himself. The pain in his arm had been growing worse and with it a deepening depression. As the bickering and arguing dragged on into the evening he'd slipped from the room. Some instinct had led him to the top of the wall. There he'd sat, watching the fog engulf the city.

"Hoy, lad. Glad I found you." A nebulous shape separated itself from the gloom.

"Ozzy?"

Barrett looked up, half annoyed by the interruption, yet glad for the company. "How did you find me?"

"Fletcher trains his lads well. They let you be, reckoning you wanted to be alone. Not much gets by them, even in this soup. Why did you leave the council?"

Barrett shrugged. "Not my affair. Will they evacuate?"

"No. They voted to stay and defend."

"Oh? Why did they change their minds?"

"Ren, bless her. You'd already left."

"Ren?"

Barrett hadn't seen Ren since that morning when Aerindir had carried her off somewhere. Later he'd felt too tired and ill to seek her out. "She's alright then."

"Some mischief, a few cracked ribs. Bors and the other knights are behind her now. With Cuchulain dead and Artos gone, Ren now holds their fealty. She's certainly proven herself. In any even, it's done. They voted to forego her maturity. She's queen now."

"Queen?"

"Soon as she can be crowned, probably in the morning. And if the queen orders Barad'An be defended, then it's to the death, if need be."

Barrett mulled this over. He was glad Ren would be well. His memories of her were strangely vague, as though he'd heard or dreamt about her, not once loved her.

"What about you?" he asked. "Will you stay?"

Even in the darkness and fog he could sense Osmodon was studying him, looking for a reaction, perhaps.

"Well now, that depends on you," Osmodon answered slowly. "Though to be honest, if I'd my way I'd be on my horse and gone in the morning."

"It's up to you."

"You forget Sianiave, though admittedly this is one of those times I curse having taken the Vow. She swore me to look after you. So where you go, I go."

"It's hopeless. They haven't a chance."

Osmodon sighed. It was a weary sound, full of regret. "Aye. Those were my thoughts as well. But Ren has put your name forward as commander. She wants you to lead the defense of the city."

Something finally broke through the grey emptiness of Barrett's thoughts. "Me? You can't be serious!"

"This is no jest. They sent me to find you. They await your answer."

Barrett slumped against the parapet. "I'm a stranger here. Bors is better suited. The others must have had something to say, Aerindir?"

"Actually they all agree. You've made quite an impression."

"I was out of my mind."

"Nevertheless."

"It's something to do with that name, isn't it? Enor or something. They were chanting it in the hall."

Osmodon hesitated, again studying Barrett with an oddly speculative look. "You know nothing, about Eanor, I mean?"

Barrett recalled the grendel's sly whispers, then shook his head. "Nothing. I've heard the name mentioned a few times."

"People in hopeless situations often draw courage from odd things," Osmodon mused, seeming relieved.

"Who is he?"

"Not is. Was. Eanor lived two thousand years ago, King Ambergin's greatest and most loyal knight. Folk still sing his tales. 'The Lay of Berengard' is one."

Osmodon began to sing. His voice was surprisingly melodious.

> *"At the king's command the knights set out,*
> *for neither gold nor fame did they ride.*
> *Eanor rode Grenfyr, and Thrandil by his side . . .*
> *Fifty followed that day, to test the witch king's . . ."*

Pain exploded in Barrett's head. "Ozzy—not now. Please."

"There are some who find my voice pleasing," said Osmodon, feigning hurt. "No matter. I can't remember all of it anyway, but the short of it is this: Ambergin was doing battle with the Corsairs in the west when he learned the witch king was preparing to take advantage by moving on Barad'An. He sent Eanor with fifty knights to Berengard, a keep overlooking Beren's Gate. We saw its ruins in the distance that day in the sled, if you recall."

Barrett nodded, though in truth he recalled no such thing. The pain in his head was too great.

Osmodon continued. "Eanor was to hold the pass until Ambergin could finish with the Corsairs. But it took twenty-one days before their fleet retreated. When Ambergin finally arrived at Berengard, he found Eanor alone still standing, so covered in blood it was impossible to tell if he was a man or some dark thing from hell. A circle of gold cloth under his sword belt was the only part of his garment not soaked red. From that day forward the Ambergin battle colors have been maroon and gold."

Barrett lowered his head and sighed. "So, that's it. I changed clothes at the inn. There was no circle of gold. People shouldn't put their faith in ancient heroes."

"True or not, that image, Eanor soaked in blood, is fixed in the memories of these people. You came storming into the wedding like that, red from head to toe, wielding your sword with a vengeance. To them, you are Eanor."

"My sword—."

Barrett's reply was bitter. The faces of the men he'd killed that morning were even now forming in the fog, anguished, accusing. He tried to raise his sword to dispel them, but his arm hung like a dead weight. The numbness was working its way into his shoulder.

The pain in his head was becoming unbearable. The sword fell from his hand, landing with a clatter on the stone. The fog had grown thicker, enfolding him until he could no longer see the shadow of Osmodon's face.

"Ozzy—."

"Guards!" cried Osmodon, sweeping Barrett up in his arms. "Sir Barrett is down!"

When he opened his eyes Barrett was lying on a narrow bed. His clothes had been stripped away and fresh sheets covered him. Ren sat in a chair beside the bed. Her face still showed cuts and bruises, but in Barrett's mind she was still achingly beautiful. A glow surrounded her, indescribably intimate. *How could he have forgotten?*

Others were there, Osmodon and Aerindir among them.

Osmodon was the first to speak. "Good to see you awake, lad. We thought we'd lost you. With the Sisters gone, Ren was the only one with the training."

"What happened?"

"You were poisoned," said Ren.

"Poisoned?"

Barrett raised his arm. The skin looked yellow and bruised where the magician's teeth had pierced his skin, but the enervating numbness was gone, and with it the emptiness that had filled his thoughts.

He looked around the room, a small infirmary in one of the wall towers. A warm glow from the corner fireplace cut the chill of the night air. Even the stones in the walls appeared to be set in some meaningful and miraculous pattern. For Barrett the world once again seemed renewed and wondrous.

This was Barad'An as Ren knew it, he realized, not the rotting carcass of a once great city, but a place of beauty and harmony, a place of the heart. And he understood the need to protect it, to protect her, for she was Barad'An.

As he looked into her eyes he saw that she was no longer a child, and he mourned the loss. But he also saw a new and unsettling strength, the wisdom of a true queen, and the awareness of her duty, a duty that would take precedence over all else. It was this love that had healed him. But it was a love that he could no longer claim as his alone.

"We need you now, Sir Barrett," she said.

"I am yours, my queen. I give you my fealty."

He wasn't sure if those were the right words, but no one bothered to correct him. Ren smiled, but there was a deep sadness in the smile, for she knew what his words meant, what they were both forsaking.

"I accept your fealty."

She reached out and stroked his head. "Rest. Let your strength return. You'll need it soon enough."

CHAPTER 61

"YOU CAN STILL CHANGE your mind," Osmodon said.

"You'd have me break my vow?"

"That wasn't a real liege vow. Truth is, I never heard anything quite like it. Besides, you can always say you weren't in your right mind, the poison and all."

Barrett laughed. He knew Osmodon wasn't serious. The big man would be the first to lecture him on the sanctity of a man's word.

They were atop a ridge overlooking the eastern plain. Dust clouds stirred up by the approaching army blanketed the horizon. Barrett saw for himself what the scouts had reported; the massive force was laying waste to everything in its path. With the arrival of refugees fleeing the devastation, the population of Barad'An had grown.

Some seasoned fighters appeared alone at the gate, but others arrived with their own companies, as many as twenty men at a time. Farm folk, woodsmen, traders, even bandits came seeking the imagined safety of Barad'An's great walls. Others came for glory, for whatever the outcome, this battle would be remembered for the ages.

At the height of its power Barad'An had housed over a hundred thousand fighting men. Long unused armories and forgotten storage rooms were reopened. Captain Fletcher's archers worked day and night feathering stores of arrows. Water was plentiful. Granaries could supply the city for some months. Remaining livestock and fowl were herded into empty stables, and the city's gardens, parks, and orchards could provide some fruit and vegetables.

"The dust makes it seem larger than it is," said Barrett. "We will have camp followers, like any army."

"So long as a morghul commands," observed Osmodon glumly, "every jack one of them will fight to the death. He'll have the Sirdar's witch men with him. Already the air reeks of their sorcery. By Asgar, I hope the Sisters are up to it."

A contingent of forty-four Sisters had arrived that morning, sent by Saolin from the Sisterhood's ancient redoubt at Marduk. They would serve as physicians and could work against the sorcery of the witch men. The two hundred or so others who remained at the monastery would, according to Saolin's letter, "—*join in battle by other means.*"

The Sisters had gone to work immediately, setting up aid stations in preparation for the coming battle, while doing their best to clean out the debris left in their tower by the priest's men. There would be a ceremony that night to resanctify the temple. Barrett had promised to attend.

Low, hovering clouds, the color of bruised flesh, were coming in from the north, carrying something unclean. Barrett had sensed it upon awakening that morning. He was familiar with it now, knew it for what it was, the first wave of the morghul commander's attack.

Never again, for I know you—.

They were outnumbered, twenty to one by some counts. There was no sign of either Ellohir or the desert people, nor any word from Sianiave, though the Sisters said the sorceress had passed through Marduk weeks before, remaining only a night before continuing on toward some mysterious destination.

"Dismal odds," said Osmodon gloomily. "The scouts say at least ten Uruk tribes have joined them, while we have fewer than three thousand men to hold twenty-six miles of wall. They can surround us, attack anywhere."

They'd been over this a dozen times. As yet Barrett had no answer. But something Osmodon had said, about the odds, set off a memory.

"*Odds don't mean much. You said that yourself—.*"

"Even should Ellohir manage to break out of Gallian," Osmodon went on. "At best he'll bring one or two thousand. It's a matter of numbers."

Barrett scanned his memory. *Numbers. Numbers—a conversation? Where?*

Barrett looked up. "*They couldn't bring their numbers to bear!*" "Of course!" Without waiting for Osmodon he reined Greywind around, spurring him back down the trail.

"Now what's gotten into him?" Osmodon asked out loud, then turned his own horse to follow.

The trail was the same as they'd taken on their journey to Barad'An. Ten days, and the world had changed. The corpses had been cut from the trees and pyres burned for days. The scent of daffodils and wildflowers had replaced the stench of rotting meat, and the songs of the robins, starlings, and mocking-birds had driven out the screeching of the crows. Barad'An's wall was turning golden in the afternoon sun, and the polluted clouds had not yet crossed over the hills.

Barrett was lost in thought. After they'd ridden for some time, Osmodon broke the silence. "I've a confession to make. Should've told you sooner, but the time never seemed right."

"What do you have to confess? You deflowered another virgin?"

"Hardly a thing to warrant confession. No—. " Osmodon hesitated. "Remember that night I said I'd reckoned Sianiave had brought you here so as you could marry Ren?"

"Yes."

"Well—I was wrong."

"Oh," replied Barrett, eyebrows raised.

"A blind man could see how you felt toward one another. Still, if I used my head instead of listening to my sentiments, I would have worked it out sooner. The truth is, I didn't want to see you hurt."

"Worked what out sooner?"

"If Sianiave meant for you and Ren to marry, why was she so set on find-ing Artos?"

"Ren's uncle? What does he have to do with it?"

"Everything. You see, he and Ren were —are, if Sianiave is right about him still being alive— betrothed."

Barrett felt like he'd been punched. "Betrothed? To her uncle?"

"Has been since she was seven. You see? So long as Artos was thought to be dead, the way was open. But if Sianiave is certain he's still alive, well, simply put, it wouldn't make sense for you to marry a girl already spoken for."

"Her uncle," Barrett repeated dumbly.

"Don't take it hard, lad. It's their way, bloodline and all. Anyway, since you pledged your fealty, it's all a bit moot."

Barrett struggled to speak. He felt bereft, the world turned on its head. As

Ren's liege knight, they could never be lovers, much less married. At best he would be allowed to kiss her hand or wear her token into battle. Despite this he'd held out hope. After all, they'd made Ren queen, despite her age. Things did change.

Maybe Artos really was dead, as everyone save Sianiave seemed to believe.

Barrett caught himself and laughed. What was he thinking? He'd be lucky to live through the week himself.

"Laughter was the last reaction I expected," muttered Osmodon.

Looking at the big man, Barrett had a sudden insight. "You know about these things, don't you? Personally, I mean. It's Sianiave. You're in love with her."

"What? Me? With Sianiave?" Osmodon's cheeks puffed out as if to deny it. Then he closed his eyes and let out a great sigh.

"Of course I'm in love with her. Have been from the night I first laid eyes on her. Clear right off she wasn't the marrying kind. How else to be with her but take the Vow?"

Barrett shuddered, seeing his own fate.

"By Asgar," breathed Osmodon. "She'll not hear it from you. Promise me!"

"I expect she already knows."

"Your oath. Please."

Osmodon looked at him with such earnest entreaty, Barrett could only nod. "I promise. Sianiave will never hear the horrible truth from me."

"Good." Osmodon straightened in his saddle. "The animals need a run. I'll race you to the gate." Without waiting for an answer, head down, he spurred his horse into a gallop.

CHAPTER 62

THE SPECIAL COUNCIL MEETING Barrett had asked for was held in a room in the Left Tower following the Sisters' ceremony. The walls were three feet thick and windowless. To remove any taint of the priest and his kind, the Sisters had scrubbed the room with vinegar and alcohol and smudged the air with sage, *suph*, and Kingsroot.

Barrett waited, impatient, while members of the Council trickled in. Bors, Aerindir, Captain Fletcher, the old pikeman Ben Shafter, and fifteen others represented various contingents in the city. They had little time.

Few had seen much sleep the past week. The enemy would be at the gate in less than forty-eight hours. Every council member had an essential roll in the city's defense.

Last to arrive was Ren. She took her seat beside Barrett at the head of the table. Without preamble, she spoke. "I know Sir Barrett would not have called for it were it not of extreme urgency, so I turn this meeting over to him."

Ren's resolve was keenly focused, all signs of girlishness gone. Barrett stood, nodding to the people gathered.

"I believe I have an alternative to our present plan of defense, one that will give Barad'An a chance for survival."

"A little late for changes, isn't it?" growled a portly man across the table. Kamleth Kendren, Barrett recalled, once mayor of Barad'An and a leader among the guilds. Kendren had an irritating habit of interrupting, whether or not he knew anything about the subject at hand.

Barrett ignored him and continued. "If what I have in mind is to succeed, we must decide on it tonight, before this meeting adjourns."

Kendren sniffed. "Just say what you have to say so we can get on with this."

Kendren's attitude caught Barrett off guard. The man was annoying, but by all accounts a useful organizer within the guilds. Yet he felt the animosity flowing from him like a toxic cologne.

If what he was about to say made its way to the enemy . . .

He put the thought aside. Kendren was an unlikely traitor.

"The morghul commander is the key," he said. "A morghul's power lies largely in its ability to influence our thoughts, its ability to control its legions."

"You dragged us away from our preparations for this?" sputtered Kendren. "To tell us something every child knows?"

"Be still!" snapped Ren, with a look that froze the man.

Kendren shrugged and sank back into his chair.

Barrett scanned the room, gauging the mood. Kendren seemed to be the only person present openly antagonistic. He knew that with his next words, that might change.

"We all know the odds are overwhelming. Using our present stratagems, it would take five times our numbers to adequately defend Barad'An. Ellohir's forces are bottled up in Gallian. We've heard nothing from either Sianiave, or the desert people. If we don't alter our position in some fundamental way, our chances for saving the city are slim to none."

He received the response he expected. No one wanted to hear the bleak truth spoken out loud, certainly not by him. He could feel their doubt creeping into the room like a physical thing.

Yet there were those in the room who understood that he only spoke the truth. The knights in particular were used to facing the reality of a situation, however unpleasant. It came with the calling. Aerindir, Bors, Ilesor, the others present, all sat silent, waiting for him to continue.

Ulawyn, the aged representative of the Sisterhood, nodded her head, as though in silent approval of what he was about to say. Osmodon, already his ally, pursed his lips. Barrett could almost hear his thoughts. *What are you waiting for, lad? Give it to them. If this thing fails, none of us will live to worry about it.*

"You say this new strategy offers more hope," Ren urged. "Please, tell us about it." He could see the trust in her eyes.

It weighed on him. He would have preferred doubt. *What if I'm wrong?*

"Get on with it," growled Kendren.

"My plan is simple," said Barrett. "We kill the morghul. Without the morghul to control the army, the Sirdar's legions will fail, a snake without a head."

There was dead silence, then everyone began talking at once. "What a marvelous idea," cried Kendren derisively, his voice rising above the others. "Just kill the morghul! I'm surprised no one's thought of it before!"

He leaned forward on the table, his face as red as a beet. "And just how do you propose to do that, Sir Knight? Are you volunteering to sneak into the creature's tent when it's sleeping and slit its throat yourself?"

"A fair question," someone cried. "How do we kill it?"

Barrett's shoulder was throbbing again. He'd been so certain. Now he wondered if he wasn't deluded. After all, what did he really know about morghuls? He looked over at Ren and saw the trust still there, and with it, encouragement.

"I considered that," he said slowly. "But it's doubtful one man, single-handed, could get into the thing's tent undetected, much less kill it."

"The tent is certainly protected," said Ulawyn. "The witch men are not there for companionship. And morghuls have their own means of protection."

"How then!" cried Kendren, "How do you plan to kill a morghul, sur-rounded by an army, protected by sorcery?"

"We attack."

Kendren's face blanched. "Attack? Are you mad? Attack an army eighty thousand strong?"

Kendren turned to the others, his arms raised. "Barad'An's walls have withstood far greater threats than this! If this is his plan he may as well be working for the enemy!"

Barrett's hand went to his sword hilt. This had gone beyond rudeness. Kendren was directly challenging his leadership.

What was the man up to?

Then, suddenly, the room seemed to fall silent and he saw Kendren as he was, shortsighted and self-seeking. But behind his bluster lay genuine fear. Fear of enemy, certainly, but more than that, fear of being seen for the trivial man he was.

Kendren was shouting now, pointing a finger at Barrett. "Who is this man? What do we know about him? Where is he from? Amra? Where is that?

Does anybody know? Has anybody even heard of it? This plan of his is suicide! We must trust the walls!"

Barrett's own anger was gone. Kendren was not alone in his fear. Everyone felt it. Kendren was simply acting it out for the rest of them.

Realizing his rant was not having the desired effect, Kendren turned back to Ren, pleading. "Your majesty, certainly you, of all people . . ."

"Sit down, Master Kendren," said Ren quietly.

Kendren stood, his mouth agape. He started to speak, then abruptly sat down.

It was Bors who voiced the obvious question. "How do you propose we attack an army eighty thousand strong?"

Barrett let out his breath. The Council sat, ready to face the truth, without illusion or false hope.

"The morghul has deployed his forces in a broad front. Ozzy . . . Sir Osmodon and I saw it from afar this afternoon. It is impressive, but strategically unwise. Its ranks are thin, no more than four or five deep. It's not a formation designed for defense. I believe its purpose is to inspire terror. It tells us the morghul doesn't expect to be attacked."

Bors nodded. "Easy enough to cut through the line."

"How many men?" Aerindir asked.

"Fifty. No more."

There was a stir. "Fifty? So few?"

"The odds don't matter. If we move quickly enough they won't be able to bring their numbers to bear."

"What about the Mongaday?" asked Ilesor, a hedge knight from Amadin. "They move quickly."

The Mongaday were the Sirdar's shock troops—Barrett knew—a light cavalry force, taken from their villages as boys for training as warriors.

"Fierce opponents," Aerindir agreed. "Abdelar and I fought against them at Ethendel."

"And the Uruks," added Bors. "Less disciplined, but still fearsome fighters."

Other of the enemy's forces were mentioned; Southerners, the Ghaad, Niburian archers, the Maerlings. Barrett waved them off. "None of them matter. If we give them time to react, we've already failed. Success depends on speed and surprise."

"And the morghul?" asked Ren. "Who will face the morghul?"

"All of us who reach its tent alive."

"Aye," muttered Osmodon, stroking his beard. "Arriving alive."

Bors was thoughtful. "Sir Barrett, I assume you intend to lead us. What others? There aren't fifty knights left in the city."

"Knights are best in the field," said Fletcher. "Others are better trained for the walls."

"The creature's tent is easy enough to spot," offered the hawk-faced Galwyn, an ex-ranger and their chief of scouts. "It's a great black thing, twelve feet high with five peaks, each flying a red pennant marked with runes of power.

"There'll be pickets," he added. "And the witch men; we've counted twelve."

Witch men? Barrett hesitated. He knew little of sorcery, less of how it would play in battle.

Sister Ulawyn interrupted. "We will deal with the witch men."

The aging Sister had been one of Ren's mentors, Barrett knew; sharp-tongued and practical, she drew near as much respect as the High Priestess Saolin herself. Ulawyn never spoke without severe purpose. She had something up her sleeve.

"A brave offer," Bors said gently. "And I don't discount your abilities, Sister. But however excellent as healers they may be, I don't see how the Sisters can hope to stand against master sorcerers."

The old woman's bright eyes flashed. "Master sorcerers? There's not a first-rate adept among them! A morghul would never allow it. It was sorcery that broke the morghuls' power, and they fear it still. The witch men are acolytes, present only to serve as its lens, to channel the creature's own power. You've all felt it, the insidious weight of doubt and failure, hanging like a poison.

"The Sisterhood has always had to deal with the black arts," she added. "One is a poor healer indeed who does not understand the source of the disease."

"My sincere apologies," said Bors humbly.

"We will not be alone, however." The old woman turned to Ren. "Gwyndolyn Ambergin, I ask permission to introduce another to the Council. He waits outside."

"He, Sister? A man? By all means."

There were no objections. A bell sounded and a man entered, tall and thin, dressed in a stained leather jerkin and faded green tights.

"By Asgar!" whispered Osmodon to Barrett. "It's the minstrel from Ardendell! Tom O'Canter! I knew there was something between him and Sianiave."

Appearing somewhat uncertain, the minstrel approached Ren and bowed. "Your majesty. I arrived only this morning. By chance, I found Sister Ulawyn before I found a room. As I'd come to offer my services in any event, I found the encounter well omened."

"A minstrel?" muttered Kendren. "What next? Dancing maidens?"

Ulawyn glared. "Master Kendren, you would be better served if you listened more and spoke less about things of which you know nothing."

The ex-mayor flushed, but held his tongue.

"A minstrel he may be," Ulawyn continued, turning to the others, "but no common one. He is of the Brotherhood, and it was in Megida where we first met. Then he was known as Maerlis."

A murmur passed through the room. Ren raised a hand. "Is this true? Are you Maerlis?"

The minstrel closed his eyes for a moment, then spoke. "Forgive me. I have not heard that name pronounced in a very long time."

"You forsook the power?"

"I could never do so, your majesty, even if it were possible. I was on an errand outside the walls when Megida fell. With the Sirdar's men searching under every bush and stone, it seemed wise to take another calling. Over time I learned to enjoy being a minstrel."

"The Brotherhood is no more, Master O'Canter . . . or should I call you Master Maerlis?"

"O'Canter please. Tom is even better. It's a name of which I've grown fond."

"Tom, then. Yet you come to us willing to help."

"Yes, your highness. Though to be honest, I wish it were otherwise."

"Why then? Why at such a time?"

"Many Brothers died at Megida, it's true. But the Brotherhood did not die with them. The Brotherhood is not a physical thing. It exists outside of time, of place. The mantle is never given without a price. Each initiate has made his own terms and time of payment. When the Lady Sianiave came into the inn at Ardendell with these two knights, asking for news of Barad'An, I knew the time had come to honor my debt."

The minstrel straightened, and seemed to grow younger. "Yes, I will join you in this fight. I have been hiding too long."

The questions continued for another hour. In the end Barrett's plan was set in motion, with the condition that among the fifty men who accompanied him, no more than ten would be full knights. The remaining knights would be needed in the city.

Even Kendren was mollified. Fifty men only, a loss certainly, but not the disaster he'd envisioned. This Sir Barrett was a glory seeker, like all knights. They were no better than himself, whatever their pretensions.

CHAPTER 63

A SCREAM, UNMISTAKABLY HUMAN, cut through the heavy night air. Somewhere nearby, a man had just died a violent death.

"Easy," cautioned Osmodon. "It's not one of ours."

Barrett was not so sure. He looked at the riders gathered in the darkness. He couldn't see their faces. He sensed anticipation and excitement, but no signs of fear.

Of the hundreds who'd volunteered, fifty were chosen, seasoned warriors, and not a shy heart among them. The meadow they waited in overlooked the plain and the enemy encampment below. They had come by varying routes to avoid the attention of enemy scouts. Now they waited for the order to attack, knowing that many of them would not live through the morning. Perhaps none.

Barrett looked up at the sky. The half moon, near to setting in the west. The order would have to be given soon.

Where was Aerindir?

Bors tightened his cinches. Nearby he could hear the creak of leather as men mounted their horses. Aerindir and the minstrel had not yet arrived. The dour knight's absence would be a serious loss.

Barrett shivered. The chill seeped its way into his padded armor. He wondered if he was making a mistake not wearing a helm. Bors had offered him one of his own. He'd tried it on, finding it heavy and confining, but it would have kept his ears warm.

Several of the older knights had arrived wearing brass or iron chest plates. Most, like Osmodon and himself, wore the common battle dress of lacquered leather. It was lighter than metal, and nearly as tough.

The horses of Anor had been bred for speed and endurance. Barrett still wondered that no one had recognized Greywind, for even among the warrior's mounts, Greywind was exceptional.

The horses' breath condensed quickly in the cold air, curling away in wisps of vapor. Somewhere an owl hooted. There was little conversation; the time for talk had passed.

Eastward the sun rose. Aerindir or no, Barrett knew that soon he would have to give the order. Greywind pulled at his bit.

"A moment longer," Osmodon advised as Barrett steadied the stallion. "Aerindir will come."

As if in answer came the sound of horses approaching at a gallop. "Six riders!" came a muffled cry. Then, with relief, "It's Aerindir!"

"*Six?*" They'd been expecting only Aerindir and the minstrel.

The riders entered the meadow, Aerindir in the lead, followed by the minstrel and four others wearing hooded capes. *Women!* Barrett realized in surprise.

"Our apologies," said Aerindir. "We encountered four enemy scouts. One managed to elude us, until Tom spelled him."

Spelled him?

Barrett recalled the scream and suddenly lost his curiosity. "No matter. But these women—?"

"The morghul has witch men, we have these Sisters," said the minstrel. "Besides, the numbers were wrong."

"Numbers? What numbers?"

"Fifty men? Fives and tens indicate confusion, upheaval. Nine is serendipitous. An end . . . and a beginning."

"Nine?" Barrett had a sudden image of the council room table in Gallian and the floor in Khagad'Oth, "Where do you get nine?"

"Fifty, plus myself and these three Sisters. That's fifty-four. Five and four equal nine."

Barrett quelled his curiosity. Now was not the time for a lecture in numerology. "The Sisters can watch from the ridge."

He stopped. There were four women with the minstrel, not three.

Ren threw back her hood. "The Sisters know the danger. They will ride with Master O'Canter."

The thinning moonlight reflected off her flaxen hair. A ripple of astonishment passed through the gathering.

"The queen is here."

"You shouldn't have come. It's dangerous," said Barrett. "If you were lost—."

Ren replied, "Galwyn's rangers are in the woods. I'll be safe. It's you who rides into mortal peril."

Barrett no longer felt the cold. His impulse was to take her in his arms, but Ren was their queen. He knew that the other men, each in his own way, felt something of the same, and he understood why she had felt it necessary to come. Her physical presence embodied all they valued in the world.

"And Tom, the Sisters? Who will look after them?"

"Don't worry on our account," said the minstrel. "We're not as vulnerable as we may appear."

Barrett studied the minstrel for a moment, then turned away. Sorcery was beyond his understanding, but he recognized courage when he saw it.

"One moment." Ren turned and loosed a slender bundle from her saddle, removing a sword from its blanket wrapping.

"Aerindir wished me to give this to you. I would like you to carry into battle."

Barrett glanced at Aerindir, who was wearing an uncharacteristic smile. "A sword? I have a sword."

"Trust me. This one will serve you better."

Barrett hesitated, then took the weapon from her outstretched hands. From the moment his fingers touched the blade he knew he held something extraordinary.

It was light, far lighter than his own sword. Even in the scant moonlight, its blade glistened brightly, the edge so sharp it almost appeared transparent. It was not made of steel, nor of any metal he knew.

He took a cautious swing. The blade cut through the air with a faint, almost musical sound, like air over harp strings. No sword maker he knew, in this world or any other, could have fashioned such a thing.

Bors and Osmodon had been watching the exchange closely. "Daemonsyr?" Bors asked.

Aerindir nodded. To Barrett he said, "It was Abdelar's, brother blade to my own. I believe you are meant for it."

"A princely gift," said Bors.

"More than princely," murmured Osmodon. "You could buy a kingdom with such a weapon."

Barrett withdrew his sword from its scabbard and handed it to Ren. "Keep this for me, if you will. It's a good weapon."

Ren accepted it. "Until you return."

Barrett sheathed Daemonsyr. He wanted to encourage the men by saying something rousing and uplifting, but no words came. Ren was there and that seemed enough. He looked up at the sky. Sunrise was upon them.

"It's time," he said.

Beside him Osmodon repeated. "Aye. It's time."

"Bors? Aerindir?"

Both men nodded.

Barrett turned to Ren to say good-bye, and instead met her gaze with a resigned smile. Ren understood, returning the smile with one of her own.

He nudged Greywind with his heels. The big horse bolted forward quickly. Osmodon, Bors, Aerindir, and the other riders followed, forming two columns, with the minstrel and the three Sisters bringing up the rear.

No horns sounded, no drums were beaten. Unable to hold back her tears, Ren wondered if she would ever see any of them alive again.

CHAPTER 64

KROSK MORGHUL, COMMANDER OF THE SIRDAR'S LEGIONS, could not sleep. The creature was troubled, and uncertain why. They had marched across half of what once had been the greatest empire in history and had yet to meet serious resistance.

The priest's death had been unfortunate but it was hardly a disaster. Subduing the city would simply take longer. His reign, short as it was, had left Barad'An in disarray, its king poisoned, its knights dead or scattered. It was not possible for the city to right itself before he arrived.

Krosk had not yet decided whether to settle in for a siege or attack immediately. He was inclined to use a frontal assault. By all reports only a few thousand remained to defend the city. The assault would cost men, but this was of little consequence. Krosk was in no mood to wait the weeks, perhaps even months, a prolonged siege would require.

The knight who had killed the priest and almost killed the magician drew his interest. It was no coincidence that he appeared at this moment. Other powers than Belliol's were at work here.

Hero or not, the knight was only a man, a monkey. Best dispatch him quickly. Unfortunately, with Gothmog's hasty retreat, getting assassins into the city proved difficult. There was new sorcery afoot, bindings the morghul couldn't break, even with the focusing power of the Sirdar's witch men.

The morghul peered down at the young girl lying unconscious on his bed. Her back was still bleeding from where his nails had torn her flesh, but she was still alive, and from this he took some satisfaction.

Morganwyn, not that her name mattered greatly, had been found hiding at her family's burnt-out farm. The girl was a virgin, it seemed, and could bear children. Few human females survived Krosk's affection.

Two others had lived, though both had gone quite mad. Krosk had ordered them kept alive, at least until it was determined whether either was with child.

The morghul cleared the girl from his thoughts and turned away. The witch men could tend to her in the morning.

It was too late to sleep, too early to begin the march over the hills.

He leaned back in a chair, breathing evenly, almost in a trance, determined to find the source of his unease, the anomaly in the pattern.

Krosk was two hundred and twenty-seven years old, the last of his kind born. Only a handful of others still lived, eight that he knew of, perhaps another half dozen scattered about the Black Mountains, feeding on passing travelers and dreaming of past glories.

Long had Krosk studied the humans. Physically inferior, venal, avaricious, fearful, prone to treachery, how had this petty race of hairless monkeys grown to such prominence? Wherefore came their power? This was the great question.

It was their cleverness, especially in the realm of the art, that was most troubling. Krosk's own kind had a capacity for sorcery far surpassing that of the monkeys, but morghuls seemed almost incapable of subduing their personal appetites long enough to complete the arduous training needed to attain true mastery. This had been their downfall.

Krosk's fascination with humans had made him an outcast among his own kind. The other morghuls even had a name for him, *Al agheth-e-benaght,* The One Who Mates with Animals, and despised him.

After much seeking Krosk finally encountered a true master, one both willing and able to teach him what he desired. And this new master hated the monkeys as much as he did.

A small price to pay—the others were doomed—he was the future.

He heard footsteps. Someone was approaching the tent. He sniffed the air. Gothmog. Who could mistake the magician's foul smell.

Gothmog peered in through the tent flap. His face, never appealing, was now hideously deformed, the wounds inflicted by the mysterious knight were just beginning to heal.

"Are you asleep, M'lord?"

"Do I look asleep? Why do you bother me?"

Gothmog lifted the flap and came into the tent. He glanced at the girl, noting only that she appeared to be alive. "There's been a disturbance in the hills. Men are gathering. A team of our scouts was discovered."

"They're probably preparing to ambush the vanguard," said Krosk dismissively. "Don't concern yourself. The captains have been alerted."

"It's not that, M'lord."

"What, then?"

"There was evidence of sorcery."

Krosk sat up in the chair. Suddenly the reason for his unease and inability to sleep took form. "The witch has returned! She was supposed to be in the west!"

"No. Not her. The signature was unfamiliar. The Sisters are involved."

"The Sisters? They're not capable—."

Krosk stopped, puzzled. Few really knew what the Sisters were, or were not, capable of. Because the priest had dealt with them so easily, he'd dismissed them as a threat.

"Wake the witch men! And find a vessel."

Gothmog's eyes shifted, furtive. "You wish to contact the master?"

"Of course. Belliol will know."

At the mention of his master's name, Gothmog cringed. Unlike Krosk, who liked to imagine he knew Belliol for what he was, and communed with him almost as an equal, Gothmog still imagined Belliol to be, if not exactly a god, then something close. Gothmog also preferred to summon Belliol in private. Perhaps it was the particularly disgusting nature of their relationship. What Belliol got out of it, Krosk could only guess. Likely it was the only means he had to control the little man's vicious and unpredictable nature.

"I'll bring a boy," said Gothmog.

The words were forced, jealous, Krosk knew.

He had no use for such gutless fawning. Belliol had knowledge, which he exchanged for obedience. This Krosk understood. But unlike Gothmog, Krosk saw Belliol as mortal, and therefore, fallible.

The time was not far off when he would no longer need a master. In teaching Krosk the secret of travel, Belliol had made a grave mistake.

Gothmog left, and Krosk settled into his chair. Once the magician was no longer needed, he would kill the odious little man, and eat his heart for supper.

The girl on the bed let out a squeak. Her body shuddered.

Morghul and human. To other morghuls the thought of breeding with humans was loathsome. But Krosk had decided that if a human female could bare him offspring, he, Krosk, would be the father of a race of powerful new beings. Unanticipated had been the pleasures involved.

The girl was wakening. The pathetic sounds were disturbing his thoughts. The witch men could take her.

A commotion outside the tent caught his attention. Cries. Horns. Men running. Gothmog burst into the tent, his face flushed a horrible crimson. "They're attacking!"

"Attacking? Who's attacking? Where?"

"The knights! The knights of Barad'An are attacking! Here!"

CHAPTER 65

AN EARLY RISING COOK STUMBLED as he ran to get out of the way. Grey-wind's metal shod hooves crushed his chest. A soldier, half naked, his eyes still blurred from sleep, stuck his head out of his tent. Daemonsyr flashed and the head fell into the mud. Horse and rider swept past before the blood touched them.

Dawn had not yet risen when Barrett's small force began their charge. Sentries, dulled by morning duty, had been slow to react. Minutes passed before any alarms were sounded.

The battle horns, the pounding of hooves, the screams of the maimed and dying, Barrett felt caught in time, as if this is how it was, and always had been. There was none of the mindless rage that had propelled him up the dungeon stairs. He felt alive, every nerve in his being tuned to one purpose, to reach the morghul.

A soldier appeared to his right, bare chested, wooden spear in hand. He looked no older than sixteen. Barrett parried a clumsy thrust and took off the boy's arm. Later he might feel regret at such slaughter, but for now all he felt was gratitude their luck had so far held.

It had been only minutes since he'd given the signal for the charge. They'd caught the camp completely off guard, sweeping through the bivouacked army like a storm.

"Can you see the tent?" Barrett cried to Osmodon as Greywind leapt over a smoldering fire pit. "We should be near!"

The enemy camp was a maze of crude tents, open latrines, and panicked soldiers. They rode over it all, cutting down anyone foolish or unfortunate enough to be in their path.

But that very disarray also proved a danger. From the hills above it had been easy to spot the morghul's black tent. It was not so on level ground, sur-rounded by chaos. If they missed the tent, all would be for naught.

"There!" cried Aerindir, swinging in the direction of a red pennant visible in the distance.

A huge bearded man clutching an axe lunged at Greywind, his left hand reaching to grab the stallion's bridle. The point of Daemonsyr's blade took him in the neck. He fell back, dropping the axe in a fruitless attempt to staunch the fountain of blood.

An arrow flew past Barrett's head. Another glanced off the pommel of his saddle. From here on out, it would be a fight. The camp was awake.

Under the clamor of the charge, Barrett became aware of another sound, a thin, discordant hum that grew in volume and intensity even as they closed on the morghul's black tent.

Breaking through a final wall of stacked weapons and small tents, he saw the source of the sound. Twelve men in hooded robes stood facing the riders. Their hoods shadowed their eyes, but their lips were visible, calling out in an eerily syncopated chant.

The keening grew until Barrett's head seemed ready to explode. The horses reared in panic, throwing their riders. Even Greywind tossed his head as though in pain.

All around Barrett men were throwing off their helms and clamping their hands over their ears. "Witch men," Aerindir cried, fighting to steady his stallion. "Where's the minstrel!"

As if summoned, Tom O'Canter, the three Sisters at his side, entered the clearing, their own horses unfazed by the dreadful noise.

The minstrel raised his arms. A blue glow had formed in his cupped palms. Swinging his arms as though he were pitching a ball, the blue light flew toward the witch men. Three of them fell to their knees screaming. Confused, the nine who remained drew together in a tight circle.

The minstrel's face was contorted by the effort. "Hurry!" he cried to Barrett. "Finish your business!" The words seemed torn from his throat.

Beside him the Sisters had grown deathly pale, their eyes tightly closed as they intoned their own sorcery. The horses steadied. Men regained their mounts.

"Barad'An and Queen Gwyndolyn!"

It was Aerindir, charging into the circle of witch men, killing three as the rest scattered.

The minstrel leaned forward in his saddle, retching. Two of the Sisters fell unconscious from their horses. The third managed to keep to her mount, but her face had turned a deathly shade of green and, like the minstrel, she voided her stomach.

More alarms sounded as a troop of horsemen arrived, lean, golden-skinned men in leather armor, curved bows across their backs, scimitars raised.

"Now we're in for it," muttered Osmodon. "Meet the Mongaday, lad."

"Forget them! The tent!"

Daemonsyr's blade sliced through the silk wall of the black tent. Barrett spurred Greywind through the opening. But before they could follow, Osmodon and Aerindir were cut off by the Mongaday horsemen.

Osmodon parried a scimitar, grabbed the tattooed hand that held it, and dragged the man from his horse.

Aerindir spitted the man as he tried to rise. "Ozzy! To hell with this! We'll be overwhelmed! It's the morghul we're after."

Osmodon hesitated. The moment that Barrett entered the morghul's tent, something had become clear to him.

In the first days after Barrett's arrival at Tor Eyrie, his shoulder shattered by a morghul's mace, Sianiave had tended him day and night, never sleeping, rarely speaking. By her concern alone, he knew the young man was important.

One evening after a long session of healing, nearing even the limits of her extraordinary reserves, she spoke of morghuls. "Their strength lies in their ability to see the worst in us," she'd said. "To feed the Toad. If one is prepared, this can be a blessing, for it forces our ancient enemy to reveal itself. Most of us refuse to even acknowledge the enemy exists. Few manage to defeat it."

All this time, in a hundred subtle ways, Sianiave had been preparing Barrett to face the morghul, and in doing so to face something even more dangerous, the Toad, the ancient enemy.

The lad had some great purpose beyond this. That was clear.

Around him Mongaday and knights were locked in ferocious battle. Bors, nearby, was taking two at a time.

"Ozzy!" cried Aerindir as he struck a man from his saddle and spun his horse to face another. "We have to get in the tent! Even Eanor couldn't best a morghul alone!"

"It's the lad's job," said Osmodon, certain now. "Ours is to hold here until it's finished."

CHAPTER 66

Barrett shifted his eyes, adjusting them to the gloom. The floor was covered in thick carpets. The furniture was oversized, built for a giant. The cloying smell of incense couldn't hide the underlying smell of sulfur, and something else, a foul smell for which he had no words to describe.

He saw a bed. A young girl lay exposed in a pool of blood. He was certain she was dead, but then, in a slight motion, she drew her hand to her breast and whimpered.

He started toward her when a mocking chuckle from the back of the tent stopped him cold. *"So. It is you. I suspected as much."*

Barrett swayed as pain shot through his head.

"I've often wondered why Belliol sent me to that accursed place. He imagined you a threat."

The morghul's voice was sly and insinuating. Barrett couldn't tell if the words had been spoken out loud or were only in his mind.

It was dressed as he remembered, black leather kilt, high black boots. He could see its features more clearly now than when they had fought at Langton Manor. Its eyes were not the fiery red he recalled, but golden, serpent-like. Its limbs were oddly jointed, its head oblong and hairless, with small pointed ears. The slit of its mouth was also that of a serpent. Its tongue, though not forked, was thin and black. It wore a long sword in a scabbard at its waist and carried a mace in its right hand, the spiked ball swinging back and forth like a pendulum.

"I thought I had done with you. You're the one who killed the priest."

Barrett couldn't speak. It took all of his strength just to remain standing.

"Nothing has changed. Everything you've done is for nothing. You're life is for nothing. You're weak. Impotent. Look at you, shaking like a slave before its master. Where is your mistress, little monkey? The whore witch? Where is she now?"

Barrett fought to steady himself. The world began to move more slowly, the clamor of battle became a distant drone. The sight had come back. The pain in his head subsided, then was gone.

He saw the creature as it was: cunning, predatory, and vicious. Its chief passions, lust and hate. Its ability to influence emotions were little more than a conjurer's trick, the sly tone, the negative words, the carefully modulated cadence, even the controlled arcs of the mace, reflecting and amplifying emotions already present. Without these it had nothing with which to work.

It was hesitating. Why? Why bother with words? Why didn't it just attack, finish him off?

The answer came from the creature's own thoughts.

Who is this human? Why does Belliol think him important? His sword is surely a weapon of power. And that spell that broke the witch men, even I could find no counter. Was that his doing?

The morgul was uncertain. Deep in its alien mind, it knew fear. Still its words struck home.

"*A fine sword, little monkey. Do you really imagine yourself worthy of it? I know who you really are. A failed soldier from an ignoble world. I saw you there, cowardly little man. I know your real nature. I know your sins, your weakness. I know you. Tell me if I'm wrong. Tell me!*"

Barrett couldn't answer. The creature wasn't wrong. It wasn't saying anything he hadn't told himself. He was weak, unworthy, an orphan. He had felt it all his life, the pain. What was he doing here?

He stood rooted, unable to respond. The morghul chuckled. The arcs of the spiked ball grew larger.

"Barrett!"

The sound of his spoken name snapped him to life. The minstrel stood at the entrance to the tent, hunched with pain. His face was strained and bloodied, but his eyes were clear and unafraid.

"Don't listen to it. It knows nothing. Only the Earth and the Sky know your true name, and they won't speak it until your last breath is gone."

There was a cadence to the words—a spell, Barrett realized—pacing the morghul's malign whispers.

The morghul screamed and swung the mace, but the attack lacked the speed Barrett remembered. Daemonsyr sliced through the morningstar's chain as easily as if it had been rope. The spiked ball flew free, missing his head by half a foot.

The morghul tossed the handle aside and drew its sword. "I will enjoy cutting off your legs, little monkey. This time you will have no wizard to help you."

Barrett glanced at the entrance where Tom had collapsed, and now lay unmoving.

The creature was big, at least two heads taller than himself. Still, it did not seem so terrifying as memory had made it. Unfortunately its strength was no illusion. The blade it had drawn was longer than his own, yet the monster handled it as if it were a willow wand.

It charged, using the sword more like a club than a blade. The force of the blows drove Barrett back toward the bed where the girl lay.

He tried to sidestep, but the morghul turned its blade, cutting Barrett's arm, then catching his right wrist in an iron grip, driving him nearly to his knees. With his left hand Barrett struggled to draw his dagger, but his fingers felt clumsy and blood made the handle slippery.

The morghul's slash of a mouth curled into a malignant grin, its golden eyes gleaming as it bore down. Its breath stank of turpentine and rotten eggs.

Barrett drove a knee into the creature's groin. The morghul screamed, its grip relaxing. Barrett pulled away.

His right wrist was either badly sprained or broken. Shifting Daemonsyr to his left hand, he regained his balance.

Snarling in fury, the morghul charged again. But its blows were wild and lacked the ferocious will of the first attack.

Barrett felt hope. It was tiring. He parried a blow, countering with a sweeping slash to the creature's midsection.

The morghul stepped back in surprise. Taloned fingers felt at the wound, staring at the blood in disbelief.

Barrett waited. He'd been lucky. His right hand was useless and the morghul wasn't the only one who was tiring.

Far in the distance, beyond the battle raging outside, came the sound of horns. More Mongaday. Or Uruks. He had to end this.

The blood seeping down Barrett's arm was a bad sign. It was only small consolation that the morghul was in no better shape. The creature was breathing heavily and blood flowed from the gash in its midsection.

The girl on the bed made a mewling sound and opened her eyes. When she saw the morghul she screamed. Absently, as though swatting an annoying insect, the morghul's sword dropped down, severing her neck.

Horrified at the casualness of the murder, Barrett took a step forward, then caught himself. It was a trap. The morghul was baiting him.

Patience. Let him come to you.

No one ever won a battle through defense alone.

Who had said that? He shook his head. Loss of blood was making him light-headed.

The muscles in the morghul's hand flexed as it sought a better grip on its sword.

Almost —almost —hold—.

A horse crashed sideways through a wall of the tent. The rider, one of the golden-skinned Mongaday, was dead. Caught in the ropes and silk of the tent, the horse thrashed wildly before finding his footing, and then bolted free.

The morghul took that moment to attack. Barrett was forced to deflect the blow with one hand. Pain shot up his arm.

The morghul turned, bringing his sword around in a sideways slash. Barrett's riposte faltered and the morghul's blade bit deeply into his left side. There was surprisingly little pain, but he knew it was no small cut.

Its breath coming in labored gasps, the morghul drew back, either too tired to press its advantage, or knowing there was no need. Outside the horns grew louder, with them the thunder of charging horses.

Horns and hooves. Hundreds by the sound of it, too many to be Mongaday. Probably Uruks.

A veil was closing over Barrett's vision.

The morghul stood, swaying on its feet. Waiting.

Barrett wiped the sweat from his forehead with the back of his hand. He could feel the blood draining down his side, soaking his breeches, filling his boot. He had nothing left.

He'd failed, failed Ren, failed his friends, failed Barad'An. A civilization. Lost.

He blinked, shaking his head to clear the fog. The minstrel lay nearby, unconscious or dead. Barrett remembered his words. *"Only the Earth and the Sky know your true name, and they will not speak it until your last breath is gone."*

A fierce anger rose up in him. He was still breathing. His last breath still to come. He was still alive, and he still held Daemonsyr.

"NO!"

Raising the sword before him, he lunged. The morghul, exhausted beyond measure, weakened by its own loss of blood and certain its last blow had ended it, was unable to respond. Daemonsyr's point struck through its ribs and heart.

Krosk looked down at the sword and shook his head. This was impossible. He was Krosk, the greatest of the morghuls.

Then, raising a hand, as if to ward the blade magically away, he took a last ragged breath and collapsed heavily to the floor.

Barrett pulled Daemonsyr free. With his last vestige of strength he swung the blade at the creature's neck. The spray of blood drenched him as the great head rolled free.

The atmosphere inside the tent was making him sick. He staggered through the torn wall into open air. He felt no triumph, but more a relief, and a mild surprise.

He'd actually killed the thing.

Outside the battle seemed to have come to an end. Enemies, who just moments ago had been locked in mortal combat, stood silent. Bors and Aerindir were there. Osmodon also, bloodied and afoot, but still alive.

The veil of fog was lifting, but he failed to see the furtive figure creeping from behind the tent.

"Lad! Behind you!"

Osmodon's warning came too late. There was a moment's pain as Gothmog's slender dagger pierced him in the back. Then nothing. No feeling at all. Before anyone thought to stop him, the magician had vanished into the tent.

Osmodon was first to Barrett's side. "Get the minstrel, the Sisters! Bors! Aerindir! Find that little rodent and kill him!"

Bors and Aerindir separated, moving in opposite directions to cut off the magician's escape. Osmodon removed Barrett's armor. "Don't worry, lad. We'll get you home!"

"Leave me. Save yourselves—the horns—Uruks—."

"Not Uruks, lad. It's Ellohir's horns you hear, and Sianiave. She's come with Artos. And the desert people as well, if I guess rightly."

"Sianiave? The desert people?" It was too much for Barrett.

There were tears in Osmodon's eyes. "You won lad! And to think only this morning I was composing my death song. Even the Mongaday are riding off, what's left of them. See? Look there. The moment you did that beast in, well, fearless they may be, but not fools. The others? Conscripts and booty hunters, the fear and greed that shackled them is gone. Few will stand now."

"And us? Those that rode with us?"

"Some still live. Bors and Aerindir. A Sister. A few others, I reckon. The minstrel is hurt, though not from any fleshly wound."

Barrett closed his eyes.

He heard Osmodon's shouts as though from a great distance, "Sister, hurry! Someone! Find Sianiave! Get her here! Wake that minstrel! Hurry! Sir Barrett's life is in the balance!"

CHAPTER 67

AN UNFAMILIAR ROCKING MOTION surfaced in Barrett's consciousness. He was lying on blankets in the back of a moving cart. Mounted men flanked him on either side, grim-faced men, their eyes fixed straight ahead.

One man in particular caught his attention, tall, with golden hair, he wore gold and maroon armor. His face was fair and noble, his eyes a startling shade of green. The round shield hanging from his saddle was emblazoned with the Seal of House of Ambergin, a lion and a unicorn, rampant.

Prince Artos. It could be none other. Ellohir rode with him, as did Bors, Aerindir, Osmodon, Penthys, Prince Bandar, and others Barrett didn't recognize. The dog, Bear, was also there, trotting alongside the cart, and Greywind was tethered behind. In a column stretching back to the forest and beyond rode others, too many to count.

They were outside the walls of Barad'An, nearing the great gate. Horns heralded their approach. The way was lined with people. Maewyn, the tavern wench, stoop-shouldered Gregory, Captain Fletcher, even wispy Will, dressed for battle. Somewhere Barrett heard a woman sobbing.

The crowd was subdued, almost reverential. Why weren't they celebrating? Wasn't the war over? Hadn't they won?

There were other carts with the column, carrying the bodies of the wounded and dead. He felt no pain from his wounds. In fact he felt mildly euphoric. Maybe it was Osmodon's goat grease salve, or something the Sisters had given him while he'd been out.

In any event, he felt well again. *Not a hundred percent, but well enough to . . .*

He willed himself to sit up, but his body refused. He wondered if he had been drugged.

Certainly he could move his head, his eyes. Otherwise how could he see what he was seeing?

Abruptly his viewpoint changed. He was looking down on himself, at his own body lying on the cart. His clothes were blood-soaked, his hands folded across his chest, the sword Daemonsyr beside him.

His eyes were closed! How could that be?

A voice came to him. *"You did well, Lieutenant O'Byrne."*

"Sianiave?"

He saw her now, to the left of Artos, mounted on a white horse. She was dressed in silver armor, her blonde hair falling over her shoulders. She looked every inch the warrior maiden. *"Don't be afraid. I'm here with you."*

The words were spoken with tenderness, but her mouth had not moved. Like the others, her eyes were fixed straight ahead. He wondered that no one else seemed to hear them, for no one turned to look.

Another voice, a boy's from the crowd, "Is that Eanor, mum? Is he really dead?'

The woman next to the boy laid a hand on his shoulder. "It's true, my son. They're building the pyres now. But his will be the largest."

Ren was riding out from the city to meet the precession. She did not even look in his direction, instead falling in beside Artos. Her face was drawn as though in grief, but she sat upright, and no tears stained her cheeks.

"It's not time! I'm not ready!"

The words had come out before Barrett realized what he was saying. It wasn't true. He wasn't Eanor. And he certainly wasn't dead. Otherwise how could he be seeing all this?

"I'm sorry," said Sianiave.

It was the compassion in her voice that told him the truth. *"But I can't die. Not now. I'm almost home!"*

"This world is not your home, Barrett. Not your real home. You have much work yet to do."

"Please—."

"Even I cannot change what is. Have faith. All will be well again. This much I know."

"Ren—?"

And with that last thought, Barrett O'Bryne, lieutenant in the American

Special Forces, known as Barrett to his friends, and as Eanor by others, passed forever from that world.

THE PYRES WERE MANY, though Sir Barrett's, a man many now called Eanor, was by far the largest. Queen Gwyndolyn herself had replaced Daemonsyr with his own nameless sword, kissing his forehead before lighting the wood.

The minstrel was forced to view the funeral from his balcony room in the Old Left Tower, where he was recovering. As he watched the flames rise, his own eyes filled with tears. Of the original fifty-four who had ridden into the enemy camp that morning, only nine had returned alive.

Nine living, forty-five passed on. Sir Barrett of Amra, Eanor, whatever the man's true name, had not died in vain. By killing the morghul, he had broken the army's will.

Nine—an end—and a beginning.

The number would undoubtedly have meant more to the sorcerer Maerlis. But Maerlis no longer existed, and the man he'd become no longer had much interest in such things. He had fulfilled his task and paid his dues. He would live out his remaining years as Master Tom O'Canter, wandering troubadour and sometime poet.

But even filled with sorrow as he was, a part of him rejoiced. Artos had returned, Barad'An was restored. What a song it would make!

In his own long and memorable journey, Tom O'Canter had learned a great secret. A poet, a true poet, is more powerful than the sorcerer. The power to change worlds rests not with those who fight the battles, but with those who tell their stories.

Epilogue

Constable Jonathan McGurdy was baffled. Twenty-seven years with the Yard and he'd thought he'd seen everything. Now, as he whiled away his retirement working as a town constable in one of England's sleepiest villages, he'd come across the strangest case he'd ever encountered.

He stood in the observation room outside the emergency unit at Langtonshire Clinic. Beyond the observation window a doctor and two nurses were doing their best to revive a man brought in by the local fire brigade medics. The man was tallish, over six-foot-two, and well built, with scruffy brown hair and bright blue eyes.

A passport on his person identified him as Barrett O'Byrne, a twenty-six year old Yank. McGurdy had run the name through Central Identification Services and come up with nothing. No British, no Commonwealth, visa had ever been issued.

And that was the least of it.

At first he'd suspected a prank, an anonymous call in the middle of the night, a wounded and unconscious man, a burning manor house. It was Samain night, after all. Halloween.

He quickly changed his mind when he'd looked out the window of his small cottage and saw the glow in the distance. When he'd arrived O'Byrne was already being loaded on the gurney. His shoulder looked like raw meat.

But that was hours ago. Other than some nasty bruising, there now appeared to be no physical damage at all. The medics had cleaned the injury up, of course, but that hardly explained what he'd seen earlier, shoulder and arm twisted, bone poking through deeply lacerated skin. And the blood, there had been lots of it, far more than was now apparent with this relatively minor bruising.

The—what? Patient? Victim? Suspect?—was deep in a coma. McGurdy had seen enough trauma in his career, had stood more often than he cared to remember while doctors struggled to save a man's life. He would have bet his pension O'Byrne was a goner.

He turned to the man beside him. "Tell me again, Mr. Winford. How did you say your friend was injured?"

"I've told you twice already, inspector," sighed Billy. "I really don't remember."

"Constable, if you please. You and your friend drove out here from Oxfordshire to answer an advertisement, you say?"

"The *London Times*. It was in Isabel, my car, an old Jaguar."

"Yes. Burned when the wall fell on it, I'm afraid."

McGurdy consulted his notes. "You arrived at the manor at approximately eleven-thirty in the evening. It was raining—."

"About to rain," corrected Billy.

"About to rain. Everything was dark. You both got out of the vehicle and then—."

"That's it. We got out, started toward the front door, and—."

"And then you remember nothing. Not until you woke up by the stone nearly an hour later. You have no memory of how the fire got started?"

"None whatsoever." Billy suppressed a shudder. What he had said was not entirely true. He did remember something, something dark and terrible. *Fire. A creature chasing them—best not to go there. Elyse was on the way with a friend.*

Billy watched the monitor through the observation window. The past few minutes the illuminated spikes of the sixth line, the heart line, had grown noticeably weaker. The medical staff had gathered around Barrett in nervous activity.

The constable's eyes narrowed. "You saw the damage to his shoulder. What do you make of it now?"

Billy didn't answer. When he first came to, he saw Barrett lying unconscious nearby, his shoulder a bloody mess. The medics had arrived soon after, driving their lorry across the field straight to the stone, though how they'd known where to go, he had no idea. But the constable was right. Barrett's shoulder now appeared nearly normal.

"Samain night," said McGurdy. "Tricksters. Except this is no joking matter.

A squire's house has burnt to the ground, and a man lies near death."

Clearly the constable did not believe Billy's claim to amnesia, though it was largely true. But Billy was no longer listening. Every line on the life signs monitor had suddenly flattened. The doctor and nurses had shifted into high gear. Oxygen pressure was increased, epinephrine given, paddles brought. He couldn't hear through the thick glass, but he could see the doctor mouthing the word "Clear!"

Barrett's body jerked. The monitor lines remained flat.

"Again."

Another charge, another jolt. More epinephrine. Seconds passed.

Inside the room desperation had turned to resignation.

"Isn't there anything we can do?" a nurse asked. "He's so young."

The man lying on the table was young, and in apparently excellent condition. Not at all like the drunks and pensioners they usually got this time of night.

The doctor shrugged. "Not if we don't know what's wrong with him."

William Niles was a good doctor. This wasn't the first time he'd lost a patient. It wouldn't be his last. He couldn't get over the feeling he'd somehow failed with this one, missed something important. "Autopsy will tell, I imagine," he said, finishing his thoughts out loud. "Get him cleaned up, would you."

Ignoring a sign that read, PATIENTS AND MEDICAL STAFF ONLY, Billy burst into the room, pushing past the nurse who tried to block him.

"Sir! You're not allowed in here," she protested.

The doctor removed his mask, a sad looking man with grey hair and a kindly face. "It's alright, Nurse Ann. It doesn't matter now."

Gently, he took Billy's arm. "I'm sorry. There was nothing we could do. Other than that bruising, there appeared to be nothing wrong with him. Any information you might have would be welcome."

"Drugs?" Billy asked, remembering the dark thing. *It had to be drugs.*

Dr. Niles sighed. "We're just a small hospital here, a clinic, really. His blood workup came back normal in all categories. We won't have more on the toxicology until after the autopsy."

"Autopsy?"

"Yes. Necessary, I'm afraid, unexplained death and all."

Billy watched as a nurse removed Barrett's oxygen tube, then the IV in his arm. *"I'm responsible,"* he thought miserably. *"If it wasn't for me—."*

"Come along, Mr. Winford. Does no good standing here. The nurses have their work to do."

Billy, fighting back tears, let himself be led away, only half aware someone else besides the constable was now standing in the observation room.

A grey-haired woman wearing a floppy hat and brown woolen greatcoat watched Barrett through the window. Something stirred in Billy, a memory.

In the observation room McGurdy addressed the new arrival. "Miss, are you a relative? A friend, perhaps?"

"A friend."

"I'm truly sorry, then. He's just passed."

The woman looked amused. "Passed? I suppose that's as good a word as any."

An odd thing to say, and an odd way to say it, thought the constable. He took another look at her. Samain brought out all the loons. Her manner irritated him. She expressed no grief, quite the contrary.

"He died just minutes ago," he said.

"Oh, I don't think he's dead."

Something in her tone—arrogance, or was it certainty, increased his annoyance. "I'm sorry, miss, but there is no doubt. You see —."

Inside the operating room the life signs monitor gave a sudden beep. The nurse who had been about to remove the monitoring electrodes from the body jumped back in alarm. "Doctor Niles!"

The first beep was followed by another beep, then another. All six lines on the monitor had resumed a steady pattern.

The patient opened his eyes. As he looked around the room, for a moment he appeared confused.

Billy rushed back into the room. "Barrett—? You're alive!"

"Billy?" It was half question. "I was worried about you. The morghul—."

Barrett stopped. Like a man coming out of a dream his eyes suddenly sharpened into focus. "Where are we?"

"A clinic outside Langton Vale. An ambulance brought us. Thank God! We thought you were dead!"

"The fire—."

"I'm sorry, but I'm going to have to ask you to leave." Looking as confused as the rest of his staff, Doctor Niles was doing his best to regain control of the situation. "He's still a patient. Please—."

Barrett ignored the doctor. His attention was fixed on the woman standing on the other side of the observation window. "Sianiave?"

"Please, young man. You've been through a rough time of it. If you would just—."

The woman gave a satisfied nod to the middle-aged man next to her and left.

"SIANIAVE!"

Barrett tore off the electrodes attached to his body, pushed away the doctor's hands, leapt from the bed, and ran from the room before anyone could stop him.

"SIANIAVE! WAIT!"

That late at night the reception desk was manned by a single volunteer, a grey-haired matron who stared indignantly as Barrett sprinted past wearing only a green surgical gown.

"Young man! What are—?"

Barrett burst through the entrance doors and stopped. A heavy fog had settled over the village. Wide steps led down to a brick sidewalk. Some thirty feet away stood a lamppost, its light a pale glow.

Sianiave stood beneath the lamp. She removed a pipe from her coat, tamped it, and lit it with a flick of a finger. She took a puff, then looked back. She raised the pipe as though in salute, turned, and walked away, vanishing as completely into the fog as though she'd never been.

A crowd had gathered on the steps. Billy was the first to break the silence. "Barrett?"

Barrett turned toward Billy and the others.

He was smiling.